Branded Hearts

ELLE MARIAH

Copyright © 2024 by Elle Mariah

All rights reserved.

No part of this publication may be reproduced, distributed, or transmitted in any form or by any means, including photocopying, recording, or other electronic or mechanical methods, without the prior written permission of the publisher, except as permitted by U.S. copyright law. For permission requests, contact authorellemariah@outlook.com.

The story, all names, characters, and incidents portrayed in this production are fictitious. No identification with actual persons (living or deceased), places, buildings, and products is intended or should be inferred.

Cover Design: Coffin Print Designs

Cover Model: Gabriel Loureiro

Editing: Indie Editorial LLC

Formatting: Indie Editorial LLC

Author's Note

Thank you for choosing to embark on the journey of Branded Hearts, the second book in the Wattle Creek Series, with me. Writing this story has been a labour of love, and I hope it resonates with you deeply.

Before you delve into the world of Bradley and Amelia, I want to take a moment to address some sensitive content within these pages. This story touches on the heart-wrenching loss of victims in a series of tragic house fires and delves into the nuanced experiences of characters dealing with anxiety. These themes are portrayed with the intention of raising mental health awareness and fostering a deeper understanding of such challenges.

Thank you for joining me on this journey. Your support means the world to me, and I hope you find Amelia and Bradley's story as touching as I did while writing it.

This book contains mature themes, and is not suitable for readers under the age of eighteen years old.

To all my quiet girls out there who dreamed of finding a man that sees the fire behind your shyness, cherishes your gentle heart, and makes you feel truly alive.

I give you Bradley Mitchell.

Playlist

Theme Song:
You & Me - James TW

Hometown - Kane Brown

Work Song - Hozier

A Bar Song (Tipsy) - Shaboozey

Footloose - Kenny Loggins

Smooth Operator - Sade

A Troubled Mind - Noah Kahan

Fast Car - Luke Combs

Like Real People Do - Hozier

Delicate - Taylor Swift
Girls Just Want to Have Fun - Cyndi Lauper
Master Of Puppets - Metallica
Chaos - I Prevail
Falling Slowly - Glen Hansard, Markéta Irglová
She Is - The Fray
Conversations in the Dark - John Legend
Latch - sped up + reverb Vocal - Covers Unplugged
My Side of the Fence - Dan + Shay
I'll Be There for You - Brent Morgan
Never Been In Love - Lauren Spencer Smith
Stand and Deliver - Patrick Droney
Enchanted (Taylor's Version) - Taylor Swift
More Hearts Than Mine - Ingrid Andress
Undertow - Bryson Tiller
Sweet Love - Myles Smith
Saturn - SZA
L-O-V-E - Nat King Cole
PILLOWTALK - ZAYN
Control - Halsey
Gravity - Sara Bareilles
Falling like the Stars - Acoustic - Amber Leigh Irish
Vienna - Billy Joel
All I Want - Kodaline
Say Something - Zhavia
Outnumbered - Dermot Kennedy

Someone You Loved - Lewis Capaldi
The Night We Met - Lord Huron
Say When - The Fray
Stargazing - Myles Smith
Go Get Her - Restless Road
Iris - The Goo Goo Dolls
Before You - Benson Boone
Forever After All - Luke Combs

Prologue

Bradley

18 YEARS OLD

The sun hangs low on the horizon, casting long shadows across our Mitchell Valley farm. The air is thick with the scent of hay and the distant hum of cicadas. It's one of those lazy afternoons that stretch endlessly, where time seems to slow down, and the only rush is the soft shuffle of our footsteps on the dirt path.

"Oi, Brad, pass me that bucket of feed," Xavier, my older brother by two years, grumbles.

He's got this idea that being the eldest makes him the boss of everything. We're out here in the fading light, tasked with the mundane chore of feeding the cows.

Buddy, our loyal dog, tails us like a shadow. I grab the bucket and hand it over to Xavier.

"You act like you're running the show, Xav," I grumble.

"Someone's gotta keep things in order round here." He smirks, a cocky expression that's been etched on his face since puberty hit.

I roll my eyes. The last thing I want is to be bossed around by my older brother, but today, I let it pass. Just then, the irritating sounds of giggles pierce the quiet evening air, and I glance over to find Olivia, my younger sister, and her friend, who I've seen around a few times, sharing some joke that's apparently hilarious. Their laughter, like an annoyingly cheerful melody, grates on my nerves.

Olivia, four years younger than me, is the baby of the family and the golden child in Mum's eyes. She's always finding new and inventive ways to drive me up the wall, and bringing her friend along for the ride makes it all the more infuriating. Her friend, whose name I don't remember, must be about the same age.

There's something about her, though—cute in a way that makes her hard to ignore. Yet, she's younger, so I force myself to push those thoughts aside.

I can't wrap my head around why everything seems so amusing to them. It's like they're scheming to crank up the annoyance level for me and Xavier. Classic little sister traits, you know? Always finding ways to do our heads in.

Xavier starts divvying up the feed into the feeders, and I glance over at my sister's friend, who's shooting me a quick, shy smile. Her bright smile, accompanied by those waves of long brown hair, catches my attention for a moment, causing something to stir in my chest. It's foreign, and I don't quite understand it.

My brother, who is currently lifting the bucket over the wooden gate, grumbles, "Whaddya want, Liv?"

It's evident that he's as irritated as I am about our sister's presence.

"Ugh, Dad sent us down here to help. Like, seriously, as if I'm supposed to know anything about cows or whatever," she whines, crossing her arms, a defiant expression etched across her face—the epitome of teenage rebellion. Classic Liv.

Xavier nods toward her brand new white Nike Air Forces, then mutters, "Of course, God forbid you dirty those shoes of yours."

Liv huffs, "Can you just say we helped out to Dad when he asks?"

Xavier looks at her with disbelief. "Abso-fucking-lutely not. Get over here and be useful."

I smirk at their bickering. My gaze then flits over to Liv's friend, who stands with her arms crossed behind her back. Taller than my sister, with long lean legs, she's dressed in denim shorts and a white off-the-shoulder shirt.

Our eyes meet briefly, and I catch a hint of her face flushing. I avert my gaze back to Xavier, who's waiting for Liv's response.

Her friend decides to break the silence, and her voice, soft and melodic, carries an air of genuine politeness. It's calming—a stark contrast to Olivia's usual dramatic tone. "C'mon, Liv. I've never fed a cow before—it sounds like fun."

"Well, at least your friend here has some brains," Xavier says, and she smiles.

"Ugh, fine," Liv exclaims, clearly defeated. She turns to her friend with a look. A look that Xavier and I have been on the receiving end of all too often.

"Thanks a lot, Amelia."

Amelia. Hm. Even in my sister's icy tone, her name sounds sweet, *feminine. Just like her.*

Xavier is busy giving the girls a rundown on how to feed the cows and fill the feeders. I hang back, my hands moving on autopilot as I pass over buckets when needed. Liv, predictably dramatic, lets out a squeal when a cow inches closer to the gate.

Amelia calmly tells her, "Relax, Liv, they're harmless."

Xavier laughs, and I can't help but smirk.

"Easy for you to say, Amelia. That cow is so calm." Liv almost throws the bucket into the pen.

Observing Amelia effortlessly follow Xavier's instructions, pouring food into the feeders, I can't help but notice how she's a natural at this. Meanwhile, Liv—who has grown up on the farm alongside us—is more interested in playing with the cows than actually feeding them, much to Xavier's dismay.

I decide to approach Amelia as she moves along the fence. The barn's fences are pretty tall, and although she's managed so far, the last bits of feed are struggling to come out because she can't lift the bucket high enough over the fence.

I sigh and mutter, "Lean over the gate a bit more—it'll come out easier."

She freezes momentarily at the sound of my voice, turning to look back at me with those big brownish-hazel eyes. There's an innocence in her gaze that I can't quite place. I feel a strange pang in my chest as our eyes meet.

I guide her in leaning over the gate, adjusting the angle of the bucket. The last remnants of feed spill into the feeders, and I can feel a small *sense of satisfaction at the successful completion of the task. The cows, content with their meal, continue chewing lazily, oblivious to the minor struggle that just took place.*

"There you go," I mutter, releasing the bucket. Amelia straightens up, offering a small, grateful smile. It's a fleeting moment, but in those hazel eyes, I catch a glimmer of something more. Maybe it's relief, maybe it's gratitude.

Amelia puts the bucket down, her hands brushing off bits of hay, and she turns toward me, her sweet smile unwavering. "Thanks, Bradley. I appreciate the help."

She remembers my name? It's one thing for Liv to have mentioned it, but for her to remember it means something different entirely. It's as if I've taken up some space in her mind, some significance. I'm baffled, curiosity now swirling in my head. I shake off the notion and grunt a nod in response, a subtle acknowledgment of her thanks.

Just then, Mum calls out, her voice loud enough to reach us from inside.

"Dinner's ready, everyone! Come and eat!" Her voice carries through, breaking through the rhythmic clatter of cutlery and dishes being prepared. Xavier packs up the buckets of feed, discarding them inside our shed, and we make our way inside.

Dad takes his seat at the head of the table, and Xavier follows suit, muttering, "I'm bloody starving," while rubbing his stomach.

With all tasks completed, the girls had bolted out of the barn after their brief stint with the feeding, leaving just Xavier and me behind. He'd exchanged a peculiar glance, but I shrugged it off, not wanting to know what he was thinking. I take a seat next to Xavier. Mum's voice echoes through the house again, calling the girls down for dinner. Soon, we hear the familiar creaking of stairs, and both Liv and Amelia appear. Liv joins us at the table, yet Amelia lingers at the stairs, glancing briefly at her phone.

"*Amelia, dear. Come and eat,*" *Mum calls, her tone warm and inviting.*

Amelia hesitates. "*Oh, it's okay, really. My mum will be picking me up soon.*"

Mum insists, her voice warm and welcoming, "*Nonsense, dear. There's plenty of food. Come, sit.*"

Amelia still hesitates, but after a bit of back-and-forth, mustering a small, appreciative smile, she takes a seat—right in front of me.

Mum plates up the food before sitting down next to Dad. Just as Mum is about to say something, Xavier wastes no time diving into his food. I shake my head at his impatience, and Mum admonishes him.

"*Xavier Mitchell. We give thanks before we eat.*"

He mumbles with a mouth full of food, "*Sorry.*"

I can't help but smirk.

Mum starts us off with a quick prayer. "*Dear Lord, we thank you for this meal and the hands that prepared it. Bless our time together as a family. Amen.*"

I glance around the table, unenthused but playing along. The others seem into it, and I wonder if they genuinely find comfort in this routine. I keep my eyes low, finishing the prayer in silence within my head.

As we start eating, Mum and Dad begin a conversation that, to be honest, I'm not overly interested in. They talk about the town, the weather, and some local gossip that I couldn't care less about. I just listen, picking at my food. Across the table, Liv is in her usual animated state, practically bouncing in her seat as she recounts some drama from school.

"Oh, you won't believe what happened in English class today! Mrs. Simmons gave us this ridiculous assignment, and I swear, it's like she's trying to torture us with boredom."

"Yeah, because your life is just so full of excitement, Liv. I'm sure an English assignment is the pinnacle of thrill for you," Xavier interjects.

Liv shoots him a playful glare. "Well, at least I'm not the one spending my days talking to cows. Honestly, Xavier, when are you going to get a life outside of the farm?"

This makes me smirk, and I chime in, "He's married to the cows, Liv. Didn't you hear? It's a serious commitment."

He shoves my shoulder, and I stifle a laugh. I just love to rile him up.

I keep my gaze anywhere but on Amelia, though I can feel her eyes on me. I refuse to meet them, focusing instead on Mum, the kitchen cupboards, Dad, the bracelets adorning Liv's wrists—anything but her. This family dinner feels like an eternity, and I'm just waiting for it to be over.

My mother's voice rings in the air. "So, how'd you all go with the feeding today?"

"Fine," I mutter.

My father's commanding voice cuts in. "I sent Liv down. Did she help out?" He raises a brow at my sister.

"Yes, Dad. In fact, we both did," Liv answers, and I shoot a glance at her and Amelia before Dad nods.

Always so intense, this bloke. He then changes the conversation to me, asking when I'll be enrolling in the academy now that I've graduated high school.

"Sent in my application last week. Should be hearing back from them soon."

Dad grins, a twinkle of approval in his eye. "Bout time you took a step outta your comfort zone. That's my boy."

I give a nonchalant shrug, not wanting to admit how his approval actually means something to me.

As the conversation shifts, Amelia, who has been quiet, chimes in, "What academy?"

I glance at her, and for a moment, our eyes lock. Before I can say anything, Mum replies, "Bradley, here, has enrolled in the NSW Police academy." Her voice is proud.

Amelia, breaking the brief silence, is shocked with awe. "Oh, wow. That's so cool," she mutters, her eyes wide with surprise.

Why is she so interested? I nod, uncomfortable with the sudden attention.

The atmosphere shifts, and I can feel everyone's eyes on me. Amelia, obviously unable to contain her curiosity, asks another question. "What made you decide on that? It seems... intense."

I glance at her, briefly meeting her gaze before looking away. "Just seemed like the right move," I reply, keeping it vague. The weight of *everyone's expectations lingers, and I shake off the feeling.*

Amelia presses further. "Do you, like, have a passion for it or something?"

I'm not a talker, never have been. I've always been the quiet one, letting the light shine on Xavier and Liv. Xavier stepped up to help out our father with the farm, and I just felt like that life wasn't for me.

I'm observant, always seeking challenges, and this career path seemed like the right choice for me. So, yes, you could say I've always had a passion for it.

But I downplay my thoughts and shrug. "Yeah. Someone's gotta do it."

Xavier, with his usual sarcasm, remarks, "Yeah, someone's gotta keep the town safe, ey?"

Liv jumps in, never one to remain quiet for long. "Well, I want to do something in business. An office job, maybe start my own company someday."

Mum nods approvingly, then turns to Amelia. "And you, Amelia? What do you want to do?"

Amelia smiles shyly. "I'd love to be a teacher. It's a passion of mine—working with kids, helping them learn and grow."

Mum beams at her. "That's wonderful, dear. You'd make a great teacher."

I look at Amelia, seeing her excitement and determination. It's clear she's found her calling, just like I have. Her eyes continue to linger, and I can't help but wonder what's going on in her head. Why is she staring? I shake off the thought with a frown, returning my attention to the mind-numbing dinner conversation.

Mum, always one to know everything, politely asks, "So, Amelia, dear, tell us about school. How did you and Liv meet? She hasn't told us much."

Amelia's smile returns as she responds, "Well, I don't go to Springbrook High. I'm at a smaller high school, about twenty minutes from town. Liv and I met at a school event not too long back. Our friendship just clicked from there."

Liv chimes in with a big smile, confirming, "Yeah, it was like an instant connection."

The girls giggle together, their bond evident.

Mum nods. "That's lovely. It's always nice when friends become family. You're welcome here whenever, dear."

Amelia's eyes light up, and she responds sincerely, "Thank you, Mrs. Mitchell. I really appreciate it."

In that moment, with the golden hues of the sunset dancing on her face, I see her young innocence—a kind of beauty untouched by the world.

She's younger, way too young, and I feel a surge of discomfort.

Stop being a bloody creep, Brad. The evening air feels heavier, and I focus on the remnants of my dinner, hoping to distract myself from thoughts that shouldn't be there.

It's just a trick of the light, I tell myself, a momentary lapse. I shift my attention back to the mundane conversations, trying to shake off the unsettling feeling settling in my chest.

Little did I know, those fleeting glances would become a subtle undercurrent in the years to come, weaving a connection I couldn't foresee at that moment.

1

Bradley

29 YEARS OLD

"Morning, Mitchell," Daniels chirps, the cheeriness in his voice echoing through the dull police station. My eyes stay fixed on the paperwork as I mumble a greeting, fighting the urge to roll them at his overly upbeat demeanour.

Dim fluorescent lights flicker above our timeworn desks, casting a feeble illumination across the small police station. Here, time meanders at a pace slower than a lazy river's gentle current, and the crime rate is as riveting as watching paint dry on a picket fence.

Yet, within the unhurried cadence of provincial life, I wouldn't barter it for the hectic life of working on our family farm or the relentless bustle of city life. Xavier still gladly takes up the mantle on the farm.

Over the years, I've progressed from a young prospect to constable and now senior constable. Offers to transfer to Sydney or pursue loftier opportunities have dangled before me like tempting carrots, but I've swatted them away, one after another. I guess I'm too rooted to this town.

There's a part of me that occasionally flirts with regret, the 'what-ifs' lingering in the corners of my mind. Yet, another part of me finds comfort in the snug embrace of this small town, where everyone knows everyone, and the rhythm of life—though it may seem monotonous, it bears the weight of a blessing in its comforting predictability.

"You look like you swallowed a lemon. What's eating at you today?" Daniels continues.

"Same old, Daniels—your perpetual sunshine presence," I mutter, the snark slipping through my usually reserved exterior.

He chuckles, taking a sip of his coffee. "Got anything exciting to deal with, or is it just the thrilling world of paperwork for you today?"

"Yeah," I grunt, offering nothing more. I can feel Daniels' gaze lingering, waiting for a more elaborate response, but I'm not in the mood for small talk or his attempts to inject excitement into the mundane.

Officer John Reynolds saunters in, a file in hand, and joins the impromptu morning gathering. "What's got Mitchell's panties in a twist today?" he asks, smirking as he eyes me.

"Oh, he's in his usual sunshine mood," Daniels retorts. "Today has dragged on, man... I need something exciting to happen," he adds with a glint in his eyes.

"Good luck with that," I quip.

Daniels jumps back in, "Well, on the bright side, you should be excited, Bradley. Less crime means more time to perfect your scowl."

"Mhm," I grumble, my tone making it clear that I'm not interested in pursuing this line of conversation.

Reynolds leans against the desk, laughing while flipping through his file. "Got anything exciting in that paperwork of yours, Mitchell?"

I give him a curt nod, not bothering to look up. "Just the riveting saga of unpaid parking tickets and noise complaints. The usual thrill."

My words hang in the air, a heavy acknowledgment of the monotony that defines our days in this sleepy town.

"Come on, Mitchell. You're just not appreciating the subtle art of small-town drama. Remember the time Mrs. Turner accused old man Mr. Whittle of stealing her prized geraniums?"

I raise an eyebrow, unamused. "Yeah, thrilling stuff. I'm living on the edge of my seat."

Reynolds smirks, his amusement unabated. "You never know, Mitchell. One day, we might get a case that shakes this town to its core." *Yeah... that'll be the day.*

I scoff, more to myself than anyone else. "In this town? The most excitement we get is when someone's cow wanders onto Main Street."

The engine hums to life as I settle into the familiar leather of the police car's passenger seat. Daniels slides into the driver's seat.

"Ready for another patrol, Mitchell?" He grins, turning the key in the ignition.

"Just drive, Daniels," I mutter, eyes fixed on the road ahead.

He chuckles, undeterred. "Come on, Bradley Bear, loosen up a bit. You might actually enjoy yourself."

I shoot him a sidelong glance, my annoyance barely contained. "I enjoy doing my job, Daniels. No need for the extra frills."

He leans back, unfazed by my clipped response. "You're a tough nut to crack, Mitchell. One day, I'll get you to crack a smile."

Good luck with that, Daniels.

The idea of me cracking a smile feels as unlikely as Wattle Creek suddenly transforming into a bustling metropolis. If anything, I've mastered the art of maintaining a stoic expression, a skill honed through years of navigating the ins and outs of this small town.

The town, basking in the soft glow of afternoon sunlight, seems to be in a relaxed state, much like the rest of its inhabitants.

The radio crackles to life with a static-filled voice, breaking the monotony of the afternoon patrol. "Attention all units, we've got a potential disturbance reported at Blossom Haven. Caller reports raised voices and some commotion inside." There's a brief pause before the dispatcher adds, "Caller also mentioned a male possibly in possession of a weapon. Proceed with caution, over."

Daniels glances at me, a flicker of excitement in his eyes.

"Looks like we've got ourselves a case, Mitchell. Ready for some action?"

I nod, reaching for the radio intercom. "Copy radio. This is Mitchell and Daniels. We're heading over. We will be red and ten."

Sirens blaring, Daniels picks up speed as we make our way toward the florist, located near our Town Square. As we pull up outside the floral shop, we exit the car swiftly, my hand steady on my taser holstered at my right side. Daniels has his gun out, ready if necessary. He glances at me, catching the subtle movement, and I offer a silent acknowledgment.

An older man, dishevelled and clearly under the influence of an illicit substance, stumbles around the shop in a daze. Daniels swings the door open abruptly, and the man's slurred words fill the air as he sways unsteadily. In his trembling hands, he clutches a small knife, adding urgency to the already tense situation.

His movements become erratic, as he incoherently demands money from the floral shop till. The woman's pleas for help, from behind the till, take on a more urgent tone.

"Officers, please, he's trying to rob us!" We approach cautiously, moving toward the commotion, and as I scan the surroundings, I am abruptly halted in my tracks. There, standing in the corner next to a frightened elderly woman, is Amelia Brown.

Amelia Brown—my sister's best friend, her face etched with pure shock.

My breath catches, as if the air has been sucked out of the room. Panic courses through me at the sight of Amelia, stirring old feelings that clutch at me, feeding the fear of seeing her in this situation.

Daniels moves with purpose, swiftly positioning himself closer to the man. His gun is up, held steady, while my hand remains firm on the taser.

"Sir, I'm gonna need you to step away from the counter. Now," Daniels commands, his voice firm and authoritative.

The man sways, his words slurred and desperate. "N-need cash, y'know? Jus' a little, okay? Jus' a l'il, mate."

Daniels' urgency is palpable, his command echoing in the tense atmosphere of the shop. "Drop your weapon immediately, sir. This is your last warning. Step away, or we'll be forced to take action."

Time compresses into a series of heartbeats in my ears.

2

Amelia

Teaching kindergarten is like being the ringmaster of a circus where the clowns are on a sugar high. Today's highlight—convincing little Timmy that crayons are not, in fact, a food group. Oh, the adventures of moulding young minds!

Post-crayon escapade, I decide to reward myself with a bouquet from Blossom Haven because, let's face it, flowers are my version of therapy.

I mean, who needs a therapist when you have lilies, right?

As I step into the shop, my mind dances among the vibrant hues of flowers, seeking the perfect bouquet to brighten up my apartment. The sweet scents of lilies and roses saturate the air, wrapping me in a fragrant cocoon as I delicately pluck each flower, weaving a masterpiece rivalling the colours of a summer sunrise.

I'm in the middle of admiring the beautiful flowers, lost in their vibrant colours and gentle sway, when my peaceful bubble is suddenly popped by the arrival of a sketchy-looking guy. He slouches in, hand buried deep in his pocket, stumbling like he's either drunk or high. The other customers, an elderly woman and a young couple, are too engrossed in their own flower picking to notice him. A chill runs down my spine, causing every hair on my body to stand at attention.

My heart pounds frantically against my ribcage as a sense of creeping dread envelops me. The once peaceful atmosphere turns ominously sinister as the man inches closer to the woman behind the counter. Without warning, he whips out a menacing blade, thrusting it toward her with slurred demands for money from the till. Panic floods through me like a tidal wave. The florist lets out a terrified scream, the young couple next to me freeze in fear, and chaos erupts all around me.

I am paralysed by terror, unable to move or think as danger looms just feet away from me.

The poor lady behind the counter is now a picture of pure panic, her eyes silently begging for someone, anyone, to step in. In the middle of this chaos, the young guy with his girlfriend catches on to what's happening and pulls out his phone.

He presses it to his ear, clearly calling triple zero for help. The sketchy guy's voice gets louder and more frantic as he demands the money again. The woman behind the counter, tears starting to well up, opens the cash register, her hands trembling uncontrollably.

The young guy, still clutching his phone, moves cautiously. His girlfriend grabs his shoulder, silently begging him to stop. He turns to the drunk man, his voice steady but tense. "Hey, man, put the knife away. I've called the cops."

The drunk guy's eyes, wild and unfocused, lock onto the young man as he points the weapon at him. The air grows thick with tension; the silence broken only by the desperate pleas of the florist trying to comply with the unfolding nightmare.

"Put it away, mate! We don't want any trouble!" the young guy stammers, fear making his voice shake. His girlfriend tightens her grip on his shoulder, her eyes begging him to stay calm.

The armed man, fueled by greed and desperation, sneers, slurring his words. "Y'think callin' the police is gonna help'uh?"

My heart pounds in my chest, fear wrapping around me like a vice. I can't believe the bravery of this young guy, standing up to the armed man and staying calm enough to call the police. He's a hero in this terrifying moment, and I silently pray that his courage won't cost him.

As the tension escalates, the man's girlfriend squeezes his hand, silently urging him to stay composed. The florist, hands trembling, continues to comply with the demands, her eyes darting between the drunken man and the young couple.

In that harrowing moment, the wailing sirens pierce through the tense air, announcing the arrival of the cavalry. A police car screeches to a halt outside, and two officers rush toward the shop, their expressions stern and determined.

The lady beside me, seeking comfort, inches closer, and I instinctively wrap a hand around her frail shoulder, offering what little reassurance I can. As the police officers burst through the entrance, my adrenaline spikes at the sight of a familiar face. But not just any familiar face… It's one that has been ingrained in my mind since I was fourteen years old.

Bradley Mitchell.

His authoritative stance emanates a sense of calm amidst the chaos. I shouldn't be so surprised. I know he's a police officer, and this is a small town, after all—yet the sight of him always takes my breath away.

Even now, in the midst of this chaos, his presence is electrifying.

Fear and shock still grip me, but a sliver of relief cuts through the terror.

Bradley is *here*.

I can't let myself feel too safe just yet, but seeing him gives me hope that this nightmare might finally end.

The florist's desperate cries pierce the air, and my heart lurches as I watch the scene unfold. The drunken man sways on unsteady feet, still clutching the knife in a menacing grip. Then, with a clatter, he drops the knife to the floor, following the other officer's request from earlier—the sound echoing loudly in my ears.

"Drop to the ground, now!" Bradley's command is firm and urgent, cutting through the tension. The man hesitates, swaying on his feet, his gaze unfocused and unsteady. Sensing the imminent threat, Bradley swiftly draws his taser and fires. The electric crackle fills the air as the man convulses and collapses to the ground, subdued.

In synchronised motion, both officers spring into action. The other officer holsters his gun and approaches cautiously, swiftly kicking the knife out of reach. With practised efficiency, they secure the man, restraining his arms with handcuffs that click sharply into place.

The scene is tense, adrenaline pumping as they immobilise the man swiftly and effectively, ensuring no further danger lingers.

My breath comes in short, nervous gasps as I watch them immobilise him, the gravity of the situation palpable in the air. The other officer meticulously pats him down, checking for any other weapons, but finds none. The sense of relief washes over me as the immediate danger subsides, though the adrenaline still courses through my veins.

"Sir, you are under arrest for attempted armed robbery," the same officer declares. "You do not have to say or do anything, but anything you say or do will be recorded and used in court as evidence against you. Do you understand this?"

The man nods hurriedly. I remain rooted in place, a tremor coursing through me as shock tightens its grip. Instinctively, I move my hands to comfort the lady beside me, offering a reassuring presence amidst the aftermath of chaos. She glances at me, hands still trembling, with gratitude in her eyes, a silent acknowledgment of shared vulnerability.

Bradley then turns to the officer beside him, who nods, before grabbing the restrained man by his cuffed arms and lifting him up to stand. Bradley pats down the man's sides, where his pockets are, before pulling out his wallet and opening it up. He extracts the man's licence and asks for his name and address.

The man mumbles a response, but I can't quite catch it.

Bradley warns him, "It's an offence not to give us your correct name and address," and asks him to repeat it. The man complies, and Bradley nods to the other officer before the man is escorted out of the shop. He then turns to the rest of us.

"Please remain where you are. More officers and paramedics will be arriving shortly," before following the suspect closely behind, his demeanour focused and professional.

As I watch, two more police cars arrive, their red and blue lights casting an eerie glow across the scene. Additional officers emerge, swiftly joining Bradley. From my vantage point at a safe distance, I observe the controlled chaos unfolding. Some officers are out on the street, surveying the area and ensuring bystanders stay clear, while others manoeuvre to block off the road.

Bradley stands out amidst the flurry of activity, communicating efficiently with the arriving officers. His demeanour is calm and collected, his training evident in every precise movement and in the way he relays information, coordinating the next steps with practised ease. The scene pulses with urgency, yet Bradley's steady presence lends a reassuring stability. Once the suspect is safely secured in a new car, Bradley returns to the shop, accompanied by a different officer. The new officer, with light brown hair, introduces himself as Detective White before approaching the owner of the shop.

Bradley's expression is serious as he makes his way over to me, and I find myself still frozen in place, the aftermath of the attempted robbery still lingering in my senses. My mind, in shock and daze, drifts to a memory from years ago.

As everyone talks around me, Olivia animated in her seat beside me, I find it hard to focus on anything other than the boy sitting across from me. Bradley. There's something about him that's utterly mesmerising. I've never been up close to teenage boys before, and I know I shouldn't be feeling this way, especially about my best friend's brother. But I just can't help it. He's quiet, almost brooding, yet there's a calm confidence about him that intrigues me. His eyes, a striking shade of blue, catch the light just right, and I find myself stealing glances, trying to understand what lies behind them. His presence is magnetic, drawing me in despite my better judgement. The way he moves, the subtle clench of his jaw as he listens to the conversation around him—it's all so captivating. I can't explain why I'm so drawn to him. Maybe it's because he's different from the boys at my school, who are loud and brash, always trying to prove something. Bradley seems... grounded, like he knows who he is and doesn't need to show off. It's that quiet strength that pulls me in, making me wish I could get to know him better, understand what makes him tick.

But I know it's wrong.

Still, as I sit across from him, my heart races a little faster, and I can't shake the feeling that this boy, with his intense blue eyes and quiet demeanour, is someone worth knowing.

The elderly woman murmurs beside me, "I think she is in shock, dear."

I try to steady my breath as Bradley approaches, his eyes full of concern and determination. Now, ten years later, I realise that those feelings are unchanged. The intensity, the pull I felt back then, is just as strong.

He shifts his attention to her, asking, "Are you okay?"

In my peripheral vision, I see her nod enthusiastically. "Yep. I am now."

"Amelia, are you alright?" My eyes are looking at him, but I'm not really focusing.

He grips my chin, his touch both grounding and surprisingly gentle, pulling my face up to face his, and mutters in a commanding tone, "Amelia. Look at me."

This snaps me out of my daze.

"Are you hurt?" he asks, his eyes searching mine for any sign of injury.

I swallow, trying to find my voice. "No. I-I'm fine. Just a bit shaken up." He frowns at me, processing my words.

I mutter a quick, "thank you," before instinctively hugging him tightly.

Bradley just stands there, his body rigid. Realising what I've done, I quickly release him. He clears his throat, and a flush of embarrassment passes through me. His expression softens, and he looks around the shop, scanning the surroundings briefly.

"We'll need to take your statement, Amelia," he says, his voice calm. "Would you prefer to do that here, or back at the station?"

"H-here. Here is fine."

"Okay. Could you tell me what happened?"

"The man came in, and he had a knife," I explain, my voice trembling slightly. "He demanded money from the till, and then the young man over there called the police. Bradley, he was so *brave*."

As I speak, I watch as Officer Reynolds does the same with the young couple. Bradley nods, listening intently.

"Did you see where the man came from? Did he say anything else?"

I shake my head, my mind still reeling from the events. "No, I didn't see where he came from. He just walked in, and then the next minute he was shouting, demanding money, and then *you* got here."

Bradley nods again, jotting down notes on a pad. "Thank you. Our detectives will need to get a formal statement from you soon, but for now, I think it's best if you let the paramedics check you over."

He guides us outside to two paramedic vans. The slight breeze outside is a welcome respite from the tension within the flower shop. A young paramedic nurse approaches me.

"Hi there, I'm Nurse Emily. Can you tell me your name and what happened inside?"

I nod, grateful for her gentle approach. "I'm Amelia. A man came into the shop with a knife and demanded money from the till. He was shouting, and then the police arrived."

Emily nods, taking notes on her tablet before giving me a comforting smile. "You're safe now, Amelia. I'm just going to check you over to make sure you're okay. Can you come with me?" I nod, following her to a van. Once seated, the nurse begins checking my vitals, asking me a series of questions to assess my condition.

"Do you have any pain or discomfort?" she asks, her voice gentle and reassuring.

"No," I respond, feeling a bit dazed, but physically unharmed. She continues her examination, checking my pulse and blood pressure. Meanwhile, my gaze drifts to Bradley. Dressed in his police uniform, he exudes a rugged stoicism that has a way of igniting a flush of nervousness throughout my body.

As the paramedic checks me over, my mind drifts back to old memories. Bradley was, without a doubt, my best friend's cool, older brother, who totally had my attention.

I'd developed a crush on him all those years ago. Now, he's become this guy who commands respect and exudes this magnetic charm that's impossible to ignore.

As I watch him, the realisation hits me: the silly crush from my teenage years hasn't dissolved; it's evidently still there. A fire I thought had long been extinguished is surprisingly still *burning*.

I chuckle inwardly at the irony of it all.

Here I am, years later, still affected by the same boy who used to make my heart race.

Funny how some things never change.

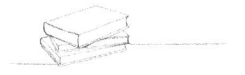

Back in the safety of my apartment, I try to shake off any lingering unease from the attempted robbery earlier today. The whole thing still feels surreal, like a scene from a crime drama rather than my quiet town's reality. I move around the kitchen, putting dishes in the dishwasher, a task that offers a semblance of normalcy.

Only a few months ago, I made the decision to move out, despite my parents' initial disapproval. Being the baby of the family, they found it absurd that I'd want to live anywhere but at home with them. But I wanted to experience living on my own, and this apartment is much closer to my school, so that's a bonus. With some convincing, and the invaluable aid of my persuasive sister, I managed to win them over.

Moving out didn't just shorten the commute to work—it also brought me even closer to Olivia *and* Bradley.

Now, as I stand in my own space, I can't help but appreciate the independence it brings. My phone buzzes, and I glance at the screen to find an incoming FaceTime call from my sister, Kathryn.

Her voice fills my kitchen with a cheerful, "Hey, Meli!"

'Meli' has been a nickname thrown around for a while now. My sister, who has a delightful three-year-old bundle of energy named Millie, decided to name her after me. I was absolutely over the moon when Kat told me this. It's a testament to our tight bond, and now little Millie, still mastering the art of pronunciations, has taken to calling me Meli, and so the nickname has stuck.

A warm smile spreads across my face as I answer, "Hey, Kat! What's up?"

Kathryn's laughter dances through the phone. "Not much. Trying to get Millie to have a bath, but she's being so stubborn."

"Sounds like you," I tease.

"Oh no, no, no. She gets it from you," Kat fires back.

"Me! No way, I'm not stubborn at all," I retort.

"Mhm," is all Kat says.

Despite the eight-year age gap, Kathryn and I have always been close. She's been a protective older sister, and I'm immensely grateful for the bond we share.

"How was your day?"

"It was supposed to be a normal day at work, bustling with the usual energy and chaos..." I shudder as I continue, my voice soft. "But... I got caught up in an attempted robbery."

Silence falls upon us like a heavy weight before Kathryn's voice breaks through with an edge of panic. "Oh my God, are you okay? What the fuck? What happened?"

"I'm okay, it's all good. Police rocked up, handled it. Paramedics came as well, to assess all of us, but I was fine. I am fine." My body still runs cold at the thought of what happened.

"Did you tell Mum and Dad?" Kat asks hurriedly.

"Yes, I rang them just after I was free to leave," I reassure her.

"Bloody hell. Well, thank goodness you're okay," Kat breathes, her voice shaky. "Was anyone hurt?"

"No, the police got there just in time to stop the man. It was pretty intense," I reply. "And you won't believe who one of the officers was."

"Who?"

"Bradley Mitchell!"

"Wait, Bradley? Like *your* Bradley, Bradley?" Kathryn exclaims. I can't help but smile, but quickly wipe it off my face.

"Yeah," I admit. "Seeing him there was a shock. Even though I know he's a police officer, it's still..."

"Intense," Kat finishes for me, her tone softening. "How do you feel about it?"

"It was overwhelming," I confess. "But I couldn't help feeling... safer with him there."

"Of course," Kat says, her voice filled with understanding. "He's always had that effect on you, hasn't he? Don't think I didn't see your *smile* before, Meli." She winks.

"I didn't... it's... Ugh, maybe? I don't even know." I sigh. But I *do* know.

The answer to her question is *yes*. He's always had this effect on me.

I look away for a moment, trying to fix my gaze on something other than my sister's inquisitive face on the screen. "This crush is... It's stupid. I'm being stupid."

"You're not stupid, just overly optimistic, I think. But hey, there's nothing wrong with a crush. It's harmless."

"Yeah, I guess," I say, more to reassure myself than my sister. I take a deep breath, deciding to shift the conversation. "Anyway, how's it going over there?" I ask, hearing Millie squealing and giggling in the background.

Kathryn catches on and shakes her head with a playful smirk. "It's going," she says with a laugh. "John is trying to catch Millie; he's on bath duty tonight."

I can just make out John's voice in the background calling out,

"Kat! Can you grab her for me at least?"

Millie's cries suddenly echo through the background.

"Ugh, I think I should go, sis. John needs my help. Again." She winks, and I chuckle softly.

"Sure, no problem. Give my love to the little munchkin over there."

"Will do. And keep me updated on how you're doing, please. Especially after everything today," Kathryn says, concern etched on her face. "Are you sure you're okay?"

"Yes, Kat! I'm fine."

"Okay, okay. I'm just a phone call away, yeah?"

"Yeah, I know. Thanks, Kat."

"Goodnight, Meli. Love you, and stay safe," she adds, blowing a kiss.

"Night, love you, too!" I say before ending the call.

As it disconnects, I find myself staring at my phone wallpaper: an image from last Christmas—Kat, Millie, and I in matching Mickey Mouse pyjamas. My heart swells at the sight.

I can't help but smile at how our conversations always feel so familiar. Sisters are like that, no matter the distance between us. I pause, taking in the quiet ambiance of my living room, softly lit by the warm glow of lamps. As I reflect on today, everything replays in my mind—the attempted robbery and then Bradley's sudden appearance. Life really does throw unexpected surprises!

Sure, I've seen Bradley around quite a bit, especially when I visit Liv. We crossed paths at Christmas and then again at Isla and Xavier's wedding earlier this year. Despite all these encounters, we've never really gone beyond a polite hello or a smile. Part of it is nerves, I suppose. Bradley has this aura about him—kind of intimidating, in a way.

And nothing has changed.

Ten years later and he still intrigues me, still excites me, still makes me nervous. It's just funny how in a small town like ours, our paths have always seemed to skirt around each other without ever *really* converging. Not that I've actively avoided it—well, maybe he has, too, now that I think about it.

But why? It's a question that lingers in my mind now.

I stroll to the window, drawing back the curtains to reveal twilight's painted sky. It's quiet outside, with the street lamps casting a warm glow. Night brings a sense of peace, a time to reflect and savour the little joys.

After closing the curtains and turning off the lamps, I slip into bed. Moonlight softly filters through the window, and I embrace the quiet of the night. Despite the peaceful ambiance, worry still lingers in the back of my mind. The events of today keep replaying—flashes of fear and adrenaline. My heart races at the memory of the robbery, the panic in the air, and the relief when the police arrived. Seeing Bradley in the midst of it all only added to the whirlwind of emotions.

I hug my pillow tighter, trying to shake off the unease.

3

Bradley

The events of yesterday loom over me like a shadow, and I can't shake the memory of it. As my pen scratches across the paperwork, my mind drifts to the unexpected sighting of Amelia. The image of her shocked face keeps replaying in my mind like a haunting echo.

She would've been terrified; and that's probably an understatement.

Witnessing something like that is bad enough, but being caught up in it is a whole different story. I remember the look in her eyes—pure fear. It's a feeling that sticks with you, no matter how much you try to shake it off.

I'd checked in with the paramedic after she'd dismissed her yesterday, just to make sure she was really okay. The paramedic reassured me that she was, but here I am, still fucking worrying about her.

I can't help it. The way she looked at me, the vulnerability in her eyes... It's not something I can just easily forget.

I try to push her image aside, focusing instead on the paperwork in front of me, but her presence lingers, a nagging distraction that refuses to be ignored. I'm a man of few words, but my mind churns with a sea of unspoken thoughts and unresolved emotions—thoughts and feelings I thought I'd buried deep ever since that night.

I usually do a good job of unintentionally avoiding her when she comes over to hang out with my sister. It's not that I don't want to see her, and I try not to be a snob or a grumpy prick, but if I don't keep my distance, I'll get caught up with thoughts of her.

Which is exactly what's happening right fucking now.

With a sigh, I stand up and make my way to the staff lunchroom, in desperate need of a break. It's only ten in the morning, and I'm already feeling the strain. The familiar routine of grabbing a bottle of water from the fridge helps to ground me, if only for a moment, before I return to my desk.

As I walk back, I pass by officers engrossed in their work or chatting too loudly for my liking. Mornings at the Wattle Creek station are usually calm, filled with reports from the night before, minor traffic issues, and the occasional retail or school-related call. It's a welcome respite from the chaos that often descends upon us during the late afternoons or nights.

I'm grateful for my shift rotation, four days on, four days off, with each fortnight alternating Mondays off. It's a schedule that allows me some semblance of normalcy, a luxury in our line of work. But as always, things can change in an instant, and I try not to take this stability for granted.

Daniels, full name Sebastian Daniels, has been working with me for the past few months, and sometimes, I forget how much older he is than me. At thirty-five years old, he acts like a fucking child most days. While I'd never admit it to him, he's grown on me. Despite his occasional immaturity, I see a good man beneath the surface—someone I can trust, much like I trust my brother Xavier. He reminds me of Xavier in many ways, and perhaps that's why I've grown to rely on him, even if it's begrudgingly.

I return to my desk, the familiar rhythm of the station lulling me back to a sense of normalcy. Yet, I can't shake the feeling that something has shifted, that the events of yesterday have set something in motion that I can't quite grasp. And amidst the chaos of police work, amidst the mundane routine of paperwork and reports, one thing remains clear—the presence of Amelia in my thoughts is a puzzle I can't seem to solve.

I pull my phone out and reluctantly type out a text.

Me: I have a question, and I need an answer and an answer only. Understood?

Xavier: Hello to you too, brother!

Me: Xavier.

Xavier: Yes, sir. Ask away.

Me: What school does Amelia, Liv's friend, work at?

The three bubbles dance as I can imagine Xavier's mind running rampant, trying to decipher why I'm asking. *Just answer the fucking question*, I chant silently in my head.

> **Xavier:** I'll need to ask Isla. Hold on.

A few moments pass before another text pops up.

> **Xavier:** Koala Creek Primary School. Why?

Ignoring his question, I just reply with a thumbs up emoji.

It's about twelve thirty now, and I'm sitting in my car, on our second round of patrolling for the day. This time, I'm behind the wheel, with Daniels in the passenger seat. We've been driving around town, observing the townsfolk, yet, somehow, subconsciously, I've ended up outside Koala Creek Primary School, about a twenty-minute drive from the main town square of Wattle Creek.

What the fuck am I doing here? The question lingers in the air.

Daniels is absentmindedly scrolling on his phone, not having noticed where we are just yet.

I had asked my brother for the details of Amelia's school, but I hadn't really thought through what I wanted to do with the information. And much to my dismay, I've ended up out the front of the school. How fitting.

I can't explain why I'm here, why I've driven to this place without even realising it. *What exactly do I think I'm going to do now?*

This is fucked.

Daniels' voice breaks through my thoughts. "Uh, care to explain why we are outside Koala Creek Primary School?"

"No."

"You lost then, mate?"

"No."

The truth is, I've driven here because my thoughts haven't stopped since the fucking morning.

It's doing my head in. I've never felt these emotions before, and rather than revel in them, I just want them *gone*.

I've tried to rationalise it, to convince myself that it's just a concern. Concern for an innocent bystander who found themselves caught in a shitty situation yesterday. I'm just doing my due diligence by checking on said innocent bystander.

Yeah, that's it.

"Just going to check up on something," I say to Sebastian, my voice terse as I open the car door, but remain in my seat.

"What?" he says abruptly, turning his attention to me, away from his phone.

"Hop in the driver's side. I'll only be a few minutes or so," I say back, not bothering to turn and face him. "Keep the car running."

"What are you doing?"

"I just told you." I grit my teeth, annoyed by his prying.

"I heard you... but is it something? Or *someone*?" he quips with a raised brow. "Since when do we do *personal* check-ins? Is this something new I'm not aware of?"

Ignoring his queries, I step out onto the footpath. The schoolyard is deserted, a stillness settling over the scene. My footsteps echo in the quiet, each step amplifying the weight of my thoughts. I walk toward the entrance, feeling the gravity of the moment pressing down on me.

As I enter the school, the cool air of the hallway washes over me, a stark contrast to the warmth of the midday sun outside. I walk down the corridor, and I can't shake the feeling that I'm walking into something I can't quite understand. An elderly woman at the front office desk spots me and stands up immediately, her expression tense. I realise that I momentarily forgot I'm in uniform, and she's probably worried that something has happened.

"Oh! O-officer. Can I help ya?" she asks, her voice stuttering slightly.

"Sorry to rock up unannounced." I nod to her. "My name is Officer Mitchell. I'm here to see one of your staff members."

"Oh, dear. Is everything alright?" she inquires, her brow furrowing slightly.

"Quite alright. Just doing a brief check-up," I reply, with a curt nod.

"Oh. I wasn't aware we'd be needing one. Shall I fetch the principal for ya?"

"No. I was after a particular staff member." Her eyes go wide as saucers, as she stutters a response back. *I'm aware that as soon as I say this, it sounds very ambiguous.*

"Nothing troubling at all. I didn't mean to alarm you. Just checking in on them," I reassure her.

"Righto. Who ya after?"

"Miss Brown."

She smiles warmly and nods, understanding dawning in her eyes. "Ah, yes, Miss Amelia Brown. She's currently in class, with her kindergartens. Just down the hall to ya left," she says, pointing in the direction.

"Thank you." I nod gratefully, starting to walk off in the direction she indicated, but before I can get far, she stops me, apologising.

"Hold on, where are my manners? Let me escort you."

"No need. I can manage just fine," I insist, but she shakes her head.

"Nonsense. I'll walk ya, dear."

As we approach the classroom door, the sounds of children's laughter and squeals fill the hallways. The sounds cracking ever so slightly at my tough exterior, warming something inside me. Amidst their joyous laughter, my thoughts linger on Amelia, her face still vivid in my mind from yesterday's ordeal. She's just a bystander, caught in the chaos of a random incident, yet there's something about her that pulls at me, something beyond duty or protocol.

I find myself wanting to ensure she's alright, more than just a passing concern. It's a tug at my conscience, a gnawing feeling that refuses to be ignored. The warmth I felt moments ago now mixes with a subtle flutter of nerves. It's not just about the incident anymore; it's about her well-being, her safety in a world where unpredictability lurks around every corner.

The office lady swings the door open, and I step into the room, immediately scanning for Amelia. What I see stops me in my tracks, my heart momentarily catching in my chest.

There she sits, poised at the front of the classroom, immersed in reading to a group of captivated children. For a fleeting second, my mind goes blank, and I forget why I'm here.

Her smile, gentle and genuine, softens her features as she brings the story to life with every word. All I can focus on is her—the way she interacts with the children, and the way she lights up the room.

It's mesmerising, and I find myself unable to look away.

4

Amelia

I sit cross-legged at the front of the classroom, holding up the colourful pages of *The Very Hungry Caterpillar* for all the children to see. Timmy and Dahlia, two of my more energetic students, are practically bouncing in their seats with excitement.

"Yes, Timmy?" I ask, smiling at the eager five-year-old.

"Miss Amelia, why is the caterpillar so hungry?" he asks, his eyes wide with curiosity.

"Well," I begin, "the caterpillar is so hungry because he's getting ready to turn into a beautiful butterfly. Just like how you eat lots of food to grow big and strong!"

Ever since I started teaching kindergarten, I told the kids to call me Miss Amelia rather than Miss Brown. I wanted them to feel more comfortable around me, and since then, it hasn't changed.

Plus, Miss Brown just sounds *plain Jane boring*.

Dahlia's hand shoots up, and I call on her next. "Miss, why does the caterpillar eat all that stuff? It's yucky!"

I chuckle at her question. "Uh, well, the caterpillar eats all those things because he's preparing to build his cocoon. It might seem yucky to us, but it's just right for him!"

The children giggle, and I continue reading, the story captivating their young minds. Then, suddenly, I'm interrupted by the sound of the door opening. I glance up and am caught off guard when Mrs. Higgins enters the room, with *Bradley Mitchell* towering behind her.

I freeze, my heart skipping a beat, and stop reading instantly. The kids all turn to look in the direction I'm facing, their eyes widening with shock. A few let out audible gasps.

"Who's that?" one of the kids whispers loudly.

"Oh my gosh, it's the police!" another exclaims in shock. I raise a hand gently, trying to calm the room.

"It's okay, everyone," I say, forcing a smile.

Mrs. Higgins says, her voice cheery, "Amelia, sorry to interrupt, dear, but Officer Mitchell would like to have a word with you."

I stand up slowly, trying to compose myself. "Oh. Um, of course. Kindy, I'll be right back. Continue listening to the story with Mrs. Higgins."

I can hear the kids start to whisper and a low chorus of "ooo's" coming from the boys. I can't help but smile at their curiosity, even in a moment like this. As I walk toward Bradley, worry gnaws at my chest.

Why has he shown up unannounced? What could he possibly want to discuss with me?

My heart races as I notice him in his uniform, the crisp lines and polished badge. *Stop, you foolish girl, before you get all flustered.*

His towering figure commands attention, and I can't help but feel a rush of nerves.

Nerves now dance throughout my body, sending tingles down my back as I approach him. He nods toward the door, indicating for me to step outside with him. I follow him out into the hallway, the sounds of the classroom fading behind us.

"Amelia," he begins, his voice serious yet gentle. "I'm sorry. I didn't mean to show up unannounced. Especially while you're at work."

"Oh, that's okay. This is the most exciting thing the kids have encountered all day today, most likely." I laugh. He doesn't. *Don't be awkward, Amelia.*

"Uh, so why are you here?" I blurt out before I can stop myself. "Oh my god, sorry, that came out so rude. What I *meant* to say was, do you normally check up on people like this? Sorry, I tend to ramble when I'm nervous. Sorry."

So much for not being awkward, loser.

A smirk appears on his mouth ever so slightly. Are my eyes deceiving me, or did Bradley Mitchell just smirk?

"You're nervous?" He says, his voice so, so deep. *My goodness.*

I feel my heart skip a beat, his words sending a jolt of electricity through me. "Y-yes," I stammer, my voice barely above a whisper. "You make me nervous, sorry."

That slight smirk remains on his face, yet his brows furrow, his eyes holding mine so intensely.

"You just apologised like four times," he drawls.

My eyes widen. *Did I?* Omg, how embarrassing. I blush furiously, feeling embarrassed at my nervousness.

"You don't need to apologise, Amelia," he says. "If anything, I should be the one apologising for showing up unannounced *and* making you nervous while you're at work."

His words catch me off guard, and I can feel my cheeks burning even hotter. I glance back at the classroom; I notice that all the children are watching us, their eyes wide with curiosity.

"Look, I... I just wanted to make sure you're okay after yesterday. And no, this isn't something I normally do. But something about yesterday... It just didn't sit right with me."

Oh. *Oh.*

It's not something he normally does? Yet he came here anyway to check up on me? *Amelia, don't get your hopes up; the man is just polite.*

I hear the kids chatter start picking up, so I look past Bradley's tall frame, and observe Mrs. Higgins trying to continue reading the story, but it's clear that the kids are more interested in what's happening over here.

"Uh, thank you, that's nice of you," I say, tearing my gaze away from the kids. "Again, I'm sorry, I didn't mean to be rude. It's just... unexpected, seeing you here."

"Amelia," he says sternly. "Stop apologising." His voice is gruff and so deep. Gosh.

"Yes, sir." Did I actually say that out loud? Omg why did I say that? What an absolute goose. His eyes widen for a split second, processing what I just said. I can see the gears turning in his head.

"That just came out," I huff out a shy laugh. "Do uh, do people call you that? ... Sir?"

"Not really."

Just as I go to apologise again, I rethink my words.

"I don't mind it coming from you, though." His words catch me off guard; again, his voice is so low, yet loud enough for me to hear.

Did he... did he just flirt? With me? A kindergarten teacher with zero experience in the dating world. Maybe I'm reading too much into it. After all, Bradley Mitchell is just being polite. *Right?*

Still, I feel my cheeks flush at his words. I take a deep breath, trying to calm my racing heart. I don't even know what to say to that? Does he expect me to continue?

I have no idea what I'm doing.

He stares at me, his gaze searching my face, his dark blue eyes intense and piercing. They're not as bright as Xavier's, but they still hold a captivating quality that makes my heart race.

"So, you're holding up okay?" Bradley's voice is low and steady, cutting through the classroom's ambient noise. "If you're not, I want you to tell me. I understand if you're still feeling some shock from what happened."

"Yeah, I'm alright," I reply softly, managing a small smile. "It was scary, but I'm really thankful you were there. Honestly, thank you for checking in."

As I speak, I notice Bradley watching me intently, his brows furrowed slightly, his eyes scanning my face.

Does he believe me? The thought flickers through my mind, but seeing his concern makes me feel at ease, reassured by his genuine care.

"I promise, I'm okay," I add, meeting his gaze directly. Immediately, I see his features soften, a subtle relief crossing his expression.

"I'm glad to hear that," he murmurs, his voice gentle yet reassuring. "You know, you've got a lot of strength, Amelia. Not everyone handles situations like that as well as you have."

My pulse quickens at his unexpected compliment, his sincerity striking a chord deep within me.

"I should probably get going," he says, clearing his throat lightly.

I nod with a smile, trying to lighten the mood. "Oh, yes, of course. I'm sure you have more exciting things to do than be here," I tease, a small laugh escaping me.

"Not really," he replies softly, his gaze steady. "This is the most exciting thing I've seen all day."

His words catch me off guard, sending a rush of warmth through me.

Before I know it, he's guiding me back inside the classroom, with a hand at my back, and his touch sends a jolt of electricity through me.

Calm yourself, Amelia.

As we enter, the children's heads turn in unison, their eyes widening with curiosity. I can't help but smile at their innocent fascination.

"Alrighty, kindy, can we all say good afternoon to Officer Mitchell?" I prompt.

In a sweet chorus, they all chime, "Good afternoon, Officer Mitchell!"

Their voices fill the room with warmth, and I catch Bradley's small smirk as he acknowledges them. I glance away quickly, feeling my cheeks flush under his gaze.

He nods to the children before stepping out, Mrs. Higgins following closely behind. And just like that, he's gone again, leaving me with a lingering warmth and a smile that I can't seem to shake.

In an instant, the kids erupt into chatter and questions, all at once. "Who was that? What happened?"

I hush them and return to my seat, attempting to calm them down.

"Miss Amelia, is he your boyfriend?" Timmy asks, his eyes wide with curiosity.

"Yeah, are you going to marry him?" Dahlia chimes in, her voice filled with excitement.

"Do you like him?" another voice pipes up from the back.

"Oh, no! He's not my boyfriend," I reply, trying to hide the blush creeping up my face. "We're just friends."

"Is that why you're smiling?" Talia asks, her voice squeaky.

Dear God. This is exactly what I was just talking about.

"Guys, guys. Shhh!" I say, trying to remain calm. My heart is racing, and I can't believe I'm having this conversation with a bunch of five-year-olds. I glance at their eager faces, and despite the embarrassment, I can't help but smile at their innocence.

They make even the most awkward moments endearing.

As the bell rings for lunchtime, the kids pack up their things and say goodbye to me before running out the door, their laughter fading down the hallway.

My conversation with Bradley from earlier triggers a sense of déjà vu, unlocking a memory I thought I had buried. We were at a party at his place. He was drinking, and he said things to me… things I've tried so hard to forget. He almost kissed me that night, and since then, I've tried to bury that memory deep down, along with my stupid crush on him.

But now, seeing him again, that night is resurfacing. Does he remember? I don't think he does. He was intoxicated, after all. But surely, he must remember something?

Why would he? You're nothing to him now; you'll always just be his little sister's best friend.

As I gather my things and head to the staff room for lunch, I can't shake the unease that has settled in my stomach. Maybe it's just my imagination, or maybe it's something more.

Either way, I can't help but wonder.

5

Bradley

18 YEARS OLD

*I*t's the first summer after high school, and Xavier and I have the place to ourselves while our parents are off visiting family friends a couple of hours away. Mingling with 'family' we don't know? Yeah, no. Not our idea of a good time.

So we've opted to stay put. Xavier, being Xavier, decided we should throw a little shindig to celebrate our graduation. To our parents, it's just a simple BBQ with a few friends. Little do they know, Xavier's definition of 'a few friends' is a bit... generous.

Our backyard is buzzing with activity, the smell of steak sizzling on the BBQ filling the air. Xavier's mates are here in full force, along with Harrison and Michael, and of course, a bunch of my own mates. People are scattered all over the place, some chilling by the barn, others lounging around the pool. The sun has set, but the warmth of the day still lingers, making the evening just right for a swim.

Jackson and Luke, two of my mates, clap me on the back as they pass by, congratulating each other and me on finally being done with school. In passing, Luke hands me a red party cup with clear liquid. Cautiously, I look at it, and Luke notices, laughing.

"Relax, bud, it's just vodka and lemonade."

"Cheers to us, mate," Jackson says, raising his beer bottle in salute.

"No more exams, no more teachers breathing down our necks," Luke adds, grinning from ear to ear.

I take a large sip of my drink and nod in response, my smile a little forced. I'm grateful school's over, but I've never been one for loud celebrations.

"Come on, Brad," Jackson says, patting me on the back again. "You're joining the police force soon. It's time to loosen up!"

Luke chimes in, grinning, "Exactly! No more studying or stress. Let's enjoy tonight!"

Their words linger in my mind, sparking thoughts about the path ahead. Joining the police force is the dream I've always wanted to pursue. My father had been ecstatic about it, and I don't want to let him down. The pressure is on to make something of myself, to prove that I can succeed. But right now, surrounded by friends and the sounds of laughter and music, I can't help but feel a sense of freedom. Tonight is about letting go of the past and embracing the future, whatever it may hold. Fuck it. What's a couple of drinks?

"I guess you're right," I finally respond, trying to muster up some enthusiasm. I down the rest of my drink in one gulp.

"Oh yeah! Let's go!" Jackson exclaims.

"Atta boy!" Luke whoops, following suit.

A couple of drinks turned into many more, and now my head has a slight buzz. I'm feeling a lot more relaxed than I was earlier. The music is loud, the atmosphere vibrant, and for the first time in a long while, I feel like I can just be in the moment. As the night rolls on, Jennifer, a girl from my year, totters over to me, clearly sloshed.

"Bradley, there you are," she slurs, before plopping herself onto my lap. Jennifer's been in our social circle for a while now. Her mates took a liking to Jackson and Luke, although Jackson has never been one for too much female attention. I'm pretty sure he swings both ways, but each to their own. I'll never judge a mate or their sexuality. This meant, naturally, I got roped in, too.

While I don't mind the attention from girls, tonight feels off. Sure, I've hooked up with girls plenty, but I've never settled down. Lately, I haven't been in the mood to chat them up. Since graduating, girls have been all over me ever since they heard I'm aiming to be a policeman.

She's made it obvious she wants me, yet I haven't done much to reciprocate the feelings, apart from an occasional kiss here and there, and I don't want to lead her on, especially since she's made it clear to others that she has a thing for me.

As Jennifer's fingers weave through my short hair, her boozy breath, mixed with a sweet perfume, envelops me. Despite these thoughts, I find myself welcoming her closeness, the alcohol coursing through my veins heightening my senses.

"I've been thinking about you all night," Jennifer whispers, her voice dripping with desire, sending a shiver down my spine. Her touch intensifies as she moves closer, her lips brushing against my neck in a seductive dance.

But amidst her advances, I can't shake this nagging feeling of unease. It's as if my body is here, but my mind is elsewhere, lost in a whirlwind of conflicting thoughts. Then, amidst the haze, I spot a group in the distance. Liv stands among a few people and next to her stands... Amelia.

I watch her as she speaks, a smile painting her face, all while Jen continues her assault on my neck, and in that moment, her eyes lock with mine. Fuck.

It's brief, but our eyes lock, and I can't look away. As I watch her, she holds my gaze, her smile fading slightly as she notices Jennifer on my lap. This feels wrong. Weird.

Why am I so caught up with this girl? She's my sister's best friend, for fuck's sake.

As I grapple with these thoughts, Jennifer's eyes lock with mine, and a wave of discomfort washes over me. This feels all wrong, weird. I gently push her away, mustering a weak smile.

"I, um, sorry, I think I left something in the house," I mutter, my voice strained as I search for an excuse to escape.

As I head off, a voice calls my name from behind, but I continue walking, my head pounding. Water, I need water. Inside the house,

I head straight to the kitchen, grab a bottle, and gulp it down, the cool liquid soothing my throat. Tossing the empty bottle into the bin, I decide I need some space to clear my head.

Outside, at the front of the house, two wooden chairs beckon. A wind chime hangs from one of the beams, swaying gently in the now-cool breeze, its soft tinkling a stark contrast to the earlier raucousness of the party. Leaning back, I close my eyes, trying to clear my mind.

But the evening's events keep pushing in. Jennifer, my unease, and then seeing Amelia again. She's off limits in every way—my sister's best friend, too good for a guy like me.

Yet, there's something about her, something that draws me in, makes my pulse quicken. I remember the way she looked at me, her eyes full of something I couldn't quite read. It's like she sees right through me, past all my bravado, and into the parts of me I try to hide.

She's different. She's... real. And it scares me how much I want to know her, really know her, beyond just the surface.

I shouldn't feel this way. It's complicated, messy. But fuck, I can't help it.

I shake my head, trying to dispel these thoughts. I can't afford to be distracted, especially not tonight. Tomorrow, I start preparing for the police academy, and I need to be focused. But as I sit here, in the quiet of the night, I can't shake the feeling that everything is about to change.

The distant thump of music from the backyard is still audible, but the sound of the front door suddenly bursting open startles me, and out stumbles Amelia.

What the?

She looks around and squeals when she spots me. "Oh, my goodness! You scared me." Her voice is so pure, melodic, and innocent. I can't explain it, but I love the sound of it.

"Sorry, I didn't mean to disturb. I was just looking for..." Her words trail off and I raise my eyebrow, prompting her to continue.

"Looking for?" I mimic her, my tone dry.

"Liv. She came back into the house, and I thought she might be out here."

As she stands there, looking lost and a bit vulnerable, a protective instinct kicks in.

"Well, she's not here. She might still be inside," I say, my voice softer. "You need help finding her?"

She shakes her head, her eyes meeting mine. There's something in her gaze that makes my heart race. "No, it's okay. Thanks," she replies, but she doesn't move. She just stands there, fidgeting with her bracelets, in the cool night air, the tension between us palpable. "I didn't mean to intrude. I'll just... I'll head back inside."

"Wait," I blurt out, surprising myself. She stops, looking at me with those wide eyes. "You don't have to rush off. It's nice out here, and honestly, I could use the company."

As she pauses, I can't help but feel a wave of uncertainty wash over me. What am I doing?

"Are you sure?" she asks, her voice soft and unsure.

"Yeah," I say, more confident than I feel. I tear my gaze away, my eyes scanning the darkened surroundings.

She sits on the chair beside me, her body swaying slightly. I furrow my brows deeper as a thought crosses my mind. *Has she been drinking? She's underage—she shouldn't be.*

"You haven't been drinking, have you?" I ask cautiously.

Amelia's eyes widen, surprise and embarrassment flickering across her features. "No," she says quickly, shaking her head. "Neither has Liv. I made sure of it."

Her response brings a sense of relief, surprising me.

But who am I to lecture her? *I think to myself, reflecting on my own past.*

I was once the same, influenced by my older brother, Xavier. We did everything together. Whatever he did, I did, too. It's not my place to tell her what to do, but she's surrounded by horny, drunk seventeen- and eighteen-year-olds.

"Okay." I nod, easing up slightly. "Smart move."

After a moment, she chuckles softly, and I raise a brow at her. "Something funny?"

"That was such a 'big brother' thing to say," she says with a smile.

A comfortable silence settles between us. Yet, her words linger in my mind.

'Big brother.'

The phrase coming from her lips just sounds... wrong. *Is that how she sees me? Like a big brother to her? She should, shouldn't she?*

After all, she's practically family. There shouldn't be anything else between us.

But why does that thought disappoint me?

Breaking the silence, she asks, "How was school for you? Besides the obvious, graduating and all. Did you enjoy it? What was your favourite subject?"

"It was alright," I reply nonchalantly. "I'd say PE was my favourite. I enjoyed playing sports."

As I talk, her eyes flicker down to my chest, then up to my biceps. My muscles tense in response, and I wonder why I'm so nervous about her admiring my body. I watch as she struggles to catch her breath, the rise and fall of her chest becoming more rapid.

She looks back at me and clears her throat.

"Why are you out here alone? Shouldn't you be with your girlfriend?" she asks. Huh?

"Girlfriend?" I repeat, puzzled.

"Oh, the girl you were with earlier. Aren't you two together?"

I shake my head, trying to hide my surprise. "Jennie? Nah, she's just a friend," I reply quickly. "Nothing more."

Despite my attempt at nonchalance, her observation lingers in my mind.

Why did she notice that? Does she think there's something between me and Jennifer? Or is she just curious?

Either way, the fact that she paid attention enough to ask surprises me.

"I see. Sorry, I didn't mean to pry. I just assumed," she mumbles, looking apologetic. I can't help but smirk at her reaction.

"No need to apologise. It's fine."

"Sorry, I tend to apologise a lot when I'm..." Her words trail off.

"When you're what?"

"Nervous," she whispers and avoids meeting my eyes.

"Why are you nervous?"

"Y-you make me nervous." Her eyes widen again, and she shakes her head. "Sorry, I'm just mumbling."

I don't know what I was expecting, but it sure as fuck wasn't that.

"I make you nervous?"

"Y-yes."

Well, fuck. A strange sense of satisfaction washes over me at her admission. Why does it please me to know that she's affected by my presence?

"Why?" I ask, genuinely curious now.

"I-I don't know," she stammers. "You just... you seem so... I mean, you're older, and... I'm just... I'm just me." Her words tumble out in a rush, and she fidgets with her fingers, unable to meet my gaze.

As I listen to her, a sense of tenderness washes over me. She's so genuine, so unassuming. "Just you? And what's wrong with that?"

"Nothing, I'm... it's nothing."

I reach out, placing a hand on her thigh. "Amelia, you're more than just you. You're kind, thoughtful, and incredibly sweet. Don't sell yourself short."

She looks up at me, surprise flickering in her eyes. "You think so?"

"Yeah, I do."

Her blush deepens, and I can't deny the rush it gives me. As much as I hate to admit it, her nervousness lights a fire inside me. Leaning in slightly, I notice she does the same, her breath quickening.

Caught up in the moment, her scent surrounds me, tempting me to reach out and touch her, to feel her skin beneath my fingertips. But I hold back, my rational side reminding me of the lines I shouldn't cross. My heart races, realising this needs to stop.

Her eyes flicker to my mouth, and the alcohol in my system doesn't help. I feel her uncertainty, mixed with something that matches my own desires.

"Amelia, you gotta stop giving me that look," I warn, trying to keep my voice steady.

She tilts her head, confusion clouding her eyes. "What look?" Her voice barely rises above a whisper.

I exhale heavily, running a hand through my hair. "Like... like you want me to kiss you," I admit quietly.

Fuck, the urge to kiss her right now is overwhelming. To feel her lips against mine. But instead of backing off, she inches closer. In my somewhat intoxicated state, my thoughts are all over the place, but seeing her respond, sober and steady, sends a thrill through me. My heart races, and I feel my cock stir in my pants, a feeling I am desperately trying so hard to ignore.

"I—"

Before I can finish, Luke emerges out front, breaking the tension with his abrupt arrival. "Mate, there you are! Fuck, I've been looking for you everywhere."

His interruption couldn't have come at a worse time. Amelia shoots up in a hurry at the sudden intrusion.

Fucking Luke.

"I'm-I'm gonna go find Liv. Thanks for the, uh, chat," she says nervously before glancing at Luke and then hurrying away back inside.

Luke looks at me, his expression questioning. "What was that about?" he asks, nodding toward where Amelia disappeared.

I ponder for a moment, choosing my words carefully. "Nothing," I finally say, shaking my head. "Just a chat."

Luke gives me a sceptical look, but thankfully doesn't push further. Instead, he claps a hand on my shoulder and gestures toward the house. "Well, come on, then. Let's head back inside."

As we make our way back to the party, my mind drifts back to Amelia. Despite the abrupt end to our conversation, her presence lingers in my thoughts, accompanied by a slew of what-ifs.

What if things had gone differently? What if we had given in to the tension between us?

Deep down, I know it's probably for the best.

Amelia is Liv's best friend, and I can't risk messing that up—or my relationship with my sister. As tempting as it is to entertain those what-ifs with Amelia, I've set these boundaries for a reason, and I need to stick to them. Besides, she deserves someone who's not a brooding mess, with a future as uncertain as mine.

That's just how it has to be, for everyone's sake.

6

Bradley

A week has crawled by, and I find myself ploughing through the endless tranquillity of Wattle Creek Police Station. Yesterday's shift dragged on into overtime, thanks to the ongoing drama at Beaumont Creek Jail. And then there's the paperwork—endless stacks of tedious speeding fines, each one requiring my painstaking focus.

Amidst all this, Amelia lingers in my thoughts like an unwelcome guest who refuses to leave. It's embarrassing to admit, but she's been on my mind every morning and every night for over a week now. Her presence is like a persistent shadow, always lurking at the edge of my mind, making it damn near impossible to focus on my job.

I keep replaying our last conversation at her workplace, where memories of that one night resurfaced—the night where the lines blurred slightly, where things almost changed. I can't shake the memory of how close I came to kissing her, how the air between us crackled with undeniable tension. If it weren't for the intrusion, I might have leaned in, closed that gap, and crossed that line I've been dancing around for years now.

Fucking hell.

That was so long ago. Years have passed, and not a single thought or itch of that night has resurfaced. Until now.

Interrupting my thoughts, our superintendent, Gary Faulkner, enters the room, his presence commanding attention.

"Mornin', Mitchell. How's your week been?" Faulkner's voice breaks the quiet of the room.

"Fine. The usual, sir."

Faulkner nods, then gestures toward me. "And your partner? Everything okay there?"

I nod. "Yeah, we're doing fine, sir. No complaints."

"Daniels," Faulkner says with a chuckle. "There's never a dull moment with that bloke."

Fighting a smirk, I nod in agreement. "That's for sure."

"Noticed you clocked off late yesterday. All good?" he inquires, his tone casual yet observant.

"Fine, sir. Just had some things to finish up," I reply, my responses succinct.

Faulkner studies me before offering, "You know, Mitchell, you can finish up earlier today to make up for the extra hours last night."

His unexpected kindness catches me off guard. "Sir, I don't think—" I begin, but he cuts me off, his tone firm and decisive.

"Look, son. You do a damn good job around here, Mitchell. It's fine. Go on, get out of 'ere a bit earlier today," he insists, leaving no room for argument.

Grateful for the reprieve, I nod. "Thank you, sir. I appreciate it."

With that, Faulkner exits the lunchroom, leaving me to contemplate his gesture. It's a rare moment of compassion in a job that often feels isolating.

Faulkner's mention of Sebastian brings another thought to mind; there really is never a dull moment with that bloke. Don't get me wrong, I love my job. It's been my passion for as long as I can remember. But lately, I can't shake the feeling that something is missing. There's a longing for excitement, a need to sort things out before I become a grumpy fuck like my father.

That man takes the definition of 'cunt' to a whole new level.

Despite Mumma's sunny disposition, which one would think might lighten his mood, he remains unchanged. I can't help but feel a pang of sympathy for Xavier, who often bears the brunt of his foul temper as his right-hand man on the farm.

> **Me:** You home?

> **Xavier:** Where else would I be? 🙄

> **Xavier:** Actually, I can think of many places other than here.

> **Me:** Ok

> **Xavier:** I'm trying to teach Liv how to shear. She 'offered' to help, which means Dad probably berated her and sent her over.

Seems like things never change with her. I snort, shaking my head at our predictable family dynamics.

> **Me:** Tough break. Good luck with that. I'm finishing early today, so I'll be home soon.

Xavier: Hectic! I'll have a cold one waiting for ya.

As Xavier and I sit on the back deck of our family home, the sun dipping low on the horizon, we each nurse a cold stubby, the reward for a hard day's work, well, for Xavier at least—mine's been cruisy. Can't complain.

"So, Liv actually did something useful today," Xav chuckles, breaking the comfortable silence between us. I raise an eyebrow, prompting him to continue.

"Yeah, she held the shearers for me while I did all the work," he says, shaking his head. "That girl, I swear." I can't help but chuckle at Liv's antics. She's always been a character.

"How was work?" Xav asks, turning the conversation to me.

"Good. The boss was pleased with some work, so I finished early," I reply.

"Good stuff. You've been putting in those extra hours, eh?"

"Yeah," I confirm, nodding slightly.

"Well, you deserve it. Cheers to that." Xav raises his bottle, and I follow suit, clinking our bottles together in a silent toast.

"How are you and Isla doing?" I inquire. "Especially, you know... after the wedding and everything that's happened."

Xavier's expression shifts, a flicker of discomfort crossing his features. "Isla's—she's good," he replies, a bit too quickly. "Yeah, we're good."

I raise an eyebrow, too perceptive to not know when something is up. Something is in fact up, and I can see it all over Xavier's face. I watch as he gulps down the rest of his beer, avoiding my gaze.

"You sure?" I press, knowing Xavier well enough to sense when something's not quite right.

Xavier downs the rest of his drink, and I can see the nervousness written all over his face. Apart from his wedding, I don't think I've ever seen him this jittery.

He clears his throat before blurting out, "Isla's pregnant."

Well, fuck.

I'm taken aback by his announcement. That's... that is definitely *not* what I was expecting.

"Oh. For real?"

Xavier responds with a snarky comment. "Nah, I'm lying, Brad," he scoffs. "Yes, for real!"

"Pregnant?" I repeat, trying to process the information. "But... how?"

Immediately, I mentally kick myself. Of course, I know *how*. That was a dumb question. Judging by the look on Xavier's face, it's like he knows exactly what I'm thinking.

"Do I really need to tell you how?" he says with a smirk.

I roll my eyes. "No, I'd rather not. What I should've asked is, *when* did you two find out?"

"A week ago," Xavier admits, looking sheepish. "It's still early days, and we weren't planning on telling anyone yet. Fuck, I wasn't supposed to say anything."

I can't help but shake my head. Trust him not to be able to keep it together. But in all honesty, fuck, I'm really happy for him. He deserves it.

"All good," I say. "I'm happy for you and Isla. Truly."

"Stop it. You'll make me tear up," he says, playfully smacking my shoulder.

Fucking idiot, he is.

"Nah, I appreciate it, bro. I really do. Fuck, I'm just—" His words trail off, as he takes off his cowboy hat—as Isla calls it—before running a hand through his unruly hair.

"You're what? Are you and Isla both… happy about all this?" I ask, frowning slightly. Fuck, now I really don't know what's going on in his head.

"Bloody oath! Of course we are," Xavier says with a full on smile. "I'm fucking stoked. It's just so—" his voice trails off.

"Unexpected?" I finish for him.

Xavier chuckles nervously. "Yeah, unexpected is an understatement. We're still trying to wrap our heads around it ourselves. But we're excited, you know? Scared shitless, but excited."

"I bet," I say, nodding. "Is Isla doing okay? You know, with everything that's happened recently?"

Xavier's smile fades, and he looks down at his beer, swirling it absentmindedly. "She's been struggling, to be honest," he admits, his voice low. "The whole thing with her dad... It hit her hard. And now, with the pregnancy... It's a lot for her to handle."

"I can imagine," I reply, my heart going out to Isla. She's been through so much, and now she's facing the challenges of pregnancy on top of it all. "She's strong, though. She'll get through this."

"Yeah, she is," Xavier agrees, a hint of pride in his voice. "And I'll be there every step of the way, no matter what."

I clap him on the shoulder, offering him a supportive smile. "I know you will, Xav. Isla's lucky to have you."

As we sit there, enjoying our cold ones, a comfortable silence washes over us. The horizon is lit up with the sun setting, casting a golden glow over everything. The air around us is warm, with a gentle breeze that carries the scent of the earth and distant eucalyptus trees.

"So... Amelia, ay?"

I'm caught off guard by his question. Fuck, it's my fault, really. I asked for her details the other day, so of course, he's curious now.

I whip my head in his direction, my brows furrowing. "What about Amelia?" I ask, attempting to sound casual, but I can feel the tension creeping into my voice.

"Just wondering how she's doing," Xavier says, his tone holding a hint of curiosity.

I shrug, attempting to play it off. "I'm sure she's fine."

Xavier raises an eyebrow, clearly not buying it. "Just fine? You did pay her a visit, no?"

"Yes. And?"

"Well..."

"Well then, what?" I reply, a bit more sharply than intended.

"Easy tiger," Xavier teases. "Just wanting to know what would have prompted you to do that."

I exhale, trying to keep my cool. "Just checking in on her. There was an attempted robbery at the florist in town, and she was there."

"Oh, fuck. I heard about that," he says, shaking his head. "So, she was *there*? Fucking hell!"

"Mhm."

"Is she alright?"

"Yes. From what I've gathered. Medics checked her out before she left."

He watches me for a moment, assessing. "That was... nice of you."

"Just doing my job," I murmur, trying to deflect.

"Mhm, sure," Xavier teases, seeing right through my excuse.

Before the conversation can continue, the back door opens abruptly and Olivia steps out. "I thought I heard your voices."

"Where'd you go?" Xavier asks, clearing his throat.

"I ran to the shops to get some snacks," Olivia explains, "and ran into Amelia. Chatted for a while in the aisles. I can't believe what happened the other day at the shop," Olivia suddenly blurts out. "How fucking scary. Amelia and I were talking about it."

My body goes rigid at the mention of the incident.

"Thank God you got there in time, Bradley."

"Yep," is all I can muster, in a clipped tone.

"Yeah, thank God," Xavier mimics sarcastically, and I shoot him a glare that says *shut the fuck up*. Xavier nods in response. Olivia furrows her brow, noticing our change in behaviour.

"Why are you both acting weird?"

"We're not acting weird."

Olivia's eyes narrow. "Righto, sure."

I exhale quietly, hoping to dispel some of the tension in the air.

"Why didn't Amelia come back here?" Xavier asks, being the nosy prick he is.

"Oh, she said something about heading to her parents' house for dinner."

Her parents' house? Does she still not live with her parents? I can't help but wonder.

"Does she not live at home?"

"Nah, she moved out a few months ago," Liv replies casually, as if it's no big deal.

Hm. *Interesting.*

Olivia shakes her head, still puzzled by our odd behaviour. "Well, I'm going inside. See you two later."

As she heads inside, I finish my beer, lost in contemplation. The image of Amelia, navigating life on her own without the safety net of her family home, weighs on my mind.

"I should head off, too," Xavier says, rising to his feet. "Need to help Isla with dinner."

I nod to my brother and follow suit, grabbing the bottles and heading inside.

7

Amelia

I walk into my classroom, and the vibrant energy of my little students instantly fills the air. The smell of paint and the sound of excited chatter fills the room. Today is art day, and the kids are buzzing with excitement as they gather around the tables, eager to get started.

I smile as I make my way to the front of the class, ready to teach my young artists the wonders of finger painting. The kids are already seated, their eyes wide with anticipation. I pick up a brush and dip it into the paint, showing them how to mix the primary colours to create new ones. Their faces light up with understanding as they follow along, mixing red and yellow to make orange, and blue and yellow to make green.

I guide them to use their fingers instead of brushes, as they are too young to handle brushes. Surprisingly, for a group of primarily five-year-olds, they're incredibly smart. They catch on quickly, giggling with delight as they swirl their fingers through the paint, creating their own masterpieces. It's moments like these that remind me why I love teaching and why I love art.

"Look, Miss, I made purple!" one of the kids exclaims, holding up their painted hands for me to see.

"That's wonderful, Tommy!" I praise, giving him a high five and instantly getting paint all over my hand. I laugh, shaking my head at the mess. "You're all doing such a great job!" I walk over to the sink, still grinning, and quickly rinse off my hands.

As the kids continue to paint, I can't help but think about my own art. Painting has always been a passion of mine, and I often dream of one day showcasing my works in a gallery. But in our small town, opportunities for artists are scarce. For now, I'm content to paint for fun and teach these young minds the joys of creativity.

No one, apart from my family and Olivia, knows that I paint. It's not like I have a big group of friends, anyway, but it's not something I just willingly share with people. *I'm too shy for that.* My art is like a secret world that I escape to, where I can express myself freely without judgement. Maybe one day, I'll have the courage to share it with the world. But for now, it's enough to know that I have this creative outlet to call my own.

Just then, my phone buzzes with a text message from Olivia, my best friend.

> **Olivia:** Hey girl! I bought you a few things for your studio at home. Can't wait to see what masterpieces you create with them! 😊

> **Me:** Ahh. Gimme, gimmie! Thank you so much, Liv! You're the absolute best!

Olivia's always been so supportive of my art, and I'm grateful for her. But every time I think of her, Bradley's right there in my mind, sending shivers down my spine.

Bloody hell. I thought by now, with a bit of age and wisdom, I'd be over this massive crush on him. But he makes it impossible. It's like he's everywhere lately, impossible to ignore.

At twenty-four, still being a virgin bothers me.

Am I doing something wrong? Do I need to put myself out there more?

I yearn for a love like my sister Kat's, to be married someday with kids. But when will that happen for me? I know I'm young, but these thoughts throw me off balance. Just as I'm lost in thoughts of Bradley, another text pops up.

> **Olivia:** Swing by this afternoon to grab them?

My heart races as Dahlia calls for help, pulling me from thoughts of Bradley. Panic sets in momentarily as I juggle Liv's request *and* my swirling emotions. Flustered at work, embarrassment floods through me—how could I let myself get worked up over a guy, especially here?

It's absurd.

The thought of seeing Bradley again, after the other day, adds to my nerves. A tingle spreads through me, excitement and anxiety swirling in my stomach.

Butterflies? Maybe. I'm not sure.

What if he's there?

Suddenly, I find myself hoping he is.

As I pull into the long dirt driveway leading to the Mitchell's house, my heart flutters like a flock of startled birds. The sight of their farmhouse nestled among the fields brings a smile to my face, despite the nervous flutter in my stomach. It's a modernised farmhouse, a converted barn with thick stone walls and oak beams, giving it a rustic charm that I've always admired.

But as I drive further up the dirt path, my questions from earlier are answered, and not in the way I wanted. My heart sinks as I realise Bradley's ute is parked right there.

Of course, he's home.

My stomach churns with nerves and disappointment, completely contradicting my earlier thoughts.

Yeah, that part of me earlier, the one that secretly wished he'd be home? It can take a flying leap, for all I care. Because right now, my stomach is doing somersaults!

I take a deep breath to calm myself, but it's useless. Sitting in the car, nerves and uncertainty whirl around me. I try again, taking another deep breath to steady my racing heart. I smooth out my skirt, adjust my shirt, and fiddle with my gold rings—all nervous habits I can't seem to shake.

Why bother? Bradley won't care what I look like.

Chuckling at my own silliness, I pull out my phone and quickly text Olivia.

> **Me:** I'm here.

Minutes pass, but there's no response.

Damn you, Olivia.

Deciding to take matters into my own hands, I step out of the car and make my way to the front of the house, up the wooden stairs. The front door is open, with the screen door closed. I tug on the handle, finding it's unlocked. Do I... just walk in?

Well, you're no stranger, Amelia.

Glancing around, I see no other cars apart from Olivia's and Bradley's, so I assume their parents aren't home. I check my phone again—still no text back from her.

Alright, let's do this.

I walk in, figuring Olivia has to be around somewhere. As I step inside, the familiar warmth of their home surrounds me, easing some of my nerves.

"Olivia?" I call out, hoping for a response. But the house remains quiet, the only sound is my own footsteps echoing in the hallway. I walk further into the large open lounge room, where the kitchen and dining room are, and find nothing. The quietness of the house unsettles me. There's no sign of Olivia.

Or Bradley.

That's a relief. For now.

Curiosity gets the better of me, and I decide to check upstairs. As I head up the staircase, I notice the main bathroom door is slightly ajar down the hallway. Olivia must be showering.

But why would the door be open? Maybe she's airing it out? Or does she just like living dangerously?

As I get closer, my heart starts pounding. What's this weird feeling? I shouldn't be doing this—I know it. But Olivia wouldn't mind, right? We've seen everything of each other.

With hesitant steps, I draw closer, the floorboards creaking under my weight.

And then I freeze.

Because the person in the shower is, in fact, not Olivia. Nope, definitely not Olivia.

Standing in the shower is… Bradley.

Oh, my god!

Internally panicking, I have no idea what to do. The floorboards creak under my footsteps, and I stop dead in my tracks. Holy crap!

I'm rooted in place, captivated but terrified of the sight before my eyes. Bradley stands under the shower, running his hands through his hair. The door is only opened slightly, ajar, so I can't see much, but I'm seeing *everything*. I move to walk away slowly, but stop myself. I can't.

I'm too... tempted. Intrigued.

I've never seen a guy naked before—sure, in porn once, but never in real life. And Bradley, right now, is every bit naked—*everything* on display. My cheeks go all warm and fuzzy, and I feel tingles zipping down to my toes. I can't tear my eyes away as he lathers up, hands gliding over those ripped abs.

My goodness, I'm seeing more dips and ridges than a mountain range!

My eyes wander lower, lower, and nearly pop out of my head at the sight of his... manhood. Why does that sound so weird in my head? *Cock?* Yeah, that's what I hear most often.

Let's stick with that.

Bradley's cock is... massive. Like, seriously huge—just hanging out there. *Jesus Christ!*

Suddenly, Bradley shifts, catching sight of me in the doorway. His face morphs into complete shock. His eyes lock onto mine, wide and unblinking, like he's seen a ghost. He raises his brows but doesn't move to cover up. I'm frozen, like a deer caught in headlights, unable to look away.

Why am I still standing here?

I gasp, the realisation hitting me like a ton of bricks. I've been caught red-handed—okay, red-faced—snooping where I definitely shouldn't be. With a sharp intake of breath, I bolt downstairs, my cheeks burning hotter than the sun.

As I tumble down the stairs, my mind still spinning, I crash right into someone with a loud, "oof!" and a startled exclamation of, "Oh, shit. What the fuck!"

Stumbling back, I try to regain my balance. "Oh my god, Liv! I'm so sorry!" I blurt out, realising I've bumped into her, who's clutching a basket of eggs.

"Dude, where did you even come from?" Olivia exclaims, clearly shaken. "You scared the shit out of me."

"I, uh," I stutter, feeling my cheeks blaze with embarrassment, hoping they're not turning as red as ripe tomatoes. "Don't you check your bloody phone? I texted you that I was here!" I explain, gesturing between us.

"I was just out back, collecting these silly eggs for Mum," Olivia says with an exasperated sigh, patting her pockets and realising her phone's missing. "Shit, I must've left it on the table inside."

"Well, that's just perfect," I mutter under my breath, feeling a mix of relief and humiliation.

"You okay? You look... all flustered," Olivia observes, her brow furrowing in concern.

I huff out a nervous laugh, trying to shake off the awkwardness. How do I even begin to tell her I just stumbled upon her brother in the shower, all wet and completely naked? Oh right, I'm definitely not telling her.

No way.

"I'm good. You just startled me, is all," I say, trying to sound nonchalant, but probably failing miserably.

"Righto," Olivia responds, her smile now more amused than curious.

Clearing my throat, I feel the awkwardness settling in. "Um, those supplies you bought? I've just come to grab them and then I'll be out of your hair." Olivia places the basket of eggs on the kitchen bench, and I follow her.

"Oh yeah, they're just here," Olivia says, heading to the dining table to grab the plastic bag sitting on top. "I saw these today and just had to grab them for you," she adds, giving me a playful wink.

Opening the plastic bag, I discover a round wooden paint palette, a set of graphite pencils, and a small pack of oil paints. Olivia's thoughtfulness strikes me, and I silently marvel, *wow*.

"This is amazing! I actually needed a new palette," I exclaim.

"I know! I remember you telling me, so I had to grab it."

"How much do I owe you?"

"What? No, don't be silly, they had a sale. It honestly cost me nothing," Liv insists.

I beam gratefully at her and go in for a tight hug. As I let go of Olivia, footsteps from behind send a chill down my spine. Oh, God, I can't possibly face him after what just happened.

Bradley steps into view, now dressed in black track pants and a fitted white t-shirt. All the air whooshes out of my lungs, and I exhale shakily.

Liv notices Bradley. "Oh, you're home," she states.

"Clearly," he deadpans, his eyes locking with mine. Oh, God. I should bolt.

His gaze holds mine, exchanging silent messages, all while pretending he wasn't just caught naked moments ago. Then, his eyes drop to the palette I'm still clutching.

"You paint or something?" he asks casually, his tone almost teasing.

I fumble with the palette, avoiding his gaze like it's a hot stove. "Um, yeah, a bit. It's a hobby, nothing important," I manage, my voice cracking slightly.

"Nothing *special?* Come on, you're seriously talented," Liv chimes in, and I feel my cheeks flush even more. Great, now Bradley's still watching me with that unreadable expression.

"I-I'm gonna go, okay?" I blurt out.

"Already? Stay for a bit," Liv insists, but I can't handle the tension.

"No, no. I-I really need to get home," I stammer, hastily stuffing the palette back into the bag and giving Olivia a quick, awkward hug. Liv looks puzzled, but explanations can wait for another time. I bolt out the door, practically sprinting to my car, where I fumble with my keys, hands shaking like I've just downed a litre of espresso. Finally, I manage to unlock the car door and flop inside.

What on earth just happened back there? Did he... enjoy catching me gawking at him?

Oh, don't be ridiculous, the voice in my head says. *He probably thinks you're a total weirdo now.*

How am I supposed to look him in the eye after that mortifying encounter? And why does it feel like my heart is still racing a marathon, even though I'm safely ensconced in my car?

Deep breaths, Amelia. Deep breaths.

I start the car, trying to calm my nerves. Life suddenly feels like a cringe-worthy rom-com.

Note to self: avoid awkward encounters with naked guys in the future.

Ugh, no wonder I'm single—classic awkward Amelia strikes again!

8

Bradley

I'm left standing in the dining room, Liv beside me, as Amelia rushes off after hugging Liv goodbye. Her sudden departure leaves a lingering awkwardness in the air. I can't shake the image of her, eyes and mouth wide open, while she just… stood there, watching.

Fuck. I never expected to see her while showering, of all times. The thought of her watching me, it was… unexpected, but if I'm being honest with myself, it was also strangely exciting.

Nah, it straight out turned me the fuck on.

And as if my dick had a mind of its own—let's be real, it does—he, too, liked the thought of it. After she sprinted off, I'd turned the cold water on, dousing my body, which had become a raging inferno, to help push away the thoughts of her and focus on catching her before she bolted out of there.

Caught up in my head, Liv turns to me, concern etched on her face. "Is she acting normal to you?"

I glance at my sister, trying to gather my thoughts. "Dunno. She's *your* friend?"

I do know something is off. Why would she be acting normal after catching me in the shower, after all? I just can't shake the uneasy feeling now settling in the pit of my stomach. And as if it can't get any worse, I feel a rush travel straight down to my dick.

Not now, wanker.

Minutes pass, and breaking me out of my thoughts, Liv asks. "You right, Bradley?" scepticism evident in her voice.

I clear my throat, shaking my head. "Yeah, just... thinking."

"About?"

"Nothing that concerns you."

She narrows her eyebrows. "You're always thinking."

I shoot back, "Well, it's a hard habit to break." *And isn't that an understatement.*

Liv rolls her eyes, but her expression softens. "True, but sometimes it's good to take a break from all that thinking, you know?"

I grunt in response, her words hitting a nerve. If only it were that easy.

She has no idea.

That uneasy feeling? I know *exactly* what it means. I should not be this attracted to Amelia. But I am. Fuck.

I've always prided myself on my restraint, but lately, it feels like I'm losing my grip.

As the afternoon drags on, Liv and I silently carry on with our routines. A buzz from my phone shatters the silence, signalling a new message. Glancing at the screen, I see a message from Xavier in our family group chat.

> **Xavier:** Dinner at ours. 6pm. Don't be late.

I inwardly sigh, realising I'll have to push aside thoughts of Amelia for now. Maybe this distraction is what I need. Being around my family, as exhausting as they can be, brings a sense of normalcy. It's a welcome break from the turmoil in my mind.

Ever since Xavier moved in with Isla, making their place our new gathering spot, they've been pushing for these family dinners. Mum used to enforce weekly dinners like it was law. Xavier seems hell-bent on keeping that tradition alive.

My phone buzzes again, this time with multiple texts flooding in from the group chat.

> **Liv:** Yay. See you then! 🖤

> **Mum:** Need us to bring anything?

> **Isla:** Nope, just yourselves 🖤

Dad:

Feeling a bit rebellious, I shoot back a text.

Me: And what happens if we're late?

Xavier's reply is swift, trying to sound imposing, but it just makes me scoff silently.

Xavier: You don't want to find out.

Me: I'm shaking in my boots.

Isla: 😂😂 Don't listen to him, Bradley. He's in a mood today.

Xavier: If you're late, you're on a dishwashing duty.

Liv: Bradley is never late??

Isla: This is true!

I read their messages with a smirk but stay silent. They're not wrong—I won't be late. It's family dinner, and I'm not about to keep them hanging.

"Liv, you haven't watched the new episode of *Fire Country* yet? I can't believe it! I just managed to get Xav to catch up," Isla exclaims.

Liv laughs, shaking her head. "I know, I know. I'll watch it soon, I promise."

Xavier nods, looking slightly amused. "Yeah, she's been saying that for weeks now."

As Isla goes on about the TV show, I tune in half-heartedly. TV isn't my thing. My mind's always racing, and sitting still for shows isn't my idea of fun. Sometimes, I need to hit the footpath to clear my head.

Isla and Xavier's place is inviting, filled with the scent of home-cooked meals. We're gathered around their hefty wooden table, loaded with a feast. There's everything—fresh-baked bread, colourful salads, juicy roast chicken, veggies galore, and smooth mashed potatoes.

Isla's got this glow about her; whether it's from the pregnancy or just being with family, I can't tell. I wonder if they're planning to spill the beans soon.

As we settle around the dining table, conversation flows effortlessly, each of us catching up on the latest happenings in our lives.

Despite seeing each other often, there's always something new to share. Xav's still managing the farm, now with extra help to tackle the workload and renovations. Isla's a constant presence, balancing her time between the farm and the clinic without ever seeming to take a break.

As Isla and Liv delve into lively discussions about *Fire Country*, and other shows I've never even heard of, Xavier chimes in with his own commentary. Amidst the chatter and laughter, my thoughts drift away, fixating on Amelia more than I care to admit.

What would it be like if she were here with us at this family dinner?

A part of me imagines her seated at the table, engaging in our banter, and for a fleeting moment, I wish it were true. But I quickly shake off the fantasy. Bringing myself back to the present, I dismiss the thoughts as pointless. I focus on the conversations around me, determined to keep my mind from wandering again.

Xavier's clearing of his throat jolts me back, prompting me to refocus on the discussion at hand.

"You good, Brad?" he asks, his gaze searching mine.

"Fine," I reply with a nod, hoping to brush off any signs of distraction. I glance around the table, hoping my momentary lapse went unnoticed.

"Bradley, you've been quiet over there. How's work been?"

Mum's curious gaze settles on me, and I shift uncomfortably in my seat. Work isn't a topic I enjoy discussing, especially here. I've dealt with my share of cases—some straightforward, others challenging—but work stays at work, a line I prefer not to blur. I clear my throat, trying to dispel the unease settling in my chest.

"It's been fine, Mum," I reply. "Just the usual."

Xavier's gaze lingers on me a moment longer, his curiosity palpable. I quickly divert my attention to my plate, avoiding him.

"So, Isla and I have something we need to tell you all," Xavier chimes. His announcement draws everyone's attention away from me, and for that brief moment, I'm silently grateful.

Mum, always eager for news, leans forward in her seat. "What is it?" she asks eagerly.

Xavier glances at Isla, and they exchange a knowing smile before he continues, "It's still early days, but—"

Before he can finish, Liv interjects with her characteristic impatience, her excitement palpable. "You're pregnant?" she blurts out, eyes widening with surprise.

Isla beams, her smile infectious. "Yes! It's still early, but we couldn't wait to tell you all."

The room fills with congratulations and happy chatter, the joy of the moment spreading like wildfire.

Despite the whirlwind of emotions inside me, I find myself smiling. It's a significant change, and despite Xavier being the older one, I feel a surge of pride and protectiveness for him.

Dad clears his throat, a gruff sound amidst the emotional atmosphere.

"Oh, don't tell me you're crying over there, old man?" I tease, trying to keep things light. Xavier chuckles.

"Fuck off, Bradley. Got somethin' in me eye, is all," he replies gruffly.

"Mhm. Sure thing, bud," I mutter, watching as Dad rises from his seat and claps Xavier on the back, messing up his hair in a playful gesture. Leaning down, he plants a kiss on Isla's tear-streaked cheek. The dogs join in, barking happily at the commotion, and Xavier bends down to give them some affectionate belly scratches.

As the initial excitement settles, Liv bombards Isla with questions about the pregnancy, and Mum gets up to hug them both, tears of happiness glistening in her eyes. I lean back, silently observing the scene unfolding before me. My family, in its evolving and unexpected ways, reminds me of what truly matters.

Seeing Xavier so content, knowing he's about to become a father, stirs thoughts about my own future. The idea of having a family of my own, of being a father someday, tugs at a deep longing inside me.

In that moment, amidst the love and laughter of my family, I can't deny it—I yearn for that one day.

My phone vibrates on the table, pulling me out of my thoughts. I pick it up and see a text from Daniels.

Daniels: Wyd later? Wanna chill at mine?

I contemplate it. Maybe hanging out with that boofhead might settle my thoughts.

> **Me:** Sure. Give me about 15.

Amelia

I'm sitting on my couch, take-away from Madison's spread out in front of me. I tap on my phone and open FaceTime, calling my sister, Kat. It's not long before her face fills the screen, and little Millie's bright eyes peek over her shoulder.

"Hey, you two," I greet them, trying to keep my voice light despite the turmoil in my head.

"Hi, Meli!" Millie chirps, her little hand waving enthusiastically.

"Hey, sis," Kat says, a knowing smirk already forming on her lips. "So, what the bloody hell was that today?"

I groan, sinking further into the couch. I had texted her earlier, and of course, she's bringing it up again. "Nothing. Shush. There are children present."

Kat scoffs. "Oh please. Hey, Millie, cover your ears for me, okay?" she says casually.

I hear Millie's little voice respond, "Okay."

I shake my head. "Is she actually doing it?"

Kat turns the camera to show Millie sitting on the floor with her ears covered while still watching the TV. *Oh, bless her.*

I take a deep breath, trying to compose myself. "He was... in the shower, but I'd thought it was Liv... so, I'd lingered, and then..." I trail off, feeling my face heat up.

Her eyes widen in amusement. "So... was it *big*?"

I blush furiously, shaking my head. "Kat, come on!"

She bursts into laughter, Millie joining in, though she doesn't quite understand the joke. "I'm sorry, I couldn't resist!" Kat manages to say between giggles. I cover my face with my hands.

"Well, at least it'll make for a good story," Kat says, still chuckling. "You'll laugh about this one day."

I nod, trying to see the humour in it. "Yeah, one day."

As I picture him in the shower, rippling muscles, water dripping down his body, his member on full display, my whole body shudders.

But the image lingers, haunting me, tempting me with thoughts I shouldn't entertain. I shake my head, trying to dispel the thoughts. This is wrong, I remind myself. He's my best friend's brother, for crying out loud. But the more I try to push the image away, the more vivid it becomes.

His deep voice, his piercing gaze, the way his wet skin glistened under the water... *Stop it, Amelia*, I scold myself. This is not what I should be thinking about.

But the butterflies in my stomach continue to flutter, betraying my resolve.

9

Bradley

The midday sun beats down on the town's park, casting harsh shadows and highlighting the graffiti scrawled across the benches and playground equipment. The colourful paint clashes with the park's muted tones, a glaring reminder of the vandal's audacity. As Daniels and I approach, a familiar sense of weariness washes over me. Another day, another mess to clean up, but hell, I wouldn't trade this job for anything.

We survey the scene, and it's a damn mess. Graffiti sprawls over everything—benches, slides, you name it. A chaotic mix of colours and shapes, the work of some punk with too much time and no sense. I glance at Daniels, already pulling out his notebook to start documenting. We'll need photos, paint samples, and maybe even a witness or two if we're lucky.

Daniels starts babbling about his weekend escapades, as if we aren't standing in the middle of a vandalised playground. His cheerfulness grates on me, but I let him talk. Sometimes, it's better to let him ramble while we get the job done.

"Man, you should've seen her," he says with a grin. "Best blowjob of my life."

I roll my eyes, unimpressed. "Yeah, I'm sure it was," I reply, my tone dripping with sarcasm. "You know, it truly baffles me that you're older than me, considering the way you carry on."

Daniels laughs, undeterred by my jab. "Age is just a number, Bradley," he says with a wink. "You should try living a little.

"Speaking of living a little, mate, when was the last time you had a good fuck, Brad? Can't be a recluse for the rest of your life, you know."

I raise an eyebrow, irritation bubbling up inside me. "That's none of your business," I snap, my tone icy. "And I'm not a recluse. I just value my privacy."

Well, isn't that the truth.

He chuckles, shaking his head. "Sure, sure. Just remember, life's too short to be alone all the time."

Alone.

Those words hit a nerve, stirring up a mix of frustration and resignation. He's right, but that doesn't mean I have to like it. I glare at him, a familiar annoyance rising.

"Drop it, Daniels," I growl. "We've got work to do."

But that doesn't stop him. "Wait! What about that girl from the flower shop? Anything going on there? You seemed pretty hung up on her the other day."

His words stop me in my tracks, my heart skipping a beat. We're at work; I don't need to be thinking of Amelia right now. I try to play it off, masking my surprise. "Nah, nothing going on there," I reply, my tone clipped and dismissive, hoping Daniels doesn't notice the slight tremor in my voice.

Daniels eyes me for a moment, clearly not convinced by my response. "Uh-huh. No worries, mate," he says, his tone teasing.

As we finish up at the park, satisfied with the evidence we've gathered, Daniels and I head back to the car in silence. The occasional passerby smiles at us, and an elderly couple strolls past, waving cheerfully. I nod in acknowledgement while Daniels drawls, "G'day folks," with a salute and that charming smile of his.

I grunt, climbing into the car. "Let's get this wrapped up," I mutter.

As I sit at my desk, the station buzzes with the boisterous chatter of my colleagues. The boys are in high spirits, swapping weekend stories with loud enthusiasm. I listen, but I don't get involved. Their laughter fills the air, momentarily lifting the sombre mood that hangs over me.

"Oi, Bradley, you coming?" Reynolds calls out, breaking through the noise. He moves over and perches on the edge of my desk, arms crossed, waiting for a response. I didn't catch what he said, so I'm confused.

"Where?" I ask, leaning back in my chair.

Reynolds clarifies, "To the pub for drinks? The Loose Lasso?"

I nod slowly, still feeling a bit hesitant. "I don't know, Reynolds. I might just head home tonight," I reply, my voice quiet amidst the lively chatter around us.

Reynolds raises an eyebrow, a hint of surprise in his expression.

"Come on, mate. You've been working hard. A drink won't hurt," he insists, leaning in slightly.

I consider his words, his voice cutting through the background noise of the station. He's right; I have been working hard, and tomorrow is my day off. I could use a break. With a mental shrug, I decide, why the hell not?

A tight smile forms on my lips. "One drink," I say, reluctantly agreeing, my voice barely audible over the lively chatter around us.

Reynolds grins, smacking his thigh in approval. "That's the spirit, mate! We won't keep you out too late."

I nod, acknowledging his words.

Reynolds winks at me before moving off my desk to join the rest of the guys. "Alright, Bradley's in!" he announces, eliciting whistles and cheers from the group.

Later that night, as we clock off from our shifts and make our way out of the station, I can't help but feel a slight sense of relief. It'll be good to unwind with the boys after a long day. Maybe a drink or two will relax me, distract me from things, from Amelia.

Anything to ease the tension that's been building up inside me.

10

Amelia

"Cheers to surviving another week!" Kristie exclaims, raising her glass. We all clink our glasses together, the sound ringing out over the din of the pub.

Jamie laughs, taking a sip of her drink. "Seriously, those kids are adorable, but they sure know how to wear you out."

Stella nods in agreement. "I don't think I've ever been so grateful for Friday night drinks."

Amanda, the oldest of our group, chuckles. "You young ones have no idea. Wait until you hit my age." We all laugh, the sound blending with the lively atmosphere of the pub.

The Loose Lasso is alive with energy, and I can't help but soak it all in, a wide grin spreading across my face. The scent of alcohol and fried delights fill the air, adding to the excitement of the evening. Seated beside me are Kristie, with her infectious laughter and vibrant spirit, Jamie, always impeccably dressed and ready for a good time, Stella, whose witty sarcasm keeps us entertained, and Amanda, whose nurturing presence brings a sense of calm to our group.

We've been colleagues for the past three years, ever since I started teaching. It's been quite the journey together. Stella might be the newbie, but she fits in like glitter on a craft project, her vibrant personality blending effortlessly with ours. Most of the other staff at Koala Creek Primary are like wise old owls, full of years of teaching wisdom. But with this crew, age is just a number, and we've formed a bond that's more like a wacky, loving family than mere colleagues.

As I glance at the drinks scattered across the table—some empty, some still full—I realise I've already had my fourth drink. Or is it my third? Well, who's counting, anyway?

Trying to keep track of how many drinks I've had is like trying to keep track of how many times little Timmy asked to go to the bathroom today. Impossible!

Working with kindergarteners is undeniably adorable and fulfilling, but let's be real, being around five- and six-year-olds all day, every day, can be mentally and physically exhausting.

And that's putting it lightly.

As we chat and laugh, my body starts to hum with that familiar buzz from the alcohol, and I welcome it with a contented sigh.

"So, any plans for the weekend, Amelia?" Kristie asks, leaning in with a smile.

I take a sip of my drink, considering her question. "Well, I was thinking of catching up on some reading. Maybe finally finish that book I started last month."

Jamie raises an eyebrow teasingly. "You mean the one you started and never got past the first chapter?"

I laugh and nod. "Yep, that's the one. I really should finish it."

But truth be told, the reason I haven't finished it is because it's just so damn raunchy, I've had to pause before getting too flustered.

Amanda adds, "Oh, the one full of cowboys and some steamy sex scenes? Don't forget your vibrator while reading." This earns a laugh from the girls, but I can feel my face heating up, blushing hard at the mention.

"Amanda!" I admonish, feeling my cheeks burn.

"What? If you're reading that cowboy or fairy porn, you gotta have some form of relief, right?" Amanda quips.

I smack my forehead, the girls' giggles filling the space between us. "How do you even know all of this?" I ask.

"Honey, I may be ancient, but I've read my fair share of romance novels over the years. I'll have you know, my sex life is still quite lively thanks to those books, and Gerry never complains, so…" Amanda's words trail off with a mischievous grin.

"Oh, my god! I don't think we need to know that," I exclaim out loud.

Jamie chimes in with a laugh, "You dirty woman, you! Don't mind her, she's a little prude." I gasp in disbelief, smacking Jamie on the arm.

"What? Hun, do you even own a vibrator?" she questions with a raised brow.

I feign embarrassment, but I can't help but wonder. I've never owned a vibrator before, never had the urge to buy one. Do I need one? Is that what girls these days have?

Jamie notices the look on my face, and hers lights up. "Oh, my god! You *don't* have one?" she says in disbelief. "We're gonna have to change that. I'm going to order you a few of my favourites."

Oh, kill me now.

"No, that's okay." I say, blushing.

Kristie then puts her hand up. "No, no. We're getting you one *or* two alright," she says with a wink.

How did this conversation go from talking about work to sex and vibrators? Good lord.

I lift my glass to take a big gulp of my drink to ease these rampant thoughts, but as I do, Amanda exclaims, "Fuck the vibrators. We need to find her a man," and the contents of my drink are spit out as I choke on the liquid.

Jamie makes a *tsk* sound. "Look what you did now! Made her choke on her drink."

"It's not her drink she should be choking on," Amanda adds, throwing in an exaggerated wink.

Oh, for heaven's sake. The girls burst out in a raucous laughter.

Jamie chimes in, turning to Amanda, "I don't think I'll ever get used to hearing you swear."

"What?!" Amanda shrieks. "I swear all the time, clearly." The girls burst into more laughter, and I can't help but join in. "Fuck, fuck, fuck!" she adds for good measure. "There ya go! How's that for swearing?" This earns even more laughter from the girls.

Amanda then turns to me, holding her thumb out. "This one never swears! I think we need to loosen her up a bit."

Jamie then adds, "In more ways than one, apparently."

"Remember that time you stubbed your toe at work and yelled, 'Oh, fiddlesticks!'?" Kristie says, trying to hold back her laughter.

"And what about the time you dropped your lunch and yelled, 'Holy guacamole!'?" Jamie adds, giggling.

"Oh, wait! What was that word you said the other day, 'Son of a what?'"

"Biscuit," I finish for Kristie, with a roll of my eyes.

Stella chimes in, "Yeah, that phrase should be 'Son of a bitch!'"

"Hey, they work just as well! Why do I need to swear?"

Amanda chuckles, shaking her head. "Oh, Amelia, dear, you're too pure for this world."

Stella leans in, her eyes sparkling with mischief. "I think we need to give you a crash course in swearing. Lesson one: the art of the word 'fuck'. It's so versatile."

"*And* 'Cunt'," Jamie adds casually.

"Oh, that one's my favourite!" Amanda joins in.

I clear my throat. "Yeah, I think I'll pass on that lesson, thanks."

"At least tell us you've seen a real dick before?" Kristie asks, her tone teasing.

Oh my. I instantly feel those tummy flutters, images of Bradley from yesterday in the shower flashing through my mind. "Th-that's none of your business, thank you very much."

"Hold the fuck up! She's blushing!! You have! She has!" Jamie exclaims, her excitement palpable.

"Amelia Brown, you better not have seen a dick and not have told us!" Kristie adds, her voice a little too loud for my liking as she scans the surroundings to make sure no one heard.

I can't help but think that she really needs to work on her no-filter mouth. Sometimes, I swear she forgets we're in public.

"Shush, would you? My goodness!" I exclaim.

"You better tell us right now. Please and thank you!" Stella insists, her words making me wish for another drink.

As if on cue, one of the bartenders comes round to collect our empty cups. I take this opportunity to order another round of drinks, asking for mine to be a double shot.

"Oh, she's sure as hell seen one alright. Asking for double shots 'n all," Amanda chirps, earning laughter from the group.

"Well…" Kristie says, waiting for me to answer. I hesitate, feeling the weight of their expectant gazes.

I feel my cheeks flush as their expectant eyes bore into me. "Um, yes! I have. There, happy?" I try to muster confidence, but I'm already second-guessing my response.

"When? Where?" Kristie's curiosity spikes, leaning in with a grin.

"The other day, on my laptop," I state matter-of-factly, hoping to steer away from the real details. Lies.

"Oh no, no, no. We don't mean porn, hunny," Jamie chastises, her tone playful. "Kristie meant in *real* life, up close and personal. Veins and all."

My mind involuntarily drifts to Bradley and his very, very large member, and I feel myself growing increasingly flustered.

"It's okay. You can tell us." Jamie nudges me, eager for details.

Kristie chirps in, "Yeah! Remember that time I told *you* about that guy Ben and how he had a monster schlong."

I can't help but snort. "Yeah, information that YOU willingly shared. I didn't *pester* you about it."

"Same shit, different smell," she fires back with a smile.

I squirm, feeling like I've dug myself into a hole.

"Well, it was the other day at Liv's house," I begin reluctantly. "I went to pick something up, and I may or may not have stumbled upon her brother, Bradley... in the shower."

The girls erupt into giggles and exclamations. "You walked in on him?"

"No, no. He left the bloody door open!" I exclaim. "I mean, who does that?"

Jamie squeals with excitement. "Was he all soapy and steamy?"

"Um, yeah," I stammer, trying to sound casual and failing miserably.

"Oh, my!" Stella exclaims amidst laughter. "Damn, girl!"

"Was it big?!" Amanda blurts out.

I swallow nervously, feeling their expectant stares. "I-I don't know, I didn't exactly look," I lie, feeling my face heat up even more. I did look. And I *definitely* noticed.

Jamie probes further, "So, who is this mysterious Bradley to you?"

"Just Liv's older brother," I say, awkwardly.

"Hold on. Olivia, your best friend? As in Olivia Mitchell? So Bradley Mitchell... the town's finest police officer?" Amanda chimes in.

The girls gasp in unison. "What?"

Stella leans in with wide eyes. "So, the hottest police officer in town, and you saw him naked? You lucky girl!"

I snort, shaking my head. "It's not like that. He's just Liv's brother. I've known him forever."

"Yeah, yeah. That's what they all say," Jamie teases.

"Did he... you know, see you?" Stella asks.

I bury my face in my hands, mortified by the whole situation. "Yes! Can we please change the subject now?" I plead, my voice muffled by my hands—hoping to move on from this embarrassing topic.

"Oh, my god! This is amazing," Kristie exclaims.

"No, it's mortifying! I don't think I can ever look at him again, without, you know, picturing his..." My voice trails off into silence.

"His dick?" Amanda finishes for me bluntly.

"His cock?" Jamie and Kristie chime in simultaneously.

"You can say the word. It's okay. Around us, there's no need to be shy, girl," Jamie croons, trying to lighten the mood.

I chuckle nervously. "Thanks, Jamie, but I think I'll pass on embracing my inner sailor just yet."

Their laughter fills the air, and I can't help but join in, despite my embarrassment. Oh, the joys of having friends who don't let you live down your awkward moments.

I love these girls, but sometimes they just have no filter or any inkling of when to stop.

After the awkward conversation about Bradley Mitchell fizzles out, we decide to move on and order another round of drinks. As the night progresses, the drinks flow freely, and soon enough, my head is buzzing, my words slurring just like the rest of the girls.

With each round of drinks, the atmosphere becomes more relaxed and carefree. My cheeks hurt from laughing so much, but I wouldn't have it any other way.

Eventually, we find ourselves on the crowded dance floor, the lively beat of "A Bar Song" filling the air. The girls are dancing, twirling each other around, laughing as we move to the music. Stella's red hair is a blur as she spins, Jamie's laughter infectious as she attempts some fancy footwork. Kristie and Amanda are in their own world, lost in the music and the moment.

I join in, letting loose and dancing like nobody's watching. The alcohol has given me a newfound confidence, and I twirl and sway with the music, my worries melting away with each step. The girls cheer me on, and I can't help but grin from ear to ear.

"I needa go to the bathroom!" I call out to the girls over the blaring music, my words slightly slurred.

Jamie, being the caring friend she is, asks, "Want me to go with you?"

I shake my head, insisting, "Nah, I'll be right. Just need to pee!" Navigating my way through the crowded bar, I stumble slightly, catching myself on a nearby table.

"Whoops," I mutter under my breath, earning a few amused glances from nearby patrons.

Finally reaching the bathroom, I take a moment to appreciate the brief silence before the door swings open, revealing a line of equally tipsy women waiting their turn. It reeks of women's perfume and alcohol. Surprisingly, for a small town country pub, this place is actually pretty clean.

I make my way to the toilet and do my business, then move to the sink to wash my hands. Glancing at myself in the mirror, I notice my once tightly wound curls have morphed into soft waves cascading over my shoulder. I freshen up my hair, run my fingers through the strands, and wipe the small beads of sweat forming on my forehead.

Before rejoining the girls, I decide to make a short trip back to the bar to order another drink. I'm feeling a little parched, and well, why not? More alcohol probably isn't the best idea, but who cares? It's Friday night, and I have no other plans for tomorrow other than to sleep in.

Might as well seize the moment.

Squeezing myself between people to get to the bar, I miraculously find a vacant spot. Leaning against the counter, I ponder what to drink next. The bartender, an older guy but very good-looking, catches my eye. He has dark hair and a short, trimmed beard, and his name tag reads Joshua.

I blink at him, suddenly feeling a flutter in my stomach.

"What can I get you?" Joshua asks, flashing me a charming smile.

I shy away at his flirtatious tone. "Uh... um, just a vodka sunrise, thanks."

"Long day?" he asks, pouring the drink.

"Long week, more like it," I mumble, avoiding his gaze.

He whisks up my drink in no time and hands me the glass. "Here you go. Need anythin' else?"

I glance back at the girls, who are laughing and dancing, and a mischievous idea pops into my head. "Actually, yeah. Can I get a round of vodka shots for my friends?" My voice is a little louder than before, the alcohol giving me a newfound confidence.

As Joshua goes to pour the shots, a group of guys come barreling to the bar, glasses and beers in hand. One of them spots me, and our eyes meet. I immediately avert my gaze, but it seems I've caught his attention. He moves closer to me, leaning in.

"What's a pretty little thing like you doing at the bar all alone?" he asks, his voice slightly slurred from the alcohol.

I feel a pang of discomfort and quickly hide my face, pretending to be engrossed in my drink.

"Oh, um, just waiting for my friends," I mumble, hoping he'll take the hint and leave me alone. *Confidence? Yeah, that went out the window.*

Despite my attempt to brush him off, the guy doesn't seem deterred. He leans in even closer, his breath smelling strongly of alcohol.

"Well, lucky for you, I'm 'ere now," he says with a smirk, his words oozing with confidence.

I squirm uncomfortably, feeling trapped under his intense gaze. "That's... nice," I manage to say, my voice trembling slightly.

He reaches out to touch my arm, and I instinctively pull away, my discomfort growing by the second. "Hey, no need to be shy," he says, his tone becoming more insistent. "Wanna dance?"

I glance nervously at Joshua behind the bar, hoping he'll notice my discomfort, but he seems preoccupied with serving other customers. Panic begins rising within me as I search for an escape route.

Feeling stuck and unable to abandon the drinks at the bar, I realise I can't carry them all by myself.

Great, I didn't think this through.

"No, I'm good. Th-thanks," I manage to stutter out. Desperate for an escape, I pull out my phone and quickly send a message to Kristie.

> **Me:** Come to the bar. I ordered shots!!

I type quickly, followed by another message.

> **Me:** Now. Quick!

The guy continues, however, "Come on, darl, don't be like that. Come dance." His accent is thick, and I can tell he's had one too many.

In that moment, a deep voice from behind me raises the hairs along my arms, and my spine stiffens. "She said no. Take the hint, mate."

The word 'mate' is laced with a warning, devoid of any friendliness. I'd recognize that voice anywhere, even blindfolded.

Bradley.

My heart skips a beat as I turn around. There he stands, towering over the guy who's been pestering me. Bradley's expression is hard, jaw clenched in a way that means business.

The guy, surprised by Bradley's sudden appearance, stammers, "Relax, mate, I was just..."

Bradley cuts him off with a sharp glare. "She said no. Now, fuck off."

The guy mutters an apology and scurries away, swallowed by the crowd. Bradley turns to me, his gaze softening.

"Are you okay?" he asks, his voice gentle.

I nod, feeling a rush of relief wash over me. "Y-yeah, I'm fine. Thank you."

As I look into Bradley's eyes, so full of concern and strength, I can't help but feel a surge of gratitude. It's probably just a coincidence that he's here at the right time again, but still, in his presence, I feel safe, protected. I take in his appearance—dark cargo pants, combat boots, and a black hoodie—I can't help but feel a flutter in my chest. He must've come straight from work. My face heats up, and I try to subtly hide my blush, hoping he doesn't notice my sudden change.

I feel all flustered and warm, and it's definitely not from the alcohol.

11
Bradley

I stand in front of Amelia, fuming at that prick who thought he could just lay a hand on her. Fucking idiots like that really piss me off. I watch as the guy scurries away, disappearing into the crowd, and turn my attention back to Amelia.

"You sure you're okay?" I repeat my question. *She said yes before, why are you asking again?*

Amelia's movements are a bit stiff as she nods, looking flustered, her cheeks tinged with pink. Despite the alcohol, her smile remains, unwavering as ever. Even in her frilly blue dress and white sneakers, she has this glow about her.

"Yeah, I'm sure. Thanks to you," she replies, her voice shaky.

I study her for a moment, taking in the way her hair falls in loose waves around her shoulders, the way her eyes dart nervously around the room. She looks so vulnerable, and it pisses me off that someone would dare make her feel uncomfortable.

But I keep my thoughts to myself, simply nodding in response. "Anytime."

Anytime? *Really, Brad?*

To my left, a group of girls come barreling toward us at the bar. A red-headed girl leads the charge, exclaiming, "We just saw your texts!!"

Her enthusiasm is matched by the blonde-haired girl beside her, who adds, "Why the urgency? I mean, we'll never say no to shots!"

I stay silent, just watching as they gather around Amelia, completely oblivious to my presence. An older woman stands behind them, and I wonder if these are her friends, or maybe work colleagues.

The girls continue chatting, animated and unaware of me, until I clear my throat. They turn, finally noticing me standing behind Amelia. The blonde's mouth falls open in surprise, and the older woman lets out a soft whistle.

The clearing of my throat snaps Amelia out of her daze. "Oh, gosh! Guys, this is Officer Bradley... Mitchell," she says, hesitating on my last name. Odd. And why such a formal introduction?

"Bradley's just fine," I murmur, keeping my eyes on Amelia.

"Wait. Bradley as in..." The redhead's voice trails off.

"Oh, shit!" This comes from the blonde, followed by another, "Oh... Holy shit!"

Amelia smacks her forehead, and it makes me smirk. I love seeing her all flustered like this.

"Oh, move out of my way, you foolish girls." This comes from the older woman behind them. She pushes the girls aside and steps in front of me, offering up her hand.

"Bradley, it's nice to meet you, son. I'm Amanda, Mills here has told us all about you," she adds with a wink. *Mills.* I like that.

So, Amelia's been talking about me, huh? Can't help but wonder what she's been saying. It's strange hearing that from her friend. Makes me feel... something. Protective, maybe. Or just curious about what's going on in that head of hers.

Either way, I like knowing she thinks about me enough to mention me to her friends.

"Has she, now?" I ask, my voice low.

"No!" she says way too quickly, almost mortified. "I mean, good things, yes, just..." She trails off, before the blonde woman cuts in.

"What she means to say is yes, your name has come up once or twice in conversation about Olivia. You're her brother, right? The police officer?"

Olivia. Of course, because why else would she be mentioning my name, other than when talking about my sister.

"I am. Yes." My tone is clipped.

"Well, it's nice to officially meet one of our officers. I'm Jamie."

I shake her hand, which is light and delicate. Jamie turns to the other two women behind her. "This is Stella," she says, pointing to the redhead, before moving to the other woman next to her. "And this is Kristie. We all work together at Koala Creek Primary."

"Nice to meet you, ladies," I murmur, making a mental note of all their names. Not that I'll likely talk to them again, but it's just a habit—observing others, remembering names. "Sorry, I didn't mean to crash whatever this is. I just, uh, saw Amelia at the bar, looking for an out, so I offered some help."

"An out? What does he mean?" Jamie exclaims.

"Was someone bothering you?" Kristie interjects with furrowed brows.

Amelia hesitates, her voice carrying the weight of discomfort. "Y-yeah, I'm fine. Just some creep making me feel uncomfortable."

"Who do we need to bash?" Kristie says.

"Now, now, ladies. It's all good," I say, huffing a laugh. "I think I scared him off," I add, winking at Amelia.

"Are you okay?" Stella asks, with concern evident in her eyes.

"Y-yeah, I'm all good now."

As the girls launch into a flurry of colourful language, expressing their disdain for the man who harassed Amelia, I can't help but feel a sense of satisfaction.

They're like a protective shield, fierce and loyal, ready to defend their own at a moment's notice.

"Seriously, what a jerk," Jamie exclaims, her voice filled with righteous anger.

"Yeah, who does he think he is?" Kristie adds, shaking her head in disbelief.

Amelia turns to me, her eyes sincere as she speaks. "Thank you again, Bradley. I really appreciate you stepping in."

I feel my rigid posture soften at her words, a warmth spreading through me. "It was my pleasure."

Jamie chimes in, her tone softened, "Yes! Thank you for saving our friend, Bradley."

I nod gratefully, acknowledging their gratitude, though my attention shifts subtly back to Amelia. I notice a faint blush creeping up her cheeks, and I can't help but feel a surge of protective satisfaction. Seeing her relieved and grateful stirs a quiet sense of pride within me, knowing I could make a difference for her.

As she turns back to the bar to grab the shots, handing them out to the girls, she turns to me, "Would you like one, too?"

I tsk with a shake of my head. "No, thanks. I'm taking it easy tonight."

She smiles and nods before the girls take their shots in unison. With that, her friends beckon for me to follow them back to their table.

I hesitate. "Nah, it's alright, thank you. I don't mean to intrude on your night." I glance out into the crowd, spotting the boys at a large booth, drinks in hand, laughing loudly.

Then, a thought occurs to me. "Wait. Why don't you ladies come join us?"

Smooth move, Bradley. *Trying to keep your distance, remember?* I steal a quick glance at Amelia, hoping she didn't catch on to my momentary lapse in judgement, but it's a silly thought.

"Us?" Amelia says with a curious look.

"Yeah, my colleagues are here," I explain.

Jamie's head perks up. "You mean there are more of *you*? Here?"

"*More* police officers? Where?" Kristie asks.

Amelia just laughs, and Amanda rolls her eyes, but a broad smile spreads across her face. As the girls show interest in joining me, I lead the way to the booth where the boys are seated. They notice our approach and greet us with welcoming smiles.

Here we go.

"Bradley! My man," Reynolds exclaims, raising his glass in greeting.

Daniels chimes in, "Ah, so this is where you disappeared off to, huh?"

I roll my eyes. Truth be told, I spotted Amelia at the bar, saw that jerk making her uncomfortable, and before I knew it, my legs were moving on their own—told them I needed to take a piss.

"Who are your friends?" Reynolds asks.

"Yes, who are these beautiful ladies?" Stokes comments, earning a round of giggles from the group. His full name is Tom Wilson, but his overuse of the word 'stoked' has about done our heads in, so now we just call him 'Stokes.'

Ignoring their remarks, I begin the introductions. "This is Amelia, Stella, Kristie, Jamie, and Amanda." The girls wave in acknowledgment. Then, pointing to the guys, I continue, "And these idiots are Daniels, Reynolds, and Wilson."

Daniels interrupts with a sudden recognition. "Wait. I know your face," he says, studying Amelia closely. I raise my brow at him, waiting for him to continue.

"You were at the shop that day, a few weeks back, right?" Amelia shifts uncomfortably in her seat.

"I was. Yes," she admits reluctantly.

"Thought so."

Clearing my throat, I decide to steer the conversation elsewhere.

"Right, now that that's out of the way, girls, now's your chance to bail, and trust me, I don't blame you if you want to," I say, my tone clipped, hoping to spare Amelia any further discomfort. Memories of that incident at the shop flicker through my mind—I don't want her to feel uneasy about it.

The guys chuckle at my attempt to lighten the mood. I mentally kick myself for bringing them here. Spending more time with her means those damn thoughts that have been plaguing me will only get worse.

"Oh, don't be silly, we'd love the company," Jamie says, and the girls all nod in agreement. Amelia just looks at me with a small smile. Her smile unexpectedly puts me at ease, and for a moment, any slight worry dissipates.

It's been a few hours, and we're all crammed into the large booth. The girls are huddled together, surrounded by the guys who are really hitting it off. Amelia's on my left, and I'm at the end of the booth, with Daniels sitting opposite me.

Jamie and Kristie are shouting over the loud music, their voices barely audible above the din. Amanda signals her departure, claiming it's past her bedtime and that her *Gerry* is waiting for her at home, presumably her husband.

As the girls sing their goodbyes, Amelia accidentally knocks over her glass, spilling it all over the table.

"I think that's enough drinking for you, missy," Kristie says, and Amelia just giggles.

"I think I'm gonna be a be'sick," she slurs, her words blending together in a drunken mumble.

Yeah, that's my cue.

I rise from the booth, helping her stand up.

"Let's get you home, then," I say, my tone firm. "You didn't drive here, did you?"

She looks up at me, her eyes glassed over. "No, I did not. We caught a taxi."

"I'm gonna take you home, is that alright?" I ask.

"Yess'sir," she slurs in response. Her calling me 'sir' sends a rush straight down to my cock; a response I shouldn't be entertaining. I glance at the girls, silently extending the offer of a lift. They beam, their smiles widening as if they know something I don't want to admit.

"Nah, we're all good, champ. You get her home safe," one of them says, their confidence in me oddly reassuring.

I nod in acknowledgment, then turn to the guys. Daniels just winks at me, his mischief evident.

"Night, boys. Stay sharp," I say.

They reply in a chorus of "Yes, sir's," and I can't help but shake my head as I guide Amelia to the doors. With a hand at her back, I lead her out, determined to get her home safe and sound.

As we step outside, the brisk air sweeps around us, causing Amelia to shiver slightly. I guide her to my Navarra, parked just down the road.

"You don't have to take me home," she says.

"I want to. I'd feel better knowing you got home safely."

"Always such a gentleman." Her voice is soft, barely above a whisper, but I catch every word. It brings a smile to my face, even though she doesn't see it.

She passes on her address, and I navigate the streets until we reach her small brick apartment, not too far from the town square. It's a familiar area—relatively safe and quiet. Not much happens around these streets, which also relieves me. The whole block is surrounded by similar small apartment buildings, giving the neighbourhood a snug, communal feel.

Amelia's place is compact. The living room is snug, with a grey couch and a small TV in the corner. A small kitchenette sits nearby, cluttered with dishes and empty bottles. There are two doors leading off from the main area, probably her bedroom and bathroom. Standing in her personal space, a surge of warmth radiates through me. It feels intimate, but at the same time, like I shouldn't be here. Like it's forbidden.

Probably because it is.

I should get out of here before I lose control and say something I'll regret, like how much I want her, how her being this close is driving me insane. Yet, I can't bring myself to leave.

"Nice place," I mutter, my tone clipped as I try to keep my distance.

Amelia takes off her shoes, leaning against the kitchen counter, all wobbly and uncoordinated from the alcohol.

"Thank you!" she says, stumbling forward, I move instinctively to catch her before she can fall.

"Do you always drink this much?" I ask, furrowing my brows.

"N-no. Never," she says, and I believe her. I fight the urge to smirk at her.

I move to her sink, finding a glass against a rack and filling it up with water.

"Drink," is all I say. She gulps it all down without a word. Amelia then sways slightly, her hand reaching out to steady herself against the kitchen counter.

I fill up her cup again and hand it to her. She drinks it, then fills it up herself, finishing another cup before excusing herself to the bathroom.

What the fuck am I still doing there?

She should be fine. I should leave. But I watch her regardless, concern evident in my expression.

"Come on, let's get you to bed," I say, taking her arm to guide her. "Which door?"

She points to the door on my right. Walking inside, I'm hesitant to invade her personal space, but she moves inside and sits down on the edge of the bed, turning a small lamp on. As she does, I take in the surroundings. A double bed covered in a colourful quilt. The scent of florals envelops me, likely from the fresh bunch of lilies on her bedside table. There is also a hint of something sweet. Cherry maybe?

I wonder if they're her favourite flower. I keep my distance and remain at the doorway, watching her closely.

"You gonna be alright?"

"Yeah," she mumbles, nodding slowly.

I turn to leave, but her voice stops me in my tracks. "Bradley," she says, her voice pulling at something deep inside me. "Can you—can you stay? Just for a bit?"

Her words hit me like a punch to the gut. I grit my teeth, feeling a mix of frustration and something else I can't name.

I shouldn't stay. It's not smart. But fuck it, I can't bring myself to leave her like this.

Part of me feels a sense of responsibility for her, especially in her intoxicated state, but I'm not sure if that's just the police officer in me, or if it's something more.

Maybe a bit of both? No. It's just *me*.

Fuck. Now I'm feeling a bit out of sorts, which is unusual for me. I'm a grown man, accustomed to private moments with women without any fuss. Yet, Amelia's presence ignites an unexpected nervousness within me, akin to a teenager stepping into uncharted territory on his first date.

"Sure. I can stay for a bit."

I step further into the room, closing the door behind me, and take a seat on the edge of the bed beside her. A wide grin spreads across her face.

"Thanks, captain grumps."

"Captain Grumps?" I echo.

"Yeah. Because you're always so serious. Grumpy," she explains with a giggle.

Am I? Yeah, I guess I am. It's not just a mood, it's a constant state of being. Everything and everyone tends to annoy or bore me.

But her? She's different.

She cuts through the noise, makes me feel something real. I want to tell her that, let her know she's the exception. But I keep it to myself.

"Right," I respond, my tone curt, unintentionally proving her point.

This earns a giggle from her, and despite my efforts to maintain composure, a small smile tugs at the corners of my lips.

"You're not so bad," she says with a yawn, her words slightly muffled.

"Pardon?" I ask, leaning in to catch her words again.

She takes off her gold hoop earrings, placing them on the bedside table. "I guess you're not so bad," she finally concedes.

I watch her, marvelling at how she manages to stay so sincere, even with the haze of alcohol. Some might argue that alcohol often leads to saying things you don't mean, clouding your judgement. But with her, it seems different—her words remain genuine.

"Yeah, I'm not so sure about that."

"I mean it."

She yawns again, and a thought crosses my mind that maybe I

should leave, let her rest. But alas, I remain seated, my gaze fixed downward, arms still resting on my knees.

"Do you think I'm too frigid?" she says abruptly, breaking the silence. I turn my head to her in surprise.

Did I hear her right?

She must see the look of sheer surprise on my face because she quickly adds, "OMG, forget I even asked that. Sorry."

Her and her *sorry's*. She has a habit of saying that too much.

"I shouldn't have asked. Never mind. That's a question for friends, I guess," she mumbles. "I'm not even sure why I said that. It just popped into my head, and I blurted it out without even thinking." She lets out a nervous laugh, fidgeting with the hem of her shirt as she rambles on.

"I'm not even sure if we're really friends, you know? I mean, apart from you being Olivia's brother, we don't know each other all that well. And even then, we've never really hung out one-on-one like this before, so…" She trails off, her uncertainty hanging heavy in the air.

Well, shit.

She's clearly flustered, her words spilling out in a nervous stream. It's endearing, in a way, how she rambles on, her face flushed with embarrassment. Despite her attempts to backtrack and apologise, I can't help but find her babbling strangely charming. It's like she's trying to make light of the situation, to ease the tension that has settled between us.

Her mention of not being sure if we're friends stings a little, though. It's true, we don't know each other well, apart from the fact that I'm Olivia's brother. That's how it should stay. But there's something about her vulnerability, her honesty in this moment, that makes me pause.

I *want* to be her friend.

Yet, her questioning our friendship makes me realise how little we've actually talked, how little I know about her. I've never been one to seek friendships easily, preferring solitude over idle chatter. Yet, with her, it's different. I should tread carefully. But right now, as she sits before me, vulnerable and uncertain, I realise I want to be more than just her *best friend's brother*.

"If you haven't already gathered, I'm a bit of a yappa. I ramble *a lot!*"

No kidding.

"My students tell me all the time. I mean, for a five-year-old child who never stops talking to tell a grown woman she talks too much…" Her words trail off, and she exhales. "Yikes. I just can't help it, I guess. It's like my brain is always on overdrive, and I just start talking before I can stop myself. Honestly, sometimes I think I should come with a warning label or something. Maybe 'Warning: Prone to Excessive Rambling,'" she finishes, and I just study her, watching her expression, not knowing what to say.

"Oh, God, I did it again, didn't I? You probably think I'm the biggest weirdo."

A smirk tugs at the corner of my mouth, and I nod. "Not at all. And I don't mind."

Oddly enough, I actually really *like* it when she *yaps* too much. I shouldn't, but I do.

She looks at me, her gaze intense yet searching, as if she's trying to decipher a hidden code in my expression. I meet her eyes, and for a moment, everything else fades away. It's just her and me, locked in this strange, unspoken connection. Despite all this *yapping*, as she put it, however, it does not detract from the fact that she asked a question; a question that was evidently so out of the blue.

I need answers.

"Amelia?"

"Mm?"

"Why do you think you're frigid?" My tone is blunt, probing deeper. Instantly, I regret it.

Just drop it, Bradley. Leave. Go home.

"Sorry. I won't pry. If that's what you want," I say, standing to leave before she cuts me off.

"Wait." She releases a heavy sigh. "I dunno, I just... I feel like..." Her words trail off, leaving a weighty silence between us.

"Like?"

"I dunno, I-I..." She hesitates. "I don't know how to really act around guys." Her admission catches me off guard. She seems to be doing just fine talking to me.

"Well, there's no rule book on how to act," I reply, trying to keep my voice casual. "Just be yourself. Anyone worth being around will appreciate that." The words feel strange on my tongue, like they belong to someone else.

"So, why hasn't a guy ever kissed me?" she blurts out, followed by a nervous laugh. "Forget it. I'm asking you as if you'd have the *answers*," she says softly, almost to herself, shaking her head.

The alcohol must be wearing off slowly, leaving her thoughts clear and raw. She's never been kissed? The realisation hits me like a ton of bricks.

"You've never been kissed?" I repeat, incredulous.

She simply shakes her head, and I'm at a loss for words. This revelation changes everything. How is it possible that someone as beautiful and kind-hearted as her has never been kissed?

It baffles me. It intrigues me. The first thing that comes to mind slips out, "When the right guy comes along, I'm sure he'll be too captivated by you to even think about waiting." She nods slowly, her gaze dropping to her hands in her lap.

"Yeah. Maybe," she whispers, almost as if to herself.

The thought of someone else being her first kiss pisses me the fuck off. If anyone is going to kiss her, it's going to be me. It's a raw, possessive thought, something I've got no right to claim, but it's there, stubborn as hell. I can't say it out loud, though.

So, I sit there, my mind racing with these selfish desires I shouldn't be having.

12

Amelia

"You know, I swear, the barista totally flirted with me," Olivia exclaims, her eyes sparkling with excitement. Liv and I are nestled in the cosy corner of Tracy's Coffee Stop, a local joint always buzzing with activity.

I chuckle. "Dude, you think every coffee boy flirts with you. It should be part of their job description by now, I reckon."

Olivia grins, nodding in agreement. "Yeah, well, it's true. But this one was really laying it on thick. Didn't you hear?"

To be honest, I didn't. My mind has been a whirlwind this morning, babbling to itself—skipping from one worry to the next like a hyperactive squirrel. Saturday had been spent nursing a throbbing headache from the alcohol I consumed, even though I seemed to sober up pretty quickly that night.

Being around Bradley's presence will do that to ya!

I find myself replaying every moment with him, and all those 'what ifs' that I've tried to bury come bubbling back up.

What if I hadn't asked him that awkward question? What if he thinks I'm a complete weirdo now?

If only I could shake off this silly crush, maybe things wouldn't feel so awkward between us. I can't help but dissect every interaction with Bradley, my mind spinning with questions and hypotheticals. But alas, my heart seems to have a mind of its own, and it's set on overdrive whenever Bradley's around.

Is there a way to uninstall this crush like a bad app? Maybe I should try hitting 'reset' on my feelings.

Oh, if only it were that easy.

Her words pull me back to reality, and I realise I've been staring off into space. "Sorry, Liv. What were you saying?"

Olivia clears her throat, drawing my attention back to the present. "I was saying there is a man at the counter who keeps staring. Don't look now!"

I try to act casual as I wait for the right moment. When Olivia finally gives the signal, I sneak a quick glance in the direction of the counter. I immediately spot the man Olivia is talking about. He's tall, towering over the other customers. His bright yellow high-vis shirt and cargo shorts make him stand out, and there's a dishevelled quality to his dark hair.

He looks older, somewhere in his mid-thirties. *Maybe?*

I have no clue.

"Oof. He's got that rugged look and the brooding vibe, no?" Liv adds.

"I suppose," I say with a shrug, not particularly interested. I'm not one to ogle men or get flustered over a guy standing in a coffee shop.

"You suppose? Girl, we need to up your game! Spruce up your love life," she insists, clearly amused by the idea.

Her comments on the man's rugged look and brooding vibe trigger an unwarranted thought in my mind about Bradley—making me blush instantly. Of course, Liv *notices*.

"Look at you blushing. I know you think he's cute." But my blush isn't about the stranger at the counter. I roll my eyes, trying to hide the flush creeping up my cheeks.

"He's *way* too old."

"Pfft, age is just a number, sweetie. Besides, I like them a little older." She waves off my comment with a smirk.

"You're as mad as a cut snake."

She grins, a mischievous glint in her eye. "What can I say? I like 'em with a bit of experience."

"Speaking of experience, when are you thinking about applying for jobs? You can't sit around on the farm all day long." I chuckle, teasing her.

"Gee, thanks. Maybe that's what I plan to do for the rest of my life, ya never know." I settle her with a look—a look that says *'as if.'*

"Yeah, nah, fuck that! I can't think of anything worse." This makes us both chuckle. "I *have* been thinking of starting up my own candle making business for now, just to get by until I can land a proper job," she adds.

"Oh, that's new!"

"Yeah, it's easy, fun, *and* I can personalise them for any customer. I just need to start up a website or Insta account," Liv adds enthusiastically.

"Sounds like a great plan," I reply, genuinely intrigued. "I'm sure your candles will be a hit."

Olivia beams. "Thanks, girl. I hope so."

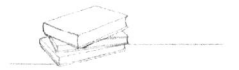

"Well! Did you gals have a good time today?" Grace asks, her hands bustling around the kitchen as she wipes down the countertops with a flour-dusted cloth. Liv and I exchange a knowing glance; her mum has always been like this, full of energy and always bustling about, even when there's no need.

After our impromptu coffee catch-up, Liv's mum asked her to grab some last-minute groceries for dinner, so we made a quick trip to the local mini-mart. Now, in the spacious Mitchell kitchen, Liv and I are unpacking the bags for Grace while she tidies up—her father, well, who knows where he is.

He's always been a bit of a mystery, but to me, Dominic Mitchell has always been like a second father. After all, I did spend quite some time here after school in our younger days.

"We had so much fun," Liv chimes in, flashing me a grin and a wink.

"What's that smile about?" Grace queries.

"Oh, she's still blushing about the guy that was flirting with her at the counter," I say.

"Oh, really now?"

"Yep! He even came past our table before we left to leave his number with her," I admit, as I recall the encounter.

Grace just smiles at me.

"Yeah, yeah. They just can't help themselves," Liv adds with a chuckle.

I can't help but marvel at Liv's confidence. She's always been so sure of herself, in the way she speaks, presents herself, talks to guys, talks about them. I wonder if I'll ever be like that. But it's not in my nature, I remind myself.

I'm just not wired like that.

"When did I raise ya to be so full of yourself, girl?" Grace says with a hand on her hip. "You know them boys like humble women."

"Yeah, exactly, boys," Liv says, making air quote signs. "I think I need to find myself a *man*."

"Olivia Mitchell," Grace says, whacking her with the cloth in her hand. "You best hope that your father doesn't ever hear this sort of yarn. Keep your voice down," she chides. Liv just rolls her eyes and shoots me a look.

I can't help but giggle.

"Besides, *men* are too old for you, young lady. You need to find yourself a nice, compassionate fella," Grace advises.

"Sure thing, Ma. You'll be waiting for as long as a wet weekend," Liv quips.

"Well, I bloody hope not. It's bad enough now I gotta wait for your brother to settle down," Grace remarks, her tone slightly exasperated.

"Which one?" Liv asks, looking genuinely confused.

"Bradley, you numbnut!" Grace says, shaking her head.

"Oh, I forgot about him. My bad." Liv's casual response makes me blush at the mention of Bradley. I hope Grace doesn't notice, but she momentarily looks at me, and I quickly look away, hoping to hide my embarrassment.

Great.

"Amelia, you're a bright young woman, impeccably polite. We should set you up with our Bradley," Grace suggests, her eyes twinkling with mischief.

My eyes go wide, my breathing falters. Laughter breaks out, but it's not coming from me or Grace. Liv bellows over, laughing loudly.

"Yeah, good one. As if Amelia here would ever date Bradley."

But... I kinda, totally *would*. I feel a nervous flutter in my stomach, unsure of what to make of this revelation.

"Oh, I-I..." I start to politely decline, but words fail me.

Grace watches me with a knowing smile.

What does that mean? Does she see right through me?

"No way, that would just be so... weird," Liv says with a forced laugh.

I nod in agreement, trying to play it cool. "Yeah, I was just thinking the same."

"Smart girl! I feel sorry for whoever falls for Bradley. He's too work-driven, too in his head," Liv adds, and her words hit me harder than expected.

I feel a pang of sadness, a sense of disappointment at her words. They only solidify the thoughts running in the back of my mind—get over this silly crush, because that's all it'll ever be.

"Now, now. No need to be rude. Your brother is..." Grace begins with a heavy sigh. "A dedicated and focused man, with a heart of gold," she finishes with a warm smile, and I can't help but feel a twinge of warmth in her words.

Maybe I'm not the only one who sees something special in Brad. But it doesn't matter. He's off limits, and I need to keep my feelings in check.

"Anywho, it was... just a suggestion," Grace says, and I look back to her, only to find her eyes on *me*.

After a few minutes, Liv mentions she has to jet, as she has an appointment in town at Imogen's salon.

"Oh, yes, Imogen! I remember her," I say, recalling our past encounters.

"How can one forget?" Liv laughs. "Blonde hair, legs for days, feisty gal," she adds further.

"True! Tell her I said hi," I say, genuinely.

Grabbing her keys from the kitchen counter, she calls out, "Will do! Hooroo!"

As Grace finishes wiping down the countertops, she turns to me with a warm smile, her eyes twinkling. "You know, Amelia, I'm sure you'll find someone who appreciates you for who you are."

I nod, feeling a surge of gratitude for her words. I'm sure I've heard my own mum say those words before. They feel like a real stretch, though.

"Thanks, Grace. That means a lot."

She then asks if I'll be staying for dinner, but I politely decline. As I make my way to leave, she calls out, "Oh, Amelia, dear. Would you mind grabbing Bradley for me? I heard him come home not long ago, and he hasn't come in yet. He'd probably be out back."

I falter for a moment, my body frozen.

Why me?

I sigh internally, realising I hadn't even realised that he'd be home. How dumb of me.

"If that's alright with you, dear? I would, but I should probably get started on cooking, especially when these Mitchell men can get quite ravenous," she says with a laugh.

Righto.

"Oh, uh, of course. No worries at all," I reply, but my voice sounds squeaky, so I clear my throat.

I find Bradley where Grace said he'd be. Out the back, reclining on one of the pool chairs. Nerves instantly start to kick in. I take a deep breath, trying to compose myself.

Approaching quietly, I remain silent, trying to muster up what to say. I scold myself internally, trying to shake off the jitters.

Come on, Amelia, you can do this.

Before I can gather my thoughts, Bradley's deep voice slices through the quiet, making me jump a little.

"You planning to just stand there all day?" he asks, not turning from his view of the fields.

My heart skips a beat at his words, and I feel a rush of panic. I open my mouth to respond, but all that comes out is a jumble of words.

"Oh, um, no. I mean, I was just... your mother, she, uh, asked me to find you," I blurt out, feeling my cheeks burn with embarrassment. I mentally kick myself for sounding so awkward. Why can't I ever talk to him without sounding like a bumbling fool?

"Well, here I am," he replies, his tone as gruff as ever. Seriously, does he ever not sound grumpy? What's got his engine revving today? I wonder why he might be feeling this way? Maybe he stubbed his toe or had a bad breakfast.

Does he even eat breakfast?

"What does my mother need?"

Trying to regain my composure, I manage to squeak out, "She said dinner will be ready soon."

He just nods, yet he makes no effort to get up, and I feel a wave of uncertainty wash over me. What do I do now? I can feel my heart pounding in my chest, my palms starting to sweat.

Oh, great, sweaty palms, just what I need right now.

Okay, Amelia, breathe. You can do this. Just act casual, like it's no big deal. But how does one act casual around Captain Grumps over there?

"I can practically hear your thoughts racing, Amelia," he says suddenly, and I realise he knows it's me. Duh, who else would it be? Smooth move, brain.

I laugh nervously. Well, at least he didn't hear the circus going on in my head. Yet.

"You gonna sit? Because if you're gonna just stand there, you might as well leave," he quips, his tone abrupt.

My goodness. Way to make me feel welcome, Bradley.

"What is up your ass today?" I blurt out before I can stop myself.

He turns his head slightly, slowly, his eyes sweeping over me, a hint of a smirk on his lips. Great, now I've probably offended him.

"Nothing. Absolutely nothing," he sighs. "Please, sit." He gestures to the chair beside him. "Sorry, I'm being a dick," he adds.

I slowly sink into the chair next to him, feeling his gaze lingering on me the whole time. Eventually, we settle into silence, and I find myself enjoying the peace. The birds chirping loudly around us drown out any lingering thoughts, and being outside in nature's embrace feels surprisingly serene. So, I close my eyes, soaking in all the sounds with a deep sigh.

"Are you... good?" Bradley's voice cuts through the quiet, with a hint of amusement.

"Are you?" I respond, keeping my eyes shut.

"Touché." He chuckles softly.

Opening my eyes, I gaze up at the tall trees above us, their leaves swaying gently in the breeze. "What are you—"

"Shh... Just look up and take a moment to appreciate the leaves,"

I gently interrupt.

He clears his throat. "The leaves?"

"Yes, Brad. Shh." We lapse back into silence.

"Listen to the birds, just breathe in the air," I continue after a pause. "I do this sometimes when my thoughts are racing, or when I feel overwhelmed."

I wonder if his thoughts are always racing like mine sometimes do. There's so much I know about him, yet so little at the same time. Over the years, I've noticed little quirks of his—how he always straightens his watchband when he's lost in thought, meticulously adjusting it until it's perfectly aligned. Or the way he slightly tilts his head when he's listening intently to someone, his eyes narrowing just a fraction, as if he's trying to absorb every word.

There's this faint crinkle at the corners of his eyes when he's amused, like he's trying not to smile too widely. Even the way he pauses before answering questions, like he's carefully considering his words, reveals layers I haven't fully unravelled. There's also how he taps his foot impatiently when he's waiting, or how he subtly clenches his jaw when he seems frustrated. Like right now, as I watch him sitting on the chair, his brows are furrowed and his jaw is clenched, clearly showing his frustration.

"My thoughts aren't racing, though," he counters, but there's a hint of uncertainty in his tone.

"Yeah, and I'm a unicorn," I retort, a playful jab lacing my words.

Bradley chuckles softly, the tension between us easing slightly.

I can't help but smile, hearing that sound. It's like a rare glimpse of a softer side of him, a side that's usually hidden behind his gruff exterior.

"Alright, just stare at the leaves, or close your eyes if you prefer, and focus on your breathing. In and out," I instruct gently, keeping my eyes fixed on the trees above.

His presence beside me is like a comforting warmth on a chilly day, but I resist the urge to steal a glance, my nerves fluttering like trapped butterflies in my stomach.

"Are your thoughts racing? Feeling overwhelmed?" he asks quietly after a moment.

"No," I reply softly. *Lies.* "I'm doing this for you."

"For me?" he echoes, surprised.

"Yes. Just try it," I urge gently.

As the sounds of just birds and the rustling of leaves fill the air, a warm breeze sweeps over me, bringing a sense of calm.

"Is it working?" I ask in a hushed tone, barely audible above the rustling leaves. He doesn't reply right away, and when I start to turn my head to meet his gaze, I find his eyes already locked on mine.

I freeze, startled by the intensity in his eyes. A faint smile quirks his lips, sending a flutter through my chest.

"Yeah, it's working," he finally answers, his voice steady and calm.

Heat rises to my cheeks. Quickly, I look away, focusing on my breathing and the serene sounds of nature around us.

But no matter how hard I try, all I can think about is how his gaze warmed me up and that quick smile on his lips.

"You look lost in thought," she says.

Liv's over at my place for a girls' night, and we're lounging on my couch, devouring Chinese takeout while *Love Actually* plays in the background. Thoughts of Bradley from today keep creeping in—his intense stare, his serious demeanour—it's all swirling around in my head.

I widen my eyes and quickly shake my head. "Oh… what? No, it's nothing."

Liv chuckles, clearly not buying my denial. "You sound just like Bradley. That's his go-to line whenever I ask what's on his mind. 'Nothing. None of your business,'" she mimics, nailing his gruff tone perfectly.

We divert our attention back to the movie. Onscreen, Hugh Grant's character is dancing through 10 Downing Street, trying to charm the girl he likes. It's a sweet and romantic scene, making Liv sigh dreamily.

"You know, girl, when are you going to let some romance into your life?" Liv teases lightly.

I shift uncomfortably. "I don't know, Liv. I'm just taking it easy. Happy as I am."

She rolls her eyes dramatically. "Oh, please, spare me the 'I'm forever alone' speech. No one is happy alone forever. I mean, maybe some people. But we're not those people. You're like a fine wine, darling. Your time will come. In the meantime, let's get you a cat."

"No way!" I say with a chuckle.

Liv grins mischievously. "Oh, come on, think of the Instagram likes!"

"No Instagram, remember?"

"Ugh. You are such a hermit. No wonder you haven't dated anyone."

I scoff playfully. "Oh yeah? What about you, then? Any love life updates?"

"Hey, no, no. Interrogation is my territory. Besides, my heart belongs to pizza and Netflix."

"But seriously, anything going on? Don't say nothing, that's my line," I tease, and Liv laughs.

"Ugh, nothing exciting since I came back from Sydney. But who knows? Maybe the right person is closer than we think."

I steal a glance at her, my mind inevitably drifting back to Bradley. Could Liv be on to something?

Could *he* be the one?

Despite my thoughts, I force a smile, grateful for Liv's unwavering optimism. "Yeah, we'll see."

13

Bradley

Seated at the dining table for our usual family dinners, this time at our place, I quietly observe my brother and Isla across from me. Isla's sporting a small bump now, barely noticeable to anyone else, but glaringly obvious to those in the know. They're keeping it under wraps from our friends and others until they hit their twelve-week scan, something about waiting in case of risk or concern, as Isla put it.

Their presence offers a welcome distraction from the chaos swirling in my head. Lately, my headspace hasn't been great. There's this weight, this constant pressure to keep it together 24/7. Sometimes, I spiral into these moods, and nothing really helps except distancing myself for a while to clear my head.

But the other day, something shifted.

Amelia.

Just being around her, experiencing something as simple and pure as a breathing exercise or staring into the sky, grounded me in a way I haven't felt in ages. It's like she brought calm to the storm in my mind.

I'm fixated on how her presence affects me, like discovering a part of myself that was missing. As the chatter around the table picks up, the atmosphere shifts.

"Isla, how's the little one treating you?" Mum asks, her eyes warm with concern.

Isla talks animatedly about her pregnancy, mentioning how she's feeling more energetic lately but still gets those occasional bouts of morning sickness. She smiles, placing a hand on her stomach.

"We're doing well. We just need to finalise the nursery, but we still have time," she replies, exchanging a glance with Xavier, who kisses her head.

"I'm slowly starting to box things up, like Mum and Dad's clothes—" Isla starts, her voice trailing off as tears well up in her eyes.

"Oh, my dear," Mum soothes, taking Isla's hand.

"Ah, pregnancy hormones."

Xav rubs Isla's arms up and down, comforting her. "It's okay, baby."

Isla composes herself for a moment. "We're getting there. I just don't want to change the house too much, you know?" she says with a sigh.

"Of course, dear. I think it's a beautiful idea to keep and hold on to the memory of your parents in your home," Mum says, wiping her own tears with her napkin. "They're always here with you."

"Thank you," Isla says warmly, squeezing Mum's hand.

As everyone finishes eating, knives and forks clatter against plates. Liv starts a new conversation, "Have you been getting any weird cravings?"

Isla laughs, eyes sparkling. "Oh, you have no idea. I've been craving pickles and ice cream at the oddest hours!" she exclaims, earning chuckles from us.

"Pickles and ice cream, huh?" Dad joins in. "Grace was the same when she was pregnant with you lot. I remember running out to get her some in the middle of the night more than once!"

Isla looks amused. "Really?"

Dad smiles fondly—a rare sight. "Oh yes, she had some interesting cravings. But it was all worth it in the end, wasn't it, love?" He looks at Mum, who nods with a smile, her eyes twinkling with memories.

"I remember she practically lived on cheese and pineapple sandwiches for weeks," Dad adds.

"Gross, man," Liv grimaces.

"Don't knock it till you try it, darling," Mum chides, before addressing Isla, "Just remember, Isla, dear, to take time to relax through it all."

"On that note," Liv continues eagerly, "I was talking to Imogen at my hair appointment the other day—"

"That can't be good," Xavier interjects, and Isla playfully smacks his arm.

"Anyway, she gave me this brilliant idea. Since you two never got to go anywhere after the wedding," she gestures to Isla and Xavier, "what better way to celebrate than to go on a small getaway? We could book an AirBnB somewhere nice and just relax and have some fun."

Isla's face lights up at the suggestion. "That sounds amazing! I'm totally onboard."

Xav, however, hesitates. "I don't know, babe. With the baby on the way, I just want to make sure everything's okay. Maybe we should hold off on big trips for now."

Isla rolls her eyes playfully. "Oh, stop being a softie. It'll be fine. We can still have a great time *and* take it easy."

This makes me snort.

Xav shoots me a playful glare. "Wait until you have kids, mate. Then you'll know what real worry is," he says, his tone teasing, but with a hint of truth. His words poke at me, but I just shrug it off. Xavier doesn't even comprehend the true essence of worry.

Worry? He couldn't grasp the weight of that word, not truly. Our concerns may differ now, but the core remains unchanged.

"I think it's a fantastic idea," Mum chimes in. "It'll be a wonderful way to celebrate this new chapter in your lives."

"Alright, fine," Xav sighs.

"It'll be fun. And plus, it's just a small getaway," Isla says with a smile.

Liv turns to me, and I can feel all eyes on me, waiting for my answer. I hesitate, feeling reluctant about the idea of a trip, but with a heavy sigh, I finally relent.

"Fine."

Liv nods, satisfied. "Great! I'll pass on the information to everyone."

"Everyone?" Xavier and I ask simultaneously.

"Yeah, the whole gang. Michael, Harrison, Imogen—" Liv's voice blurs as I anticipate the next name she's about to say. "And Amelia!"

Isla chuckles. "Oh, this should be interesting."

Xavier adds sarcastically, "Stuck in an AirBnB with everyone, especially with Harrison and Imogen's bickering. Can't wait."

As the conversation swirls around me, the reality of spending a weekend in an AirBnB with Amelia sinks in. I'm already regretting this decision, but there is a part of me that's intrigued.

This could be an interesting turn of events.

14

Amelia

Saturday morning rolls around, and I start packing my stuff for our little impromptu weekend getaway. I've got Olivia on FaceTime, and she's giving me the rundown of what to bring.

"So, just the basics, right?" I confirm, folding a few shirts and tossing them into my bag.

"Exactly, just the basics," Olivia confirms, watching as I hold up a couple of shirts for her approval.

"Should I bring this one?" I ask, showing her a colourful top.

"Yeah, that looks perf! And don't forget your cozzie, just in case we decide to hit the lake," Liv suggests. I nod, making a mental note.

"Got it. What about shoes?"

"Comfortable ones for walking, and maybe something a bit dressier for the night," Liv advises.

"Okay, I'll pack a pair of sneakers and some sandals," I say, adding them to the growing pile in my bag.

"You're all set, then. Oh, and don't forget your charger!"

I chuckle, grabbing my charger from the bedside table. "Wouldn't want to be without that."

Suddenly, Liv's face lights up. "Oh, by the way, Bradley will pick you up. We're all meeting at my place before we head out." My heart skips a beat at the mention of Bradley.

"O-oh, are you sure? I can drive to yours?" I stammer, trying to hide my jittery nerves.

"No, no. Don't be silly," Liv insists, her smile comforting. "Saves you having to leave your car here."

This is just a weekend trip with friends. I've got this.

Thinking that, a rush of nervous excitement washes over me. I can't help but feel all bubbly at the thought of seeing him again.

Liv says she's gotta run, but assures me Bradley should be here in about twenty-five minutes. She adds he'll text when he's outside. With a quick goodbye, she hangs up. I finish zipping up my bag, my mind still buzzing about Bradley. Then, my phone starts ringing, and my heart jumps to my throat.

Could it be Bradley already? But Liv said twenty-five minutes, right?

I check my phone in a hurry, only to see it's my sister, Kat, FaceTiming me. Relief floods over me as I answer the call. Millie's bright face pops up, instantly lighting up mine.

"Auntie Meli!" she chirps, all excited.

"Hi, Millie!" I match her excitement. "What are you up to?"

"I'm playing with my dolls!" Millie beams, showing off her doll.

"That sounds fun! What are their names?"

"This one's Sawah!" Millie points proudly.

"Sarah looks lovely. What's she doing today?" I play along with her game.

"She's having a tea party!" Millie moves her dolls around.

"That sounds like a lot of fun!"

"Alright, Mumma's turn now," Kat says as she takes over the call from Millie.

"Hey, Kat!"

"Hey, Meli. Mum told me you're going away for the weekend. Who's going?" Kat asks, looking curious.

"Yeah, Liv organised a little trip. It's going to be Liv, Xavier, his wife, a few other mates, and... Bradley," I reply, a slight nervousness creeping into my voice at the mention of his name.

"Ooo. Bradley's going?" Kat asks, her eyebrows raising in surprise.

"Yup. He's coming, too," I confirm.

"Everything all good?"

"Yeah, yeah. Just... you know, going away with everyone, it's a bit... different," I explain, trying to brush off my nerves.

"I get it. It's like a big group outing. Should be fun though, right?" she says, trying to reassure me.

"Yeah, you're right," I reply, trying to sound more confident than I feel.

"Well, have a great time. And let me know if Bradley does anything cute," Kat teases.

"Kat!" I exclaim. Just then, a text pops up from an unknown number.

> **Unknown:** It's Bradley. Hope you don't mind, Liv gave me your number. I'm outside.

It's Bradley. Hope you don't mind, but Liv gave me your number. I'm outside.

My heart leaps, butterflies going wild again.

"Kat, I've gotta go—my ride's here."

"Okay, okay. Have fun!"

"Thanks! Talk soon," I say quickly before hanging up. I grab my things and hurry out to meet Bradley.

Bradley leans casually against the passenger door of his white ute—dressed in jeans and a white t-shirt that clings to his muscular frame.

Holy cow!

I stop for a moment, ogling him, struck by how attractive he looks. My heart flutters in my chest, and I have to remind myself to breathe.

"Hey," he greets me as he takes my bag, effortlessly tossing it into the backseat.

"Hi. Thanks for picking me up," I say, grateful for the gesture.

He just nods, a small smile playing on his lips, before opening the door for me. I slide into the passenger seat, feeling a flutter of excitement mixed with nerves as he closes the door behind me. He gets in and starts the engine. As we pull onto the road, I try to break the silence.

"So, uh, how's your morning been?"

"Good. Fine," he replies, eyes on the road. "You?"

"Good. Fine," I echo his statement with a smirk.

The tension's thick, and I fiddle with my bag strap. After a bit, Bradley speaks again.

"You excited for the trip?" he asks, glancing at me before focusing ahead.

"Yeah, definitely. It should be fun," I reply, my voice a little more steady now.

As we drive, my gaze keeps drifting to him, mesmerised by the way his big hands confidently grip the wheel, fingers tapping out a silent rhythm. Sunlight filters in, casting a gentle glow on his strong jaw and the hint of stubble. The t-shirt he is wearing does wonders for his muscular physique, revealing the bulging muscles and the dark hair that dusts his tan skin.

He's so incredibly attractive, it's hard not to notice.

Blushing, I glance out the window at the blur of green trees rushing by. Before long, we arrive at Liv's place. Bradley parks, and I spot everyone outside, busy loading up cars.

"Looks like everyone's ready to go," Bradley remarks, turning off the engine.

As I step out of the car, the familiar faces of Liv, Xavier, Isla, Imogen, and Harrison greet me with smiles and waves.

"Hey, girl!" Liv chirps, giving me a quick hug before turning to Bradley with a grin. "Thanks for bringing her, bro." Bradley nods, his usual serious look softened just a bit as he acknowledges everyone.

Isla and Imogen both envelop me in warm hugs. The guys nod in acknowledgement, and I return their gestures with a wave, suddenly feeling a bit shy amidst the lively group. They then begin discussing the logistics of the trip, and Liv announces that we'll be splitting into three cars.

Imogen pipes up, "I'll drive with anyone, as long as I'm not stuck with him," pointing toward Harrison.

This elicits a round of laughter.

Liv quickly gathers everyone's attention. "Alright, fine, so here's the plan. Isla and Xav are driving up together. Imogen, Amelia, you're with me." She glances over at Harrison with a mischievous twinkle in her eye. "Harrison and Michael, you're with Bradley."

"Who put her in charge? Aren't you like twelve or something?" Harrison teases.

"Ha. ha," she mocks.

I grab my bag from Bradley's car as everyone starts moving. Xavier's parting comment brings a small smile to my face as he pats Bradley on the shoulder.

"Good luck with those two," he says, nodding toward Harrison and Michael in the back seat. Bradley just shakes his head, unfazed.

As I settle into Liv's car beside Imogen, I sneak a quick glance at Bradley. Our eyes meet unexpectedly, and a wave of warmth washes over me. For that moment, it's like time stands still, and there's this electric connection between us. But then he looks away, and the moment slips by.

Even so, my heart is doing cartwheels, like a kid on a trampoline.

15

Bradley

The drive here was something else. Stuck in the car with Michael and Harrison, it's always a rowdy affair. They're Xav's mates, but after enough time, they've become like mates to me, too. Bloody hell, we're almost like brothers.

At least, that's how my brother would see it.

Yeah, Harrison can be a handful, but I get it. He's been through some rough patches, but that's not my story to tell, not by a long shot. I pull up in the driveway of our temporary home for the next two days.

The house is right on the riverfront, a decent view of the water. The land around it is green and lush, typical Aussie countryside. Liv really nailed it by finding this place, especially at such short notice. I had my doubts about this trip, but now that we're here, away from the grind, I feel the tension slipping off my shoulders. Maybe a change of scenery is just what I needed to clear my head.

"Fucckk me. Look at this shit! Where did Liv find this place?" Harrison calls out as he practically leaps out of the car, and I can't help but smile.

I shrug, scanning the surroundings. "No idea."

"Does it really matter? It's a nice change of scenery," Michael retorts, getting out of the car and slinging his headphones around his neck before lighting up a cigarette.

Harrison strides off toward the river. "I'm gonna check it out!" he announces eagerly.

I watch him go, shaking my head. "He's like a kid in a candy store."

Michael nods in agreement, his expression relaxed. "Yeah, but I think we all needed this break."

These two couldn't be more different—Harrison's always bouncing around like a golden retriever, while Michael's the steady one, the rock in the storm. It's an odd pairing, but it works for them.

After a moment, I step out of the car and meet Michael around the back. Harrison returns from around the front of the house.

"This place really goes down to the river," he exclaims, clearly impressed. I turn around and notice that we're the first ones here. Michael seems to read my thoughts.

"Where are the other slow pokes? We actually beat them here?" he asks.

"Yeah, because *he* was speeding the whole way here," Harrison quips, nodding to me.

"Was not. I'm a responsible driver," I reply, a hint of defensiveness in my tone.

"Sure, mate. Just because you're a cop doesn't mean you can't have a bit of fun," Harrison adds.

"Fun?" I give him a sceptical look, raising an eyebrow. "Yeah, I don't think so."

I pull out my phone and call Xavier. He picks up on the second ring.

"Yeah, we're about ten minutes away," he replies. "Isla needed to pee, so we stopped off at the servo."

I smile at Xavier's knack for anticipating my questions. We've always had this unspoken understanding. Mum used to joke that we were so in tune, we might as well be twins with our telepathy.

"Alright, no worries. We're just waiting in front."

"See you soon," Xav says before ending the call.

I consider calling Liv but decide against it. I don't want to distract her while she's driving, so I scroll through my recent texts and decide to message Amelia instead.

Me: You guys far?

Moments later, her response comes in, and I can't help but smirk at her bubbly energy.

Amelia: Hi! Not too far, about 10 minutes out.

Me: Ok. Everything all good?

Amelia: Absolutely. Why wouldn't it be?

> **Amelia:** Liv has been driving the speed limit, BTW! We should be there very soon.

> **Me:** Good to hear.

> **Amelia:** Yep. See you soon 😈

> **Amelia:** Omg! Sorry. Please ignore that emoji!

> **Amelia:** I was supposed to click on the smiley face, but that was right next to it.

As I read her messages, I can practically hear her reprimanding herself in her head. Despite her quirks, I've actually become quite fond of her. Weird as it may seem, I find her babbling and fumbling of words endearing. It's cute.

> **Me:** Lol. All good.

Moments later, another text pings in.

> **Amelia:** I'm just glad it wasn't a winky face. That would've been awkward...

> **Me:** Yeah... maybe.

I pocket my phone away just as Xav's black Tacoma pulls up, followed by Liv's Yaris, blaring some girly song. I hope she doesn't drive around with music that loud on main roads. Then again, it's her call. I need to ease up; I'm starting to sound like Dad.

The thought wrinkles my face.

"How loud is your *music*, Liv? How do you even concentrate on driving?" Harrison blurts out, voicing what I was just thinking.

"Surely that's not legal," Michael says, as he turns to me for confirmation.

I just shrug.

"It wasn't that loud!" Liv defends herself.

Harrison snorts. "It's bad enough you're listening to that sappy shit."

"Sappy shit?" Imogen exclaims, placing a hand to her heart. "Taylor Swift is NOT *sappy shit*, you barbarian."

"Taylor what?" Harrison looks genuinely confused, and Imogen scoffs in disbelief.

Xavier then steps in. "Now, now, children. That's enough."

"Anyway, Liv, where did you even find this place? It's bloody amazing!" Isla eagerly interjects, changing the subject.

"I know, right?" Liv's eyes light up. "I found it online at the last minute. Couldn't believe our luck!"

"It's perfect, secluded away *and* there is a river! We can go swimming!" Isla says, wrapping her arm around Xav, all giddy.

"Exactly! Now, let's get settled in. Who's up for a drink?"

Imogen, Michael, Harrison, and Amelia all chorus their agreement, eager for a drink. With the decision made, we begin to unload our bags from the cars and make our way inside.

As we head inside, I spot Amelia out of the corner of my eye. Her hair's all windswept, and she's tucking loose strands behind her ears. While she's caught up in conversation, I take a moment to really look at her. It's March, so it's still warm. She's wearing denim shorts and a loose white t-shirt tucked in, with 'AC DC - The Razor's Edge' written on it.

AC/DC, huh? Didn't peg her for a fan.

The band's a favourite of mine. Growing up, Dad would always blast their music on an old vinyl record player—we still have it. I can almost hear the riffs and feel the nostalgia. I smile to myself, amused by the unexpected connection.

Liv starts unloading the esky and filling the fridge, offering me a beer. I take it, nodding my thanks. The banter continues around me until Imogen calls out, "Alright, what's everyone else having?"

"Beer for me, thanks," Harrison replies.

"Same here," Michael adds.

"I'll have a cider, please," Amelia requests politely.

"Isla, what about you? Cider?" Imogen asks.

"No, thanks. I'm not drinking," Isla responds with a nervous smile.

"You're not drinking? But I thought you liked cider," Imogen says, surprised. "Have one drink with me."

"She said no, Midge," Xav interjects, his tone firm but gentle.

Suddenly, recognition dawns on Imogen's face. Her eyes widen, and a gasp escapes her lips. Amelia, standing beside me, picks up on Imogen's reaction and mirrors it, her hand flying to her mouth in disbelief.

"No way!" Imogen exclaims, her voice filled with excitement.

Isla, now smiling knowingly, nods gently.

"No freaking way!" Imogen squeals, unable to contain her joy. "Are you pregnant?"

Isla nods again, her gaze meeting Xavier's. He smiles back at her, eyes shimmering with happiness.

"Surprise!" she announces, her hands stretched out in a gesture of excitement, and the room erupts in cheers and laughter. Harrison whistles loudly before clapping Xav on the back. Imogen steps forward, her voice laced with emotion.

"Congratulations! OMG!" she says, wrapping Isla into a tight hug before stepping back, tears glistening in her eyes.

"Hey, what about me? I took part in the conception, too. *Multiple* times, must I add," Xavier says, loud enough for only Isla to hear, but we all catch on to it. Isla blushes, feigning embarrassment.

"Xav!" she says, playfully swatting his arm.

"Didn't realise you'd become such a softie now," Imogen teases before wrapping him in for a hug, standing on her tiptoes to reach him.

"I've said it before, but I just can't wait to be an auntie and spoil the little cutie," my sister says, giving Isla's small bump a gentle rub

"This definitely calls for a celebration!" she calls out.

"Absolutely," Amelia agrees, grinning from ear to ear as she gives Isla and Xav a hug. "Congrats, you two!" Her warmth is evident in her words.

"Cheers to the newest member of the gang," Michael toasts, the group echoing his excitement.

Harrison jokes, "So, does that mean we can start calling you Daddy Xavier?"

"Absolutely not. His head's big enough already," Isla teases, and behind her, Xavier nods, mouthing the word *yes*, making everyone laugh.

As the jokes fly, I can't help but feel a deep sense of warmth. Their news brings a surprising lightness to the evening, underscoring the raw, real joys of family and the tight-knit bonds we've got.

I shift my gaze to Amelia, catching her staring at me. Her cheeks flush as our eyes meet, and she quickly looks away, but not before I see that shy smile. It's a fleeting moment, but it tugs at something deep inside me. In her presence, I feel a flicker of something unfamiliar, something that chips away at my guarded exterior. Maybe it's her genuine nature or the way she brightens a room—at least, for me.

As the group sorts out the rooming arrangements, I find myself in a familiar tug-of-war. My eyes keep drifting toward her, no matter how hard I try to resist. It's like they have a mind of their own, drawn to her like a magnet.

This is exactly what I've been trying to avoid, but here I am, struggling to tear my gaze away.

Grabbing my bag, I use the excuse of needing to settle into my room to escape this internal battle. As I make my way down the hall, I try to focus on the task at hand, but thoughts of Amelia linger, stubborn and relentless. Isla, Xav, Michael, and Harrison are taking the upstairs bedrooms, leaving Liv, Amelia, Imogen, and me on the ground level—and thank fuck, I end up with my own room.

The place is spacious, with well-laid-out rooms and wide corridors. It's a relief, considering we paid just shy of two-thousand dollars. Split between the eight of us, it was affordable. The house itself is a classic Australian riverfront property, with large, tall windows letting in plenty of natural light. Floor-to-ceiling curtains offer privacy when needed.

As I start to settle in, Liv comes barreling into my room, breaking my concentration.

"Oi, we're heading down to the river for a quick dip. You coming?"

I ponder the thought. The river outside looks inviting, and a swim sounds refreshing.

"Sure. I'll be down in a minute."

"Righto!" Liv chirps before heading out, leaving me to finish unpacking before joining the others.

After a while, I make my way down to the river. The group has dispersed—Liv, Harrison, and Imogen are splashing around, their laughter echoing across the water. Isla's lounging on a towel while Xav fusses over her, making sure she's got enough sunscreen. Michael kicking back in a foldable chair, soaking up the sun.

The scene should feel peaceful, but my thoughts are a storm. Amelia's presence stirs something in me, something I'm not ready to face. I don't do feelings. I don't do complications.

But here I am, caught in the undertow of emotions I can't control, all because of one woman.

I notice Amelia sitting on her towel next to Michael, a book in hand. Something about seeing her lost in a book warms me in a way I can't explain. It's simple, but it makes her more endearing. As I approach, I lay my towel down next to Michael and glance at Amelia, curiosity getting the better of me.

"What are you reading?" I nod toward her book.

She closes the book, answering vaguely, "Uh, it's, uh, a romance book."

Michael smirks. "What she means to say is that it's porn on page."

"What! Uh, no, it's just a light romance," she stammers.

"Mhm," Michael hums, not sounding convinced.

"How would you even know that?" I ask, raising my brow.

"Dude, it's what every chick reads these days."

I'm curious about how Michael knows about romance novels, but I don't care enough to question it. Instead, I raise an eyebrow. "What's it about? The book, I mean."

Amelia hesitates for a moment. "It's about a woman who finds love in a small, charming town. It's... it's kind of like those cowboy romances, but not as... dramatic."

"Interesting," I reply, nodding slowly.

Harrison yells for us to get in the water, cutting off the conversation. Imogen squeals when he splashes her, and we all laugh.

"Ugh. I fucking hate you," she yells, trying to splash him back.

Xav and Isla join the chaos, their laughs ringing out. Xav slaps Isla's ass, and she shoves him hard. Grinning, he picks her up and splashes into the water.

I stand, stretch, and yank my shirt off, tossing it onto my towel. As I turn, I catch Amelia's gaze fixed on me, her mouth slightly parted in surprise. Her staring doesn't go unnoticed, and it gives me a jolt. There's a primal satisfaction in knowing she's looking. Her shy smile and blush stir something I've tried to bury—an attraction I can't shake. And the fact that she's never been kissed still replays in my mind, bothering me to my core. Ever since she blurted it out, it's been gnawing at me.

Fuck, I want to kiss her so bad, and seeing her look at me like that makes me want to toss aside my own fucking rules.

I raise my eyebrow, smirking slightly. "You coming?"

She nods, scrambling to her feet, her cheeks flushing deeper. I wink before jogging down to the water. The coolness of the river has a refreshing bite to it as I dive in, relishing the sensation against my warm skin.

As I resurface, I see Amelia peeling off her cover-up, revealing a simple pink bikini. Watching her walk into the water, I'm momentarily stunned, speechless. It's the first time I've seen her like this, so exposed, and her and her body is fucking breathtaking.

Her curves are just right, the bikini hugging every inch in a way that makes my pulse spike. With each sway of her hips, a wave of heat slams into me, my cock stirring to life, straining against my swimmers. I try to remind myself that she's my sister's best friend.

Off limits. But damn, she's making it impossible to stick to that rule.

The bikini showcases her curves perfectly, from her ample breasts to her toned, flat stomach. I'm momentarily stunned, lost in admiration, caught up in her. But then Michael splashes me, snapping me out of it.

"The fuck?" I snap, irritation roughening my voice.

He just shakes his head, a teasing glint in his eyes. I roll mine in response, forcing all thoughts of Amelia's perfect body aside. At least I'm already in the water, so hiding the semi I've got won't be a problem.

This girl is seriously testing my limits.

16

Amelia

The back balcony is a slice of heaven. The setting sun casts a golden glow over everything, making the river shimmer like a sea of diamonds. I wrap my arms around myself, the soft, oversized sweater hugging me as I breathe in the crisp air.

The BBQ sizzles in the background, the smell of grilled meat mingling with the earthy scent of the trees. It's a perfect spot to relax, with the wooden planks warm under my feet and the Adirondack chairs set out like a Pinterest dream. But all I can think about is Bradley's body... up close and personal. Sure, I accidentally saw him naked a few weeks ago, but seeing him shirtless up close, with time to admire?

Totally lethal.

It felt like a guilty pleasure.

Those chiselled abs, the light dusting of hair on his chest trailing down, down to his... Oh, my gosh. Why am I even thinking about this? I'm such a dork. I just sat there staring at him, ogling him like a total idiot. He caught me, and then he winked.

My brain short-circuited.

Honestly, I'm a complete disaster when it comes to him.

As I sit here, the girls beside me are totally engrossed in a conversation about the latest TV show obsession. My phone vibrates on the table next to me, and I glance down to see it's a message from my work friends.

Jamie: Hey, how's your little stay-cay going?

Me: Good 😊

Kristie: Just good?

Jamie: Yeah, we need details, girl! Is it relaxing? Are you having fun?

Me: Yeah, it's relaxing. The river is beautiful.

Kristie: And? Who's all there?

I hesitate for a moment, not wanting to give too much away, but I know they'll pry it out of me eventually.

Jamie: Wait! You went with Liv, right? And other friends? OMG! Does that mean Bradley is there???

Me: Umm... yep.

> **Kristie:** Oh, shittttt. Now THIS is getting interesting. 👀 Wait till Amanda sees these messages and that you're on a stay-cay with BRADLEY! 😈

> **Me:** I am not just with him!!! Everyone is here, too!

> **Jamie:** What's happening? Please tell me you've bonked.

> **Kristie:** I mean, surely 👀

My cheeks flush as I read their messages. No way. I can't do that to Liv—go behind her back and sleep with her *brother*.

Holy moly, this is tough.

But really, I got myself into this mess.

Despite how wrong it is, I can't stop thinking about him. He's everywhere I look, invading my thoughts and making my heart race. I want it so bad, it's driving me crazy. His chiselled abs, that smirk, the way he looks at me... It's all I can think about. The more I try to push him out of my mind, the stronger the pull becomes.

This is impossible. How can something feel so right and so wrong at the same time?

> **Me:** OMG! Stop.

> **Jamie:** Lameeee. Seriously, what's stopping you? He's HOT!

I sigh, feeling my cheeks flush as I think about how to respond. Liv, Isla, and Imogen are still deep in conversation, and I don't want to be rude by ignoring them.

> **Jamie:** I mean, it's clear he's got a thing for you, so like... why not?

> **Me:** And what made you come to that assumption?

> **Jamie:** The way he looks at you. What he did for you the other night at the pub? Girl, come on!

These texts definitely need to wait for another time, especially not now, while I'm sitting at the table with Liv. And to top it off, Bradley is right there, mere metres away. I glance up at the guys, observing them work the BBQ. Bradley is casually sipping his beer, engaged in conversation with Michael. Suddenly, he shifts his gaze in my direction, and our eyes meet once more. I swiftly avert my eyes, a rush of nerves tingling through me.

I hastily type, "Gotta go! Talk later!" and hit send, hoping to end the conversation before it gets any more awkward. I put my phone into my pocket, feeling it vibrate with more texts, but I don't pull it back out. Taking a deep breath, I join the conversation between the girls.

They're discussing our plans for the day tomorrow, with Liv suggesting a hike along the river trail.

"That sounds like so much fun!" I chime in.

Liv nods eagerly. "I've heard the views from the trail are breathtaking."

"And it'll be great to get some fresh air and exercise," Imogen adds.

"I should probably get some exercise in before I become too big to walk," Isla quips, and Xavier jumps in, teasing.

"Don't worry, doc, I'll make sure you get plenty of exercise," he says with a cheeky wink.

"Oh, shut it, you," Isla retorts, playfully rolling her eyes at Xavier. Bradley saunters over, his tall frame casting a shadow as he sets down the sizzling foil trays of snags, ribs, and vegetables.

"Dig in," he announces, his voice carrying the warmth of a friend ready to share a meal.

"Finally!" Isla exclaims, her enthusiasm palpable as she bounces in her seat. "I'm starving!"

As we all start serving ourselves, the atmosphere relaxes, and I'm relieved to be distracted from my buzzing phone and thoughts of Bradley.

"We should make this a tradition," Harrison declares, breaking the comfortable silence.

"I'm all for it. A yearly getaway sounds perfect," Liv agrees, her eyes sparkling with enthusiasm.

"Cheers to a fun weekend, and to the newest Mitchell member!" Xavier announces, raising his beer before taking a swig.

Now fully satisfied after the meal, we're still gathered around the wooden table, discussing things we're too scared to try. I tune back in just in time to hear Isla say, "I'm excited to have this baby," clutching her stomach, "but giving birth terrifies me."

Imogen chimes in, "Oh gosh, that's a good one. I'll never understand how our bodies can do that." She shudders at the thought.

Xavier wraps an arm around Isla, reassuring her, "You'll be fine, babe. You're so strong."

Liv turns to me, and I freeze, trying to think of something. Finally, I say, "I've always dreamt of moving to the city to be with my sister, maybe owning my own art gallery."

This sparks up a conversation about my artworks. Imogen asks me, "Ooo, I didn't know you're an artist. What kind of artworks do you create?" causing me to blush.

"Not many people do, and well, I paint portraits mostly, and some still life, here and there," I explain.

Harrison looks intrigued and asks, "What's still life?"

I smile. "Paintings of inanimate objects, like fruit, flowers, or objects."

Harrison nods, impressed. "Oh, mad."

Liv turns to Bradley. "What about you, Bradley? What's something you'd love to do but are too scared to do?"

He shrugs. "I don't know."

Xavier nudges him playfully. "Oh, come on, mate. There's gotta be something."

Bradley thinks for a moment before saying, "I don't know. I guess just doing something, or anything, for myself for once. I have to put others before myself a lot of the time, especially with work, so…"

He stops talking, allowing his words to trail off. "Anyway. Enough about me," he finishes in a dismissive tone.

The group falls silent. Isla makes an aww sound before saying, "Well, I think that's a really good one. Doing things for yourself can be scary sometimes."

Everyone voices their agreements, and I find myself nodding a little too enthusiastically because, well, hearing him say those words just sends a dull ache to my heart. His admission hits me right in the feels.

Who knew the strong, stoic Bradley had such deep thoughts?

It's like discovering there's a whole new layer to him that I never knew existed. The stoic guy who always seems to have it all together is admitting he doesn't always put himself first.

It's like finding out Superman has a weakness or something.

And of course, it makes him even more attractive, which is the absolute last thing I need. He's Liv's brother, for crying out loud. Completely off limits. Yet, my heart insists on doing these ridiculous cartwheels at the thought of "something more" between us.

Maybe his confession is a sign—a sign that we could connect on a deeper level, even with all the complications. But then I have to give myself a mental shake. Focus on the now, Amelia. Focus on anything but Bradley and those deep, soulful eyes that seem to see right through me.

This is so, so hard.

I can't sleep. I've been tossing and turning since around ten thirty.

Liv decided to sleep at the same time, but she's been out like a light since her head hit the pillow. Our room is cosy, with two single beds comfortably apart, providing ample space around them. A large door opens to a small balcony overlooking part of the river. The soft moonlight seeps through the curtains, bathing the room in a gentle, silvery light.

Even at twenty-four, sleeping anywhere other than my own bed makes me feel like a little kid at a sleepover, missing home. The unfamiliar sounds, the different smells—it all keeps me on edge. I glance at Liv, peacefully asleep, and feel a twinge of envy.

How does she fall asleep so effortlessly, no matter where we are? Ugh.

To make matters worse, the events of today keep replaying in my mind like a loop, especially those moments with Bradley. I can't stop over-analysing every interaction, every glance.

I sit up slowly, careful not to disturb Liv, and swing my legs over the side of the bed. The cool floor against my feet sends a small shiver up my spine. I tiptoe to the balcony door and gently open it, stepping outside. The night air is cool and refreshing, and the sound of the river below is soothing. Leaning against the railing, I take a deep breath and let the calmness of the night wash over me. Maybe some fresh air will help clear my mind and ease my nerves. The stars twinkle above, and for a moment, I forget all my worries and just enjoy the beauty of the night.

My thoughts drift back to Bradley. What could he be doing right now? Is he asleep, too? Maybe a cup of tea will help calm my racing thoughts. I make my way to the kitchen. The house is eerily quiet, amplifying the sound of my footsteps as I tiptoe down the hallway. Raiding the cupboards, I find a small tin with tea bags and take out a peppermint tea. The familiar scent of mint fills the air as I fill the kettle with water and set it to boil. The soft hiss of the kettle is oddly comforting in the stillness of the night.

While I wait for the water to heat, I lean against the kitchen counter, hugging myself tightly. Despite the house's warmth, a chill runs down my spine, making me shiver. As I pour the hot water over the tea bag, I watch the steam swirl up, feeling my tension slowly melt away. The warm mug in my hands feels comforting, and I take a cautious sip. The soothing taste of peppermint spreads through me, easing my nerves and wrapping me in a gentle calm.

Suddenly, I sense a presence behind me, and my heart skips a beat. I spin around quickly, nearly dropping my tea. Bradley stands there, bathed in the soft glow of moonlight streaming through the window. My breath catches, and I can hear my pulse pounding in my ears.

"You scared me," I say, voice shaky.

"Sorry. I didn't mean to."

I take a deep breath, trying to steady myself. "Can't sleep?"

"Something like that."

Silence fills the room, the kettle's hum the only sound. I shift uncomfortably, unsure of what to say. He joins me, leaning against the counter. I offer to make him tea, but he shakes his head. The tension is palpable.

"It's a beautiful night, isn't it?" I gesture to the window.

"Yeah, it is." He frowns, eyes distant.

"What's on your mind?"

"A lot."

"Like what?" I inquire.

He sighs. "Work, mostly. And... you."

My breathing hitches, and I freeze. Being this close to him does things to me—dangerous things. "Me? What do you mean?"

My heart pounds loudly. The air feels charged, and I'm hyper-aware of every inch between us. His gaze is intense, making my stomach flutter. I'm caught between wanting to flee and wanting to close the gap. The tension is suffocating, yet thrilling.

His gaze darkens as he studies me, always so deep in thought. I want to know all his thoughts.

"I'm just trying to figure you out. I haven't been able to stop thinking about you," he says, voice low and intense.

Holy crap. So, he's been feeling the same.

He exhales heavily, as if struggling to find the right words.

"I keep replaying every moment, every glance, every conversation we've had. Wondering what might be next," he adds, eyes locked onto mine. He steps closer, gently taking the mug from my hands and placing it on the counter. His touch sends a shiver down my spine, and I can feel the heat radiating off his body.

"Bradley," I whisper, barely audible.

He reaches up, brushing a strand of hair behind my ear. His touch is electric, sending tingles down my neck. I'm frozen, lost in his gaze. The intensity of his stare is almost too much, but I can't look away. I'm completely captivated. Bradley grabs my chin, tilting my head up to meet his eyes.

"Fuck, I shouldn't be doing this," he mutters, abruptly letting go. "Go to bed, Amelia. It's late," he says, looking torn.

"No," I say firmly. I need to know more. I want to be desired. I crave a love like Xavier and Isla's. I may be naïve, but I am not stupid. I'm attracted to him. I have been since I was fourteen.

"Amelia, go," he repeats, softer now.

"No, Brad. Not until you explain what you meant," I say, hand on my hip, determination fueling my words.

He repeats, "I shouldn't want this."

"Shouldn't want *what*?" I ask again, surprising even myself.

"I shouldn't want to *kiss* you," he finally says, voice deep and gravelly. "Ever since you mentioned you haven't been kissed, it's all I can think about. Part of me wants to be the first to give that to you."

Holy cow. Bradley Mitchell wants to *kiss* me?

"What if I want you to kiss me?" I ask, my voice surprisingly steady. It's not like me to be so forward. A muscle in his jaw ticks, and his eyes become hooded. He steps closer, and my breathing hitches. But before he can close the distance, the sound of a door opening breaks the spell.

I gasp, quickly grabbing my mug and dumping its contents in the sink as I walk away. Glancing back, I see Bradley watching me, his expression unreadable. Then he turns away.

Imogen appears out of nowhere, exiting the bathroom with a sleep mask around her neck and her hair slightly dishevelled. She spots me and sucks in a breath.

"Shit! You scared me!" she whispers.

"Sorry," I mutter quickly. Imogen gives me a curious look, but then walks back to her bedroom. My God, that was close. She could have easily seen us in the kitchen.

I quickly head into the bathroom, closing the door behind me. I splash water on my face and neck, trying to cool my nerves. My heart is racing.

I should get to bed. Tomorrow is a new day. I should focus on that and forget everything that just happened. It's for the best—for me, for Bradley, and for Olivia. My face scrunches up at the thought of my best friend.

But God, how I want him to kiss me. To feel his lips on mine. The thought makes my stomach flip, and I feel a longing I've never felt before.

Ugh. Just stop, Amelia.

I take a deep breath and leave the bathroom, cautiously checking around before closing the door. I make my way to my room, but just as I reach for the handle, the door adjacent to mine opens. Bradley steps out, and before I can react, he gently grabs my arm and pulls me into his room.

"Brad—" I whisper-shout, my heart pounding. "What are you doing?"

"What I should have done before," he replies, eyes locking onto mine. Before I can process his words, he moves closer, his intent clear. "I'm going to kiss you now," he declares, his voice firm.

It's not a question; it's a statement.

"But I-I don't know how," I stutter.

"I'll show you. Just follow my lead," he says, his voice softening. My eyes widen, but I nod slowly, unable to form any coherent words.

Then, his hand is caressing my cheek, and his lips press against mine, soft at first, testing the waters. I respond by leaning into him, running my hands slowly up his sides, across his sculpted chest. A low groan erupts from deep in his chest, and he deepens the kiss, sending shivers down my spine.

It's intense—so intense and passionate.

Bradley's lips are firm yet gentle, moving with a confidence that makes me feel safe. He tastes like mint and something distinctly him. When his tongue brushes against my lower lip, asking for entrance, I part my lips, welcoming him. His hands cup my face, his thumbs stroking my cheeks softly, contrasting with the passionate way his mouth claims mine. A deep, rumbling growl escapes him, vibrating against my lips. I can feel the heat radiating off his body, and it's overwhelming in the best way possible. He hums softly against my mouth, the sound of approval and pleasure making my heart race even faster.

I don't know what I'm doing, but he makes it easy, guiding me with every movement, and I willingly follow, mimicking his actions. His touch is a blazing fire, consuming me, and I melt into him. My mind spins, thoughts jumbled as I try to process the overwhelming sensations. All I know is that I never want this to end.

His kiss is everything I never knew I needed.

Another groan rumbles from his chest, and it's intoxicating, sending waves of desire coursing through me.

After a minute that feels like an eternity, he breaks the kiss, and I'm left in shock.

"Holy crap!" I blurt out, my eyes wide. Bradley smirks, then a full-blown smile lights up his face, and he lets out a breathless laugh. His fingers brush gently against my cheek, a tender gesture that sends a thrill through me.

"How was that for a first kiss?" he asks, his tone soft, eyes searching mine.

I'm completely thrown off by his smile. It's the kind that makes you want to melt, like the emoji that's partially melting. Yeah, that's me. My brain is doing somersaults, trying to process the fact that Bradley "Captain Grumps" Mitchell just kissed me.

"I... uh... yeah," I stammer. "Wow."

"Was it how you'd imagined?" he asks.

Without hesitation, I reply, "No. It was everything and more."

He tilts my chin up, and my heart does a little dance. His lips meet mine again, this time softer, lingering, and it feels like he's pouring every unspoken word into that kiss. My toes curl, and I'm pretty sure I've forgotten how to breathe.

"Good. You should get some rest now," he suggests softly, his thumb brushing my cheek.

"Yeah, you, too. Goodnight, Brad," I say, feeling a warmth in my chest, my heart fluttering like a butterfly on caffeine.

"Goodnight, Amelia," he replies, his voice gentle, almost tender. I can't help but smile as I head quietly back to my room, my mind buzzing with thoughts of him.

Sleep comes peacefully, wrapping me in dreams of what tomorrow might bring. I imagine more stolen kisses, secret smiles, and maybe, just maybe, finding out what it feels like to have a real relationship with someone like Bradley. As I drift off, I smile to myself.

Who knew my first kiss would turn out to be this epic?

17

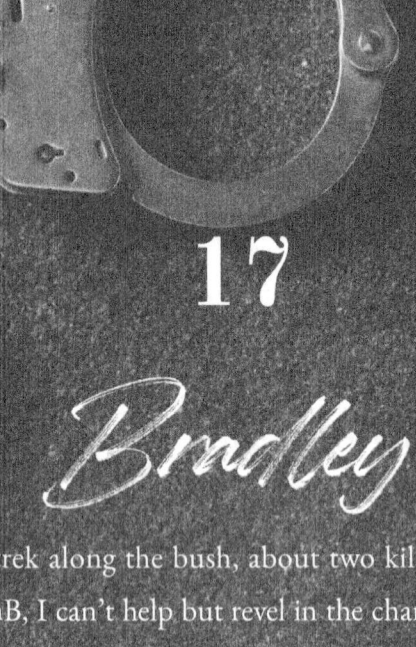

Bradley

As we trek along the bush, about two kilometres from our AirBnB, I can't help but revel in the change of scenery. Liv found the trail on Maps and thought it'd be a great idea to go bushwalking. Thank fuck, the weather today isn't a scorcher. Although I'm accustomed to being outside most of the time for work, being knee-deep in nature is a refreshing shift. The weather is a pleasant twenty-three degrees, with a slight chill in the air that the warm sun balances perfectly.

My mind drifts back to that day at my place when Amelia guided me through a breathing exercise, focusing on the leaves. It had a surprisingly calming effect, quieting the relentless thoughts that have plagued me for so long. The feelings of being undervalued, of something missing in my life, of not measuring up.

But fuck if Amelia hasn't eased the load on my chest, even if it's just a bit.

Last night... Well, last night was intense. That kiss, that simple kiss, was life-changing—mind-altering. It left me with a fucking raging hard-on, leaving me no choice but to blow my load into my hands, like a pubescent teen, to avoid a dreaded case of blue balls. As we continue along the trail, Amelia walks in front of me, giving me a perfect view of her ass.

Have I mentioned how much I love her curves? Fuck, she's perfect. The way her hips sway as she walks, especially in those tight purple tights she's wearing. Fuck, I sound like a perv.

I should stop.

Yeah, right. Wasn't saying that last night when I was kissing her, was I? From behind, Imogen's voice breaks my thoughts.

"How much farther do we have to go?" she gripes.

Harrison pipes up, "I can carry you if you like, sugar."

"Over my dead body," she snaps back. He chuckles, and then I hear the unmistakable sound of a slap echo in the air. I can only assume he slapped her ass.

"Don't fucking touch me," she throws back.

I can't help but smile. Harrison really is such an idiot. He gets so much satisfaction from stirring her up. He's been like this since the moment he met her. Honestly, their constant bickering is becoming a little boring.

As we reach a lookout over the water, Liv calls out, "We can stop here for a breather before heading back down."

The warm sun's getting to us now. Sweat drips down my neck and back, and my t-shirt clings to me. Harrison and Michael already ditched their shirts halfway through.

I decide to follow suit, pulling off my shirt and slinging it over my shoulder. All the intense training at the police academy has made me accustomed to rigorous activity, so I'm feeling good, apart from the heavy burn in my calves and hamstrings—which I welcome; it makes me feel liberated.

I spot Liv's water bottle sticking out of her backpack and steal it.

"Hey! Get your own," she snaps.

"I just need a sip," I lie, before chugging down half the bottle.

"Yeah, a sip, my ass," she mutters, wiping the lid. "Gross," she feigns disgust.

"You'll be right," I fire back, smirking.

I turn to find Amelia eyeing me up and down shamelessly. I watch her until she catches me, and I give a subtle wink. She quickly turns away, cheeks tinged with a blush, and tries to hide it behind adjusting her backpack. Fuck, she's adorable when she blushes like that. It makes me smile, seeing her try to play it off.

"Why are you… *smiling?*" my sister blurts out, her expression one of pure confusion.

Great. Just what I needed—being caught off guard like this.

"Are you feeling alright?" She reaches out to touch my forehead, but I swat her hand away.

"Piss off."

"Bradley, smiling? Yeah, right," Xav scoffs.

"I wasn't. Fuck off," I snap, my voice clipped.

"You were! I saw it with my own eyes," Liv adds sceptically.

"Yeah, well, get your eyes checked because you're seeing shit," I retort.

I catch Michael eyeing me, his smirk irritatingly knowing. What's with everyone today?

Despite the jabs earlier, I can't deny the playful ease that comes over me whenever I'm around her. As we head back down the trail, Amelia hunches over, hands on her thighs, gearing up for the trek back.

"Want me to carry you, *sugar?*" I tease, using Harrison's words from earlier. Her eyes widen in surprise before she playfully shoves me.

"Shh." She grins, and we press on along the trail. I lightly nudge her shoulder, our height difference making it more of a playful tap.

"Having fun?" I ask, my voice low and teasing.

"I don't think I'm cut out for all this," she huffs, wiping sweat from her forehead. "I'm a sweaty mess."

"Don't worry, being a sweaty mess suits you," I tease, a smirk tugging at my lips. In my head, that sounded much cleaner. I shake my head, chuckling softly, realising it might have come off dirtier than intended.

Amelia shoots me a surprised glance, her cheeks reddening. "Yeah, right," she scoffs, but her eyes twinkle with amusement.

I lean in a bit closer, my voice dropping to a whisper. "It's true," I reply with a wink, surprising even myself with the playful confidence.

Fuck, who is this guy? He's so unlike me.

Imogen's voice breaks our moment. "You two alright?"

I turn my head, my heart dropping as I realise the group has continued walking down the trail, and I hadn't even fucking noticed.

All eyes are on us, and Olivia watches with a confused expression.

Fuck.

I look at Amelia, her eyes slightly widened as she fidgets with her bag straps.

"Yep," I call back, throwing up a thumbs-up.

"Just needed to catch my breath," surprisingly, Amelia calls out, and the group turns back around.

"Righto. Chop chop," my brother says, waving us to continue.

As we walk, I can't shake the feeling that I might have crossed a line. Should I have flirted like that? Should I have made those comments? Am I being too friendly with her? Maybe it was the kiss that did it, making everything more complicated. Now, I find myself acting differently around her because of it. So much for those fucking rules I put in place. And now, all I can see is Olivia's confused face.

As we catch up to the group, my heart pounds fiercely in my chest, a rhythm of guilt and confusion. Or maybe it's clarity I'm denying. It's wrong, what I'm doing. Kissing my sister's best friend behind everyone's back. But every time I see her, it's like I'm shedding a layer of my armour.

Feeling less... guarded.

That kiss... It's astounding how such a seemingly simple act can flip everything. But deep down, I know it's not just about that kiss.

It's something that's been simmering, ignored for years. A longing, a connection I never acknowledged.

Fuck.

Sitting by the fire outside, near the balcony, I stare into the flames, lost in thought. Citronella sticks flicker, keeping mosquitoes at bay. Crickets chirp, and the river flows steadily. What a life it would be, living out here—secluded, peaceful. My mind drifts to an idyllic vision: a wife, kids, dogs, and family visiting occasionally.

But just as she has lately, Amelia intrudes on these thoughts.

Why am I picturing her like this suddenly? Could I see myself spending my life with her? It's only been a few days and one kiss.

Settle down, champ.

Goosebumps prickle my skin, and I reach for my beer, taking a big sip to quiet my thoughts. The girls start talking, their voices tinged with disappointment.

"I can't believe we have to go back to work soon," Isla sighs.

"Ugh, I know," Imogen groans. The guys chime in with low grumbles of agreement.

"Yeah, back to the grind," Harrison mutters, taking a swig of his beer. "Joe will have our asses if we don't."

"Tell me about it," Michael adds, shaking his head with a smile.

I listen quietly, the crackling of the fire and the distant sounds of nature forming a soothing backdrop. Truthfully, I don't mind the idea of returning to work. The routine, the busyness—it's grounding. It gives me purpose, a sense of structure that I've come to rely on. While the others express their reluctance about going back, I find solace in the prospect of normalcy. But I keep that to myself, sipping my beer and letting the conversation wash over me.

"Has anyone seen my phone?" Isla asks out of the blue.

"Think I saw it on the table inside," Xavier answers.

"Gee, thanks for grabbing it for me," Isla says sarcastically, rolling her eyes.

"Sorry, ma'am. I'll get that right away for you," Xavier retorts, equally sarcastic but unmoving. Harrison makes a whip-cracking noise, and Xavier responds with a middle finger, eliciting a snort from me.

Amelia breaks the banter, saying, "I'll grab it for you. I'm heading to the loo, anyway."

"Oh, you're a gem, Amelia. Thank you!" Isla says with a genuine smile.

I watch as she stands and disappears inside. I want to follow her, but I can't. Since our kiss yesterday, all I've wanted is another moment *alone* with her. I pause, unsure whether to follow her. The group has settled into conversation again, so slipping away shouldn't raise eyebrows, right?

Ah, to hell with it.

What was that bullshit I spouted the other night about doing something selfish for myself? Yeah, this feels like one of those moments.

"Anyone else want another beer?" I ask, already heading toward the screen door. Harrison and Xav nod, so I step inside and close the door behind me, making my way quietly to the kitchen.

I hear the faint sound of Amelia washing up, and soon enough, she emerges from the bathroom. Our eyes meet in the dim light of the house. Outside, the fading daylight offers us privacy unless someone stumbles upon us. The situation feels tense, my instincts at odds with reason. Yet, I can't deny the pull toward her, like some damn magnet defying all logic and caution. She walks up to me, looking timid.

"Hey," I say, my voice lower than I intended.

"Hey," she replies, almost in a whisper.

I step closer, the beers forgotten on the counter. "You know, since yesterday..."

"I know," she interrupts, surprising me with her preemptive understanding. She feels it, too.

The light filtering in from outside catches on her face, illuminating those brown irises with golden specks. They're captivating. Beautiful.

She is beautiful. *Fucking hell.*

"I can't stop thinking about... about how you kissed me," she says innocently, her fingers moving to touch her lips. My gaze drops to her mouth, and I watch as she rolls them inward, making them slightly parted and glistening under the light.

The sight sends a jolt through me; fuck, I want to kiss her.

"Me, too," I respond, my voice gravelly and low. Amelia bites her lip, a simple gesture that sends a thrill down my spine.

"What do we do?" she asks, barely audible over the pounding of my heart.

"I don't know," I whisper, unable to resist the magnetic pull between us. "But I do know I want to kiss you again."

Closing the distance between us, I press my lips to hers.

My senses are immediately overwhelmed by the feel of her hands on my chest, fingers gripping into the fabric of my shirt. With one hand firmly on her waist and the other tangled in her hair, I pull her closer to me, unable to resist the magnetic pull between us. She gasps against my lips, and her breath becomes shallow and rapid as I tug on her hair gently, eliciting a gasp from her.

I feel myself getting lost in her—her touch, her taste, her scent. It's like nothing else exists in that moment except for the two of us. Her tongue is soft and warm on mine, dancing in a silent, tantalising rhythm that sets my senses ablaze.

Fuck, despite her never having kissed anyone before, she's a fucking natural.

But then, a small sound escapes her lips, breaking the spell and reminding me of where we are. Reluctantly, I break away from her embrace, feeling the cold air hit my skin as I step back.

"Fuck," I rasp, my voice rough as I step away. "I'm sorry, I should have asked first."

"It's okay," she breathes, her voice barely above a whisper. "Don't be sorry."

But is it really? I can feel the tension between us, the hesitation in her touch. Yet, there's something else there, too—a spark that ignites with every brush of our skin. She reaches out for my hand, her touch grounding me in the reality of the moment. I look into her eyes, searching for any sign of regret or discomfort, but all I find is a raw honesty that mirrors my own feelings. The air crackles with unspoken words as we stand there.

"We should probably head back outside," I say, my voice more steady than I feel.

"Yeah, you're right." She sounds disappointed as she turns to leave, and I let her pass. She grabs Isla's phone from the kitchen bench before walking back outside. As I watch her leave, a whirlwind of emotions swirls within me. Regret, desire, uncertainty—all battling for dominance in my mind. I know I should follow her, rejoin the group outside, but my feet remain rooted to the spot. Their laughter and music drift in from the balcony, starkly contrasting with the heaviness in the air around me.

"Hey, Amelia, have you seen Bradley? Did he get lost?" Michael's voice cuts through the evening air, followed by Harrison's teasing tone.

"Yeah, and where are our beers? He left us high and dry!"

Well, that's the cue I need. I completely forgot about those damn beers. Seems like I've developed a habit of that whenever she's around.

Forgetting shit.

I force my legs to move, shaking off the haze of conflicting emotions clouding my head. Grabbing the three beers, I stride outside.

"Did you get lost, Bradley? We were about to send out a search party." Michael looks at me with raised eyebrows.

"Got a call from work. Sorry," I lie smoothly, handing out the beers before settling next to Liv, who eyes me curiously. I shoot her a glare, silently warning her to mind her own damn business.

Amelia is already seated next to Liv, sipping wine. Despite my best efforts to avoid her gaze, I can't help but feel drawn to her. It's fucked up how much I want her. The way she looks at me, the way she makes me feel—it's like nothing else matters.

I wrestle with the urge to act on it, knowing I should keep my distance.

At least for now.

18

Amelia

I take a sip of my steaming coffee, savouring the warmth spreading through my hands as I cup the mug. Liv and I are at Tracey's Coffee Stop, our usual spot for morning coffee and catch-ups. The aroma of freshly brewed coffee mingles with the faint scent of baked goods. Liv is cupping her own mug, a content smile playing on her lips as she takes a sip.

"Wasn't it so nice to go away with everyone this weekend?" she asks, breaking the comfortable silence.

I nod, a small smile playing on my face. "It really was. And celebrating Isla and Xav's announcement was the icing on the cake. Such exciting news."

Liv beams, taking a sip of her coffee. "And even more exciting that I'm going to be an aunty." We both laugh, enjoying the moment of lightness, yet the mention of our weekend away stirs up thoughts that I hadn't realised I buried inside.

It's been seven days since I last saw Bradley—since he kissed me. *Twice.*

After our weekend away, we'd left early in the morning on Monday—luckily, I had taken the day off. Bradley had dropped me off at home after getting back to Liv's house, and the drive home had been filled with tension, like a thick fog we couldn't see through. Unspoken words hung in the air, heavy with meaning. He'd seemed stuck in his head, lost in his thoughts, and I wanted nothing more than to know what was running through his mind.

We'd said goodbye; he kissed me on the cheek, and that's it. Not a word from him since. Just when I thought I'd finally made peace with the fact that nothing would ever happen between us, that it was all just a silly little crush, bam!

He kisses me and throws everything into chaos. Now, I'm back at square one.

Oh, and I've been swearing lately, too. It's like he's rewired my brain. The other day at dinner with my parents, I casually dropped the word 'shit,' and they looked at me like I'd grown two heads.

Maybe I have, who knows?

All I do know is that it's been a hectic week, and all I want is for things to go back to the way they were, or for something *more* to just happen between us. *Does he want me or not?* I wouldn't even know the first thing about 'wanting' a guy, let alone dating one. I'm too hesitant to ask Liv because she'll want to know who it is, and knowing me, I'd blurt it out. She's my best friend, and I can't even talk to her about this because it's her bloody brother.

Olivia's mood changes suddenly, and her face sours. "Bradley has been in a mood since we got back."

My face drops, and I ask a little too eagerly, "Oh. Why? How?"

before clearing my throat and trying to sound casual.

She watches me for a moment before answering. "He's just been *extra* standoffish these last few days."

I add, trying to sound nonchalant, "Maybe he has a lot going on at work?" She shakes her head, shrugging.

"Not sure. Maybe. He's just been a real prick."

Clearing my throat, I continue, "Weird. He'd mentioned that he was looking forward to the trip. I wonder what changed his mood."

Liv's eyes narrow slightly, and she asks, "Did he? Have you two become *friends* now? You seemed oddly close on the trip."

My blood runs cold, and I quickly try to play it off. "Oh, no, we just spoke a bit on the bushwalk, got to know each other a bit, that's all. He seemed nice. Wasn't rude at all."

Liv nods, her brows furrowing in thought. "Yeah, I noticed that."

Oh, no, does she know something? Were Bradley and I that obvious?

"N-noticed what?" I ask, my words stuttering slightly.

Liv seems lost in thought for a moment before she responds, "That he was acting strangely over the weekend. Happier maybe? Did he say anything else to you?"

I shake my head quickly. "Nope."

Liv nods, taking a sip of her coffee, seeming satisfied with my answer. I force a neutral expression, yet my heart sinks at the thought of Bradley being distant. *So, it's not just with me.*

Am I the reason? Oh, goodness me.

Clearing my throat, I circle back to Liv's previous mention. "Well, hopefully, whatever it is that he's going through, he snaps out of it soon."

Liv smiles. "Yeah. Hopefully," before changing the subject to lighter topics. But I can't shake the worry that settles in the pit of my stomach.

At recess, I find myself in my classroom amidst the cheerful chaos of kindergarteners. Crayons and drawings litter the tables, and the walls proudly display their latest artistic triumphs. The familiar scent of glue and crayons fills the air, creating a strangely comforting atmosphere.

As I diligently mark our weekly spelling test, placing yet another shiny star sticker next to a correct answer, I can't help but find my thoughts drifting back to Bradley.

Why does he have to be so confusing? One minute he's kissing me like I'm the only woman in the world, and the next, he's completely silent. I glance at the clock. Only fifteen more minutes left until the kids come back, and I've barely made a dent in these tests. I should be focusing on these adorable attempts at spelling, not on a guy who's turned my brain to mush.

How hard can it be to get a sign from him? *A text? A call?*

I mean, he has my number now!

Anything to say that kiss meant something. But nope. Radio silence.

I sigh, leaning back in my chair, staring at the ceiling. I need to talk to someone about this, but Liv's off-limits. I can just picture her reaction if she knew I was crushing on her brother. The horror!

Maybe I could talk to Imogen or Isla, but even that feels risky.

No. Maybe I just need to be patient. Maybe he's just sorting out his own feelings. But how long am I supposed to wait? How long can I keep pretending everything is fine when all I want is another moment with him, to understand what's really going on between us?

"Focus, Amelia," I tell myself, shaking my head.

My door bursts open and Jamie comes barreling into the room, huffing and puffing like she's just run a marathon.

"I swear, if one more ten-year-old tries to outsmart me, I'm going to lose it," she says dramatically, flopping into the chair opposite my desk. I chuckle, grateful for the distraction.

"What happened this time?"

"Do you remember Jason? The one who thinks he's a mini Einstein?"

"What did he do now?" I ask, incredulously.

"He corrected my maths. My maths, Amelia! I was explaining fractions, and then he stands up and says, 'Actually, Miss Smith, that should be seven, not eight.' The worst part? He was right!"

"Oh." I laugh. "Is that it?"

She throws her hands up in the air. "Yes! What do you mean? I've been outsmarted by a ten-year-old. The sass on that kid! He even gave me a look, like, *'What kind of teacher are you?'*"

I shake my head, still laughing. "Kids these days, huh? They keep us on our toes." Jamie leans forward, lowering her voice conspiratorially.

"And you should've seen the way the other kids looked at me after that. Like I'd lost all credibility. They were practically ready to take over the class."

"Sounds like you've had a day."

She groans, leaning back in her chair. "You have no idea. And here I was thinking Year five would be easier than Year six."

We both laugh, the tension of the day easing a bit. I look back at the spelling tests, but my mind wanders again to Bradley. Maybe talking to Jamie about him wouldn't be such a bad idea, but I hesitate.

Jamie stretches, clearly not in any rush to get back to her classroom. "So, how are things with you? You seem... distracted."

I shrug, trying to play it cool. "Just a lot on my mind. You know how it is."

Jamie knows exactly what happened over the weekend because as soon as I got back to work on Tuesday, Kristie, Amanda, and Jaime bombarded me with questions. They never miss a thing.

"Still nothing?" Jamie asks, her voice soft yet curious..

I shake my head, feeling a knot tightening in my stomach. "No, nothing."

Jaime leans forward. "Have you tried reaching out to him?"

"I'm not sure if I should," I confess, uncertainty lacing my voice. "What if he doesn't want to talk?"

"Amelia, if he kissed you—twice—clearly, he feels something. Maybe he's just figuring things out," she suggests gently.

"Maybe he's feeling guilty because I'm Liv's best friend." I sigh heavily, my thoughts racing with guilt and uncertainty. We've both done something sneaky, and now it's weighing on me. "I mean, shit. This is bad."

Jamie frowns. "Why would it be bad? You just kissed him. If anything, he initiated it first, right?"

"Yeah, but I kissed him back."

"Well, I'd bloody hope so," Jamie scoffs, laughing. "Sure, keeping it under wraps might raise eyebrows for some, but what happened between you two isn't wrong! You're a grown woman, Amelia."

She takes a breath before continuing, "This is your life, your experience. No one should stand in your way, not even your best friend."

True. Ugh, she's right. But it doesn't stop me from feeling like a shitty person. Still, Jamie is right. I am a grown woman with needs and desires. I want to experience things, to live my life.

The bell rings, signalling the end of recess. Any minute now, the kids will come barreling back into the classroom. Jamie stands up, stretching.

"Well, that's my cue. Time to face the sass again."

"Good luck," I say with a smile. She grins, giving me a quick hug.

"You, too. And remember, you've got us to support you. Whatever happens."

"Thanks, Jamie," I say, the weight of my thoughts pressing down on me. "I needed to hear that."

"Anytime," she replies, heading to the door.

I nod, trying to internalise her words. Maybe I just need to let go and see where this goes. Even if it scares me, even if it feels wrong, I can't deny what I want.

And right now, I want Bradley.

It's a quiet afternoon, and I'm lost in the world of oil paints in my apartment. After a long day at work, this is my sanctuary. I'm working on my latest collection of portraits, currently painting Millie blowing bubbles, her face lit up with the biggest smile.

I flick my eyes to the small photo beside the canvas, the one Kat took of Millie. Capturing that joy in paint is both a challenge and a thrill. I internally pat myself on the back for the progress I've made so far. The features are coming together nicely, though getting everything realistic and proportional is tricky.

Painting is my escape, but it isn't always easy. Each brushstroke requires precision, patience, and a lot of love. I pride myself on my ability to paint realism, a skill I've honed over the years.

Placing my brush in the cup of water beside me, I pull out my phone and snap a picture of the portrait. I quickly send it to my sister with a smile. The sense of accomplishment fills me as I look at Millie's joyful face on the canvas.

As I think about whom to paint next, Bradley's face pops into my mind. He has such striking features—from his sculpted jaw to his full lips, the stubble that frames his face, and those piercing blue eyes.

My goodness, I'm getting all flustered just thinking about it!

But how would I do that?

It's not like I have a photo of him. Not that I need one. I could probably draw him from memory. I mean, I've had ten years to admire him from afar, so he's practically ingrained in the back of my head. I giggle to myself, feeling a mix of excitement and nerves.

Could I really paint Bradley? The thought is both thrilling and terrifying, but it might be worth a try.

Maybe, just maybe, I'll finally capture those dreamy blue eyes on canvas.

19

Amelia

Music fills the large lounge room, pillows are scattered everywhere, creating a cosy, laid-back vibe. Isla sent out an SOS text the other night, begging for some girl time away from Xavier because, as she put it, he's been just a little too much lately. Not in a bad way, but still, too much. So, naturally, we rallied for an emergency gathering in our girls' group chat: *The Real Housewives of Wattle Creek.*

Imogen came up with the name and insisted we stick with it, even though Isla's the only one who technically qualifies as a housewife.

Now, here we are, dressed in our comfiest pyjamas, at Isla and Xavier's house, surrounded by snacks on the coffee table, bottles of wine, and juice pops for Isla. I'm on my third glass of red wine, Liv is nearly sloshed, and Imogen is belting out the chorus to "Girls Just Wanna Have Fun," lounging on the couch with a bowl of strawberries in her lap. Imogen, however, is only on her first glass, wanting to take it slow as she'll be needing to drive home.

This is our kind of therapy.

"This wine is amazing, Isla," Liv says, her words slurring slightly.

"Where did you get it?"

Isla grins, sipping from her juice popper. "Xavier found it. He's been on this wine kick lately, trying to find the perfect one for when the baby comes."

Imogen snorts. "For the baby? Are you planning on giving the baby wine?"

We all burst into laughter, the kind that comes easy with good friends and a bit too much alcohol.

"Oh, you know what I mean," Isla says, giggling. "For *after* the baby is born. A celebratory wine."

"Speaking of babies," I say, trying to keep the conversation light, "I heard that pregnancy cravings can get really weird. What's the strangest thing you've craved so far?"

Isla thinks for a moment, then laughs. "Pickles dipped in peanut butter. It's actually really good; you guys should try it. Oh, and cheese. Lots of it."

"Hard pass," Liv says, making a face. "I'll stick to my wine, thank you very much."

"Cruel Summer" by Taylor Swift comes on the speakers, and Imogen's eyes light up. "Oh my god, I love this song! Let's do karaoke!"

We all jump up, grabbing whatever makeshift microphones we can find—hairbrushes, empty wine bottles, even a cucumber from the snack tray. We belt out the lyrics, our voices mixing in a chaotic but joyous mess. Liv, with her slightly tipsy state, is the loudest, and her exaggerated dance moves have us all in stitches.

After a few songs, we collapse back onto the couch, breathless and red-faced from laughing so hard. Imogen says something that makes us all burst into laughter again, though I can't quite remember what it was.

"That was amazing," Isla says, wiping tears of laughter from her eyes. "We should do this more often."

Imogen nods, still giggling. "Absolutely. This is the best therapy ever."

Isla takes a deep breath, looking a bit more serious. "Speaking of therapy, can I just vent for a second? Xavier has been so careful around me lately. He's reading up on everything—what diet I should be eating, what to avoid. He won't even have sex with me on a regular basis because he's worried he'll impale the baby!"

We all stare at her for a moment before bursting into laughter again. Liv scrunches up her face. "Thanks for that image."

Isla throws her hands up, flustered. "Sorry, Liv, but come on. A girl has needs. And the doctor even encouraged it, saying it's safe to resume all sexual activities. I don't understand what his problem is."

I blush at this, feeling my face heat up.

"Why not just spring it on him? Instead of asking for it, just do it. Throw on some lingerie, set the mood, and then fuck his brains out," Imogen suggests.

Isla thinks for a moment before releasing a sigh. "You know, you might be right. I will try that and let you know."

Liv says, "Let *them* know, not *me*, please," she says, pointing to herself, and we all laugh in unison.

Somewhere amidst the laughter, I ask, "Hey, where is Xavier, anyway? Is he with Bradley?"

I immediately regret my question, but we're all tipsy, so who cares? Isla shrugs. "I have no idea. Probably, otherwise, he'd be with Harrison or Michael."

The conversation shifts to sex and dating, and Imogen voices her exasperation about the dating pool in town. "It's like trying to find a needle in a haystack," she complains.

Isla grins mischievously. "What about Harrison?"

Imogen chucks a pillow at Isla. "Don't start, Isla."

We laugh, and Liv turns the conversation to me. "We need to help Amelia find a man. I've told her so many times, but she just won't budge."

"Oo. Yes," Isla chimes in, her eyes lighting up.

Imogen leans forward, curiosity piqued. "When was the last time you were with a guy?"

I feel my face flush as I mumble, "Um, well, I'm actually a virgin. So never."

Imogen gasps dramatically. Isla hits her with a pillow this time. I hide my face in my hands, feeling embarrassed.

"But you're stunning, Amelia! You could have any guy," Imogen adds in disbelief.

I scoff. "Yeah, if I knew how to talk to them."

"But you do! You talk to the guys all the time—Xav, Harrison, even Bradley. You seem to be close with Bradley," Isla points out.

"Oh, no. We're just civil... I guess," I say, trying to downplay any potential implications.

"Hm, he seems to have warmed up to you recently," Isla insists, her observation making me squirm inside.

Imogen nods, looking at me intently. I glance at Liv, who's also watching me, waiting for me to say something.

How have I been that obvious? Is it that obvious? I hope to God Liv hasn't noticed anything.

Before I can dwell on it further, Imogen practically jumps out of her seat, almost tumbling over, and we all laugh. "I just had a brilliant idea," she exclaims. "Amelia and Bradley should hook up. Two single people, two *good-looking* people. Why the fuck not?"

Olivia bursts out in laughter, and I giggle nervously as heat rises to my cheeks, feeling a flutter inside.

"No fucking way. As if," Olivia retorts. "I don't think anyone could handle Bradley's mood swings. He's worse than me."

I look down nervously and find Imogen and Isla watching me. "Yeah, no."

Imogen, still elated at her idea, smiles. "Why not? I mean this in the friendliest way possible, Olivia, but Bradley is *hot*. Sexy officer vibes. Tall, grumpy, so polite."

She's not wrong.

Isla nods enthusiastically, adding, "I love Xav, but I agree with her. Brad's a catch."

Suddenly, all my tipsiness goes out the window, and I'm immediately sobered up as Olivia's words sink in.

"Would you? You wouldn't actually consider dating Bradley, would you?" she asks, her face slightly flushed.

"Uh, n-no. I mean, it's just... not something I've *thought* about." I stumble over my words, feeling a rush of awkwardness flood through me. *Crap, this is awkward*, now suddenly wishing I could take back what I just said.

"Yeah, that would be a bit weird, wouldn't it?" she says with a huff of laughter.

"Not really. Why would it?" Isla says, and I only feel my embarrassment deepen further.

"Well, she's my best friend. It's just weird."

I can't handle this conversation anymore. It's like being under a spotlight with no way out. Imogen's looks are inscrutable, and they only add to my nerves.

This whole situation is a minefield, and I'm standing right in the middle of it, sweating bullets. It's probably the sudden attention, but the alcohol isn't helping either.

I need an out.

I clear my throat. "Uh, I'm just going to use the bathroom," I say, standing up quickly.

Imogen quickly joins in, rising from her seat. "Well, then... I think that calls for a refill and more music," she declares, and Olivia chimes in with, "Yes, please!"

As the night wears on, Isla's large lounge room buzzes with laughter and chatter, blending seamlessly with the upbeat music. Imogen has moved on from strawberries to chocolate, and Liv, clutching a juice pop, is dancing with wobbly enthusiasm.

I, on the other hand, feel a knot of tension growing inside me.

Olivia's comment about Bradley has left me feeling exposed, like everyone in the room can see right through me. I'm conflicted, unsure of what to do next.

Should I tell Bradley about this conversation?

But how can I when he hasn't spoken to me since that weekend? The thought of messaging him out of the blue makes my stomach churn with nerves.

Imogen's gaze occasionally lingers on me, her expression unreadable. The thought that she might know something, something about Bradley and I, sends a shiver of nervousness down my spine. I try to shake off the feeling of being under a microscope and join in the conversation. We chat and laugh, and for a moment, I manage to forget about my worries.

Soon enough, we slowly start to sober up, the laughter giving way to tired smiles. By the time we're ready to leave, the fun chaos of the evening has quieted down. Liv is staying the night, so it's just Imogen and I saying our goodbyes. She offers to drive me home. We make our way to her blue Volkswagen Polo, and once inside, she puts the car into gear.

"Sorry for putting you on the spot earlier," Imogen says, breaking the silence.

Nervousness creeps up again. "I don't know; what do you mean?"

"You know... you, Bradley, hooking you up, our weekend away..." Her words trail off, and my pulse picks up. *Weekend away?*

I freeze.

"Weekend away? What do you mean?" I ask, downplaying the

unease emanating from me.

"You know, that night in the kitchen while we were away. You were talking to Bradley, no?" So she did see us that night. Panic flares up inside me, my heart racing. What else did she see? Does she know everything?

"Uh, well, yeah. We... We were just talking. Nothing happened." I blurt out, my eyes widening immediately.

"Seemed like you two were cosy that night in the kitchen."

Shit.

"Mhm. No point trying to fool me, girl. I wasn't sleepwalking; I saw you both but didn't want to disturb your... moment."

I realise I said that *out* loud and not *in* my head.

"Oh, God, it's... I..." Words fail me, and I stutter, at a loss.

"Hey, it's okay. I'm not Liv. I don't care. I'm just pointing out what I saw." Tears prick at the corners of my eyes, embarrassment flooding through me. Imogen turns to look at me.

"Hey, please. I didn't mean to make you upset."

"No, it's not that, it's just... I'm so screwed. I don't know what's happening."

Everything's such a mess. Bradley and I were supposed to be careful, but now it feels like the whole world is closing in.

"Well, what has happened?" She's curious but calm, and it only makes me feel more tangled up.

"Nothing!" My hands fly up in frustration. "Well, maybe something. We kissed twice."

"Twice! Well, I'll be damned."

Confiding in Imogen just feels right. God, it feels so good to get this off my chest. I don't know why, but there's something comforting about sharing this with her.

"Ugh. I'm so torn, Imogen. It's just that I've crushed on him for as long as I can remember, and now it's all…"

"Weird?"

"Yeah," I say as she pulls up out the front of my place.

"Does anyone know about this crush?"

"No. No one. So you can't say anything, please!" I plead.

"I won't," Imogen says, then takes a breath. "But I think you'll need to tell Olivia soon. Maybe once things between you and Bradley settle or become clear."

Her words hang heavy in the air.

Tell Olivia?

The thought makes my stomach churn. How can I even begin to explain this to her?

"I know. You're right. Gosh, this is so weird. I just don't know what to do with all of this." My thoughts spiral. Should I reach out to Bradley? But how can I when we haven't spoken since that weekend? The idea of messaging him out of the blue twists my stomach with unease.

What if he doesn't want to talk? Or worse, what if he regrets everything?

Imogen gives my hand a reassuring squeeze. "Hey, take it one step at a time. You don't have to figure everything out tonight."

"Thanks, Imogen. I really appreciate it. Getting this all off my chest feels..." I pause, searching for the right words. "It feels like a huge weight has been lifted."

She smiles. "Good. Now go get some rest. Things will look different in the morning."

I smile back, a bit more at ease. "Yeah, I hope so."

"Goodnight, chica. And don't hesitate to call if you need to talk more."

"I will. Goodnight, Imogen. Thank you for everything." I open the door and hop out, but Imogen stops me just before I close it.

"You know, for what it's worth," she says, her voice gentle, "I really do think you and Bradley would make a great couple."

I nod nervously, my heart pounding in my chest. Her words echo in my mind as I watch her drive away. Inside, the reality of the situation settles over me. What do I do now? Should I call Bradley? Text him? But what would I even say?

The knot in my stomach tightens. I wish I knew what he was thinking.

I close the door behind me and lean against it, letting out a deep sigh. This is so complicated. My fingers itch to type out a message.

Maybe tomorrow.

For now, I need to try to get some sleep, though I know my thoughts will be consumed by Bradley and the mess we're in.

20

Bradley

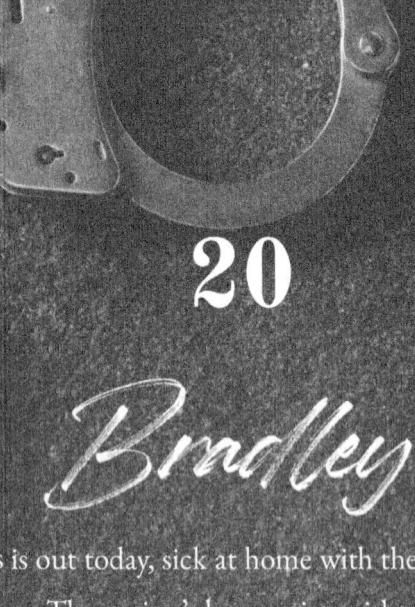

Daniels is out today, sick at home with the flu, leaving me on my own. The station's been quiet, with most officers out on their scheduled duties or responding to random 000 calls. I'm at my desk, catching up on paperwork for cases that popped up over the weekend while I was away. A part of me feels guilty for being away when so much was happening.

There was the break-in at Mrs. Jenkins' bakery early Saturday morning, some teenagers causing a ruckus at the local park on Saturday night, and a missing dog report from Sunday afternoon—nothing too extravagant, just typical small-town incidents. But I can't shake the feeling that I should've been here handling it all.

Lately, it's like I'm wrestling an uphill climb to prove myself, to be the rock-solid officer this town leans on. Each day I suit up, the weight of duty settles heavy on my shoulders. It's not just about upholding the law; it's about being a foundation for this community, earning their trust. I've been striving to forge my own path, to step beyond my father's shadow and carve out a name. Yet, with every case, every call, I question if I'm measuring up, if I'm truly making a mark that counts.

And on top of that, Amelia won't leave my fucking thoughts. It's been a week since I last saw her. She swung by the house when I was out back with Xavier, but we missed each other. Liv's been going on about dinner and a girls' night that they had at Isla's place all week, but that's about it.

It's probably my fault. I know she won't make the first move. Why would she? I should be the one to step up. Shouldn't I?

But what do I even say?

It's not just about wanting her—though, fuck, I do, with a fierceness that catches me off guard. It's about doing right by her, making sure this isn't just some goddamn fleeting thing. She deserves more than half-assed moves and my fucking indecision. She's too damn important, too fucking special. I've spent years keeping her at arm's length, telling myself she's off-limits, too young, too innocent. But after Sunday night, all those walls I built are crumbling.

And she's Liv's best friend, which makes it all feel fucking wrong. I should know better, should have control, keep those lines clear. But I'd be lying if I said I wasn't interested. Because I am.

More than I want to admit.

It's the way she looks at me, the way her eyes light up when she's into something, the way she genuinely gives a shit about people. There's this purity to her I've always wanted to protect, but now... now I can't help but want to be close to her, to shield her, to be the one who puts that smile on her face. I miss how she felt in my arms, her lips on mine, the sounds she made.

Fuck, I *need* to stop.

Last thing I need is to get caught with a hard-on at work. I've got responsibilities here, a job to do. But fuck, it's hard to concentrate when all I can think about is her. I lean back in my chair, stretching my arms overhead. The station's quiet, just the hum of the AC cutting through the silence. I take a deep breath, let it out slowly, and focus back on the pile of paperwork on my desk. But the tension's still there, coiling tighter by the minute.

I need an outlet, something to blow off this steam. If I can't fuck it out, sweating it out's the next best thing.

The old-school way.

Mid-rep, I push the barbell up, the weight heavy and unyielding. My muscles burn with the effort, but I welcome the pain.

It means I'm here, in the moment, not lost in my thoughts. The gym is quiet this late in the afternoon, which surprises me. Usually it's pumping.

Metallica's "Master of Puppets" blares through my AirPods, the aggressive riffs fueling my intensity. I'm working on my chest and back today, pushing myself harder than usual. The bench press bar holds 120kg, the weight a familiar challenge. I bring it down slowly, feeling the strain in my chest and arms, then push it back up with a grunt.

After a set of ten, I rack the barbell and sit up, wiping sweat from my brow. I move to the pull-up bar next, grabbing it with a firm grip. I pull myself up, feeling the muscles in my back engage, then lower myself down slowly. The pull-ups are brutal, each one a test of strength and endurance.

But I need this.

I need to exhaust myself, to drown out the chaos in my mind.

The physical exertion helps, but it doesn't fully silence my thoughts. I grab the dumbbells next, going for the heavier set. I start with chest flies, the weights heavy in my hands as I stretch my arms out and then bring them back together. The motion is controlled, deliberate, each rep a way to focus my mind.

I finish my last set and sit down on the bench. This time, "Chaos" by I Prevail starts playing, the heavy, driving rhythm matching my need to stay focused.

I stand up, take a deep breath, and move on to the next exercise, determined to keep my mind occupied for a little while longer. As I run on the treadmill, my headphones announce a phone call, and Siri reads out the number, signalling that it's not saved into my contacts.

My heart drops when I recognise those digits.

I quickly take my phone from my pocket to read the number, confirming it's Amelia's—the one I hadn't saved in my phone because, well... I wasn't sure if that's something I should do.

Panic sets in. *Why would she be calling?*

My intuition tells me something isn't right. I answer after it rings again, and say, "Hello," but what I hear on the other end freezes me to my core.

"Bradley, oh, my god, I don't know what to do," Amelia's voice comes through, shaky and panicked, her voice an octave higher and more hurried than normal. "I didn't know who else to call. I panicked, so I called you."

My mind races. "What's wrong?" I demand, trying to see if I can hear anything in the background. I can hear water running and an echo. Is she in the bathroom?

"Oh, my god, it's getting closer. Shit, shit, shit!" she says in a state of panic. She's *swearing*. That means something is definitely wrong.

What is coming closer?

"Please, c-can you come here? I'm t-trapped. I can't move," she pleads, and I don't have to be asked twice. I stop the machine, grab my stuff, and storm out of the gym.

"Just stay there. I'm coming."

"Okay. There is a spare key under the mat," she says, before I hang up and speed to get to her place. I don't care at this moment if I'm breaking the law.

I'll run every red light if it means I get to her sooner.

21

Amelia

I'm in the shower, the steam thick around me, my heart pounding as I stare at the massive fucking *snake* on the floor.

A SNAKE.

Where did it even come from? I'm on the first floor. Can snakes even slither up walls? All I do know is that I *definitely* screamed my apartment down when I saw it. I didn't know who else to call. So, I called the first person I could think of, despite my internal panic.

I called out to Siri to call Bradley on speaker, praising the lord I had saved his number under a contact and that I'd brought my phone into the shower with me.

After just getting off the phone with him, reality sinks in. I'm standing here, completely naked, my towel innocently hanging on the rack near the door—the same spot the bloody snake has now decided to make its resting place. Dread tightens its grip on me.

What if it moves? What if it comes closer?

I'll simply pass away.

The thought sends a shiver down my spine, and a wave of dizziness washes over me. I can't stay here, but every instinct tells me not to move. My breaths come in short, shallow gasps, and I can feel my heart pounding in my chest.

But amidst all this panic, one thought consumes me—Bradley. He's going to come rushing in here, only to find me standing here, all exposed. Thank goodness the steam has fogged up the glass a little, but it doesn't change the fact that he'll see me, *all* of me. My mind races with scenarios of embarrassment and awkwardness, adding to the chaos of the situation.

This can't be happening. Not now. Not like this.

As I stand there, my mind racing with embarrassment and fear, I hear the front door open and Bradley's deep voice calling out, "Amelia? Where are you?" Before I can even answer, he comes barreling into the bathroom, and I squeal in surprise.

"Are you hurt? What the fuck happened?"

"Oh, my god! Cover your eyes!" I shout, instinctively trying to shield myself from his gaze. On cue, he turns his head away, his voice loud and deep.

"What are you doing?" he asks, clearly taken aback.

"What does it look like, Brad? I'm trapped in here, and there is a snake right there," I say, pointing at the glass, where the snake has now moved a centimetre or two.

"Can you—can you grab it?" I ask, my voice trembling with worry.

"How am I going to grab the fucking thing with my eyes closed?" he retorts, frustration evident in his voice. He looks down and spots the snake, muttering, "Oh. Well, fuck."

Yes, indeed.

"Just grab my towel," I suggest, desperation creeping into my tone. "Please."

"Nothing I haven't seen before, sunshine," he says with a smirk. Oh. *Oh.*

"Don't kill it, please. Can you... pick it up? Grab it? I don't know!" I plead, hoping he understands the gravity of the situation.

"It's a fucking brown snake, Amelia," he replies, his voice serious, emphasising the danger. He takes a step forward.

Oh, is that bad? How does he know that? How do *I* not know that? I've been living in the bush, literally, all my life. I am ashamed to say that I did not recognise it.

"Is it really that dangerous?" I ask, my voice small.

"Yes!" he responds firmly. "They're the second most venomous snake in the world."

I gulp, feeling a wave of fear wash over me. Now that I know it's very venomous, I panic even more.

As Bradley processes the situation, he grabs my towel and throws it to me. I quickly open the shower door slightly, just enough to catch it in time.

"Thanks," I mumble, wrapping the towel around myself, feeling a bit more secure. Bradley, on the other hand, seems to find the whole thing amusing.

"Fucking hell," he says with an exhale, before releasing a soft chuckle. "I thought something bad happened," he exclaims, his voice raised in mock concern. I am dumbfounded. How does he find this amusing, and yet here I am, mortified and utterly embarrassed? But I guess in the grand scheme of things, it can be seen as... well, to him, kind of comical.

I roll my eyes, trying to ignore his teasing.

"Well, something bad did happen. There's a snake in my bathroom," I retort, and he laughs softly, clearly unfazed by the situation.

"Relax. I'll take care of it," he says confidently, stepping closer to the snake.

I watch nervously as he approaches the snake, his movements slow and deliberate. Suddenly, the snake moves quickly for a moment, and I squeal in sheer terror.

"Oh, God!" I cry out, my fear escalating. "What if it bites you?"

"Shhhh," Bradley chastises, his tone amused but firm. "Stop screaming, woman."

"I'm sorry," I gasp, trying to calm my racing heart. "I'm just *really* scared of snakes."

Bradley laughs, and with a steady hand, he reaches out and grabs the snake behind the head, careful not to startle it. And I watch in awe. The sight is doing all sorts of things to me, but being *aroused* was the last thing I ever expected to be. Why is Bradley manhandling this snake so incredibly hot? *Goodness me.*

"What are you going to do with it?" I ask, my voice shaky.

"I'll release it outside," he replies, already opening the door, before disappearing.

With the snake safely removed, I cautiously step out of the shower, looking around at... well, nothing, now. Hey, you can never be too sure. I quickly grab my things and walk back out into my living room. After a few moments, Bradley comes back in, closing my front door.

"All taken care of," he announces.

And what a relief that is.

"T-thank you so much," I say, rushing up to him to give him a tight hug. He clears his throat, and for a moment, I forget that I'm still in my towel and very, very *wet*.

"Oh, my god. Sorry," I say, gripping my towel like my life depends on it.

As his gaze intensifies, I feel a flutter of something unfamiliar in my chest. I try to brush it off, chalking it up to the adrenaline of the situation, but his proximity and the way his eyes linger on me make it hard to ignore.

"You're welcome," he says, his voice low and husky. "Just glad I could help."

It is now that I notice he's in gym gear—black shorts, a tank top, and Nike sneakers. A film of sweat marks his skin, and his tank top clings to him, outlining every ridge of his pecs and abdomen, where I know that six-pack is hiding. The mood around us changes. The air that was once cool, now warm, warming up my skin, my cheeks.

As he steps closer, the air between us seems to crackle with an electric intensity. I can feel my heart racing in my chest, my breaths coming in short, shallow gasps. His eyes are dark and intense, boring into mine with a hunger that sends a shiver down my spine.

"I'm... I'm glad you called me," he admits.

He is?

"I couldn't think of anyone else," I say softly. His eyes soften for a moment, as if he can understand my thoughts. Bradley takes another step closer, and I decide to bite the bullet.

"You never called? I just... after last weekend, after we..." My voice trails off, and I swallow, watching his expression. "I just thought you'd text me," I say, my voice almost a whisper.

"I wanted to. Fuck, believe me, I did," he confesses, his gaze unwavering.

I frown softly. "Well, why didn't you?"

"I-I don't know. I needed time to process it all," he says, his voice gravelly.

"But... you kissed me. What did you need to process?"

The tension between us is palpable, the air thick with desire. His gaze is intense, his proximity even more intoxicating. I can feel my heart racing, my breaths coming in short, shallow gasps.

"I don't even know," he says, shaking his head. He stops talking, and I wait, realising he's stuck in thought. His brows are furrowed, eyes distant. I study him, feeling a mix of frustration and curiosity.

Why is he always so stuck in his head?

"What are you thinking right now?" I ask, probably a little too abruptly.

He looks stumped. "Right now?"

"Yes, Brad. Right now." I lean in slightly, my eyes searching his face. I can see the conflict in his eyes, and it intrigues me. What's going on in that head of his? Why does he always seem so distant, yet so present?

"I'm thinking that you should get changed," he says, glancing at the towel clutched tightly between my hands.

Oh crap. The towel. *Why haven't I changed yet?* This is so awkward. One wrong move and it'll slip. Would I let that happen? *Should I?*

"Why?" I question, my voice shaky.

"Because it's fucking distracting," he admits, his voice low and filled with restraint. "And I'm trying really hard not to do something that I know I won't be able to stop."

His words send a chill down my spine, the hairs on my arm shooting straight up. *Please do,* I plead in my head. God, I want nothing more than for him to kiss me.

He moves closer, his eyes dark, the once shade of blue now almost black, his pupils dilated. He leans in, his breathing sharp, and I watch his chest rise and fall. My gaze shifts from his lips back to his eyes. Bradley towers over me, forcing me to tilt my head upward to meet his intense gaze.

Just when I think he's going to kiss me, he doesn't. "We can't keep doing this."

Disappointment washes over me in full force. I can almost feel my shoulders slump, the weight of his rejection heavy and confusing. I nod slowly, having no choice but to understand and go with it, even though I don't really understand. He's right, of course. We shouldn't be doing this.

"Okay, sorry. I'll go get changed and walk you out," I say, plastering on a smile before heading into my room. I change in record time—seconds, really. I don't want to risk him leaving before I get to say goodbye.

In my haste, I stub my toe on the corner of my bed and scream out, "Ouch, cheese and crackers!" I curse out loud, the silly words escaping before I can stop them.

I guess old habits die hard.

"You right?" Bradley's voice comes from near the door, and relief washes over me to know that he's still here.

"Yep. Coming out," I say, quickly giving my foot a rub before joining him outside.

"Cheese and crackers?" he teases with a smile. "No more swearing?"

I blush deeply and roll my eyes. "No, those are only saved for serious moments." I fiddle with my ring, my fingers tugging at the hem nervously.

Bradley's voice grabs my attention. "Would you maybe like to go out to dinner?"

I freeze, panicking momentarily. "When? Now?" I blurt out.

He huffs a laugh, shaking his head. "No, sometime soon, maybe?"

How can this man be so confusing? Is this how all men are? Sheesh. One minute he's saying *'we shouldn't do this'* and the next he's asking me out to dinner. Maybe just as... friends.

I can work with that.

"Like a... date?" I ask softly, my heart pounding in my chest. Bradley's smile falters for a moment, and I can almost see the gears turning in his head.

"Well, it can be whatever you'd like it to be."

"I'd love that," I respond, the words slipping out before I even have a chance to consider them. There's no need for consideration, though; this feels right.

"Okay," he replies, his voice slightly hoarse. "I'll text you soon to figure out the details."

As he heads toward the door, I trail behind to show him out. Opening it, I pause, a sudden urge pulling at me.

"Bradley?" I call out, and he turns back to me, his eyes searching mine.

I stutter slightly but manage a, "Thank you for, um, coming so quickly when I called." I honestly thought he wouldn't answer, but for him to actually show up, I was completely surprised. His eyes soften for a moment, and he falters, as if he's pondering what to say.

"I'll always be there when you need me," he says, his voice holding a deep, unwavering certainty, yet carrying a softer, more meaningful note. It's not a question of if, but when. His words wash over me, enveloping me in a comforting warmth.

This means something, right? It has to.

"Night, sunshine," he adds, and I feel a rush of warmth at the use of that nickname.

"Make sure all your windows and doors are closed and locked," he reminds me as he closes the door behind him.

"Okay. Goodnight," I whisper, watching him leave. Leaning against the door, I let out a sigh, feeling a whirlwind of nerves.

"I need tea. No, I need something stronger," I mutter to myself, making my way to the cupboard in search of a bottle of wine.

Tonight has left me with so much to think about.

It's finally Friday, a relief in itself. I'm on lunch duty today, basking in the sun while a refreshing breeze plays with my hair. Despite the warmth, I wrap my cardigan tighter around me for comfort. From my vantage point overseeing the playground, a group of year six girls approaches me, their mischievous grins immediately raising red flags in my mind. These girls are notorious—always causing a stir, testing the limits with their teachers. I brace myself, knowing their reputation well.

"Hey, Miss Brown," Kellie, always the blunt one, starts, innocently enough.

"Hi, girls," I reply cautiously, not having any inclination where this conversation may be headed.

"Do you know Bradley Mitchell?" Kellie asks, curiosity tingling in her voice. Well, crap. It definitely wasn't that. Why would she be asking?

"Uh, I do. How do *you* know Bradley Mitchell?" I counter, my curiosity piqued.

Kellie shakes her head. "I don't. But I do know he's a police officer."

"Everyone knows that, Kellie," Briony retorts, her tone dismissive. "Anyway, *soo*, my sister Dahlia told me he came to visit you," she says, air-quoting the word *visit* and raising her eyebrows playfully.

Heat rises to my cheeks at their teasing. "Uh, yes, he did. And?" I respond firmly, meeting Briony's gaze head-on.

"Well, why would he be hanging around you? I mean, isn't he, like, important or something?" Briony asks casually, her tone laced with scepticism. "And aren't you kind of... like, a loner?"

Her little friends giggle at her words, and I furrow my brows in surprise.

Being called out by an eleven-year-old. *Ouch.*

I am a loner in a sense, yes. But maybe not to the extent she's implying.

"Because we're friends, and what makes you think I'm a loner?" I ask, genuinely curious.

"Well, you're always by yourself," she retorts, her smirk widening. "I never see you with anyone else, just off doing your own thing."

I can't help but inwardly roll my eyes.

Is *that* it?

Children these days just have too much confidence. What she's trying to gain out of this conversation, I'll never know, but who cares?

"First of all, Briony, I'm *not* a loner," I retort, my voice stronger than I expected. "Secondly, I do have friends, and *thirdly*, it's none of your business why he would be hanging around," I say with a smile.

Briony narrows her eyes at me, but I continue, not backing down.

"*Especially* not the business of an eleven-year-old."

She steps closer, her hand on her hip, trying to assert dominance. "I'm *twelve*," she corrects me with a smirk.

"Same, same," I reply with a nonchalant shrug, flipping my hair over my shoulder. The girls exchange surprised glances, caught off guard by my unexpected assertiveness.

Probably not used to being challenged, Briony huffs with attitude, "Whatever."

The other girls exchange disappointed looks, realising they won't get the gossip they were hoping for. As they disperse, their interest wanes, leaving me with a mix of relief and pride. It's not easy standing up to older kids, especially those with a reputation like theirs.

But I did it.

And strangely, I feel liberated, as if I've proven something to myself.

I glance around the bustling playground, filled with the chaotic energy of children at play. Perhaps dealing with older kids wouldn't be so daunting after all. Yet, for now, I'm content with my kindergarteners—they may be small, but they teach me resilience and courage every day.

As for those girls, maybe they've learned a lesson, too. Not everyone is willing to be pushed around, regardless of age.

And as for Bradley, well, maybe he'd be proud of me standing my ground.

22

Bradley

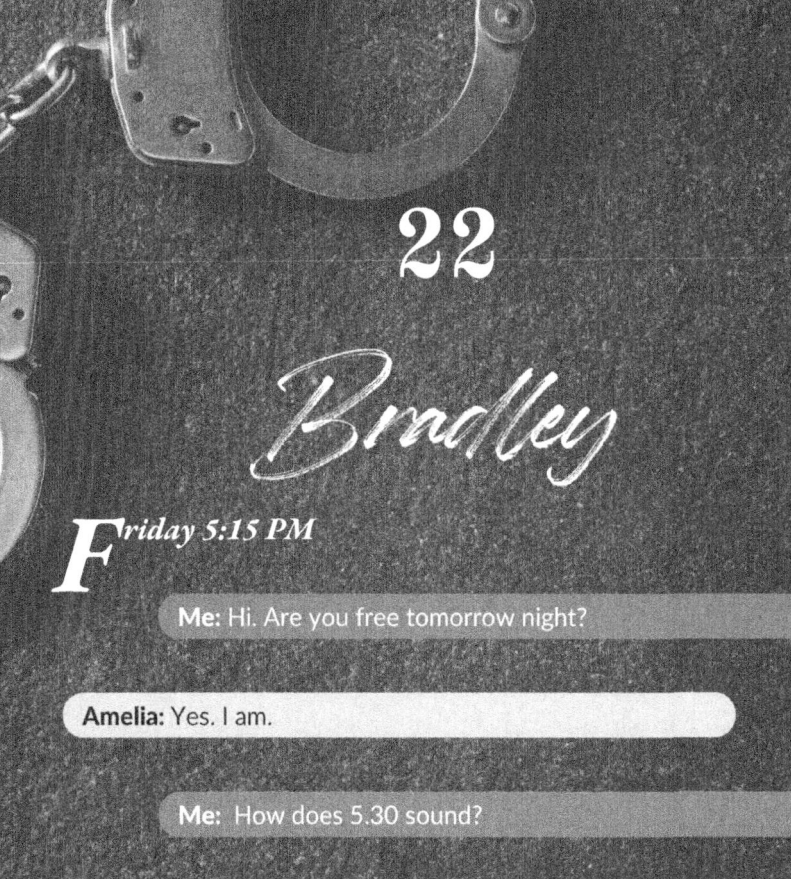

Friday 5:15 PM

> **Me:** Hi. Are you free tomorrow night?

> **Amelia:** Yes. I am.

> **Me:** How does 5.30 sound?

> **Amelia:** Sounds good!

> **Me:** Ok. I'll pick you up.

> **Amelia:** Okay xx

I reread our texts and can't help but feel a bit embarrassed that I had to search up what 'xx' meant.

She'd sent me *kisses*. It made me smile.

I'd thought long and hard about where I wanted to take her. I ended up opting for a small fancy diner about thirty-five minutes or so from Wattle Creek, in another small-ish town called Clifftop Haven, perched on a mountaintop. It's a stunning little joint they've got there. An old friend of mine from school, Jackson Hill, moved out there years ago and has been running his own orchard and livestock farm ever since. I've been meaning to catch up with him, but haven't for a while now.

I should.

I found out about this diner because a colleague from work, Grant, was raving about it after he went up there with his wife. I pestered him for the details, and here we are now. I get changed, throwing on a pair of jeans, a henley shirt, and my favourite denim jacket lined with sherpa. As I check myself in the mirror, I feel a mix of nerves and anticipation. Is this really a date? I hadn't thought of it that way, but now, as I think about it, it pretty much seems that way, doesn't it? Grabbing my keys and wallet, I head out of my room.

"Heading out," I call to Mum.

"Where to?" she pipes up from the couch, giving me a curious look.

"Out," I mumble, not wanting to go into detail.

As I head to my Navarra, I see Dad coming from around his car, wearing a tool belt and holding a hammer.

"Son," he says with a nod. I nod back.

"Where ya off to?" he asks as I unlock my car.

"Dinner. With a friend."

He gives me a once-over, then nods with a knowing look.

"Bout time," he mumbles, but I don't give much thought to what he means.

"Bye," I say, hopping into my ute.

I rock up to Amelia's house just shy of five thirty. I'm a man who's always on time.

I quickly send her a text to let her know I'm here, and a response comes shortly after, letting me know she's coming down. Stepping out, I round the car and lean against the passenger door, waiting. Then I see her. It's a sight that takes my breath away.

Amelia walks toward me, and fuck, she's stunning. She's wearing a yellow dress that falls just above her knees—the bodice is tight, like a vice, accentuating her small waist. Over the top, she has a thin cardigan, and on her feet are her usual white sneakers, that I've seen her wear countless times now.

She's a true beauty.

How I never noticed these things about her before is beyond me. Her hair falls in soft waves around her shoulders, catching the light just right. There's a hint of nervousness in her smile, but her eyes sparkle with excitement. She's got this way of looking at me, like she sees right through all my walls.

Fuck that. Deep down, I *know* I've *always* noticed.

"Hey," she says, a bit breathless as she reaches me.

"Hey. You look... beautiful," I reply, opening the passenger door for her. I'm almost speechless as she tucks a strand of hair behind her ear, her smile radiant.

"Thank you. So do you!" she blurts quickly, then corrects herself, "I mean, not beautiful, but handsome. You look... good." She hides her face before hopping into the passenger seat.

I can't help but smile at her adorable awkwardness.

She really is something else.

A warm feeling settles in my chest as I shake my head, smiling to myself. Yeah, I really am just out here smiling to myself like an idiot.

We're driving with the radio playing softly, just the way I like it. I don't understand people who need their music blaring while they drive. Amelia sits quietly beside me, her phone occasionally pinging with a text message. I glance over at her without turning my head, watching her type away.

"Someone's popular tonight," I remark, breaking the comfortable silence. Because that's what it is.

Comfortable.

The air between us has shifted, changed. I no longer feel like an awkward pre-teen around a girl; I feel comfortable. I can only hope that she feels the same way.

She sighs. "Sorry, it's my work friends."

"Uh huh," I say, keeping my eyes on the road.

"Are they the same girls from the pub?" I ask, looking at her quickly.

"Yeah," she answers with a nervous smile. "I told them I was going out for dinner, and they're pestering me for details."

"Right. And did you tell them?" I ask.

"Tell them what?" she responds, and I glance over to find her eyes watching me with such an innocent expression. Fuck, she has those doll eyes. Not the sultry come-hither eyes. No, Amelia's brown orbs are wide open, warm and inviting.

"That you're going to dinner with me?" I say, my voice steady.

"Yes. But they won't say anything. I promise," she says quickly.

This makes me feel... odd. She makes it sound so forbidden. And while, yes, it's probably not the most ideal, given the situation with her being Liv's best friend and all, however, there really is nothing wrong with two friends hanging out. Right? I frown at the thought. Friends. We are friends, yes.

But is it enough? Can it be more?

"I don't mind," I reply, trying to keep my tone casual. I swear I hear her exhale, almost as if she's relieved to hear that.

We continue driving, the comfortable silence wrapping around us once more. As I focus on the road, my mind wanders to what this night might bring. Friends hanging out, sure, but something tells me this could be the start of something more. We reach the border, passing the sign that says *Welcome to Wattle Creek,* when Amelia softly asks.

"Uh, where are we even going?"

"You'll see soon." Amelia shifts slightly in her seat, glancing over at me.

"Are you always this mysterious?" she asks, a hint of teasing in her voice.

I smirk, keeping my eyes on the road. "Only when I need to be."

She laughs softly, and it's a sound that makes me smile. I like hearing her laugh. It's genuine, like everything about her.

The sun is beginning its descent, casting a warm, golden glow across the outback landscape. The sky is painted with hues of orange and pink, the light making everything look almost magical. I don't need my sun visor, but I notice Amelia squinting and raising her hand to block the sun.

Without thinking, I reach over and pull her visor down before returning my hand to my thigh, gripping the steering wheel with my other. As we pass through the small towns and open stretches of road, I steal glances at her. She's fiddling with the gold ring on her finger, a habit I've noticed before.

I wonder what she's thinking, if she's as nervous as I am. Maybe more. Maybe less. Her right hand rests beside her thigh, and I suddenly have the urge to grab it. To quell her nerves, if she's feeling them. But how do I do that without it coming off weird?

I mean, fuck, we've kissed twice, and it almost feels like we haven't. She's just so modest, and I'm, well, just me—not exactly the most exciting guy around. But damn, I want to be exciting for her. The way she makes me excited.

The landscape changes as we approach Clifftop Haven. The rolling hills give way to steeper inclines, and the road winds upward. I can feel the excitement building in me, a mix of nerves and anticipation.

Finally, we reach the restaurant; *The Haven*. It's a small little place, perched on the edge of a cliff, with a stunning view of the valley below. The lights from inside cast a warm, inviting glow, and I can see a few other cars parked outside. I pull into a spot and turn off the car.

She looks around, her eyes wide with wonder. "This is... wow. It's beautiful."

I smile, feeling a sense of pride. "Thought you'd like it."

Amelia nods, still taking in the view. "I more than like it, Bradley. This is amazing."

I step out of the car, circling around to open her door. "Glad you think so. Come, let's head inside."

The sound of our footsteps on the gravel mixes with the gentle evening breeze. As we enter, the warmth of the diner envelops us, along with the scent of home-cooked meals and coffee. The interior is quaint, with chequered tablecloths and old-fashioned diner booths. A waitress greets us with a smile.

"Table for two?"

I nod, and she leads us to a table by the window, overlooking the breathtaking view, offering us menus. We settle in, and I flick my eyes to Amelia, who is busy staring out the window, where the sunset catches the horizon, and just below the clifftop, the town of Clifftop Haven is lit up by house windows and streetlights.

This place feels like our own little world, where the only things that matter are the present moment and the person sitting across from you. Eventually, we both decide on our orders, and another waitress arrives in time to take our orders. Amelia orders the chicken parmigiana with a salad, and I order the T-bone steak, medium-rare, with a side of mashed potatoes and chips.

Yeah, I like my carbs.

I can't be too lean for work, so I make sure I'm eating a more than sufficient amount of red meat and carbs to maintain my physique. She gives me a curious glance, before smirking, and I just know she's thinking what I am, no doubt. The waitress lingers for a moment, and I feel her eyes on me, but I avoid her gaze.

Clearing my throat, I say, "That'll be all. Thanks," before handing her back the menus.

Amelia wastes no time diving into conversation as we wait for our food to arrive. I know she's nervous because she's rambling.

"So, I have a sister," she begins, her words tumbling out in a rush. "Her name's Kathryn, but I call her 'Kat.' She's eight years older, lives in Sydney with her husband, and they have a daughter—named after me, actually." She laughs softly, a nervous edge to her voice. "It's kind of surreal, you know? To have a little niece named after you."

"Are you close with your sister, even though she moved away?" I ask, trying to keep my tone casual, though Amelia's mention of her family stirs something deep within me.

"Oh, so close. Have been since I was born," she replies warmly. "I'm really close with her husband, John, as well. He's great. You'd get along well with him, I think."

Her words strike a chord. It's as if she sees a future where we're more intertwined, where meeting her family isn't just a passing thought, but a possibility. For someone like me, who's kept people at arm's length, it's both comforting and unsettling.

"Family means a lot to you, huh?" I say, noting the warmth in her eyes.

Amelia nods. "Yeah, they're everything to me. Kat has always been like a second mum to me."

Her sincerity softens my gruff exterior. I find myself drawn to her openness, her willingness to share these personal details with me. It's a side of her that makes me want to know more, to understand what makes her tick beyond the surface.

One particular fact seems to be lingering, however. A stark reminder as I calculate silently. I realise Amelia must be around twenty-four. Literally my sister's age. This isn't news to me, more like something I just chose to ignore.

I'm pushing thirty, and she seems so... youthful, full of life. What could she possibly see in a guy like me?

"So, you're twenty-four, then?" I manage to ask, my voice attempting nonchalance.

"Yeah," Amelia replies, her tone soft, tinged with a hint of nervousness. "Turning twenty-five in July. A quarter of a century old," she adds, a small smile playing on her lips.

I watch her closely, taking in the way she holds herself, the subtle movements of her hands as she speaks. Before I can delve deeper into my thoughts or say anything more, the waitress interrupts, her presence jarring in its closeness.

"Can I get y'all something to drink?"

The waitress's hand lands on my shoulder, and I subtly shift away, feeling the weight of her touch linger. Amelia's eyes track the interaction with a fixed intensity, her gaze unwavering. Ignoring the waitress, I turn to Amelia, a flicker of amusement in my eyes as I ask what she wants to drink.

Her cheeks flush, and she hesitates for a moment.

"Um, I'll just have a glass of rosé," she murmurs softly, glancing briefly at the waitress and then back at me.

Keeping my focus on Amelia, I reply casually, "Corona for me, thanks." The waitress scurries off hastily.

"Well, she wasn't subtle at all," she comments, her voice carrying a hint of amusement.

"What do you mean?" I inquire.

"That waitress." She gestures toward where the waitress disappeared. "She was flirting with you."

I meet her gaze squarely. "Was she now? Didn't even notice."

Amelia's cheeks deepen in colour, but a small smile plays on her lips. "Really? It seemed pretty obvious to me." I smirk in response.

"Hm. Guess I was too busy looking at someone else," I say, accompanied by a playful wink in her direction.

She shakes her head, laughter bubbling up lightly. The tension eases between us, and we slip into an easy rhythm of conversation. As we talk, I find myself captivated by her presence, content just to listen to her voice for hours.

"So, how was your day at work yesterday?" I ask, leaning forward with genuine interest.

Amelia smiles, a playful glint in her eyes before she giggles.

I raise an eyebrow, curious. "What's funny?"

She leans in closer, shaking her head. "My day was... interesting. Quite funny, actually, now that I think it over. There's this group of girls, troublemakers, at my school. They're known to be quite bratty, and they, uh, well, they tried to intimidate me today during my lunch duty."

My eyes widen with surprise as I listen intently. "Intimidate you? How?"

Amelia leans back, recounting the incident with animated gestures. "They were teasing me, calling me a loner, and questioning why you would even bother with someone like me."

I'm baffled.

"Are you serious? But that was what, a while ago? And that came from year six kids?"

The thought actually bothers me, as weird as it may sound. The fact that young children are pestering her about me, teasing her. That's wild.

"Yep. But I put them in their place." She shrugs. "You should have seen their faces. I'm actually really proud of how I handled it. Usually the older kids make me nervous, but not then."

"Good on you. I'm proud of you for sticking up for yourself. Kids these days, huh? That's crazy," I say, shaking my head in disbelief.

Amelia chuckles softly, a mischievous glint in her eye. "Yeah, who knew I'd have to fend off interrogations from pre-teens?" She grins.

"Well, you handled it like a pro."

"Thank you," she says, her smile turning sincere.

As we sit there, the restaurant buzzes around us, but our conversation stays focused and intimate. I find myself admiring Amelia even more, not just for her dedication to her work, but also for her grit in handling unexpected challenges.

Amelia leans forward, her eyes bright with curiosity. "So, how was your day at work yesterday?" she asks, a playful smile tugging at her lips.

I exhale with a sigh, contemplating her question with mock seriousness. "Work was..." I pause, then shrug nonchalantly, "fine."

She eyes me closely. "Just fine?"

I chuckle softly, running a hand through my hair. "Yep, just fine. Sounds like your day had more excitement than mine," I say with a grin.

Opening up about my day isn't something I typically do, especially not in detail, but with Amelia, it feels different. It feels easy, like talking to an old friend who can appreciate a good joke.

"But seriously, I'm certain your day was more interesting," she says.

"Not really. I was on highway patrol most of the day with my partner Daniels." She nods, recognizing the name.

"Did you pull over many people?"

I smirk, feeling comfortable enough to share more. "Yeah, a few. Speeding mostly. You'd be surprised how many people think they can get away with it." I pause, shaking my head. "One guy was doing over a hundred in a sixty zone. Claimed he didn't see the sign."

She laughs softly, her eyes sparkling with interest. "And what did you say to that?"

"I told him that the sign wasn't the only thing he missed," I reply with a smile. "He wasn't too happy about the ticket."

She smiles, leaning in closer. "Must be interesting, seeing all kinds of people on the job."

"It is. You get the full spectrum—from genuine mistakes to people just being plain reckless. It's a mix of frustration and fascination. Keeps me on my toes."

It's not like me to have conversations about my day, or work in general, but I find myself freely opening up to Amelia.

It feels... natural.

Without hesitation, I answer, "I like the hands-on stuff, anything that requires my full attention. As a Senior Constable with the NSW Police, I usually lead the boys on bigger operations. I handle everything from organising raids to coordinating with other units."

I glance at her, noting the awe in her expression. "Even though I'm up in the ranks, I still like to get out on the field with Daniels for general duties. There's something about the adrenaline, the strategy... I enjoy the thrill of it all. Keeps me sharp."

Her genuine interest catches me off guard. Most people either nod politely or change the subject, but she's different. She actually cares about what I do, about who I am.

Feeling this kind of connection so soon is so unexpected for me, but it's also refreshing. It makes me want to open up and share more with her.

"Can you see yourself doing that for the rest of your life?" she asks, her curiosity evident.

"You mean being a police officer?" I raise an eyebrow.

She smiles, the kind without showing teeth, the kind that reaches the eyes. "Sorry, I meant being a Senior Constable."

I chuckle softly. "To move up in the ranks from this position, I'd need to be awarded a promotion. That would place me as Sergeant. So, I wouldn't be out in the field as much. I'd be working with a logistics team and coordinating things from behind the scenes."

She tilts her head slightly, clearly intrigued. "Do you think you'd like that?"

I pause, considering her question. "It'd be different. Less action, more strategy. But who knows? I might actually enjoy the change. It's all part of the job, right?"

She nods thoughtfully, her gaze never leaving mine. "I think you'd be great at it, no matter what you do."

Just as the moment lingers, the waitress arrives with our plates of food. Amelia's eyes light up at the sight, her excitement contagious. She's so cute.

She politely thanks the waitress, and I can't help but smile at her enthusiasm.

"You must have some incredible stories," she says, her voice tinged with wonder.

"Yeah, there are a few. Maybe I'll tell you some of them one day."

"I'd like that," she replies softly.

As we start eating, I watch her, fascinated by the way she immerses herself in the moment. She seems to savour every bite, her eyes twinkling with delight. It's these little things that draw me closer to her.

At this moment in time, I realise just how much I want to spend more time with her.

There's something about Amelia that feels right, like she fits perfectly into my life in a way I hadn't anticipated.

23

Amelia

The plates have been cleared away. My glass has been refilled *twice*, yet Bradley remains on his first bottle of beer. Surprisingly, our conversation flows effortlessly, with me doing most of the talking. Big shocker there, right? But it's different tonight.

He's opened up more than I've ever seen him, and it's amazing. Underneath all that gruff, there's a genuinely kind-hearted man. I feel a sense of pride knowing I might be the only person who gets to see this side of him. It's like a privilege, and I'm grateful he's chosen to share this with me.

As the minutes tick by, my phone screen flashes 7:15 PM.

We've been engrossed in conversation for nearly an hour, and neither of us has hinted at leaving. I wonder if I'm babbling on too much, filling the air with more stories about my kindergarteners—not exactly the typical dinner date conversation, right?

But Bradley seems engaged, and that surprises me. Maybe he finds my tales amusing, or maybe… just maybe, he's enjoying this as much as I am. His eyes, usually guarded, reflect genuine interest and warmth.

It's a side of Bradley Mitchell I never expected to see, and yet here we are, sharing this moment.

"I really love my art classes with the kids," I mention, trying to keep the enthusiasm in my voice. "Watching them paint is so rewarding."

He's quiet, his gaze intense, yet oddly comforting, as he listens. Is he really interested in my school talk? Or am I boring him to death? Maybe I should switch gears, ask him about his hobbies or something.

Yeah, that might lighten the mood.

"Anyway, I guess that might not sound too exciting for everyone, so, enough about that—"

"Hold on. I wasn't done listening," he interrupts, his voice gravelly and unexpectedly attractive. How can someone's voice be both deep and alluring at the same time?

Oh my.

Those piercing blue eyes hold mine, and a ripple of excitement dances in my gut.

"Tell me more about *your* paintings," he continues.

Does he really want to know? No one has ever shown this kind of interest before. Maybe that's because I've always kept this part of me to myself. Silly me.

"Oh," I say, trying to steady my voice. *Come on, Amelia, focus.* "Uh, well, I like to use oil paints, occasionally watercolour. I like to paint subjects that will evoke strong emotions from them."

He nods slowly. "What sort of subjects?"

Goodness me.

"People. I paint people. Well, *portraits*, technically speaking." His eyes widen for a moment, taking in what I've said. Is that bad? Is that not what he was expecting to hear?

"Just random people?" he asks.

He's been studying me ever since we sat down, as if trying to unravel a mystery. He's good at it, too. Maybe too good.

"Sometimes I use models I find online. Other times, I create characters in my head. But usually, I'll paint someone I know, like a family member or friend," I explain, taking a sip of wine to steady my nerves.

"I've started this new series of portraits," I continue, my voice brightening with excitement. "But I've been stuck on finding a new model for my next canvas..." Then, without warning, the thought pops into my head.

"I could paint you," I blurt out, freezing mid-sentence. My eyes widen involuntarily, and his brows arch in surprise.

No, I didn't just say that.

That was definitely an intrusive thought. Intrusive thought 1 - Amelia 0.

Oh, gosh, why would I even suggest that?

Sure, I've thought about it before, but now that I've actually said it out loud, I'm embarrassed. What if he thinks it's weird? He's such a private person.

"Kidding. I don't... I won't do that," I quickly add, my words stumbling over each other in my haste.

"Why not?" he asks, a faint frown crossing his face. "Am I not a good enough model?"

Oh my.

Now I've made him feel inadequate.

"What? No!" I blurt out, flustered. "You most definitely are. I mean, look at *you*. You'd be a great subject... You are... very handsome."

His mouth quirks up into a smirk, his eyes crinkling slightly, as if he's suppressing a laugh, before a genuine smile spreads across his handsome face. Is he teasing me?

No, scratch that. That smile—it's all real.

"I'm just joking, sunshine," he says, and I exhale in relief, trying not to smile back too broadly.

"That's... not funny," I say, trying to sound stern, but feeling a smile tugging at my lips as I playfully smack his arm from across the table.

The bastard, *affectionately, of course,* bursts into laughter, a rich, warm sound that sends a shiver of delight through me, like sinking into a warm blanket on a chilly night.

"So, you think I'm very handsome, huh?"

I let out a nervous giggle. "Well, I mean... It's just... obvious, isn't it?"

"Well, if it's *that* obvious, maybe you *should* paint me, after all," he suggests, leaning forward again with a slight smirk. "I'd be more than happy to model for you."

His suggestion catches me off guard, and I blink, momentarily surprised by his confidence. His playful demeanour makes my heart flutter, and I find myself smiling back at him, intrigued by his sudden openness.

"You'd really model for me?" I ask, my voice a little breathless.

"Absolutely," he replies, his tone teasing but sincere. "Anything for you, sunshine. Remember?"

My heart flutters at his words, and I take another sip of my rosé.

"I'll hold you to that, officer." A smile tugs at my lips.

"I'm counting on it."

As our conversation becomes more relaxed, I can't help but ask the question that's been on my mind.

"Can I ask you something?" I say hesitantly.

"Of course."

"Why do you call me sunshine?" My heart pounds in my chest. He takes a moment to study me before answering.

"Because you light up any room," he says simply, and my stomach does backflips at his words. He doesn't know this, but his words mean *everything* to me. More than he probably ever *realised*.

"I... thank you," I manage to say through a shaky breath.

And just like that, without realising it until now, I know that I am falling for him—hard and fast. Panic sets in as I realise this could end badly, but then he flashes that genuine, heart-stopping smile and any doubts melt away.

Despite the risks, I am helpless to resist him.

This is not good.

24

Amelia

As we finish dinner, the waitress brings the bill. I reach for my wallet, ready to split it because, hey, it's the twenty-first century. But before I can hand him the cash, his voice stops me.

"Amelia," he says, shaking his head firmly and dropping his card on the tray. Well, okay, then. I tuck my wallet back into my bag.

Bradley stands up, and I quickly follow. The waitress returns with his card and a polite smile. He places a hand on my back, guiding me out of the diner. His touch sends a shiver down my spine, and I feel giddy as we step into the cool night air. As we walk along the footpath, he gently taps my shoulder, pulling me to his left, away from the road. My heart skips a beat.

Bradley Mitchell knows the *sidewalk* rule?

We reach his car, and he moves to open my door. I stop and turn to face him.

"Bradley?" I say softly.

He makes a soft *hm* sound. I step closer and give him a kiss on the cheek. "Thank you. For dinner."

Bradley's eyes darken, a smirk forming on his lips.

"You call that a kiss?" he says, voice low and gravelly.

Before I can respond, he gently cradles my face in his hands, his touch tender yet firm. His lips meet mine in a kiss that ignites a fire within me, a passion I never knew existed. The world blurs as his tongue gently teases my lips, asking for entrance.

I melt into him, trying not to think about how this feels like one of my daydreams. My hands slide up to his chest, feeling his heartbeat thumping under my fingers. He guides me backward until my back presses against the side of the passenger seat. A deep, rumbling sound vibrates from his chest, sending shivers down my spine and eliciting a soft, completely involuntary whimper from me. His touch is electric, like a live wire, sparking a fierce desire that zips through my body. And then, way too soon, he breaks the kiss, leaving me breathless and a bit dizzy.

"We're in a public car park," I whisper, my voice shaky.

He grins that infuriatingly charming grin. "And?"

I try to steady myself, glancing around at our surroundings. "And... people can see us!"

He must sense my apprehension because he turns to look around. About two metres away, an older couple strolls by, their eyes glued to us.

My face flushes, and I wish the ground would swallow me whole.

He turns back to me, his expression softening. "Hey, don't feel embarrassed. If I wanna kiss you in an open car park, I'm gonna do just that. I don't give a fuck what people think, and you shouldn't either. Understood?"

I nod quickly, biting my lip to stop the words *Yes, sir* from escaping.

"Good girl. Come."

With swift movements, he lifts me up and gently places me on the seat, closing the door behind me. I watch as he rounds the car to the driver's side, his actions deliberate and confident. Just as we settle into the car, my phone rings. Fishing it out of my bag, I see it's my mum calling.

Panic grips me.

Why is she calling now?

Bradley notices my wide eyes. "Everything okay?"

"Sorry, it's my mum," I say, glancing at Bradley. "Should I step outside to take this?"

He raises an eyebrow, shaking his head. "Amelia, stay in the car and answer it."

I fumble to answer the call. "Hi, Mum!"

Her familiar voice brings instant comfort. "Hi, darling. Is this a bad time?"

"Uh, sort of." I glance at Bradley, who just gives me a pointed look. "But it's fine. What's up?"

"Meli, I have such exciting news!" Her voice brims with excitement. I blush, praying Bradley didn't catch the nickname.

"What news?" I ask, trying to match her enthusiasm.

"Kathryn is coming up from Sydney with little Millie and John!" Her announcement sends a thrill through me.

"When? Why didn't she tell me?"

"Friday afternoon, for the weekend!" Her joy is contagious. "I just spoke to her. She'll probably call you soon."

A squeal escapes me, and I glance at Bradley, who's clearly amused. I clear my throat. "Thanks for letting me know."

"What are you up to?" Mum asks. I wince. *How do I explain this?*

"Just had dinner," I say casually.

"With who?"

"Uh, just a—" I start, but Bradley interrupts, taking the phone from my hand. My eyes widen in shock. *What are you doing?* I mouth to him, and he just holds up his hand with a wink.

"Hi, Mrs. Brown." His voice is calm and collected.

"Bradley? Is that you?" She sounds surprised.

"Yes, ma'am. Hope you're doing well." He smirks at me, clearly enjoying this.

"What are you doing with my Meli?" she asks, and I slump in defeat.

"She wanted chicken parmi, so I took her to get some," he says smoothly.

"Oh, how sweet. Is Liv there, too?" she asks, and I snatch the phone back.

"Uh, yeah, she's just in the bathroom," I lie quickly.

"You're such a good big brother," Mum says, and I can almost hear her smile.

"Mhm, yep," I mumble, trying to keep my cool. "How did you know it was Bradley?"

"He's the only one who calls me Mrs. Brown. I've told him to call me Sophie a million times," she laughs.

"I'm just trying to be polite," Bradley says, leaning closer, his shoulder brushing mine. His breath is warm on my face, sending chills down my spine.

"Alright, Mum, gotta go. Talk soon. Bye!" I hang up quickly, my heart racing from the unexpected turn of events.

"Why did you do that?" I ask, half-exasperated, half-amused.

"What? I just said hi," he says, raising his hands in mock innocence.

I roll my eyes. "You know exactly what I mean."

He grins. "Just being polite."

"Polite? More like nosy," I tease, nudging him with my elbow.

He chuckles. "Okay, maybe a bit nosy."

"You tryna score brownie points with my mum?"

He laughs. "Nah, she already adores me."

I want to argue, but he's right. Mum's always liked Bradley, ever since we introduced the Mitchells to our family. She's always said he'd turn out to be a fine man. My skin tingles with heat, and I shift in my seat, the corners of my mouth twitching upward.

"So, Meli, huh?" he asks, smirking.

"It's just a nickname," I mumble, feeling shy. "My niece couldn't say Amelia when she was learning to talk, and it stuck."

"I like it. It's cute," he says, his tone low and teasing.

He starts the car, and we pull out of the parking lot. The drive is quiet, the tension between us palpable. I steal glances at him, his profile illuminated by the soft glow of the dashboard lights. I can't help but feel a pang of longing. It's so easy to be around him, to lose myself in his presence. I didn't ramble too much tonight, so that's a win.

Maybe he doesn't think I'm a complete mess after all. The song "Stick Season" by Noah Kahan plays on the radio, and I can't help but smile.

"Oo, I love this song," I say, moving to put the volume up a little louder. At the same time, he moves to do the same thing, and our hands brush. It sends a jolt through me, but not the usual spark of electricity.

"Fuck, your hands are freezing," he says, turning on the heating in the car. He grabs my hand and places it in his lap, trapping mine with his.

"You should have told me you were cold," he says so casually, holding my hand in his warm grasp. I sit there stunned for a moment, feeling the warmth of his hand seep into mine.

"I, uh, I didn't realise," I stammer, trying to regain my composure.

It's such a *simple* gesture, yet it ignites a whirlwind of emotions within me. My heartbeat quickens, my breath catching in my throat, but he remains focused on the road ahead, seemingly unaffected by the intimacy of our touch. I wonder if he feels it, too; this electric current that seems to crackle between us whenever we're close. I feel a sense of peace settle over me, a feeling of being right where I'm supposed to be. But all too soon, we arrive at my apartment, and he pulls into the driveway. He turns off the engine and looks at me, his gaze intense.

"Home sweet home," he says softly, his hand still holding mine.

Home.

I wonder what that would feel like with him. To come home to *him* every day, to share my life with him. The thought stirs something deep inside. Reluctantly, I withdraw my hand, feeling a sudden chill in its absence.

"Thank you for tonight," I murmur. "I had a really great time." His smile is genuine, heart-stopping.

"I did, too," he replies softly. "We should... maybe do this again sometime."

I nod, unable to find the words to express what I'm feeling. After a few moments of silence, I reach for the door handle, whispering, "Thanks again."

Just as I start to exit, his voice stops me. "Wait."

Before I can speak, he leans in, his warm hand cradling my cheek, and places a quick, tentative kiss on my lips. It's not as passionate as earlier, but it's sweet and leaves me smiling. When we pull apart, I'm left breathless, my heart racing in the most pleasant way.

He leans back, his eyes locked on mine, and a small, satisfied smile plays on his lips.

"Goodnight, *Meli*," he whispers.

"Goodnight, Brad."

I step out of the car, my legs feeling like jelly, as I watch him drive off—the memory of his kiss lingering on my lips.

25

Bradley

I sit at my desk, surrounded by the usual chaos of the station. Despite the hustle and bustle, I can't help but be amused by the banter between Daniels and Reynolds. Daniels' cocky attitude always sparks a response from Reynolds, and their exchanges are a welcome distraction from the grim realities of our job.

There are good days, of course, but when things go south, they go south fast. In my years as a senior constable, I've seen things that would make your blood run cold. From domestic disputes spiralling out of control, to the aftermath of violent crimes, the job exposes you to the darkest sides of human nature. There was this one time, a grisly scene at a remote farm, and another incident involving a drug bust that turned violent. But it's not just the violence; it's the raw emotion, the despair in people's eyes, that stays with you.

You have to be tough to make it in this profession.

I've never had to take a life in the line of duty, and I'm grateful for that. But there have been moments when the thought crossed my mind. I pray I'm never put in a position where I have to make that choice.

Amidst these thoughts, Daniels is currently boasting about his ability to charm anyone, while Reynolds remains sceptical. Stokes, always eager for entertainment, prods Daniels to demonstrate, much to Reynolds' reluctance.

"You're going to make me do this, in a room full of men?" Daniels protests, his scepticism evident.

Reynolds responds with a smirk, "Oh, come on, big boy. Too shy now?"

"Fuck, no. You're lucky Faulkner isn't around," Daniels retorts before reluctantly agreeing. "Just go along with me, yeah? Pretend you're the woman." Reynolds frowns at the suggestion.

"What? Why the fuck am I the woman?"

"How else am I going to demonstrate? *You* asked for it," Daniels explains, and I can't help but shake my head at their antics.

Daniels moves closer, picking up a bottle of hand cream from Reynolds' desk to kick-start his gambit. Trust Reynolds to have hand cream on his desk. Ever since his wife said his hands are too rough, he's been using it any chance he can get.

Reynolds dismisses the idea and says, "Forget it. Don't worry," before turning to walk back around to his desk, but Daniels' words halt him before he can go further.

"Hey, the other day, I came across this word," he says, pretending to study the label. "And for the life of me, I just can't pronounce it. Is it Jo-jo-ba?" He exaggerates the 'J's' harshly.

"No. It's pronounced Ho-how-ba. The J is pronounced kinda like an H," Reynolds replies.

"Oh, wow. I didn't realise. What language is that?" Daniels feigns interest, moving closer to Reynolds.

"It's a Spanish term. Not many people actually know about it."

"Mhm," Daniels says, moving even closer to Reynolds and giving him a once-over. Well... this is playing out a lot differently than I thought it would. Is this his attempt at picking up a chick? If it is, then Reynolds is completely oblivious.

"You must have a good ear for languages, then," Daniels continues, nodding slowly, with a cocky smirk on his face. He looks like the biggest tool right now. In a room full of grown men.

"Nah, not really. My wife is—" Reynolds starts, but his voice trails off as he begins realising what's happening. Now, I can understand how this would play out differently if Reynolds were a female. I can see this working.

Stokes interrupts with a drawn-out wolf whistle, followed by Woody's unexpected compliment, "Fuck, I'm going to regret saying this, but that kinda... turned me on, a little."

The laughter that ensues, coupled with Woody's embarrassed blush, adds to the amusement of the scene, and I can't help but smirk behind my computer screen.

"All good, brother. I know I'm good," Daniels says with a wink.

"How did you even do that?" Reynolds asks, shock evident on his face.

"It's a talent, mate. Gets all the ladies," Daniels says, slapping his chest. "I'll teach you a few things."

I shake my head. Such a *cocky* prick.

"I'm married, you dickhead. I don't think I *need* it," Reynolds exclaims, and Daniels' eyes go wide.

"So fucking what? Just because you're married doesn't mean you can't keep your woman on her toes." And begrudgingly, I have to admit, the fucker has a point.

"Hey, you even got Bradley smiling," Stokes says, pointing at me.

"No way. Fuck off," Daniels interjects, looking over at me. I immediately wipe the smile off my face, trying to maintain a neutral expression.

"Did I make big ol' Bradley Bear smile?" Daniels says, attempting a baby voice that is more cringe than cute.

"Piss off, cunt," I reply, trying to sound annoyed, but failing as a chuckle escapes me.

Daniels grins triumphantly, clearly pleased with himself for breaking through my facade of indifference. Little do they know, it has nothing to do with them. Seeing Daniels spark up his pickup lines had me thinking of Amelia.

Reynolds adds in, "You know, I think I caught a smirk on his face earlier, too. Either Bradley is in a somewhat better mood today, or my eyes are deceiving me."

I roll my eyes. "It's the latter, trust me."

As much as I appreciate my mates' attempts to analyse my mood, they're missing the mark. The truth is, my improved spirits have everything to do with Amelia. Lately, thoughts of her have been a constant presence in my mind, her smile and laughter playing on a loop in my thoughts. I find myself looking forward to seeing her, as pathetic as that may seem.

It's a feeling I can't quite explain, but one thing's for sure—it has nothing to do with my mates.

I pull up outside my house and turn off the ignition, exhaling slowly. As I step inside, Liv is lounging on the couch, her AirPods in, lost in her own world. I drop my keys on the table by the door. The aroma of a chicken roast and vegetables wafts through the air, letting me know Mum is busy in the kitchen.

Fuck, if I thought I was hungry earlier, I'm starving now.

Dad sits at the dining table, meticulously cleaning his shotgun rifle with a microfibre rag—a routine that is both familiar and calming. I walk up to Mum and kiss her on the cheek. She startles, nearly dropping the wooden spoon she's holding.

"Jesus, Bradley. You gave me a bloody fright!" she exclaims.

"Sorry, Ma." She turns to look at the clock just above the window overlooking the side of our property.

"You're home early today."

"Yeah, got everything I needed done early. The big boss said I could clock off sooner." She shoots me a weird look.

"What?"

"Nothing. You're unusually chipper this arvo."

"Just hungry. Excited for dinner."

"Oh, well, you're just in time for tucker, then," she says with a smile, holding a mixing bowl in one arm while the other flips chicken pieces on a pan.

"Mhm." I walk past Mum and head over to where Liv is lounging on the couch. She spots me before I can scare her, but I still manage to ruffle the top of her hair and flick out one of her AirPods.

"Get up and help your mother," I mutter with a stern look.

She gives me a look that clearly says, *Sure thing, bud,* but my tone is serious, not teasing. I shoot her a glare, still standing over her, and she lets out a dramatic sigh.

"Fine."

"Good idea," I say, this time *with* a teasing edge.

She gets up, walks into the kitchen, and grabs an apron from the rack. My eyes meet Mum's, and she winks at me, mouthing, *thank you.* I nod in approval, feeling a small sense of accomplishment. I head to the steps, calling out to Dad.

"Xav gone home?"

"Ye. 'Bout fifteen minutes ago."

Slight disappointment kicks in. For once, I'd actually been looking forward to seeing my brother this arvo. Lately, my mind's been all over the place. One minute, I'm fine, and the next, I'm worried about everything. Seeing Xav would've been a good distraction, a way to break free from my own thoughts for a while. But he's gone, and I'm left with my restless mind.

What if I mess things up with Amelia? She's young, with her

whole life ahead of her. She might want to travel, chase her dreams, while I'm stuck here—duty-bound, living the same routine. I can't stop thinking about dinner the other night. How fucking natural it felt being around her, how easy it was to open up. And that's not even half of what I want to tell her. Fuck, there's so much more I want to share. But then the worry kicks in.

I'll just drag her down. She's Liv's best friend, for fuck's sake.

These thoughts, these doubts—they're just excuses, masking deeper fears. I need to face this head-on, sort out my shit, and figure out if I'm willing to risk it all for a chance with her.

But, fuck. I'm so tired of these endless questions. I'm sick of the doubts that keep screwing with my head. Just a few minutes ago, everything felt fine. Now, my mind's gone and fucked it all up. I'm pissed at myself for letting this spiral out of control.

Welcome to my brain.

I need a distraction. With a frustrated sigh, I grab my phone and hit Xavier's number.

The scent of sweat and metal fills the air as I step into the town's local gym, Xavier by my side. After I rang him up, I asked if he'd be down for a sparring match. Xav never turns down the opportunity for a brawl—and let's be real, I'm better at sparring than he is. Where else would he have learned how to fight? We're taught basic self-defence at the academy, and from there, I taught myself more advanced manoeuvres so I'd be prepared at all times. As Xavier and I circle each other in the ring, the scent of leather fills the air. Our gloves connect with a satisfying thud as we trade punches, each movement calculated and precise.

"You're getting slow in your old age, Xav," I tease, ducking under a swing and landing a jab to his ribs.

"'*Old age*,' this cunt. I'm a year older than you—relax."

We circle each other again, my muscles tense and ready. The gym's fluorescent lights cast a harsh glow over us, highlighting every drop of sweat and every flex of our muscles. I throw a feint, trying to catch Xav off guard, but he reads it and counters with a swift right hook. I block just in time, feeling the impact reverberate up my arm.

"Nice try," he says, a smirk playing on his lips.

I don't respond, focusing on my footwork. Shifting my weight, I look for an opening. Xavier's quick, but I've got experience on my side. I fake a left hook and then drive a right jab into his side, making him stagger slightly.

"Lucky shot," he mutters, regaining his balance.

"Keep telling yourself that," I reply, my breath steady.

"So, what prompted today's session?" Xav asks, moving in a circle, hands up.

"Nothing," I grunt out, throwing a quick jab. "Does something need to prompt it?" Xav gives me a look, not buying it. He sidesteps and counters with a left hook that I block just in time.

"What, can a guy not spar with his brother just because? Fuck me," I mutter, dodging his next punch.

"No thanks. And no. Especially not if it's you," Xav retorts, his eyes narrowing as he throws another punch.

"What's that supposed to mean?" I grunt, feeling the sting of his hit on my shoulder.

"It means," Xav says, circling me, "you've got something on your mind. You always do when you call for an impromptu session."

I dodge his next punch and land a solid hit on his ribs, making him stagger. "Maybe I just wanted to kick your ass today," I say, a smirk tugging at my lips. Xav recovers quickly, his expression serious.

"Yeah, right. Spill it, Brad. What's really going on?"

I sigh, throwing another punch. "Just... stuff. You know how it is."

Xav blocks my punch and lands a quick jab to my side. "Yeah, I know. But it's better to talk about it than let it eat you up."

"I don't want to talk about it." Regret tugs at me for asking him to come.

"But you need to. You can't keep shit bottled up. Something's bothering you."

"Just need to let off some steam. Shut up now," I say through gritted teeth.

I throw another series of jabs, putting more force behind each one. Xav doesn't move quick enough, and I land one on his chin, but he recovers fast, grabbing me around the midsection and shoving me to the ground with an oof. He pins me down with his elbow, all up in my personal space, feeling like dead weight on me. The restrictive hold makes my blood boil, and I'm seconds away from kicking him in the balls if he doesn't get the fuck off me.

"Nah, I know you better than that, bro," Xav says, his face too close for comfort.

"Get. The. Fuck. Off. Me." My annoyance reaches a peak. With a grunt, I shove him off me with all my strength, and he falls to the floor beside me.

We both lie on the rubber mats, breathing heavily. The ceiling lights above us seem blindingly bright in the silence that follows. Xav breaks the silence first.

"So, is this about work?"

"No." I let out a frustrated sigh.

"Dad again?" he tries, turning his head to look at me.

"No," I mutter again, staring at the ceiling.

"Well, fuck. Give me something, mate," Xav sighs, exasperated. "Does this have anything to do with a girl?" I stay silent, my fists still clenched at my sides.

"Ah. I see," he says, a knowing tone in his voice.

"I don't know, okay? I don't know what the fuck is wrong with me." The words spill out before I can stop them.

Xav turns onto his side, propping himself up on one elbow to look at me better. "This is about Amelia, isn't it?"

I look at him in disbelief. "What? No," I say quickly. Then I pause, feeling the weight of the words I'm about to say. "Wait. How do you *know?*"

Xav snorts. "This all sounds way too familiar. Like déjà vu or some shit."

I frown, turning my head to look at him. "How?"

"Mate, you're acting just like I did when I first met Isla—confused, conflicted, scared shitless of messing it up," Xav says with a smirk.

"I don't know what it is," I sigh. "All I know is its confusing as fuck."

Xav chuckles. "Yeah, love'll do that to ya."

"This isn't love," I protest.

"Yeah, maybe not yet." He shakes his head. "Look, whatever it is, I think you're overthinking it, mate. If you like Amelia, then go for it."

I shake my head, frustration creeping in. "I shouldn't, though. She's Liv's best friend."

"So fucking what? She'll get over it," Xav exclaims with a frown.

"It's not that simple," I argue.

"Brad, listen to me," Xav says, his tone serious. "If this is a chance at actually finding someone special, don't let your misguided sense of duty stop you. You'll regret it. You don't get many shots at something real. And besides, Liv will understand." He stops, pondering his words. "Eventually... somehow."

I scoff a laugh. "Gee, thanks."

Xav shrugs. "Eh, how bad can it be?" There's only one way to find out, I guess.

"Look, I'm not one to talk," he continues. "But I think you're making it more complicated than it needs to be. Just trust your gut."

How can I trust my gut when it's all mixed signals? My mind's a mess, constantly flipping between yes and no. We sit there on the mats, silence hanging between us.

"So... Amelia, eh?" Xav shakes his head with a smile. "You know. I saw it coming. She's cute, in her own quirky way. Can't blame you. She's got this whole shy, good-girl-next-door kinda vibe," he says, and I shoot him a glare, picking up my glove.

"You gonna keep going, wanker? Or do I need to shut you up?" I warn.

He starts laughing, raising his hands in surrender. "Relax, shittt." As I turn away, I hear him mutter, "Yeah, not in love, my ass," and I'm on my feet in seconds, gloves ready. He scurries away, still laughing.

"Dick," I mutter to myself, unable to stop the smirk spreading across my face.

26

Amelia

I wake up feeling like complete dog poop. The light seeps through the blinds, only adding to my nausea, and the room spins as I try to sit up. I groan and reach for my phone to call in sick for work, resigned to the fact that I'll be stuck at home for God knows how long. My sister is supposed to visit on Friday, and it's *only* Tuesday!

I've vomited twice already, dreading the thought of having to go to the toilet. So far, I've avoided that particular joy. I check my phone to find a text from Liv, the usual each morning.

> **Liv:** Good morning, boo. Coffee?

Every morning for the past few weeks, Liv and I have been meeting at Tracy's Coffee Stop for a quick coffee fix before work. I swallow down a nauseous bubble and reply.

> **Me:** Currently dying in bed.

> **Me:** No coffee for me.

Liv reads my text but doesn't reply. Instead, she FaceTimes me *immediately*.

"What part of *currently dying* didn't you understand?" I struggle to mutter. My voice is hoarse from vomiting, and if I make any sudden movements, my bowels will contract. I can't even sip water, for heaven's sake, because even that will spur on a vomiting spree. I have to take small sips instead—I am so dehydrated, it's beyond a joke now. Liv's face pops up on the screen, concern etched in her features.

"Shittt, you look wrecked. Are you okay?"

"Thanks." I let out a weak chuckle.

"Seriously, what's wrong? You never get sick," she sighs, running a hand through her hair.

It's ironic, yes, that I work with kids and 'never' get sick. Just my luck now, though. But this doesn't feel like your average flu. No, this feels worse. It's got to be food poisoning. But from what? I recall what I had in the last couple of days, ruling it out to be the sushi from my lunch break yesterday. The school canteen is trialling out new menus for the kids, and I just so happened to have reluctantly tried the sushi. Now look where it's gotten me.

"I don't know, Liv. Food poisoning, maybe? I tried that sushi from the school canteen yesterday."

Her expression turns to one of horror. "Oh, God, that sounds terrible. Do you need anything? Should I come over?" Before I can respond, I hear someone talking in the background on her end of the call. Then a deep voice cuts through, making me shiver despite my nausea.

"Who are you on the phone with so early?"

Liv rolls her eyes and snaps back, "Mind your own business." She tries to move the phone away, but not before I catch a glimpse of Bradley, his hair damp, towel drying his hair.

"Is that Amelia?" he asks, sounding curious. My eyes go wide for a split second, and instinctively, I tilt the phone upward to keep my full face out of the frame. I'll be damned if I let Bradley see me looking like complete and utter dog poop.

Liv glares at her brother. "Yes."

Bradley's brow furrows. "What's wrong?"

I quickly clear my throat, trying to sound less pathetic. "I'm fine. Just a cold." I can see the frown etched on his handsome features. That man is always frowning. *Always.* He needs to smile more. And I've seen him smile; it's devastatingly adorable.

"You weren't saying that before," she insists. "Seriously, I don't have much planned. I'm here if you need anything."

"Thank you, Liv, but seriously, I'm fine," I say, and she sighs before looking back at the screen.

"Alright, alright. Just get some rest and text me if you need anything."

I'm not fine. No. Definitely not.

Whatever mentality I had this morning? Gone. Out the window. It has now almost been a whole day, and I have gotten progressively worse. After I got off the phone from Liv, I fell back asleep and didn't wake up until lunchtime, to which I proceeded to vomit multiple times. What, you ask?

Nothing! Literally just stomach acid.

Disgusting.

I have always hated vomiting, and it's not like a bad case of emetophobia, just the whole feeling you get afterward. Scratchy throat, severe chest pains, and fatigue. The clock ticks away, and it's already four thirty in the afternoon. Earlier, I had the sense to call Mum for advice on how to shake off this sickness in record time. Her remedy? Hydration *and* soup. A big *yes* to soup! She offered to whip up her famous chicken broth soup and promised to swing by before five. Instantly, a wave of gratitude washed over me.

Bless her.

I'm draped over the couch, and yes, I say draped because that's exactly how I am. I can't lie down flat without feeling like I'll spew, and sitting up straight is just uncomfortable. So, here I am, stuck in this awkward in-between, half sitting, half lying down, with my blanket tucked up under my chin to help with the shivers. A glass of

Hydralyte sits within arm's reach on the coffee table, while the familiar banter of *Friends* provides a faint distraction from my misery. Suddenly, I hear a hard knock on my door.

I drag myself off the couch, blanket still wrapped around me, and shuffle slowly to the door. With a sigh, I reach out and twist the doorknob, not expecting much. But as I swing the door open, a gasp escapes me. Standing there, on my doorstep, is not my mother.

No. It's *Bradley*.

I stand there in shock, staring at Bradley as he holds out a plastic bag and a large Tupperware container filled with a brownish liquid. Is that my mum's soup? I blink, trying to process the sight.

"Hi, sunshine," he says, leaning against the door frame. His hulking frame fills the entire space. Holy crap. "You gonna let me in, or?" His words trail off with a smirk, snapping me out of my stupor. I quickly close my gaping mouth. Is it... rude if I *politely* decline? Can I even do that?

My mind races as I internally panic. I mean, look at me. I'm a mess—baggy pyjamas, hair a ratty nest, skin as pale as a ghost. The last person I ever wanted to see me like this is Bradley, and yet, here he is, gracing my doorstep, with all his ruggedness and muscles. He's dressed in dark blue cargo pants, Stanley boots, and a black t-shirt. He must've come straight from work. I blink a few more times, hoping maybe he'll disappear if I blink hard enough.

Nope. He's still here.

Looking as real and as handsome as ever.

27

Bradley

"Uh, what... what are you doing here? Where's my mum?" Amelia asks weakly, her voice barely above a whisper.

"I ran into her at the supermarket. She told me she was coming by to bring you soup, so... I offered to bring it for her instead. You know, since it's on the way home and all," I explain.

"Oh. That's... that was nice of you. Thanks, Brad," she says, her cheeks flushing as she tries to hide her face. She wraps the blanket around herself tighter, and it's only then that I notice her appearance. Normally, I'd find this amusing, but right now, I'm more concerned. She looks really sick. She's in her pyjamas, her skin so pale. I've never seen her like this before. She's always so vibrant and full of life. Seeing her like this, so vulnerable, it tugs at something inside me.

"Are you gonna let me in, or are you planning on standing there all day?" I repeat my question, trying to lighten the mood. She gives me a weak smile and steps aside, allowing me to enter.

As I step inside, I can't help but notice the slight mess in her apartment. Amelia quickly starts apologising, her words tumbling out in a rush.

"I'm so sorry about the mess. I haven't had the energy to clean, and everything's just—"

I manage a small smirk, cutting her off. "Amelia, don't apologise. Please. It's fine." I glance around, taking in the surroundings. "Have you seen Liv's room when she's in a state of panic? Absolute brothel. This," I say, fanning my hand out, "this is nothing."

Amelia's features soften for a moment. "Okay."

Is there ever a moment where the mention of my sister is not brought up? As much as I love my sister, the thought of her lingering in my mind, whilst being around Amelia, isn't exactly what I want to be picturing or thinking about right now. I clear my throat, moving to place the plastic bags on her small kitchen counter.

"Your mum insisted I bring her *famous chicken soup*," I say, smiling as Amelia laughs softly. "And I grabbed a few things from the shops. She mentioned something about food poisoning."

I start pulling out the items and placing them on the counter: a tissue box, Panadol, GastroStop, and some Hydralyte ice blocks. As I set down the last item, I turn to see Amelia standing there, a look of surprise on her face.

"What?" I ask.

She looks so innocent, with those doll eyes of hers piercing into mine. Damn, she has the prettiest eyes. Girls always used to fawn over mine, Xavier included, yet there's a sense of warm comfort emanating from her brown eyes. I've said it before, but every single time, it hits me anew.

It's strange. When we're together, it feels like there's a deep connection, one that has always been there. But when we're apart, it's as if we're strangers.

"Thank you," she says, her eyes glinting in the light. Is she... crying?

"Are you crying? What's wrong?" I ask, moving to her in two strides, my eyes searching hers for any sign of distress.

"Nothing! Don't get too close. I might infect you!" she says, stepping back, and it makes me uneasy for some reason.

"Amelia, I couldn't give two fucks if you have a cold *or* food poisoning. Why are you upset?"

She shakes her head before laughing softly. "I don't... know. That was... that was so nice of you. To bring all these things."

I furrow my brow, caught off guard. "Well, I—" Shit, I don't even know what to say. It was just instinct to bring them; I wasn't thinking much when I did it.

"Thank you, Brad."

Fuck, I could kiss her right now. I like it when she calls me just *Brad*.

It's different when she calls me Brad. The only other person who does is my brother, and it doesn't evoke the same feeling. Amelia looks up at me, her eyes still shimmering.

"Would you like to stay for dinner? There's more than enough soup to share."

I hesitate for a moment, not because she's sick, but because... should I?

Take a chance. Be selfish. Do something for yourself.

"Sure," I say, finally deciding.

We just finished eating our soup, which was fucking phenomenal, if I say so myself. I'm not much of a cook, besides knowing the basics and how to throw a mean grill, but that was delicious. And I hate soup. Always have, since I was a kid. But sharing it with Amelia was nice.

We're nestled on her small two-seater couch. I've discarded my boots, which sit beside the couch, and we're both under the blanket—more so for her than me. It's not freezing outside, so that means she's probably fighting a temperature. I made sure she took a GastroStop, just in case. She hasn't chucked up since I came, which is a good thing, I guess.

Friends is playing on the TV, and Amelia's soft laugh fills the room occasionally. It's like music to my ears. This is nice. Comfortable.

Again with that word.

But it really is when I'm around her. I didn't have the best day at work today, yet instantly, the sight of Amelia has lifted my mood, even if it's just temporarily. My mind drifts back to work.

And what a fuck-around that was.

Dealing with a bunch of young men, armed, and with drugs in

their possession. We had a local anonymous tip-off about where this group had been hanging around, so Daniels, Reynolds, and I were sent off to handle it.

We cornered them in an alley, and things went south fast. One of the blokes pulled a gun, and suddenly, we were in a standoff. Daniels tried to talk them down, but it was like talking to a brick wall. Tensions escalated, and before we knew it, backup arrived just in time to defuse the situation. But not before a scuffle broke out. I copped a hit to the ribs—nothing serious, but enough to put me in a foul mood.

Daniels kept cracking jokes about it afterward, trying to lighten the mood, but I wasn't in the mood for laughing. All I could think about was how close we came to something worse. The memory of the barrel pointed at us, the tension so thick you could cut it with a knife; it all plays over and over in my mind. It's not just the physical hit that stings; it's the reality check that hits harder. Every time we have a close call, it wears on you. Makes you question why you're doing this, why you put yourself in these situations.

I frown at the thought. It's not just fear; it's the constant grind of knowing that one misstep, one wrong move, could change everything. It's the weight of responsibility, the knowledge that every decision you make could have life-or-death consequences. And sometimes, that weight feels unbearable. Daniels' jokes are his way of coping, but they fall flat with me. I can't shake the feeling of how fragile it all is, how quickly things can spiral out of control. It's a reminder that no matter how much we train, or how prepared we think we are, there's always an element of unpredictability that can turn everything on its head.

"What's wrong?" Her voice breaks me out of my thoughts.

"Huh?" I ask, confused.

"You're frowning," she says, concern in her eyes.

"It's nothing," I say, downplaying my rampant thoughts.

"Don't lie to me. What's bothering you?"

"Just had a rough day at work."

She watches me intently, not satisfied with my vague answer. "Could you elaborate, or is it confidential?"

I take a deep breath and inform her of the incident in the alley, detailing everything. She listens, her eyes wide, hand covering her mouth. Talking to her about it makes me feel something different. Safe, maybe. Cared for in a way I can't quite explain. Her presence is grounding, pulling me out of the dark places in my head.

After I finish, I sigh, running a hand down the back of my head. "It's just crazy, you know, if things had gone just a bit differently, one of us might not have walked away."

Amelia's eyes widen in concern. "Brad, that sounds terrifying. Are you okay?"

I smile at her. "Yeah, I'm all good."

"You seem tense, though. Want me to massage your shoulders?" I look at her, trying my best not to scoff in disbelief. She's literally fighting a bad case of food poisoning, has a temperature, and yet she's more concerned about me and wanting to give me a massage.

She's too selfless, too caring.

"I'm good. I promise." I give her a small, grateful smile, shaking my head. "Thank you, though."

Her words hang in the air, and I feel a warmth spread through me. The way she looks at me, with genuine concern and belief, it does something to me. Her hand finds mine, squeezing gently. "I'm glad you're okay."

"Yeah, me, too," I murmur, feeling the tension ease slightly. Talking to her makes it all seem less daunting. It's a strange feeling, one I'm not used to, but one I think I could get used to. She shifts a little, and I look over at her. Her cheeks are flushed.

"You good?" I ask softly.

She nods, giving me a small smile. "Just feeling a bit tired. But this... this is nice."

"Yeah, it is," I agree, my voice barely above a whisper.

And it really is.

28

Amelia

We lapse into a comfortable silence, and I find myself basking in the unexpected intimacy of the moment. Yet, my thoughts are consumed with concern for Bradley. The challenges he faces at work only deepen my worry. While his work is his own, I find myself drawn to hearing about it. His strength, both physical and mental, is truly admirable. In fact, it's more than that—it's compellingly attractive. My attraction to him is undeniable, almost overwhelming in its intensity.

Despite these thoughts, that same feeling from earlier hits me like a ton of bricks. The impending dread, and a bubble forms in my throat. I swallow hard, hoping the urge will pass.

Oh, no. God, please not *now*. But no matter how hard I try to push this feeling down, a new wave of nausea creeps up my oesophagus. Bradley seems to notice almost immediately.

"What's wrong?" he asks quickly.

I can't even respond. I leap up and dash to the bathroom, barely making it before flipping open the toilet lid and letting out the most unladylike noise as I empty the contents of my stomach, including my mum's soup. Tears start welling up from the pressure, and I feel utterly miserable. Bradley's presence looms behind me, and mortification washes over me.

"No, Brad," I say, holding up a hand to stop him, before hunching over the toilet again, spewing out more liquid. I could cry from the embarrassment of it all. "Brad—" I choke out between heaves. "Please, get out."

"No, Amelia," he says firmly, kneeling behind me.

"What are you doing?" I manage to gasp out, utterly bewildered.

"What does it look like? I'm taking care of you," he replies. And at that, my heart does somersaults.

"You don't need to take care of me." I protest weakly.

He replies quickly, without batting an eyelid. "I know, but I'm here, so you don't need to." I can't help but think that *this* is Bradley in the *flesh*.

Enthusiastic and bubbly? Rarely. Protective *and* caring? *Always*.

He is so selfless, always willing to help others in need. In a way, I see a bit of myself in those traits—always ready to lend a helping hand, always willing to nurture someone else. I take a few deep breaths, but the heat intensifies. I feel like I'm burning up. I try to take off my hoodie, but fail miserably. It gets stuck halfway over my head, squishing my face. I let out a frustrated laugh. This can't get any worse.

Bradley's hands are near mine, gripping my hoodie and pulling it off in one quick movement. The relief is immediate, but it's short-lived as he places the back of his hand on my forehead. His brows furrow, concern etched on his face. "You're burning up, Mills," he says, his voice soft yet worried.

Everything about his touch feels both intimate and not at the same time. Hearing him call me 'Mills' sends a flutter through my chest. Amanda's the only one who calls me that, so for him to pick up on it feels strangely personal.

"This is not a good look. I'm sorry," I mumble.

He holds my gaze, his expression serious. "What have I said about apologising?" I offer a half-hearted smile, but before I can respond, he continues, "And trust me, you could make anything look good."

Well, flip me sideways. His words make my heart skip a beat. I look away, feeling shy under his steady gaze. The room seems to shrink around us. Despite literally spewing my guts out, my body still knows how to react to his touch and his words. I shiver slightly, not from cold, but from the sensation of his hand on my skin and the warmth of his presence.

Another wave of nausea hits me, and I grip the toilet, feeling disgusted with myself. Bradley quickly grabs my hair with both hands, sweeping it away from my face and holding it at the nape of my neck. My mind starts wandering—imagining his hands running through my hair in a more sensual way, his touch sending shivers down my spine for a completely different reason. The contrast between the reality of this moment and the fantasy playing out in my head is jarring.

If there was ever a time to feel even more embarrassed, it would be right about now. Yet, oddly enough, I don't feel so embarrassed anymore. No, what I'm feeling is far more intense. I feel his strong palm at my back, rubbing soothing circles, attempting to calm me.

Wiping at my face with my hands, I flush the toilet quickly—locking eyes with the most incredibly caring man, who just held my hair and rubbed circles on my back while I most likely look absolutely horrid. He's watching me, his gentle movements still ongoing, his eyes softening. I can feel mine starting to well up. *Why?* I haven't got a clue.

"It's okay, Mills. I'm here," he says, his voice smooth, deep, and... sexy. "I've got you." Sexy? Yeah, at this moment, it's most definitely not supposed to feel that way, but it does.

I'm here.

I've got you.

Such simple words, yet they ignite a kaleidoscope of butterflies inside.

"You should shower. It'll make you feel better," he suggests, leaning casually against the door frame, his arms crossed and biceps straining through his t-shirt.

"Is that your subtle way of telling me I reek?" I tease, grinning playfully.

He chuckles softly, his eyes crinkling with amusement. "Well, I didn't want to be the one to say it..."

"Gee, thanks," I quip, rolling my eyes with mock indignation.

He raises an eyebrow, his smirk widening. "Hey, you said it, not me."

"Mhm," I reply with a playful nod. "Now, if you'll excuse me, I'll go rescue my reputation from the clutches of potential stinkiness."

"Take your time," he says, his voice low and teasing. "I'll be waiting inside."

As he turns away, I feel a rush of butterflies fluttering around in my stomach. I can't help but giggle at myself inwardly.

29

Amelia

Finally recovering from a bad case of food poisoning, I've sworn off sushi for good.

On top of that, my period decided to make an appearance later that night when Bradley came over, which explains all the heightened emotions. It hadn't occurred to me in the moment, when I was tearing up at little things, but now it all makes sense. Although, calling Bradley coming over to look after me a 'little' thing, is a stretch. It was *everything*.

Liv had called and sent some texts to check in, and it's safe to say that we have now resumed our early morning coffee runs.

After a long, stressful Thursday wrangling kindergarteners, I retreat to my study, seeking solace in painting. Today has been one of those days—kids testing my patience to the max. But now, brushes in hand and my palette of oil colours at the ready, I can finally release all that pent-up frustration.

I mix the oil colours carefully, each stroke a deliberate expression of my feelings. As I apply the paint to the canvas, my mind wanders to my quest for exhibition opportunities. Local galleries don't quite match what I envisioned. Then my sister suggested Sydney's art scene. A few applications later, I was accepted to showcase my series at a well-known gallery there. It's thrilling, but also adds a new kind of pressure. For now, though, painting lets me lose myself in the colours and shapes, finding peace in creating. Oil paints are great—they practically blend themselves. Their slow-drying, creamy consistency makes blending a breeze. I manipulate the colours on the canvas, effortlessly creating smooth transitions and soft gradients.

Beside the canvas, clipped to the edge, is a candid photo of Bradley. One I took without him noticing. That night at dinner, walking to his car, I sneaked my phone out and discreetly snapped a picture before he could catch on. There's something about capturing the moment that feels more intimate than posed pictures. In this painting, he's turned away, his strong jawline and furrowed brows giving away his deep thoughts. Bradley in all his grumpy glory. I chuckle to myself, thinking of how he'd react if he knew I'd painted him like this. My phone buzzes on the table beside me, and I see Kat's name flashing. Without missing a beat, I answer the call, tucking my brush behind my ear. She's supposed to land around six fifteen-ish, she'd said.

It's only five twenty-eight now. I swipe to answer the FaceTime call, wondering why she'd be calling right now, and her face fills the screen, with our parents peeking in the background.

"Surprise!" Kat exclaims.

"Oh, my goodness. Are you here already?" I squeal, excitement bubbling up.

"Yep! Early flight," Kat says, grinning from ear to ear.

"Hi, sweetheart!" Mum's voice chimes in from behind.

"Hey, Mum. This is amazing, Kat," I say, feeling my heart swell with happiness. "How was the flight?"

"Pretty smooth, actually. We landed early, so we thought we'd surprise you."

Seeing Kat feels like it's been ages, but it's only been a few months. The last time I saw her was last Christmas. It's April now—four months. Four months too long. Sometimes, I just really need my big sister. Dad leans into the frame, waving.

"We figured you could use a little surprise after a long day," he says with a grin.

"You have no idea how perfect this timing is. I've missed you all so much."

"We've missed you, too," Kat says warmly.

"Where's Millie?" I ask, noticing her absence.

"She's out cold, on the couch with John," Kat replies with a soft chuckle.

"Poor thing," I say, my heart melting a little.

"Well, are you coming over or what? We have so much to catch up on," my sister retorts with a smirk. I laugh, pulling the paintbrush from behind my ear.

"What ya painting, kiddo?" Dad asks, peering over Kat's shoulder. I playfully roll my eyes at him. He knows I hate being called kiddo, but I'll always be his baby girl. "Something new," I reply, keeping it vague.

"Well, show us," he urges.

"Not yet," I say, blushing. "They're not ready."

I know I won't be showing anyone these works until I submit them to the gallery. And definitely not Dad. No way he's seeing the portrait I'm painting of Bradley.

"Okay, dokey," Dad says, raising his hands in mock surrender. "We'll wait."

"See you soon!" I say, ending the call with a smile.

"I'm sorry, excuse me!" Kat says, swallowing down her sip of wine. "You're telling me you've *kissed* Bradley, and I'm only just hearing about this now?" She shakes her head. "Poor form, sis. Not good."

I laugh and smack her on the arm. "Oh, shush. It's been such a busy month, between work, going away, and recently getting hit with friggin' food poisoning. I haven't had much time to do anything, really. Not even paint. I haven't been coming past home much, either."

My expression sours. I miss hanging out with my parents. Living away from them is *hard*. You easily forget to do all the things that used to be routine, normal. It's so easy to get caught up in everything, until suddenly you're realising things too little, too late. The thought upsets me. My parents aren't getting any younger.

"It's okay. Mum and Dad understand," Kat says, patting my knee. "They just want you happy, healthy, and safe. And preferably married by now with kids."

I gasp, widening my eyes before laughing. "Yeah, right. By the time that happens, everyone will be *old*."

"Don't say that! I think it may be closer on the horizon than you think."

"Pft. Okay, Kat."

"So, when am I going to see Bradley, properly, in the flesh?"

I blush again. "Uh, I don't know. It's not like we're dating or anything. I can't just invite him over."

"Why the fuck not?" I laugh at her cursing. If Mum heard her right now, she'd cop a smacking. Twelve or thirty-three—it doesn't make a difference to our mother. Swearing has always been a no-go for us since we were young. I've grown up learning every variation under the sun of swear words that aren't 'technically' swear words. But I'll be honest, it's exhausting trying to think of them.

"I don't know. Things are weird. We're tiptoeing around this newfound friendship, when neither of us has said anything."

"So say something. *Do* something. You can't stay a virgin forever. You're missing out, sis. I promise you."

"Thanks, that makes me feel better."

"Sorry." She laughs half-heartedly. "I didn't mean to make you feel worse. I'm just saying. Stop wasting time. Bite the bullet and go for it. *He* has initiated the kisses. Maybe he's waiting for you to do the same." I didn't think of it like that. She might be right. "Does he know you're a virgin?"

"Uh... not sure. I've never outright said it."

"Okay, one step at a time."

One step at a time.

It seems like I've been doing that my whole life. Tiptoeing around Bradley, my best friend's older brother, since I can remember. Harbouring this crush. Ugh. I am tired.

"Yeah. I guess."

Her eyes light up. "Oh, I can't wait to show you so many tips and tricks. I've learned a lot over the years, but John and I have found our sweet spots."

Oh, nice. Now I'm picturing my sister and her husband... you know. That's not a sight I wanted to see. Just then, Mum comes outside, interrupting my thoughts.

"We're gonna have a BBQ tomorrow night. Dad's gonna head to the butcher tomorrow morning to get some things."

"Oh, fun. John loves BBQing. He'd love to help."

This makes me think of Bradley. He'd told me he can throw a mean grill, and I can't help but think he'd fit in so well here. With us.

"Oh, Meli, darling, you should tell Bradley to come by. It'd be nice to see that boy."

"Oh—" My words trail off as I stutter.

"That's a great idea! I'd love to see your new *friend*, Meli." My sister nudges my knee with a wink.

"I don't think he'll be—"

Mum cuts off my words. "Great! It'll be a party of six."

"What about Liv? Can't leave her out," I say wearily because, well, she is my best friend, after all.

"Oh, she won't be home, love. She's babysitting a friend's kids in the evening." *What?* I frown.

"H-how do you know that?"

"I spoke with Grace this morning. I saw her in town."

"Since when do you two hang out?" I ask with a sceptical look.

"Well, lately we started our yoga sessions together, and I've been seeing her around more." I just nod slowly, and Mum retreats back inside.

"That woman is always one step ahead, I'm telling you," Kat says before sculling the rest of her wine. I have a sinking feeling in my stomach that my sister might be right again.

As I settle into bed, ready to sleep, my phone vibrates. My heart stops when I see Bradley's name on the screen.

Bradley: Hey

My heart races. He's texting me.

Me: Hi 😊

He replies almost instantly.

Bradley: How have you been feeling since Tuesday?

Me: Much better! Thank you again for everything! 😊

Bradley: Anytime, Mills :)

My cheeks flush with warmth. I should probably tell him about the BBQ now, shouldn't I?

Me: So, we're kinda having a small little BBQ at mine tomorrow arvo, you know, because Kat is here. Mum wanted me to ask if you'd like to join us?

Bradley: So your mum is asking?

Me: Uh, well, no.

Me: I am asking you.

Bradley: That's better. I'd like that.

Holy crap! That was surprisingly easy. Bradley is actually coming to my house! My dad will be there, and John. Oh, God. What if Dad starts noticing my *crush* on Bradley? He's always been good at reading between the lines, especially when it comes to me. And John, oh dear John, with his sly grins and knowing looks. He's definitely going to pick up on something. What if I start blushing like a tomato every time Bradley looks at me? What if I say something completely embarrassing or spill paint on myself?

Ugh, why did I agree to this?

Just breathe, Amelia.

> **Me:** My dad will be there...

> **Bradley:** I'd hope so.

> **Me:** And John... Kat's husband. The two of them together can be a bit much.

And they really can. My dad alone is intimidating, but when John is with him, they become overprotective of everything. And when they drink together, forget it. It's like trying to stop a runaway train.

> **Bradley:** Amelia, if that's your attempt at intimidating me to 'not come'...

> **Bradley:** It's not working, sweetheart.

Oh my. Okay, then.

> **Me:** Just a fair warning. 😊

> **Bradley:** Not needed. But your concern is cute.

A warm flush spreads across my cheeks as I read over his texts. I can't help but imagine his smirk as he typed those words. He always knows just how to tease me, and here I am, blushing like a schoolgirl caught passing notes in class.

> **Bradley:** Should I bring anything?

> **Me:** Just you. That's enough xx

> **Bradley:** xx

If my heart could leap out of my chest, beating rapidly, it would happen right about now.

30

Bradley

It's Saturday morning, about six fifteen, but it doesn't matter if it's a weekday or the damn weekend—I can never sleep in. Never have been able to. The morning air is crisp, biting at my skin as I step outside. The house was silent before I slipped out the back, seeking the familiar presence of my father. I head to the stable, the scent of hay and horse shit hitting me like a punch in the gut. *Fucking hell, it reeks.*

Inside, I find him, shuffling bits of hay on the ground. The horses in their stalls whinny and shuffle, sensing the movement. I walk over to Blue, reaching out to stroke his mane. I've never been much of an animal person, but I can see why Xavier took to these creatures so quickly. They're majestic, calming in a way I can't quite explain.

It's quiet without the dogs here all the time. Xav took them home with him, bringing them over every day when he's here. The barn feels different without their constant presence, but there's a certain peace in the stillness.

"Morning," I say, breaking the silence.

Dad looks up, a smile tugging at his lips. "Morning, son. Couldn't sleep?"

I shake my head. "You know me."

He just nods, a silent understanding passing between us. I've become like him in many ways, communicating through nods, grunts, and actions instead of words. In a way, I'm proud to be like my father. He raised my brother and me with our heads screwed on straight, leaving no room for fuck-ups.

It was his way of teaching us to be disciplined and reliable.

But part of it bothers me. Sometimes, I don't want to be so tightly wound. I want to feel free, have some fun. Xavier did, and look where it got him—married with a baby on the way. Sure, he was a bit of a dick along the way, but a carefree dick nonetheless.

Carefree. I crave that sometimes.

We fall into a comfortable silence, the only sounds being the soft rustle of hay and the occasional snort from the horses. Blue nudges my shoulder, and I can't help but smile.

Dad breaks the quiet. "Wanna go for a ride?"

"Me? Ride?" I say, pointing to myself, eyes wide.

"Yeah, mate. Come. I'll teach ya." Dad moves slowly to the horses. Age has slowed him down, and I can't help but worry about the day he won't be around. My thoughts drift to Isla, enduring so much on her own. Losing both parents—no child should face that. Pushing these sombre thoughts aside, I focus on helping Dad prepare the horses.

After we've stabled the horses, I can confidently declare that I'm never doing that again or volunteering to be a mounted police officer. Fuck that. My groin is aching, and I rub the tender parts of my inner thighs, letting out a groan. Dad chuckles, and I roll my eyes. How Xavier manages this 24/7, I've got no fucking clue. Just then, my phone rings, and my heart drops when I see the caller ID: *Faulkner*.

I answer after the first ring.

"Mitchell."

"Mitchell. I need you to get over to two-fifteen Koala Road. It's not good, mate, and I need my best men," Faulkner says urgently.

With no questions asked, I hurry back inside, grab my things, and go.

Dread eats its way through me as I do.

As I arrive at the scene, it's definitely not what I was expecting, so early in the morning.

The accident scene is a fucking mess, lights flashing and sirens blaring, casting a creepy glow over the wreckage. Two cars, a Toyota Hilux and a Holden Commodore, are all mangled up. The Hilux is smashed next to the Commodore, metal twisted and crumpled. Inside, a young guy and girl are trapped, metal crushing around them. From a glance, I have a sinking feeling that the woman is no longer breathing. The Commodore is scrunched in from the passenger side, and I head over with Faulkner beside me.

The elderly man inside looks disoriented, blood trickling from a gash on his forehead. Paramedics rush past us, their voices urgent as they assess the situation and attend to the injured.

"Clear the area!" one of the paramedics shouts, directing other officers to block off the road. I lean by the window of the Commodore.

"Sir, my name is Constable Mitchell. Can you hear me?" I ask, my voice firm and direct. The man looks at me with wide eyes, nodding slowly.

"Ye-yeah," he stammers, his voice trembling.

"Alright, champ. Don't move, paramedics are here," I reassure him, signalling for the paramedics to come over. Faulkner and I head to the other car where the young couple is. Paramedics are already there, assessing the scene. One of them checks the girl's pulse, but she just shakes her head. My heart sinks as I realise she's gone. I exchange a grim look with Faulkner before focusing on the young man. He's starting to come to, eyes bloodshot, pupils wide, words slurred. He's jittery, shaking like a leaf. Faulkner's nearby, radioing for backup and coordinating.

"Get him tested. And the old guy, too. Just to be sure," Faulkner orders, nodding toward the man in the car. I acknowledge him and call over Stokes, who's nearby.

A paramedic leans in, talking gently to the young man as he wakes up. "Sir, can you hear me? What's your name?"

The man blinks rapidly, his eyes darting around in confusion.

"Where... where'm I?" he slurs.

"You were in a car accident," the nurse explains calmly. "We're here to help you. My name is Jenny. Can you tell me your name?"

The man struggles to focus, eyes darting around. He starts to panic, movements erratic.

"Yeah, Mitchell?" Stokes interrupts, finally reaching me.

"Run some tests," I instruct. "Check for alcohol or other substances in his system. We need to know what we're dealing with here."

Just by the look of him—dilated pupils, shaking body, and track marks on his arms—I have a sinking feeling. This can't be good.

He looks to be under the influence of something, and it's only adding to the chaos of the situation.

Meanwhile, paramedics pry open the Hilux's doors and extract the woman, covering her with a sheet, shielding her. They move to the young man next, easing him out onto a stretcher. Stokes moves in, explaining the testing process.

I turn to the old man next. "What's your name, sir? Is there anyone we can call?"

"My name... is Hank Parkinson," he croaks out. "My wife, Lorelai—she's at home. I've got a daughter, Zoe, but she don't live round here no more. Please, call my wife." I nod, noting down the information, and move to make the call as the chaos of the scene continues around us.

Stokes returns with a grim expression. "Positive reading for drugs." I nod, acknowledging the information, and then turn to alert the paramedics. They quickly make arrangements to transport all victims to the hospital, with Faulkner and I accompanying them.

At the hospital, we wait outside the young man's room, our expressions reflecting the gravity of the situation. Faulkner leans against the wall, arms crossed, deep in thought.

"This is messed up, mate," Stokes comments, joining us. "Never a dull day in this job."

I nod, my gaze fixed on the closed door of the hospital room. "Yeah."

As I stand there, my mind replays the events that unfolded after the accident. Once they cleaned up the gash on his head and bandaged his broken arm, we informed the young man of his actions under the influence of drugs, driving recklessly, and endangering innocent people. Another series of tests were conducted to confirm drug use, and they came back positive, *again*. Now, the young man puts up a fit, trying to wriggle out of the handcuffs that hold him to the bed.

Faulkner steps in, his tone stern. "You're being charged with dangerous driving resulting in death, which is a criminal offence under the Crimes Act. You'll be taken back to the station to be processed. There'll be an upcoming court hearing, and a decision will be made on your bail, if granted," he continues, detailing the process.

Given the seriousness of this offence, it's unlikely he'll be receiving bail.

As Faulkner continues to speak, I zone out for a moment, fixating on the thought that a young woman lost her life today due to this bloke's negligence. An innocent elderly man was injured because of his recklessness. The weight of it all settles heavily on my shoulders, a stark reminder of the fragility of life and the devastating consequences of careless actions.

I give Stokes a nod, then head out, back to the station to sort through the damn paperwork and deal with the courts—leaving Faulkner to deal with the rest. The weight of the day settles hard on my shoulders as I make my way back. I get lost in the grind, minutes stretching into hours, til it's twenty passed five in the fucking afternoon. My heart sinks when I realise I was supposed to be at Amelia's by five, and I haven't had a damn minute to message or call her. I quickly pull out my phone to call Amelia, but it goes straight to voicemail. Fuck. I shoot her a text.

> **Me:** I am so sorry. Got caught up at work. I will be there soon.

> **Me:** I promise.

But there's no reply. I rush to finish up at work, making the necessary calls to Beaumont Creek jail before leaving the station right at five thirty. On my way, I stop at the local florist, picking out their largest bunch of white and pink lilies and grabbing a bottle of rosé.

Inside the shop, I notice a few odd looks from the locals. Some greet me, and one young woman even strikes up a conversation. I'm too preoccupied to figure out if she's just being polite or flirting, so

I move quickly. As I leave, it dawns on me why they were giving me those strange looks: I'm in my officer's uniform, carrying wine and a massive bouquet. Didn't think that through too well, did I? But honestly, I couldn't care less.

I pull up beside Amelia's Holden Barina. My heart pounds fiercely in my chest as I walk up to their door and knock. I can hear conversations and squeals from inside, likely from her niece. For the first time in what seems like forever, I'm fucking *nervous*.

When the door opens, my breath catches as I meet Amelia's gaze. Surprise flickers across her face, evident in the way her big brown eyes widen as she takes in my presence. She's dressed casually, in blue jeans, a green top, and a white apron, her hands instinctively wiping on the apron as she gazes at me.

"Hey, sunshine."

"Brad," she says, all breathy, the sound travelling straight down to my groin.

"I'm so sorry I'm late. I got called into work at the last minute."

"I-I can tell," she stutters, glancing down briefly before meeting my eyes again.

"I left you a text and a voicemail."

"Oh, God, did you? I-I haven't been on my phone. I'm so sorry. I-I just assumed you couldn't make it. Wait. You got *called* into *work*? Is everything okay? And you-you still came?"

Her barrage of questions hits me, and for a moment, annoyance prickles at the back of my mind. As if I'd ever blow her off. Not a fucking chance. It bothers me that she'd even think that.

She continues, her voice growing more frantic. "I didn't mean to seem so distant. I just thought—"

"Amelia. It's okay. Take a breath. Breathe."

She takes a deep breath, her chest rising and falling as she steadies herself. Her shoulders relax, and a bit of the tension in her eyes eases.

"Atta girl," I say once I see she's calmed down, a soft smile tugging at the corners of my mouth. I gently bring the bouquet of white and pink lilies from behind my back, holding them out to her. Her eyes widen further, and a smile breaks across her face.

"You got these for me?" she asks softly, her fingers brushing over the delicate petals.

"Yeah."

"Lilies are my favourite. How did you know?"

Because I saw them sitting on your bedside table that night I brought you home, I think. But instead I reply, "Just a guess."

Her smile deepens, and she leans in to press a kiss on my cheek. "Thank you, Brad. They're beautiful."

"I also brought this," I say, lifting the bottle of rosé. "I know you said *not* to bring anything, but I remember you enjoyed this on our dinner date."

Her eyes soften as she takes the bottle from me. "You remembered," she murmurs, a hint of surprise in her voice. I remember everything about *her*.

"I pay attention," I reply with a smirk.

Amelia steps closer, closing the gap between us. "You really are something, Bradley Mitchell."

I tuck a loose strand of hair behind her ear, my fingers lingering on her cheek. "Only for you, Mills."

She leans into my touch. "Thank you for coming, Brad. It means a lot."

"Always," I say quietly, my gaze locked with hers.

31

Amelia

I can feel unshed tears brimming at the corners of my eyes. God, I've been so emotional lately. And it's definitely not my period anymore. Just his presence here, it's overwhelming. In the best kind of way. The moment is interrupted when Millie comes barreling in between us, her excitement palpable.

"Meli, Meli. Who's dat?" Her innocent curiosity pulls me out of the emotional whirlwind.

"This is Bradley, Millie. He's a—" My words trail off.

"Hi, Millie. I'm a *very* good friend of your Auntie Meli," Bradley finishes for me, crouching down to Millie's level. She hides her face behind my leg, a shy reaction to his playful introduction.

Millie notices the flowers in my hand, and her face lights up. "Flowas, flowas!"

I bend down to hand her the bunch, almost the size of her. "Bradley bought them. Aren't they beautiful?"

Millie nods quickly. "Yes, yes!" I smile, my heart warming at the sight.

Bradley speaks up, "Millie, your Auntie Meli tells me all the time that you're a princess." His grin is infectious, and Millie's eyes light up with delight. "And do you know what princesses need?" Millie shakes her head.

"Flowers," he declares, and Millie's mouth goes wide before she hides her face behind the flowers.

Bradley winks at me, and butterflies erupt in my core. Who would have thought grumpy, brooding Bradley Mitchell would be such a natural around kids? It's a side of him I've never seen before, and it's *enchanting*.

Grumpy Bradley is sexy.

Playful, caring Bradley is downright captivating.

My ovaries are practically screaming for him.

Millie runs off, clutching the flowers, and I coax Bradley inside. Nerves wrack through my whole body; it feels like he's my boyfriend and I'm bringing him home for the first time. Hah. Boyfriend. What a concept. Yeah right.

Kat spots him first from inside the kitchen and rushes up to us, wiping her hands.

"Bradley! Welcome," she says, giving him a soft hug. He seems momentarily taken aback before putting one hand around her back and giving her a pat.

Mum is next. "Bradley, darling. It's so lovely to see you."

"Mrs. Brown. Sorry I'm late."

"Nuh uh, what have I said? Sophie, please," she urges him, before pulling him in for a hug, and he smiles. I can't help but smile, watching their embrace.

I hand the bottle of rosé to my mom. "Ma, this is from Bradley," I say.

She eyes Millie, standing beside me, still clutching the flowers like a vice. "And the flowers, I see. You didn't have to bring anything, dear. We're just glad you came, especially looking all fine in your uniform, too."

"Yeah." He huffs a laugh before running his hand down the back of his neck, causing his muscles to bulge through his shirt. "I got called in at the last minute and didn't have time to change."

"No worries at all, love. The boys are outside at the BBQ. Amelia, show him outside."

As we walk off, I catch Kat's gaze, her mouth wide open, fanning her face dramatically. I roll my eyes, trying my best to hide my now burning cheeks.

As we approach where Dad and John are chatting at the barbecue, a nervous bubble forms in my chest. I swallow hard, steadying myself before introducing Bradley.

"Dad, John, this is Bradley Mitchell," I say, trying to keep my voice steady.

John is the first to react, offering a friendly handshake. "Good to meet ya, mate."

Bradley takes his hand, giving a firm shake. "Good to meet you, too, John."

Dad's gaze lingers on Bradley for a moment, assessing him. I hold my breath, watching closely for their reactions.

"James," Dad finally says, extending his hand. Bradley shakes it firmly, maintaining eye contact. "Bradley Mitchell, ay? Dom's boy?"

"Yes, sir. Nice to meet you."

Dad nods in acknowledgment, a subtle smile forming on his lips. "Nice to meet you, too, son."

I exhale slowly, relieved that the initial meeting seems to be going well. Seeing Dad's approval lifts a weight off my shoulders. Bradley, true to form, remains calm and composed, not showing any signs of intimidation. The way he handles himself, standing tall and confident, makes me admire him even more. This is the first time I've brought someone home like this, and it feels significant. I'm amazed by how seamlessly Bradley fits into my world. I can't help but feel a surge of pride and affection.

John glances at Bradley's uniform. "Looking sharp there, Bradley."

Bradley smirks, a glint of amusement in his eyes. "Guess I took formal dress a little too seriously," he jokes, making John chuckle. Dad just watches, his expression unreadable.

"Well, you wear it well. It suits you," John says, clapping Bradley on the shoulder.

Bradley's smirk softens into a genuine smile. "Appreciate that."

Dad nods, his expression approving. "Takes dedication to be in your line of work. We respect that 'round here."

"Thank you, sir," Bradley replies with a nod.

Dad turns to me. "Amelia, why don't you head inside and help your mumma with the food?"

I falter for a moment. Welp, that's my cue to get outta here so the men can chat. I glance at Bradley, looking for any sign that he's okay with this. He meets my gaze and smirks, giving me a subtle nod to go ahead.

"Okey dokey," I say with an awkward wave before turning to head back inside. The kitchen is bustling with activity. Mum is at the counter, slicing vegetables, while Kat is mixing a salad. I join them, trying to steady my racing heart.

Mum looks up, nodding to the bouquet, now in a vase. "He got your favourite flowers," she comments, a knowing smile on her face. "Seems like someone takes a lot of notice. Lilies and rosé, hm."

I blush. "He's just being thoughtful."

Kat sidles up to me, her eyes twinkling with mischief. "Thoughtful, *sure*. He's quite the catch, isn't he?"

I nudge her playfully, trying to hide my embarrassment. "Stop it."

She laughs, giving me a wink. "Just saying, Amelia. He's a keeper."

Mum smiles warmly, her hands pausing in their work. "He seems like a good man, Amelia, and a good *friend*, at that," she adds, her tone suggesting she might have other thoughts about our *friendship*.

I help Kat finish preparing the salad, and as I do, I steal a glance out the window, watching Dad and Bradley chatting by the barbecue. A sense of warmth settles over me, grateful for Bradley's presence and the support of my family.

As the evening progresses, my mum calls out that dinner is ready. We all sit around the dinner table, Dad occupying the head, with Mum and Kat on either side. John sits beside Kat, keeping Millie entertained in her high chair. I find my place next to Mum, with Bradley seated to my left. Mum serves up the food, and we all dig in, the atmosphere relaxed and warm.

"So, Bradley," Dad starts, his tone casual yet probing, "how did you and Amelia become friends?" I freeze in my seat as Dad's question lands squarely on Bradley and me. His casual probing has the unsettling effect of making my heart race. Thankfully, Bradley steps in smoothly, his answer keeping things vague and safe.

"We've known each other for a while now," he says, his voice calm and measured. "Amelia is friends with my sister, Olivia."

Dad nods, his stoic expression unchanged. "Olivia, that's right. She couldn't make it tonight?"

My pulse quickens. Oh, God. "No, she's babysitting tonight, apparently," I manage to say, my voice betraying a hint of nervousness.

"Oh, is she?" Bradley's voice is quiet, with a touch of surprise.

"Apparently. That's what your mum told mine," I reply, hoping to keep the conversation from veering into uncomfortable territory.

Mum seizes the opportunity to inquire, "How's your family, dear? I heard your brother got married earlier this year. That's very exciting." I praise the Lord for the subject change.

"Yes, in February. They're now expecting their first child."

"Oh, how lovely!" Mum exclaims, her eyes sparkling. I notice Kat watching Bradley, a soft smile playing on her lips.

"And what about you? Marriage and kids on the cards for you, Bradley?" Dad asks, his curiosity plain.

Bradley's gaze flickers briefly to me before answering, "I'm taking things as they come, Mr. Brown. Focused on my career for now."

Dad nods, seeming satisfied with the response. "Good to hear. Career first, that's responsible."

I clear my throat, sensing the tension building. "Dad, that's a bit personal," I interject, my voice wavering. Dad looks at me with a frown, as if just realising he might have crossed a line. Underneath the table, Bradley places a discreet hand on my knee, a gesture that momentarily stops my heart.

"It's alright, Amelia," Bradley says softly, his voice reassuring. "Happy to answer."

The conversation shifts to lighter topics as we continue our meal, laughter and stories filling the air. I steal glances at Bradley, grateful for his presence and the way he effortlessly navigates my family dynamics. His hand remains on my knee, a silent reassurance that anchors me amidst the lively chatter.

As we start packing up our plates, the men retreat to the lounge, but Bradley lingers near me. Kat, Mum, and I gather in the kitchen to wash up, and Bradley, bless him, collects the remaining plates from the dining table. He places them on the counter, discarding the leftover food into the rubbish bin.

"Bradley, that's fine. I've got it," my sister insists, taking over.

"Bradley, love, why don't you go and join the boys inside?" Mum suggests.

"I will soon," he replies, locking eyes with me.

I offer him a smile in return. Millie bursts into the kitchen, grabbing Bradley's hand.

"Bwadey, Bwadey, come," she exclaims, tugging him toward the living room. Bradley chuckles and follows my little niece inside, leaving me alone with my thoughts and a sinking feeling in my stomach.

As Mum and Kat exchange knowing looks, I catch on to their silent communication.

"What?" I ask with unease.

Kat responds with a sheepish, "Nothing," before Mum cuts in.

"It's quite obvious, Meli."

"What's obvious?" I press, my confusion growing.

"It's *obvious* how smitten Bradley is with you, dear. And you, him." Her tone is laced with amusement and a hint of motherly knowingness.

"Yup! You light up whenever he's around. It's cute," Kat adds, a playful grin on her face.

My cheeks burn, and I can't help the small smile tugging at my lips. My heart flutters, caught between wanting to protest and secretly enjoying their teasing. The memory of Brad's comment from the other night flickers in my mind. *Sunshine.*

My skin tingles as if his words are a touch I can feel.

"Stop it, you guys," I mumble, trying to hide my growing smile. But the warmth in my chest is undeniable. A fuzzy sensation. We eventually finish washing up and join the rest in the lounge.

"Bwadey was showing me his horthies, Mummy. Can we get horthie?" Millie asks, bouncing in front of us. Her pronunciation is still adorable, and I know that nickname is going to stick for a while.

"I don't think so, munchkin. But you can have a toy horse," Kat replies.

"O-kay," Millie says with a little frown, her disappointment clear. She then comes up to me, tugging on my hand.

"Do ya know Bwadey is a bear? He is Bwadey Bear." Her pronunciation is endearing, and I can't help but smile at her.

I furrow my brows, smiling at her, then look over at Bradley, who just shrugs with a grin. His hair is slightly tousled, and he sits on the couch so casually. He's masculine, yet so warm and inviting. I feel myself falling for him, and I can't do anything to stop it.

"Bradley Bear?" I ask, intrigued.

"Yeah! When you hug'im, he feels like a bear," Millie explains, her explanation bringing laughter to the room.

John mutters, "She doesn't say that about me."

Kat smirks and quips, "That's because you're more like a grumpy old possum, John."

Everyone laughs some more, and Millie's little face lights up with joy as she joins in the laughter.

As the evening starts to wane, I feel the fatigue setting in, my eyes heavy and my yawns more frequent. I decide it's time to head home. Bradley seems to have the same idea because he stands up right away. "I should probably head off, too," he says, exchanging goodbyes.

Dad surprises me by stepping forward, offering his hand to Bradley. "It was good to have you here, Bradley. You're welcome back anytime."

My heart races at Dad's unexpected approval. Bradley shakes his hand firmly. "Thank you, sir. I appreciate that." At the sight of Dad's smirk, I can tell he's loving being called *sir*. He won't ever mention it, but his face gives him away.

Mum calls out, "Yes, dear! Please don't be a stranger."

Bradley smiles. "I won't. Thank you for a wonderful evening."

I say my goodbyes, hugging my sister goodnight, then lean down to plant a big, wet kiss on Millie's cheek. She turns to Bradley, her eyes wide with innocence, and asks for a hug. My heart melts at the sight. Kat's face lights up with a smile, and she sends me a knowing wink. Bradley doesn't hesitate to scoop Millie into his strong arms for a hug that nearly makes my heart burst.

"G'night, Bwadey Bear," Millie chirps happily.

"Night, princess," Bradley replies affectionately.

As Bradley walks me to my car, the evening air feels cooler, making me shiver slightly.

"Thanks again for having me over," he says, his voice warm.

I can't help but tease him. "Well, technically, it was Mum's idea."

His smirk is irresistible. "Oh, so *you didn't* want me to come?"

I roll my eyes, trying to hide my smile. "Of course I did. Don't get a big head."

"Hm, that's what I thought," he teases back, leaning in closer.

Before I can process what's happening, Bradley leans forward and kisses me softly. My eyes flutter closed, a contented sigh escaping my nose as his lips meet mine. His cologne surrounds me, intoxicating and comforting all at once, and I just want to sink into the moment.

When he pulls back, I blink up at him, feeling dazed. "What was that for?" I ask, trying to sound innocent.

"Just 'cause," he says, tucking a stray hair behind my ear. "Goodnight, Amelia."

Be still my heart.

"Goodnight, Bradley Bear," I say with a playful wink.

He rolls his eyes, but his smile gives him away. "You're never going to let that go, are you?"

"Nope," I reply, grinning mischievously. "Consider it payback for calling me Meli."

"Fair point," he chuckles softly. With that, he turns and heads toward his car. I watch him go, lingering for a moment before opening my car door. Just as I'm about to step inside, his voice stops me.

"Amelia."

I turn to face him. "Yeah?"

"Drive safe, okay?" His concern is evident in his voice. I furrow my brows for a moment, touched by his unexpected worry.

"Always," I assure him.

He nods, a small smile playing on his lips, and then he gets into his car and drives off into the night.

I lie in bed, snuggled up against my pillows, the soft glow of my bedside lamp creating a warm cocoon in my room. Sleep eludes me, my mind swirling with the events of tonight. Bradley meeting Dad, bonding effortlessly with my sister and sweet Millie—it's like something out of a movie.

The way Bradley interacted with Millie... It's heart-melting. He has this natural ease with kids that makes me imagine a future where he's a dad, whether it's with me or someone else. It's a thought that both excites and scares me in equal measure. I'm in this strange limbo of wanting to move forward, yet feeling hesitant to take that leap.

But maybe Kat's right; maybe it's time I stop overthinking and just go for it. I need to find the courage to make my feelings clear, even if it feels a bit daunting. Determined, I grab my phone and text him.

> **Me:** Hey. You up?

I know he's probably awake, but I want to check just in case he's exhausted after a big day—though I still have no idea what his day was like. His reply comes almost instantly.

> **Bradley:** I am. It's only 9:15...

I smile before replying.

> **Me:** I know that, Einstein. Just checking. I don't know your sleep routine.

> **Bradley:** It's nothing special.

> **Me:** Okey dokey. Well, I usually go to bed around 10-10:30 on a good night, and I'm up at 6:30.

> **Me:** Care to share yours?

> **Bradley:** Whenever I fall asleep, and always up before dawn.

> **Me:** Interesting.

I can work with that. I wonder if he has trouble sleeping at night. Does his mind keep him up, too? Feeling peckish for a snack, I decide to push my nerves aside and ask.

> **Me:** So, random thought. But I'm kind of in the mood for ice cream.

Those three little bubbles appear, and I stare at them. They disappear, and I frown, waiting for his reply. If he replies. Maybe he doesn't like ice cream. Maybe he wants to sleep.

> **Bradley:** It's almost 9:30. What could possibly be open?

My heart does a little flip. At least he's still replying.

> **Me:** There's a 24-hour convenience store not far from mine. Wanna join me for an ice cream run?

Those three dots appear and stay there before disappearing again. *Hm.* Minutes pass and no reply comes.

> **Me:** It's okay if you're not up for it.

I close my phone, trying not to be too discouraged. Padding into the kitchen to fill up my water bottle, a gentle vibration in my pocket sends a wave of butterflies fluttering in my stomach. I open the text message.

> **Bradley:** I never said no.

Hope surges through me. Suddenly, there's a soft knock on my door, and panic shoots through me. *Who on earth could that be?*

I hesitate, approaching the door cautiously, wishing I had a peephole. I slide the security chain off before opening it slowly, and my jaw drops.

Bradley stands there, filling the doorframe, looking absolutely adorable in black trackies and a matching hoodie, holding *two* pints of Ben and Jerry's ice cream.

Oh, my goodness.

I'll never tire of seeing him looking so laid back.

I'm speechless.

32

Amelia

"Hi," he says.

"Hi. How did you... When did you?" I stammer.

He huffs a laugh. "I'd left before you'd even mentioned the twenty-four-hour convenience store."

I stand there, feeling a mix of surprise and delight. How can he be so thoughtful? It's almost too good to be true. As he steps into my apartment and closes the door behind him, he towers over me in all his six-foot-something glory, holding out the two pints of ice cream.

"I didn't know what flavour you liked, so I got both," he says casually, shrugging as if it's no big deal. I try to contain my bubbling excitement.

He offers me the pints to choose from—vanilla or choc chip cookie dough. My mouth waters instinctively. I reach eagerly for the choc chip cookie dough flavour, my eyes lighting up with delight.

"This is my all-time favourite!" I exclaim, unable to hide my enthusiasm.

His eyes soften. "Mine, too."

I grab two spoons from a nearby drawer. "Wanna share, then?" I ask playfully, offering one to him. He nods with a small smile, accepting the spoon.

We settle on the couch together, the ice cream between us, and I can't help but steal glances at him when he's not looking. I notice how his smile flickers as Maverick's jet flies across the screen from Top Gun, a movie I've just discovered is one of his favourites. It feels intimate, and I'm hyper-aware of his presence beside me. Stealing glances at him, while engrossed in the film, I notice the subtle movements: how his Adam's apple bobs with each swallow, how his lips wrap around the spoon as he savours the ice cream. It's these small details that draw me in, and I can't deny it—he turns me on so much that I can literally feel my core pulsate, fluttering like it has a beat of its own and matching the rapid beat of my heart.

I shift, trying to ignore the way my body responds to his proximity, but it's impossible. The air between us crackles with tension.

I steal another glance at him, catching his eyes this time. Heat pools in my stomach, spreading through me like wildfire. I can't look away, and I don't want to. He sets his spoon aside and leans in closer.

"What are you thinking right now?" he asks, his voice husky with desire.

"I think you know," I reply, my breath catching in my throat.

"I want you to tell me."

"I want you," I admit, my voice barely above a whisper. "I want you to kiss me."

He hums softly at my words, then leans back against the couch, legs spread wide, his demeanour relaxed yet commanding. "Come here," he says, nodding toward his lap.

My heart races in my chest as I slowly straddle his thighs, feeling the firm bulge beneath his pants. Every subtle movement sends a delightful friction through me, awakening a sensation I never imagined.

I settle in his lap and instantly feel his bulge pressing into me. I bite my lip to suppress a moan. The tension between us is palpable, and I know that this moment will change everything.

"Do you still want to kiss me?"

"Yes," I reply, my voice a breathless whisper. I ache for his touch, for the connection of our lips, for the heat of his body against mine. I adjust over the bulge in his pants, and he tilts his head, his eyes locking onto mine as a low groan escapes him.

"Well, then, what are you waiting for?" he teases, his voice low and gravelly. It sends shivers down my spine, stirring my desire even more. Without hesitation, I lean in and press my lips to his. His mouth opens, tongue seeking entrance. I wrap my arms around his neck, pulling him closer to deepen the kiss, and my tongue swirls around his. His hands roam my body, up the sides, before moving down toward my arse, giving it a firm squeeze. I gasp at the sudden sensation of his hardness rubbing against me through my *thin* pyjama pants, so I'm feeling everything. *Everything.*

Every touch of his, every caress, builds the tension between us to an unbearable level, and I never want it to end. Without breaking our kiss, I guide his hand to the hem of my shirt. He doesn't hesitate, his fingers tracing the curve of my waist, his warm hand on my skin sending shivers of pleasure down my spine. I moan softly into his mouth. Being around him gives me a sense of *confidence* I've never felt before. Without another word, he gently lays me back on the couch, his body hovering over mine.

His hand travels further up my stomach, but stops before he can reach my breast. "Can I touch you?"

"Yes, please," I say in a breathy moan, my heart racing.

In quick movements, he's on me, fondling my breasts through my shirt, before sliding a rough palm underneath to touch one directly. "Oh, my," I manage to gasp out. I'm not wearing a bra, and my eyes widen at the feeling of that first contact. Realisation finally hits me; I am actually very inexperienced. I have no idea what I'm doing. What I'm *supposed* to be doing. Should I be touching him back? Insecurity roots itself in my stomach, and my breathing hitches. He brushes a strand of hair from my face and pauses, locking eyes with me.

"Hey," he says gently, withdrawing his hand. "We can stop. I didn't come here for this. I just… want you to know that."

"No, no," I blurt out, flustered. "God, no. Don't stop, please. It's just…" My words trail off, my breath hitching in my throat.

"Just what?"

"I don't really know what to do," I admit, feeling so vulnerable. The last thing I want is for Bradley to be turned off because I'm a twenty-four-year-old *virgin* who has never fondled with a guy before. His lips curve into a gentle smile.

"That's okay," he says softly. "Just relax and feel. Follow my lead."

I nod nervously, my heart racing. As he leans in again, his lips meet mine in a slow, deliberate kiss. It's different from before—less urgent, more exploratory. His tongue brushes against mine, and I tentatively respond, trying to match his rhythm.

God, he can kiss.

And his tongue... wow. He *really* knows how to use his tongue.

The thought of him using it elsewhere ignites the already roaring fire inside me. My skin feels like it's on fire. I'm ready to burst out of it any second, but I'm too lost in the moment to care. I squirm a little, squeezing my thighs together against his, which rests in between. His hands move back under my shirt, and he pauses, his eyes meeting mine. "Is this okay?"

"Yes," I breathe, my heart pounding in anticipation. "I trust you."

He continues to explore, his touch sending little tingles through me. "Tell me what you like, Amelia. I want to make you feel good."

I bite my lip, blushing a little. "I like everything you're doing."

"Good," he murmurs, his hands moving lower to grab hold of my thighs, placing them behind his back, so he's nestled in between me. My thighs grip him tightly as I urge him closer, my lips finding his. His hand slips back under my shirt and he pinches my nipple between his forefinger and thumb. A wet rush floods between my legs.

"Brad," I gasp, my fingers digging into his shoulders. "Oh, God..." I can feel his hard erection pressing into my stomach.

"You like that, Amelia?" he asks, his voice thick with lust. "You like me pinching your nipples?"

I flush at his crude question, but I nod quickly. "Yes."

I close my eyes, relishing in the feeling of being touched. Touched by a man. By *Bradley*.

In an instant, his warm breath hovers tantalisingly close over my left breast, and a soft gasp escapes my lips as he captures my nipple between his lips. His tongue swirls around the sensitive bud, sending a jolt of pleasure straight through me. My hips instinctively buck toward him, seeking more of that electrifying feeling.

"Oh... that feels... so good," I murmur breathlessly. Each flick of his tongue, each gentle suckle, builds a delicious tension that coils tighter within me.

A soft whimper escapes as Bradley moves to my other nipple, mirroring his actions with delicate precision—squeezing, swirling, and sucking. I can't help but squirm in his embrace, feeling overwhelmed by the sensation. With a *pop*, he releases my nipple, and I feel his lips trailing down my chest with slow, open-mouthed kisses.

My breath hitches as his tongue touches my navel, and a surge of nervous excitement floods through me as I realise where his kisses are leading—to the heated space between my thighs.

He pauses, his eyes meeting mine. "Have you—" he hesitates. "Have you orgasmed before?"

I shift uncomfortably, feeling my cheeks heat. "Uh, a few times, I think. Well, I've tried, but I'm not really sure what it's supposed to feel like."

His gaze softens, and he reaches out to touch my cheek gently. "Hey, no pressure," he reassures me, his voice calming. "We'll take it slow and figure out what feels good for you." Oh, God. *Orgasm?* In front of Bradley. What has my life come to?

"Can I pull these down?"

I swallow the nervous bubble in my throat. "Yes."

Bradley hooks his fingers into the waistband of my pants, and I hold my breath as he eases them down, exposing the delicate lace of my underwear to the cool air. It's not the chill that makes me shiver, but the intensity of his hungry gaze. With another gentle tug, he slides my underwear down, leaving me completely bare before him. His closeness is intoxicating as he leans in, placing soft, teasing kisses along the sensitive skin of my inner thighs. I tremble at his touch, anticipation coiling tight in my belly.

"Relax, sunshine," he murmurs, his voice husky with desire. "I'm going to make you feel so good."

I nod, unable to find my voice. His hand moves with purpose, brushing over my apex, and his thumb wastes no time finding my clit, circling it in tight, rhythmic motions. The sensation makes my back arch involuntarily.

"You're so responsive," he murmurs, his voice filled with admiration. "So perfect."

As Bradley continues to work his magic on my sensitive clit, he slowly slips a finger inside me. The sudden intrusion startles me, and a soft gasp slips from my lips, drawing his eyes up to meet mine.

The feeling is intense, a mix of pleasure and slight discomfort, but I push past it, craving more of his touch. I've touched myself before, but this is different—his touch is electrifying, filling me with a depth of sensation I've never known. The way he touches me, the way he looks at me, it's like he knows exactly what I need.

"Fuck. You're so fucking wet," he groans, his voice thick with need.

33

Bradley

I'm hit with her scent, intoxicating and heady. It's a mix of arousal and innocence that damn near drives me wild. Her pussy looks perfect, all pink and wet with her arousal. I keep rubbing Amelia's clit with my thumb, slipping another finger inside, and fuck me, she's tight.

There is no way I'd be able to slip inside her comfortably. If we go further, I'll have to stretch her out a bit. Not to toot my horn or anything. A soft gasp escapes her lips, drawing my eyes back to her face. She looks at me, her lips forming a perfect 'o', while she props herself up on her elbows to watch me work.

"Such a good girl," I murmur. "Taking my fingers so well." I gaze up at her, taking in how beautiful she looks at this moment. The fact that she trusts me overrides any concerned thought I had lingering in my mind. There's no turning back after this. I've crossed that line, fuck the boundaries and the voice in my head screaming *off limits*.

Right now, all I care about is pleasuring Amelia. I can't help but feel a surge of protectiveness toward her. The fact that she's allowing me to do something so intimate warms me to my core. I turn my palm so it's facing upward and curl my fingers inside her, feeling the soft, spongy part of her walls inside.

"Yes," she chokes out, tilting her hips up. "Goodness me, yes. Whatever you're doing, keep doing that."

I smirk. "Are you going to come for me if I do?"

"God, I hope so. Yes."

"Hm. That's my good girl." I move my fingers in and out faster, with deliberate care, not wanting to rush and hurt her, all the while rubbing her clit with my thumb. She's so close; I can feel her walls starting to contract.

Her soft moans fill the room, spurring me on as I maintain a steady pace with my fingers. Her breaths quicken, each one coming out in short, ragged bursts. I can feel her body tensing beneath me, and I know she's close. I lean forward, using my tongue to trace circles around her clit, *needing* to taste her.

She cries out, calling my name as her orgasm washes over her, "*Bradley.*"

I can't help but groan as she releases herself onto my fingers. She pants heavily, her chest rising and falling rapidly. After a few moments, I slowly remove my fingers and insert just my index finger back inside her. Her walls clench tightly around me, pulsating from the intensity of her orgasm. She watches me as I withdraw my finger, which glistens under the soft lighting. Without hesitation, I bring my fingers to my mouth and suck them clean, savouring the taste of her on my tongue. It's tangy *and* sweet, like a forbidden fruit that only makes me crave more.

She nervously traces her lips with her tongue before asking, "What does it taste like?"

I lean in closer, my breath warm against her ear. "Like fucking honey," I say, my voice low and husky. "It's warm and sweet." A blush instantly colours her cheeks.

She sits up, and I offer a hand to help her put on her underwear and pants. But as she looks down, her gaze lingers on the noticeable bulge in my pants, and my cheeks flush with heat.

"Do you want me to—" she starts to say, but I cut her off with a soft laugh.

"Don't worry about me, Mills. This was just for you," I reassure her with a gentle smile.

"But are you... sure?" she asks again, concern evident in her voice.

"Yes. It'll settle down in a moment," I say, pulling her flush against me to take her lips again. She leans in with a sigh, kissing me back softly. *If you keep kissing her like that, it won't, you idiot.*

I pull away reluctantly, and Amelia nestles herself at my side. I wrap my arms around her, holding her close as we both catch our breaths. The glow of the TV catches my attention for a moment, and the screen is lit up on Netflix, showing: *Are you still watching,* as well as the *Continue watching or go back* option.

I huff a laugh at the interruption, and Amelia catches on, giggling beside me. The sound is music to my ears, and I can't help but smile at how content she seems at this moment.

We linger there, soaking in each other's presence. Eventually, she lifts her gaze to mine, mischief dancing in her eyes. "So, does this mean... you know... we're a thing now?"

I smirk, placing a gentle kiss on her forehead. "I'd like that," I admit, feeling lighter than I have in ages. It's thrilling, the way we're navigating this connection between us—just going with the flow.

It feels... carefree.

In this moment, nothing else matters except the beautiful woman beside me.

"I'd like to do... you know... that again. Soon, maybe?" She pauses, her lips twisting as she considers, and I resist the urge to pinch her cheeks and kiss her senseless.

"Soon, definitely. One step at a time."

"One step at a time," she echoes.

She rests her head on my chest for a few more moments, not long before looking up at me again. "Hey, Bradley Bear?"

She's always so inquisitive. It's what I love about her. *Love?* Settle down there, mate.

I hum in response, a smirk playing on my lips as I look down at her. She hesitates, nerves flickering in her eyes.

"I kinda... like you."

My smirk widens into a grin. "Only kinda?" I tease.

She ducks her head, hiding her blush. "Maybe more."

"I like you too, sunshine," I murmur, brushing her hair back gently. And in that instant, wrapped up together, I realise this is just the beginning.

I hope.

34

Amelia

"Okay, Millie girl, now we add the flour," I say, holding the measuring cup out for her to pour into the bowl. Millie giggles, grabbing the cup and trying to pour it in. Some flour ends up on the counter and on her little apron, but she's having a blast.

"Good job! Now we mix it all up!"

Kat and John dropped her off about an hour ago for their much-needed 'date night.' The last time they had any real time to themselves was before Millie came along. So, when Kat asked if I'd like to watch Millie instead of Mum and Dad, I just couldn't pass it up. Now, here we are, attempting to bake cupcakes in my kitchen, with Disney songs playing in the background. "Be Our Guest" is currently filling my apartment with a lively, fun mood.

She eagerly starts stirring, but most of the flour ends up flying out of the bowl and onto the floor. We both burst into giggles, and I quickly grab another cup of flour to salvage our cupcakes. As I watch Millie mix the batter, my mind drifts back to last night, and I can't help but smile to myself, lost in the moment.

"Why ya smiling, Meli?" my niece asks, her eyes wide and curious.

I chuckle, feeling slightly embarrassed. Trust me to be caught out by my almost four-year-old niece. "Well, Millie, I'm just thinking about something that happened last night," I say, trying to keep it vague.

"What happen?" she presses, tilting her head to the side.

I smile at her innocence. "Oh, just something fun."

"Fun? Like baking?" she asks, her eyes lighting up.

"Sort of," I reply, unable to contain my smile.

Millie seems satisfied with my answer and returns to mixing the batter, singing along to the music. After a few more attempts, we finally manage to mix everything together properly. I scoop the batter into the cupcake tin while Millie watches, her eyes wide with excitement. Meanwhile, my mind wanders back to last night, recalling the warmth of Bradley's embrace, the softness of his lips on mine, his groans. The way he held me afterward. His words.

Definitely soon.

One step at a time.

I like you too, sunshine.

My core vibrates at the thought of seeing him again. I want him so bad. I *need* it. I need to feel him inside me—to experience that deep connection with him. The thought makes my heart flutter, and my body aches with longing.

As we fill up the rest of the cupcake batter in the tins, my phone starts ringing. I glance at Millie, who's happily singing along to the music, and then reach for my phone across the counter. Butterflies erupt in my stomach when I see it's Bradley calling.

"Stay there, Millie. One sec," I say, holding my hand out to her before answering the call. Trying to steady my nerves, I bring the phone to my ear. "Hello."

"Hi, sunshine," his deep voice comes through the phone, and instantly, a blush spreads across my cheeks. "What are you up to?"

"I've got Millie for the night, so we're baking cupcakes for dessert later," I explain, smiling at Millie, who's now attempting to lick the spoon. "And you?"

"Just wrapped up from the gym."

"Ah, nice and sweaty," I say, a teasing tone in my voice.

"So sweaty." His voice lowers an octave, sending a shiver down my spine.

Just then, Millie calls out, "Who's that, who's that?"

"It's Bradley. Want to say hi?" I ask her.

Her face lights up. "Bwadey, Bwadey." I press the button to turn on the speaker, and his voice fills the room. "Hi, princess. What are you doing?"

"We're making cupcakes!" Millie exclaims, her excitement contagious.

"Cupcakes, huh? That sounds yummy," Bradley replies warmly. I can't help but think he's yummy, too, and I can't wait to get a taste of him.

"Yeah! I mixing!" Millie says proudly, covered in batter. "Bwadey, you come bake with us?" she asks eagerly.

I quickly interject, not wanting to force him into anything. "Bradley might have other things to do, sweetheart." Even though

I'd love to see him.

"I'd love to come and help. If your Aunty Meli doesn't mind."

My heart flutters at his words. "Of course, I don't mind," I say softly, trying to hide my excitement. Millie cheers, and I can't help but feel a warm glow inside.

"I'll see you girls soon," Bradley adds, and just hearing those words come out of his mouth sounds so natural.

I can't help but picture a life with him—me cooking in the kitchen with our daughter or son, him coming home and finding us. Flour fights in the kitchen, leading to other naughty things. *Ah, what a dream.*

Two trays later, and a complete mess of the kitchen, the three of us are seated on the couch, watching *The Lion King* and munching on chocolate cupcakes with vanilla buttercream frosting. I'm perched on the couch with my legs outstretched across Bradley's lap. Millie sits between us, making a complete mess, with icing and chocolate crumbs all over her face. Kat will probably murder me for giving her sugar before dinner, but oh well. That's what aunty duties are for.

"Hakuna Matata" starts to play, and Millie sings along. I giggle at her enthusiasm, then turn to look at Bradley, only to find him already watching me. He does that often, always watching me.

Butterflies erupt in my stomach. He winks at me, and my heart just about skips a beat.

I grab some baby wipes from Millie's overnight bag and clean up her messy face. Then I head to the kitchen to start preparing dinner for Millie and me—and maybe Bradley, too.

"Hey, I'm going to start cooking dinner. Did you want to stay and eat?" I ask him, not wanting to impose, but hoping he'll stay.

"How about I head over to Madison's and grab us a quick dinner?" he suggests.

"Oh, you don't have to do that. I'm more than happy to cook," I say, though the thought of not having to cook is tempting.

Bradley gives me a reassuring smile. "It's fine, really. I'll grab a few burgers and chips for us to share. Sound good?"

I nod, feeling relieved and grateful. "That sounds perfect. Thank you."

"Be back in a bit," he says, standing up and giving Millie a playful ruffle of her hair before heading out. Millie and I finish cleaning up the kitchen mess together, and I can't help but feel a sense of warmth and contentment. Bradley's presence has added a new level of joy to our evening, and I can't wait to see what the rest of the night holds.

Millie is extremely well-fed, having polished off a small cheeseburger and a plate of chips. Now, she sits on the couch, yawning like there's no tomorrow.

"Tired, princess?" Bradley asks.

"Yeah, too much food," she says, patting her round little belly.

"Ready for bed, then, munchkin?" I say, and Millie just nods, rubbing at her eyes.

"Okay, say goodnight to Bradley Bear," I urge her, and Millie pads over to where Bradley is sitting on the edge of the couch and plants herself in his arms. He squeezes her before letting her go.

"Bwadey Bear and Meli," she says, looking at both of us. I watch her, feeling a bit confused. "Like Mummy and Daddy," she adds innocently.

Oh. She thinks we're... *together*, together. I feel a blush creep up my cheeks.

"Bradley and I are good friends," I clarify quickly. Technically, though, we are. Friends *with* benefits.

"Yeah, Meli loves Bwadey, like Mummy loves Daddy," Millie says matter-of-factly, completely unaware of the explosion she's now caused inside me. Kids and their lack of filter. I clear my throat and find Bradley watching me with a curious expression, the corner of his mouth tugging upward.

"Mhm, come on. Bath and then bedtime," I say, trying to change the subject quickly. I carry Millie into the bathroom, running the water and adding some bubbles. She giggles, splashing around, while I gently wash her hair. Once she's clean and wrapped in a towel, I bring her to my room. Despite only having the one bedroom, Kat assured me she's a good sleeper and would be fine sharing my bed.

I tuck her in, wrapping her up tightly with the covers, and kiss her on the forehead before saying goodnight. I leave the small night light on near the door, creating a slight glow in the room for Millie. With that, I leave my bedroom, leaving the door slightly ajar.

As I walk back into the living room, I'm taken aback. Everything has been cleaned up—rubbish gone, cupcakes put away. Bradley is in the kitchen, throwing out the last of the trash before moving to load my dishwasher. I just about melt on the spot. *He cleaned everything up for me?*

Little does he know, this man has stirred an uproar of emotions inside me. How am I not supposed to fall for him when he does simple acts of service like this?

He looks so domesticated, so at ease. He does it so effortlessly. Why is watching Bradley fill a dishwasher turning me on?

There's something incredibly attractive about seeing him take care of things so naturally, fitting into my space as if he belongs here.

As he finishes up, he catches me staring and raises an eyebrow. "What?"

"Nothing," I say, shaking my head and grinning. "Just... thanks for dinner, for spending time with Millie, and for cleaning up."

"You're welcome, sunshine," he replies with a warm smile. "It's nothing."

I bite my lip nervously, my eyes dropping to his mouth. God, I want to kiss him.

"Something else on your mind?" he asks, watching me closely.

I swallow hard. "Maybe," I admit softly, unable to tear my eyes away from his.

He steps closer, and I instinctively take a few steps back, only to bump into the kitchen island behind me. The air crackles with tension, and my heart races as he moves even closer, trapping me in the best way possible.

He leans in, his lips just a breath away from mine. "Care to share?"

"Well, I'm… I'm dirty from all the baking," I say, my voice barely above a whisper. "Pretty sure I have flour in my hair."

He smirks, his eyes darkening with desire. "Then maybe we should do something about that."

"Mhm," is all I can manage, nodding as my throat tightens, rendering me speechless. He takes my hand, leading me toward the bathroom. The anticipation builds with each step, and by the time we reach the bathroom door, my pulse is racing. He turns to face me, his frame towering over me.

In slow, deliberate movements, he begins undressing with a confident ease. My breath catches as his shirt falls to the floor, revealing the chiselled lines of his torso. His hands move to his shorts, and he looks up at me with a reassuring smirk.

"There's no need to be shy, sunshine," he says softly, his voice a soothing balm to my nerves. "You're beautiful."

His words give me the confidence I need. I start undressing, my movements hesitant at first. But with his eyes on me, filled with admiration and desire, I feel a surge of bravery. I let my clothes fall to the floor, piece by piece, until I'm standing before him, bare and vulnerable.

He steps closer, his gaze never leaving mine. "See?" he whispers, brushing a strand of hair from my face. "Absolutely beautiful."

I take him in, *all* of him. I'll never tire of the sight of him naked. I mean, I've only seen him once before, and that was by chance, a complete accident. This is all for me.

Oh, how the tables have turned.

I move my gaze back to him, catching the corner of his mouth tugged up in a smirk. He leans over and turns the hot water on before grabbing me and pulling me into the shower, underneath the cascading water. The warmth of his body against mine is intoxicating, and I melt into his embrace. His hands roam over my skin, washing away the remnants of our baking session while igniting a different kind of heat between us.

"You have no idea how much I want you," he murmurs, his lips grazing my ear.

"I think I do," I say, feeling his rock hard cock rub against my stomach, making me shiver.

He chuckles softly, a deep, resonant sound that sends shivers down my spine. Then he grabs hold of my hair at the nape of my neck, gently tugging it down before capturing my lips in an open-mouthed kiss. His tongue instantly caresses mine, and I lose myself in the intensity of the moment, the heat of the shower matching the heat between us.

Without taking his mouth off mine, he grabs a bottle of body wash from the rack, squirts some into his hands, and works it into a lather.

He starts to wash my body in slow, deliberate movements, his touch tantalising and sensual. As his hands glide over my skin, his breathing becomes heavier.

"*Fuck*, look at you," he murmurs, his hands roaming over every curve, now slick and slippery. I can only whimper in response, my body trembling under his touch.

He starts at my shoulders, his fingers moving slowly down to my breasts, my stomach, and the curve of my ass. Each deliberate movement ignites a fire within me, and as his hands continue their journey downward, the anticipation builds until he reaches my core. I bite my lip, trying to contain the moan that threatens to escape, my restraint barely holding.

"You're incredible," he breathes, his lips finding the sensitive skin of my neck. He sucks and nibbles, his teeth grazing my skin in a way that makes me gasp.

"Bradley," I moan, my voice shaky with desire.

His fingers find that sensitive spot in no time, rubbing circles that drive me wild. When he inserts not one, but two fingers inside, stretching me, I almost come undone right there.

"I love how you respond to me," he murmurs against my neck, his voice husky. My body arches into his touch as his fingers continue their maddening dance.

He takes my lips in another kiss, before they drift from my mouth, across my chin, and down my jaw. He kisses his way down my body, his mouth hot and hungry. I hold on, caressing his muscled back, sliding my hands up toward his shoulder blades. His mouth closes over my left nipple, and I can't help the moan that escapes me as he sucks it hard while pinching my other nipple with his forefinger and thumb.

"Brad." My fingers dig into his shoulders. "Oh... Oh, God."

He lifts his head, his eyes dark as he moves against me, his dick pressing between my legs, creating a delicious friction. I can't help but rub back against him.

A low groan escapes his mouth before he says, "Do you trust me?"

I nod quickly, without hesitation or doubt. He pushes the showerhead back, so it's not directly on top of us, before dropping down to his knees on the tiled floor.

He looks up at me, and it's the most delicious sight I've ever seen. His once blue eyes, now darkened by his pupils, hold my gaze. My breathing hitches as I anticipate what he's about to do.

I know what to expect this time; I've felt his mouth on me before. Yet, a burst of butterflies still erupts within me, mingling with the excitement and the memory of his touch. The anticipation is electric, and I can't wait to feel him again.

He grips my thigh, gently placing it on top of his right shoulder. My breathing hitches.

"Relax for me," he murmurs, sensing my apprehension. "I'm going to make you feel so fucking good."

35

Amelia

The sight of him looking up at me, eyes filled with desire, erupts the feeling of butterflies in my stomach. He slides a finger inside me, and a soft, surprised mew escapes my lips, and Bradley's eyes flick up to my face. His fingers slip out and then back in so easily. Despite being in the shower, I'm wet for entirely different reasons. My hips push against his fingers, trying to catch his rhythm.

"You're drenched, Amelia," he groans, his voice thick with desire. "You're so wet and ready for me."

"Yes," I choke out, tilting my hips up.

With a growl of satisfaction, Bradley dips his head again. His fingers slip out of me, but before I can mourn the loss, he spreads me open and I nearly squeal at the feel of his tongue on me. I gasp, my hands finding purchase in his hair as he works his magic. He circles my clit, teasing and pressing until he finally sucks it, and I can't help the moan that escapes my lips.

He hoists one of my thighs up, placing it over his shoulder, holding me steady as I cry out, feeling my orgasm building faster than it ever has before—the sound echoing in the bathroom. Bradley gently places a hand to my mouth to muffle my sounds, his eyes intense as he looks up at me.

"Can you be quiet for me, sunshine?" he whispers.

I nod, moaning against his hand, and when he presses his fingers inside me, curling them upward, like he did last night, I burst apart, crying out his name—my voice muffled by his palm as my eyes flutter shut. I'm a writhing mess against his talented mouth, my fingers gripping his hair.

The orgasm rolls through me in waves, until I finally go limp, leaning against the cool tiled walls.

If I thought my orgasm yesterday was good, then this... this is sensational.

Coming down from my high, I pull Bradley up to stand, craving his lips on mine again. Kissing him feels like a dream, and I can't get enough. He moans into my mouth, nibbling on my bottom lip before pulling away with a pleased, cocky smile on his face. He brushes his fingers across my cheekbone affectionately, his eyes searching mine.

"Holy... shit!" I exclaim, breathless—not caring about the swearing. "That... that was amazing." I enjoyed that way too much, and I think I'm now obsessed.

I take it he enjoyed that, too.

No. That's an understatement.

He *loved* it just as much as I did because, just when I thought his dick was hard before, it's an absolute rock now, jutting upward and rubbing against me. I want to repay the favour, but... how? What do I even do? Just as I'm about to ask, he says, "Come, let's finish washing up and head inside."

Does he not need to take care of... that? Surely, he does. He must be painfully hard at this point. But I follow his lead as he starts washing his body quickly, so I grab my bottle of shampoo and wash my hair—the scent of cherry blossom filling the space around us.

I finish washing up before Brad, but I wait for him to finish before we step out of the shower, each grabbing a towel from the rack. Lucky I'd laid out two earlier. Drying off quickly, he only puts his shorts back on, leaving his t-shirt draped over the rack. I wrap the towel around my body and hurry into my bedroom to grab a pair of pyjamas.

I peek in on Millie, who is now sound asleep, curled into a ball on my side of the bed. Smiling softly, I close the door and head back to the living room, where Bradley is waiting on the couch.

"All good?" he asks, a playful glint in his eyes.

"Yeah."

I join him on the couch, snuggling into his side. He wraps an arm around me, pulling me close. Bradley gives me a once-over, his eyes twinkling with amusement.

"Cute PJs," he says, brushing a stray hair behind my ear. I glance down at my Mickey Mouse-inspired Christmas pyjamas, the ones my sister bought me last year. They're my favourite.

"Thanks," I say, blushing slightly. "I-I still can't believe what just happened."

He chuckles, his fingers tracing patterns on my arm. "Believe it,

Mills. And get used to it, because I'm not going anywhere."

His words fill me with warmth, and I nestle closer to him, feeling a sense of peace. "I'm glad," I whisper, looking up at him. "I don't want this to end."

"Neither do I," he murmurs, pressing a soft kiss to my forehead.

A sudden feeling of apprehension washes over me. "Bradley, I'm worried about Olivia. Going behind her back like this... it doesn't feel right."

He sighs in response. "We'll tell her soon. When we find the right time."

The right time? But when exactly will that be? I push these thoughts aside, noticing the evident bulge in his shorts. I really want to return the favour.

"Bradley, um, can I..." My words trail off. *Just say it, Amelia.* "Can I... return the favour?" I ask tentatively. His expression shifts, a brief flicker of surprise crossing his face. "It's just, I've never—" I begin, my voice trailing off with uncertainty.

"I know, Mills. And you don't have to. I only want you to do what you're comfortable with," he reassures me, his tone gentle and understanding.

My gaze shifts to his lap, noticing the growing bulge straining against his shorts.

Gathering my courage, I continue, "I want to at least try. Can you... teach me?" I admit, the words come out with newfound determination. I'm shedding my shyness; I genuinely want to learn how to please him, for both his sake and mine.

His gaze softens in response, a silent acknowledgment of my request, before he nods in agreement.

Bradley

As I sit here, her request echoing in my mind, my thoughts drift back to our shower. I can't help but recall how beautiful she looked, her body bathed in water, her curves enticing and mesmerising. Her eyes, so round and captivating, held a depth that drew me in.

The memory of her surrendering to me, her taste lingering on my lips, ignites a fire within me. Now, as she sits before me, eager and willing, I feel a surge of affection and admiration. Her desire to learn, to please me, fills me with a sense of gratitude.

I love the sight of her, on her knees, looking up at me with those beautiful eyes—ready to explore this new experience together.

With deliberate slowness, I lift my hips and pull my shorts down my legs, my cock springing free and resting against my abdomen. I take a deep breath, trying to calm my racing heart.

Why the fuck am I nervous?

This is the first time I've had to teach someone, so I guess for both of us, this is a first. Her eyes widen at the sight of me, and it only stirs me more; then her brows crease.

"How..." She looks back at me wide-eyed. "I..."

"Tell me. Tell me what's on your mind."

She smiles nervously before starting to ramble. "Well, it's just that you're... huge, like really huge," she says, her eyes widening. "And well, despite my tendency to ramble, my mouth is pretty small, and I don't think it'll all fit in it, and I have a gag reflex, so that might be a problem. I don't know how—"

"Amelia," I command softly, trying my absolute hardest to not grin like a fucking cheshire cat. "Take a deep breath. We'll go nice and slow."

"Okay, but I want it to feel good, so, you know, you can... come," she says, nodding. I smirk at her.

"Anything you do to me, baby, will feel good." She tries to hide her blush, but I see it.

"Give me your hand," I instruct softly, my voice gentle yet firm. She grips me softly, and I inhale sharply at the first contact of her hand on me.

I wrap my hand around hers, guiding it up and down my shaft. She moves her hand with a perfect rhythm, the pressure just right, and it sends tingles down to my balls. I can't help but let out a low groan, the sensation overwhelming.

"That's it, Mills," I murmur, my voice husky with pleasure. "Just like that." Her confidence grows with each stroke, and she starts picking up the pace, her hand moving more freely.

The pleasure builds inside me, a delicious tension coiling tighter and tighter.

"Now, take me into your mouth, and while you suck me off, pump the root with your fist. The key is to grip it firmly, but not too hard. Suck hard when you get to the top." She nods, eager to continue, but I don't want to force her.

"Amelia, we seriously don't have to do this—ahh," I hiss as she cuts me off by wrapping her warm mouth around me. She freezes momentarily, probably adjusting to my size in her mouth.

"Easy, baby. Go slow," I murmur.

She's hesitant at first, applying a soft pressure, and I have to grab her hand, pressing harder to show her how much to squeeze at the base. I'm not delicate. I don't mind it being a little rough, but it's her first time, so I lay off a bit. And for a first timer, she's doing a fucking stellar job.

As I guide her, she grows more confident. "That's it, now swirl your tongue around the tip," I say, my voice strained with pleasure. "And suck harder when you get to the top and use your hand to pump the base."

Her hand pumps the base of my shaft while her mouth works on the rest, her tongue swirling and teasing. The combination of her soft, warm mouth and her hand is driving me wild. I groan, my fingers tangling in her hair as she finds a rhythm. "You're doing such a good job."

Her eyes flick up to meet mine, and the sight of her, mouth full, open wide, is enough to bring me over the edge. She picks up the pace, her hand and mouth working in perfect harmony.

The pleasure builds inside me, intense and overwhelming, until I'm teetering on the edge.

"Such a good girl. Taking my cock in that pretty little mouth."

She whimpers at my words, and I wonder if I'm being too direct, too vulgar. She hums on my cock in approval, and that's all the validation I need.

"Amelia, I'm close," I warn her, my voice husky. She doesn't falter, continuing with the same determination and focus. "If you don't want to swallow, pull off before. I'll tell you when," I say through clenched teeth, my jaw clenching at the euphoric sensation waving over me. She nods, with her mouth still full, while she pumps me again, applying suction at the tip. Finally, the tension snaps.

"I'm coming," I pant, sliding my hand into her hair, gripping it tight to hold it out of the way, and she pulls back just in time, my spurts of cum hitting my stomach.

I let out a deep, guttural moan as the pleasure washes over me in powerful waves, shuddering through my climax. The release is overwhelming, and I close my eyes in a euphoric state. I can't remember the last time my orgasm was that intense.

I also can't decide if it's because it's been a while, and by a while, I mean a good month now, or if it's because Amelia was the one to bring me to that state.

Something tells me it's the latter.

It's been about an hour since the mind-blowing orgasm Amelia gave me, and I'm still winding down from it. After I finished, I cleaned up, and I'd pulled her in for a kiss. She was so happy and shocked at her efforts; her face lit up when I praised her and covered her in more kisses.

Now, it's starting to get a little late, and we're under the blanket on her couch. The TV is playing on low, almost inaudible, with *Friends* episodes running on Netflix. It's been playing quite often since I've been around here; it must be a comfort show for her, and I love that. It's so fitting for her. She sighs contentedly, and I smile, more to myself. Despite all the stresses from work, I also feel content. Content being here, in her presence, in her safe space, just with her.

After a moment, she announces, "So, I received some good news the other day."

"Oh, yeah? What news?" I ask, curious.

"I've been invited to go to a gallery in Sydney to show some of my works." She sits up, her excitement palpable.

I can't help but smile wider. "That's amazing, Mills. I'm so proud of you," I tease, raising an eyebrow. "Though I still haven't seen these *said* artworks."

She laughs, a sound that feels like sunshine. "Soon. I promise."

That's all I need to hear. I won't press her further; I respect her privacy and request.

"Seriously, though, you deserve it. I can only assume your work is fucking mint if they've accepted you in."

Her eyes light up, and she leans in to kiss me softly. "Thank you, Bradley. It means a lot to me."

"When do you need to be there?" I ask.

"June, sometime. I'll head down and stay with my sister while I'm there. They said I could invite whoever I wanted, so..." Her words trail off as she twists her lips.

I can read between the lines. "I'll be there if you want me there."

She beams. "Of course I'd want you there."

"What about your parents? Are they coming?"

She shakes her head. "They've never been fans of flying, so most likely not. But it's okay, I'll have Kat, John, and Millie. *And* you, if you come. I know you have work."

"I'll be there," I promise.

With that, we settle back into the couch, the warmth of the blanket and the comfort of each other's company making everything feel just right. I can't help but think how perfect this moment is. Stress just melts away when I'm with her, and everything else fades into the background.

It's moments like these that make me realise how lucky I am to have someone in my life to ground me during these weird times. The other day, I'd been off, dry as shit, just in a foul mood.

Daniels is used to my moods by now, but the other boys, not so much. Some of the young prospects take it too seriously. I feel bad looking back at it. But fuck, it's *hard*.

To get out of your head sometimes, you know?

I glance over at Amelia, nestled against me, her attention half on the TV and half on our quiet conversation. Lately, she's been my anchor, pulling me out of my head when the darkness creeps in. I never thought I'd find someone who could see past the rough exterior, who could handle my moods and still want to be around. I think about how I snapped at one of the new recruits just the other day. Kid looked like a deer in headlights. I regretted it the moment it happened, but sometimes, the weight of everything just gets to you. The pressure, the expectations, the constant need to perform—it's exhausting.

But then there's Amelia. She doesn't expect anything from me other than to be myself. And somehow, that's enough for her. It's more than enough for me.

I hold her a little tighter, grateful for this moment, this quiet evening on the couch. The TV hums softly in the background. Amelia sighs contentedly, snuggling closer, and I smile to myself.

Content.

That's what this is—and for now, it's all I need.

36

Bradley

It's been a couple of days, and things have lightened up a bit. I'm walking with a bit of a spring in my step, though I try not to make it too obvious, or the boys might have a field day.

This week at work has been easy—not many tough gigs, just the usual public disturbances and a bit more vandalism around town. I even did a couple of shifts on highway patrol, catching more than a few reckless teenagers speeding along the A16 and the joining highways.

Amelia has come by a few times to see Liv, and I couldn't help but pull her aside when no one was watching to kiss her. I've been missing her mouth since that night. Any chance I get when she's over, I take it. This whole sneaking around makes it all worthwhile. It's the most excitement I've had around here in a while. Amelia's asked more than once if we could take things further, but I don't want to rush into it. Just because she's had her first taste of anything sexual doesn't mean we should jump straight into having sex. It's a big thing, and I want it to be special for her. She rolls her eyes every time, completely disagreeing, but deep down, I know she gets it.

I want to make sure everything feels right for her. Amelia deserves the best, and I have every intention of giving her that. It's two forty-eight in the afternoon when Reynolds strolls over to my desk.

"Mitchell, you free this Friday night?" he asks, his tone casual but his eyes keen. I glance up, curiosity piqued.

"Depends. Why?"

"Well, Rose and I were thinking about grabbing dinner and were wondering if..." he lowers his voice, "you and your... *missus* wanted to join us?"

I raise an eyebrow, looking around to make sure no one else is listening. Ever since my mood picked up, Reynolds, with his usual observant self, has been pestering me about it. He had a 'gut feeling' it had to do with a woman. I reluctantly told him about seeing Amelia, and he'd sworn to keep it to himself. So, I'm not surprised he's asking now. His use of the word 'missus' sets off a flurry of conflicting emotions in my mind. That territorial voice in my head screams, *mine, mine, mine.*

"I'll, uh, let you know."

"Mhm. Don't keep me waiting, Mitchell," he replies with a smirk.

I flip him the finger, and he walks away, laughing to himself. I clock off at exactly three oh five and a thought springs to mind. Faulkner's been on us about keeping our skills sharp, so I decide to head to the shooting range. I pack up my things and call out to the guys, "Laters."

On my way, I stop by Madison's Diner to pick up a few sweets, just because. Then I head to my next stop before the shooting range, hoping to catch her just before she leaves.

With any luck, I'll see that smile that's been stuck in my mind since the other night.

I pull up outside Koala Creek Primary School, right near the staff car park. It's open, by the way. Not very safe at all. I spot her small Barina and park beside it. Hoping she doesn't get called to stay back, I mentally cross my fingers, praying she's available right now.

As if answering my prayers, I spot her in the distance, wearing blue flared jeans and a fluffy white knit top. My heart skips a beat. I wonder if she'll notice it's my car parked next to hers. She looks around, and when she sees me, a wide smile spreads across her face. She breaks into a run, and I open my arms just in time to catch her.

She hugs me tightly, and I lift her in the air, a shit-eating grin on my face.

I inhale her scent, that familiar mix of cherry blossom and something floral filling my senses, and I sigh contentedly.

"What are you doing here?"

"Thought I'd surprise you," I reply, holding up the bag from Madison's Diner. "Brought some pastries. Figured you might need a pick-me-up."

She gives me a funny look. "What?"

"Who are you, and what have you done with grumpy Brad?" she says, looking around cautiously. I chuckle, shushing her, my tone serious.

"Can't have anyone finding out." I wink at her, and she scrunches up her adorable face shyly. "Come on, I want to take you somewhere," I say, pulling her to my car.

"Now? Where?" Her face lights up. "But I'm in my work clothes," she says, pointing to her outfit.

"You look fine, Mills."

She quickly puts her stuff into her car, locks it, and hops into my ute. "You guys should really have an automated gate to this carpark, you know," I say with all seriousness.

"That was so *police officer* of you," she giggles.

"Well, I'm just stating facts. It's not safe. Anyone can just park up here and waltz onto the school grounds."

"They close the metal gate during the day and open it in the mornings and afternoons," she states. While personally, I'm not satisfied with that answer, I let it go for now.

We drive for about twenty minutes, heading out of town toward the shooting range. The place closes around five, so I don't plan on her being here for too long. I just had a strong urge to bring her here.

It's not the most romantic spot, I guess, but it's meaningful to me.

From a young age, my father had taught my brother and me how to shoot, and when Liv got older, Xav and I taught her, too. Probably not ideal, but it was *our* norm. Her face is marred with confusion as she looks around.

"Shooting range? What are we doing here?"

"My boss makes us come here every so often to sharpen up our skills, so I decided to come by this arvo and thought I'd bring you along with me. You know, to show you... what I do?" I say, scratching the back of my neck.

She looks at me, a mix of curiosity and excitement in her eyes. "Okay, sounds cool."

I smile. "Okay. Let's get inside before they close up."

We make our way inside, the familiar smell of gunpowder and metal hitting my senses. I spot Mark, the owner, behind the counter, and I give him a nod. "Hey, Mark."

"Bradley, good to see you back," Mark says, a smile spreading across his face.

"Thanks. I brought a friend along. She's just going to watch for a little while," I explain, glancing at Amelia. Friend just sounds so out of sorts. I guess we're a *thing* now, but what does that entail?

Mark looks at her, then back at me, his smile widening. "She's more than welcome to give it a go if she wants. I trust you, Bradley."

Amelia's eyes widen. "Really? I've never done anything like this before."

"No pressure," I say, squeezing her hand. "You can just watch if you're not comfortable."

"It's a safe environment here. Bradley knows what he's doing, and I'll be here to help, too," Mark says.

Amelia nods, her curiosity clearly piqued. "Alright, I'll give it a shot—no pun intended."

We all chuckle, and a surge of pride runs through me. This might not be the most conventional date, but it's something special to me, and sharing it with Amelia feels right. We walk over to the range, and I pick up my pistol, placing it on the tray in front of me. Grabbing two sets of earmuffs, I put one on my head and then gently place the other on Amelia. Next, I hand her a pair of protective glasses and put mine on as well. I get myself sorted, checking my glock, making sure everything is in order.

"I'm just going to warm up," I say, giving a thumbs up to Mark behind the counter. A board appears with a round target about twenty-five metres away.

I take a moment to focus, feeling the weight of the gun in my hand. I glance at Amelia and warn, "It's going to get very loud."

She nods, giving me a thumbs up, her eyes wide and filled with awe.

I position myself, holding up the gun, my grip firm but relaxed. Turning my head slightly to the side, I focus my eye through the iron sights. I take a deep breath, steadying my aim. The first shot rings out, a loud crack echoing through the range. The bullet hits the target around the middle, somewhere in the eight ring. It's not always about hitting the ten ring; it's about the grouping. Keeping the bullets within the same area is what matters.

That's what I was taught. I pride myself on the consistency of my shots, a skill honed over the years, with both training at the academy and lessons from my father. I know I can confidently shoot and hold my aim. But I also know that under dire circumstances, this can change.

At the academy, we're drilled on never pulling out our gun unless it's a life-or-death situation. Our tasers are for stopping someone, preventing things escalating further. We only draw our guns if we or others are in immediate danger. Each shot I take sends a powerful jolt up my arm, the recoil controlled and expected. My breathing is steady, my heartbeat a steady drum in my ears. Each shot hammers into the target, the paper puncturing and tearing with every hit.

The satisfaction of accuracy, the control, the power—it all feels incredible.

Once I've fired my round of fifteen, smoke trails from the small barrel. I flick the safety on and place the gun flat on the counter. Removing my earmuffs and glasses, I turn to find Amelia staring at me, open-mouthed. I shoot her a confused look.

"What?"

"I'm not going to lie to you... that was *sooo* hot," she says, fanning her face. I can't help but chuckle, a full-on hearty laugh. When I finish, she's smiling from ear to ear, a blush staining her round cheeks.

"I'm being serious," she says, clearing her throat, and my smile drops before turning into a smirk.

"Yeah?" I say, moving closer, tilting her chin up to face me. "You know, you can't be saying these things to me in public, Mills."

"Why not?" she counters.

Hm, she's feeling frisky now, huh? I make a humming noise, deep in my chest. "Hm. Don't tempt me, sunshine." I press my hardening cock into her stomach so she can feel what she does to me. She gasps, her breathing quickening. "That's why."

I step away, needing to regain composure before I throw her over my shoulder, take her back to my car, and fuck her senseless. But nevertheless, I digress.

I shoot her a wink before readjusting myself and clearing my throat. "Alright, you're up."

Amelia

"Uh... there is no way I can do what you just did."

He laughs. "I'm not asking you to. I'll just teach you a few things."

Am I really about to do this? The most uncoordinated person, attempting to shoot a gun. Yeah, this is gonna be fun. I nod slowly, walking over to where he's standing at the range. "Okay, show me."

He places his muffs back on before guiding me through the basics, explaining each step carefully. I watch as he reloads the gun, his muscular, veiny hands pushing the slide back with practised ease. Holy crap, that's hot. I could have literally moaned out loud.

If I could, I'd put that moment on replay. I'm just watching him like a dog in heat, *panting* for him. I clear my throat, trying to focus, before moving to stand in front of him.

"First, grip the gun firmly, but don't squeeze too tight. It's all about control and balance. Now, stand with your feet shoulder-width apart, one foot slightly forward."

I follow his instructions, my hands trembling slightly. He places his hands over mine, his touch warm and steady, helping me hold the gun properly.

"Alright, now line up the sights with the target. Take a deep breath, and when you're ready, squeeze the trigger gently. Don't jerk it."

I take a deep breath, focusing intently. He presses up against my back, his body solid and reassuring. The way he's gripping my hands to move them into position sends shivers down my spine. He gently grabs my hips, turning me slightly to get my stance just right. His cologne wafts in the air, overpowering the smell of gunpowder and metal, enveloping me in his scent. My body tenses up, and I turn to look back at him.

"I'm scared!"

He looks at me, his eyes softening. "Okay, we don't have to do this, Mills. Whatever *you* want. It's your call." I'm scared but also *curious*. I want to give it a go. I want to make him proud.

I take a deep breath. "No, wait. It's okay. I can do this."

He nods at me, his encouragement steadying my nerves. "Alright, keep your grip firm, but relaxed. Focus on your breathing. When you exhale, that's when you squeeze the trigger. Just a gentle squeeze."

I line up the sights again, taking another deep breath. I exhale slowly, and when I feel ready, I squeeze the trigger. The gun fires, my body jerking slightly from the recoil.

Holy shit! I just shot my first gun!

"Fuck. Good job!" His voice is full of pride. "Not bad for a beginner."

I look at him, a mix of relief and excitement flooding through me. His praise makes me feel warm inside, and I can't help but smile back at him.

"Really? That was... intense."

He chuckles softly. "You did great, Mills. I'm proud of you."

"Can I try again?"

"Of course," he replies, stepping back slightly, but still close enough that I can feel his presence. "Take your time and remember what I showed you."

After a few more rounds each—yes, rounds, plural—we pack up and head back out. Bradley thanks Mark again, and I do, too. We walk to the car, the cool evening air brushing against my skin.

As we reach the car, he suddenly grabs me by the belt loop of my jeans and pulls me backward, spinning me around.

"Wha—" I start to say, but I don't get to finish because his mouth is on mine in a hurry, his lips moulding to mine like they fit perfectly, as if they belong there.

Maybe they do.

The kiss is intense, filled with a mix of urgency and tenderness that sends my heart racing. His hands find my waist, pulling me closer, as

I lift up on my toes to wrap my arms around his neck, losing myself in the moment. His scent, his taste, the feel of his strong hands against me—it's overwhelming and exhilarating.

I can't help but melt into him, responding to his kiss with a hunger of my own. His hands skate down to cup my ass, lifting me even further on my tiptoes, pressing me tightly to his rock-hard body. A groan escapes my lips, and he does the same.

Every part of me is on fire, our bodies perfectly aligned, and I can't get enough of him. The world around us fades away, leaving just the two of us in this intense, passionate moment.

When we finally pull apart, we're both breathing heavily, our foreheads resting against each other.

"Wow," I whisper, my voice barely audible.

"Yeah," he murmurs back, his eyes locked on mine. "By the way," he says, breaking the silence, "my colleague from work asked if you and I wanted to join him and his wife for dinner tomorrow."

I turn to him, curiosity piqued. "Like, as in, a *date?*"

He scoffs, a playful smirk on his face. "Yeah. What else would it be?"

"But, aren't double dates what you would usually take a girlfriend on? You know, with other people?" I ask, the words slipping out before I can really think about them. And now they have me thinking. The thought of officially being his *girlfriend* sends a thrill through me. But what does he think? Am I just over analysing everything?

"Technically, double dates can be for anything. But in this case, yes."

I frown, trying to read more into what he's saying. "So, you said yes. To a double date?" He nods, his expression serious.

"With your... girlfriend?" Is he saying what I think he's saying?

"It would appear so."

I point to myself and then back to him, my eyes widening as a smile breaks out on my face. Heat rushes up my spine, straight to my cheeks.

"So, does my *girlfriend* say yes? Or will I have to cancel on him?"

Holy crap! He's asking me to be his girlfriend. *Is this even real life? Am I dreaming?* I realise I've been stuck in my head for too long, so I blurt out, "Uh, y-yes! Yes."

"Fucking finally, woman," he growls before kissing me senseless again. This time, it's filled with a sense of finality and beginning all at once. His lips move against mine with a hunger that makes my knees weak. Wrapping my arms around his neck, pulling him closer, I get lost in the moment. Funny thing is, I've been falling for him long before all this started picking up.

Like, *ten* years long. It's crazy, right?

But deep down, I know that 'like' has morphed into something more. A decade of waiting, and finally, here we are. Sure, he hasn't taken my virginity yet, and neither of us has said those three little words. But this?

This is a start.

The kitchen is filled with the clinking of dishes and the soft hum of the dishwasher as Mum and I finish washing up from dinner. Occasionally, I glance into the living room, where Bradley and Dad are deep in conversation. It warms my heart to see them getting along so well, but it also sends a nervous flutter through my chest.

Earlier this afternoon, after we wrapped up our time at the shooting range, Dad texted me to invite Bradley over for dinner.

> **Dad:** Mum's making her famous shepherd pie. Salad. Tell Bradley!!!

For this to come from my dad, who for years had been so strict about not letting anyone in our house unless he trusted them completely, was huge. I couldn't help but laugh at his spelling, though. A few years ago, Kat and I got Dad a new iPhone, and he just loves to text—but his grammar? Not too good. His unexpected eagerness only added to my nerves.

Mum looks up from the sink, her curiosity piqued. "So, what did you two get up to this afternoon?"

I glance at Bradley, who catches my eye and gives me a reassuring smile. "He took me to the shooting range," I say, trying to sound casual. "Taught me how to handle a gun."

Mum's eyes widen with surprise, and a smile tugs at her lips. "Really? That's quite something. Your father did the same with me when we were younger. It brings back such fond memories."

I feel my cheeks warm at her words. "Oh, really? I didn't know that."

Mum's eyes twinkle. "Yes, he took me out huntin' all the time, too. It was our special time together. Our little camping trips. I remember feeling so proud and a bit intimidated, but he was always so patient."

"That sounds *really* nice, Mum."

She places a hand on my shoulder, her expression softening. "You know, love, you seem more... alive when he's around. Like you're shining a bit brighter."

I shift, feeling a mix of embarrassment and happiness. "Oh, stop it. Kat's not here, so you don't need to be saying these things. She's the one who usually says stuff like this. She has no filter."

Mum chuckles softly. "No, I'm being serious, Meli. I've always liked him—comes from a good family."

I let out a sigh. "I feel... I don't know, Mum. Is it wrong to be hanging around him, you know, without Liv? It's just... he's really special."

She looks at me with understanding, her gaze gentle but firm. "Oh, I can see that. But look, it's not my place to get involved. I just want you to be happy. If that man in there is the one to bring that happiness, then I see nothing wrong with it. But when the time presents itself, you need to be honest."

I nod, a lump forming in my throat. "I understand."

Mum continues, her voice steady. "Just don't sweep it under the rug. Liv's a great girl. Hell, she's your best friend. I'm sure she'd understand, especially when she sees what we're all seeing now."

I take a deep breath, absorbing her words. "Thanks, Mum. I really appreciate your support."

Mum's gaze softens further, and she squeezes my shoulder. "Come on, let's not keep them waiting. Help me bring out the coffee."

I grab a glass and fill it with cold water. "Bradley's not a coffee drinker, Mum," I explain, giving her a small smile. We walk back into the lounge, balancing the drinks carefully. The TV is on, the Nine News playing in the background. Dad is settled in his recliner chair, looking relaxed, while Bradley sits on the two-seater with one foot over his knee, looking so effortlessly attractive.

I hand Dad his coffee and pass the glass of water to Bradley, who mouths a "thank you" to me. I smile back, feeling a flutter in my chest.

"Heard you went shooting today?" Dad says, taking a sip of his coffee.

"Uh, yep. Bradley taught me," I reply.

Dad grins. "Heard you also kept hitting the eight rings. Not bad for a first-timer," he says with a wink.

Bradley's eyes twinkle with pride. "That's what I said. I think she's a natural."

I laugh, shaking my head. "Yeah, I don't think *I'll* be doing *that* again. As fun as it was, that's a one-time kinda thing for me."

Bradley smirks at me, his eyes softening.

"Ah well, that's a shame," Dad chimes in, placing his glasses on his head. "You know, it reminds me of when your mum and I used to go on our camping trips. I used to take her out in the bush, just the two of us. Taught her how to shoot. Those were some good times."

I smile, remembering Mum's earlier words. She smiles back at me, a glint of nostalgia in her eyes. Bradley's face brightens at the mention of hunting. "I'd love to hear more about that. I've done a bit of hunting myself, with my dad and brother, but I've always wanted to try it in different terrains."

"You know, years ago, your dad and I went hunting together," my dad says, shocking me.

"Oh, really?" Bradley leans forward.

"Yeah. We used to be a part of the same gun club," Dad says, his voice warm with memories.

Bradley looks to me for some form of confirmation, and I just shrug, giving him a sheepish smile. This is news to me, just as it is to him. My mind races, piecing together this new information about Dad's past that I never knew. It's strange, realising there's so much more to learn about the people you think you know best.

Dad's eyes gleam with enthusiasm. "How about this? If you're up for it, maybe one day we could plan a hunting trip together. I think we'd have a great time."

Bradley's expression is earnest. "I'd be honoured, sir."

Dad claps Bradley on the shoulder, his smile broad. "Great. It's settled then. I'll hold you to that."

I glance at Mum, who winks at me, her look saying more than words could. A warmth spreads through my chest, seeing Dad's genuine smile as he claps Bradley on the shoulder. The easy bond forming between them is a surprise, one I hadn't anticipated. It's as if the universe is aligning in our favour, making our secret relationship even more precious. The anticipation of our journey together stirs inside me, mingling with a quiet joy.

Bradley catches my eye and smiles, and I can't help but beam back at him. This moment, this connection—it's everything I hadn't realised I wanted.

37

Amelia

The restaurant's warm ambiance envelops us as soon as we step inside, promising a memorable evening. Soft lighting casts a gentle glow over rustic wooden tables adorned with flickering candles, while local artwork adds charm to the cosy space.

"Good to see you both," John says, his smile genuine as he and his wife, Rose, greet us. John leads us to a table by the bar.

The menu at Harbour Lights offers a delightful mix of modern Australian cuisine, with a focus on fresh, local ingredients. Known for its exquisite seafood dishes and extensive wine list, the restaurant's reputation is well-deserved. The song "L-O-V-E" by Nat King Cole softly plays in the background, a nostalgic melody that brings memories of my parents.

Earlier in the evening, I FaceTimed Jamie, who helped me choose the perfect outfit—a red paisley dress paired with my favourite heeled ankle boots to give me some height around Bradley's towering frame. Excitement buzzed within me until Olivia's message came through, asking to hang out.

Dread washed over me.

I'd told Liv I was going out for dinner with the girls from work, and she'd been understanding. Yet, inside, my gut was in shambles, twisting and turning with guilt. Bradley pulls out the chair for me, and it causes my heart to flutter. I know we need to sort this out, find the right time to tell her. For now, I push those thoughts aside and focus on the evening ahead, hoping that tonight will be a chance to forget about my worries, at least for a little while. Conversation flows easily. John, who's been at the station long before Bradley, shares stories from work. Rose, vibrant with her Spanish background, exudes a confidence I admire. She works at a real estate agency not far from my job—a nice coincidence.

As we enjoy our drinks—my second wine, while the guys stick to their first beers—Bradley drapes his arm around my chair, twirling a strand of my hair. His touch sends a pleasant shiver down my spine.

"So, John, how did you and Rose meet?" I ask.

John grins. "At a salsa dancing class in town. Rose was a natural, and I... well, let's just say I needed a lot of practice."

Rose laughs. "He was so charming, though. Kept stepping on my toes, but I couldn't help but be drawn to him."

I glance at Bradley, who's smirking. "Didn't know you were into salsa, John," he says, teasing.

John protests, "I'm not," but quickly adds, "Rose changed my mind. It's actually pretty fun."

"I'm not *into* salsa dancing," he protests, but then catches the glare Rose shoots at him and quickly changes his tune. "I mean, I *wasn't*, but Rose changed my mind. It's actually pretty fun."

Bradley and I laugh, the sound mingling with the soft background music and the chatter of other diners. The easy camaraderie among us feels comfortable and natural.

A smile spreads across my face. "It sounds like fate brought you two together."

Rose nods, looking fondly at John. "Absolutely. Sometimes, you just know when you've found the one."

Bradley glances at me with a soft smile, making my heart skip a beat. His hand slides under the table to rest on my thigh, my pulse quickening. As his fingers trace gentle patterns on my leg, I struggle to keep still, the desire for him intensifying.

"Amelia, how do you like working at Koala Creek Primary?" Rose asks, her eyes genuinely curious.

"I love it," I reply. "The kids are great, and the staff is wonderful. It's challenging, but rewarding."

Bradley squeezes my thigh gently, a silent show of support. I glance at him, and his eyes are filled with pride and affection, making me feel like the luckiest woman in the world. The night progresses with more laughter and shared stories, the atmosphere relaxed and inviting. As dessert arrives—a decadent chocolate fondant for the table to share—John raises his glass. "To new friendships and unforgettable nights," he toasts.

"To new friendships," we echo, clinking glasses.

There's a slight buzz from the two glasses of wine I've had, but not enough to call myself tipsy. I just feel warm inside. Arms linked with Rose, we make our way outside, the boys trailing behind.

"So, you and Bradley, huh?" Rose asks with a knowing smile.

I blush. "I guess so," I say, feeling the warmth spread to my cheeks.

"You two suit each other so well, and that man is so smitten."

"Thank you. It's still fairly new, but it feels like it's been forever, you know?" At least for me.

"I do know." She smiles warmly. "And that man has eyes for *only* you. And I'm talking *heart* eyes. I think John needs to take some notes." We both laugh just as the guys catch up to us. Bradley's eyes catch mine in an intense gaze before he winks at me. John and Rose bid their farewells, and Rose pulls me in for a hug before whispering, "Heart eyes. I'm telling you." It makes me laugh softly.

We wave them goodnight before heading to Bradley's car.

"What was so funny?" he questions with a curious look.

"Oh, nothing. Rose is just... she's great."

"Mhm," he says, coming up to me, trapping me against the passenger door. He dips his head, planting a kiss in the sensitive spot between my collar and jaw, and I shiver. He trails kisses up the column of my neck to my jaw before capturing my lips in a soft kiss.

I wrap my arms around his neck, pulling him deeper, coaxing his tongue with mine. He plants one hand on my jaw and the other wraps around my hair, tugging on it to tilt my head upward.

"Brad..." I moan, exhaling. "I think... I'm ready."

"Ready for?" he asks, his voice husky.

"I think you know. Please. I need you," I say, pressing myself against his thigh, which is firmly nestled between my legs. With that, he picks me up, puts me into his car, and drives off, heading straight for my apartment.

38

Amelia

The moment we burst through the door, it's like a dam breaking. Our hands are everywhere, tugging at clothes, desperate to feel skin against skin. Bradley's lips never leave mine, his kisses hot and urgent.

"Fuck, Amelia," he murmurs between kisses, his voice rough with need. "Are you sure this is what you want?"

"Yes," I gasp, trying to tug his shirt off. "Yes, Brad. I want this. Right now."

He pulls back slightly, a soft laugh escaping him as he helps me with his shirt. "Thank fuck," he says before bending forward and hoisting me up into his arms. My legs wrap around him instinctively, and I can feel his hardening erection through his pants. I rub myself against him as he carries me into my bedroom, the anticipation building with each step.

In the dim light of my room, he sets me down gently on the bed. He strips off his clothes first, every movement deliberate and controlled, his eyes never leaving mine. Seeing him naked, with his cock on full display, is something I don't think I'll ever get used to.

The fact that I've tasted him, had my mouth full of him, is beyond me.

"Clothes, baby. Off," he instructs, his voice low and commanding.

I nod, my fingers trembling slightly as I stand and begin to undress, peeling off my dress, leaving on my matching red lace set—which, fun fact, had shown up on my doorstep this morning from Jamie and Kristie. Those two conniving little witches ordered me a whole bunch of 'goodies', as they put it, and I could have killed them.

But, nevertheless, I couldn't not wear this set.

And judging by the look Bradley is giving me right now, I'd say it's worked.

He watches me like he wants to devour me. There's something in the way he looks at me. He's controlling, but in the most delicious way—never overpowering, just enough to motivate me to do what he asks. And let's be honest, I'd do just about anything if he asked me to.

I slowly peel off my bra, tossing it aside, and my underwear follows next. Bradley watches me intently, his gaze heating my skin. My mouth gapes open as he lifts a hand to palm his hard cock, giving it a tug and squeezing the tip. "You're beautiful," he whispers.

He towers over me, pressing me into the bed, his touch so arousing. His hands roam over my body, igniting a fire within me. I arch my back, craving more of his touch.

"You like when I touch you like this?" he murmurs, his voice low and husky.

"Yes," I breathe out, my body responding to his touch.

He takes a nipple into his mouth, sucking and biting, before moving to the other. As he does this, his hand trails down, his fingers finding my clit easily. He dips a finger inside, and I finally feel how wet I actually am.

"So fucking wet, fuck," he groans. "Is this all for me, sunshine?"

I nod, my breath coming in short, excited gasps, barely able to contain a whimper of pleasure.

"It's all for you," I manage to say.

"Fucking oath it is," he says before capturing my mouth in a passionate kiss. Our tongues tangle, and his hand coasts up my torso. I arch into his touch, a blaze of heat lighting me up from the inside out as he rubs his thumb over my clit. I start feeling that familiar tension build up at my core. As he continues to coax my clit to attention with his thumb, his erection strains against me, and I can't stop looking at it.

I snake a hand down my stomach to palm his rock-hard erection, and he groans loudly. "Fuck, Amelia."

Suddenly, he stops, pulling back slightly. "What?" I ask, a mix of frustration and concern in my voice.

"I don't have a condom," he admits, his expression serious.

A smile tugs at my lips, embarrassment coursing through my veins. "I have one."

His eyebrows shoot up in disbelief, but I turn to my bedside table and grab the three foiled packets that had also been an added surprise in the parcel from Jamie and Kristie this morning. Maybe a thanks needs to go out to the girls, after all.

"Don't ask, just know they came from Jamie and Kristie."

He laughs softly before nodding, taking one of the packets and ripping it open with his teeth. He sheathes his impressive erection, and I watch in awe.

He positions me comfortably on my back, gently pushing my legs further apart before bracing himself over me. He leans down to kiss me, his kiss long and deep.

I whisper against his mouth, "I'm nervous."

"I've got you," he murmurs reassuringly. As he begins to move closer, I stop him, placing my hands on his chest.

"Wait. What if it doesn't fit?" I blurt out, my anticipation of potential discomfort evident.

He chuckles softly. "We're going to make it fit, Mills. Nice and slow." His words soothe the tension, calming my nerves. "Just keep looking at me," he whispers against my lips, his hand slipping between our bodies again, his thumb finding my clit. Sitting up, positioned in front of me, with my legs wrapped around his waist, I watch as he grips his impressive erection, rubbing the crown up and down my folds. I arch my back at the sensation.

Oh, that feels so good.

He positions his tip at my entrance, and I can only nod, locking my eyes with his as he pushes forward. I grip the sheets at my sides, bracing myself against the tight resistance of my body. I bite my lip to stifle a whimper, my breaths turning ragged. He encounters more resistance, and I hold my breath. "Oh, God. I don't think I can take it."

"You can take it, baby. Breathe. Deep breaths. Once the crown passes through, it'll be smooth sailing from there."

My eyes widen. "Oh my god. You mean that's only the tip?"

Sitting up, I look down to see our bodies joined, confirming that not even half of him is inside me yet. God help me.

He chuckles, the sound deep and warm. "Still have another six inches to go."

Despite the discomfort, I want *more*. I want to feel more of him. I squeeze my eyes shut, bracing myself for the pain.

"Hey. Eyes on me, Amelia." His voice is strained but gentle, and I lock my gaze with his. "I'll go slow. You tell me when it's too much, and I'll stop," he reassures me. I watch as he bites his lip, his brows furrowing, and the tension in me eases a bit.

"Are you good?" I ask, and a breath of laughter escapes his lips.

"Yeah," he manages. "It's just... You're so tight, and I'm trying to be gentle. Just bear with me, okay?"

I nod quickly. "Of course."

Surprisingly, the anticipated pain doesn't come. Once his head passes through, the rest of him eases in much smoother. I finally exhale when he's buried to the hilt. There's a dull ache, but it's manageable. His movements are gentle and measured, and the discomfort gradually gives way to pleasure, deeper and more intense.

"You okay? Can I start moving?" His concern for my well-being warms my heart.

"Yes. Please," I say, lifting up and grabbing hold of his muscular arms. He hovers just above me, his palms resting on either side of my head. Leaning down, he captures my lips with his as he pulls out slightly before moving back in, sending a delicious sensation through my body.

Goodness me.

The connection between us feels electric. Each slow, deliberate thrust builds a new kind of pleasure inside me. My fingers glide over his back, soothing and reassuring, and I realise the discomfort is fading away.

Oh. This... this is different.

Suddenly, I'm eager to learn more. My hips lift instinctively, seeking movement, and Bradley growls, pulling back. Instead of pulling all the way out, he thrusts back in. I gasp as a beautiful tension stirs inside me. I focus on his face, captivated by the mix of lust and tenderness in his eyes, the way his jaw tightens, like he's holding back just for me. He leans down and kisses me softly.

"You're doing so good," he murmurs, his breath warm against my lips. "Keep your eyes on me, okay?"

His blue eyes lock onto mine, taking in every pant, every bounce of my breasts with each thrust. Suddenly, he pushes harder, moves faster. "I'm so close, Brad." A loud whimper escapes me, but I don't care.

Bradley growls, "Such a good girl. Come for me." His dirty words send a rush of heat through me, spurring me on even more. My moans get louder, and he picks up the pace—not too hard, but more intense. Each thrust sends waves of pleasure through my body, building a delicious pressure that's almost too much to bear.

"Fuck, I don't think I can hold out much longer," he says through gritted teeth.

"I'm coming, I'm coming," I gasp, lifting my hips to meet his thrusts, feeling the tension coil tighter and tighter. And when Bradley's thumb presses down on my clit again, I shatter. Loudly. It's so intense, I can't stop moaning his name, over and over.

Bradley, Bradley, Bradley.

My eyes flutter shut as my body shudders uncontrollably, jerking hard against him. He grips my hips tight, following me into climax with a loud groan, his movements becoming more erratic. As the waves of pleasure slowly subside, he pulls out of me gently, wincing a bit. I lean up on my elbows, glancing down at the bed. There's a small pink stain on the sheet, and panic sets in.

"It's okay, sunshine. That's perfectly normal," Bradley reassures me. I nod, trying to calm my racing heart. He gently tilts my chin up. "Hey, I didn't hurt you, did I?"

I shake my head quickly. "No, not at all. That was incredible."

He hums his approval before hopping off the bed to toss the condom. When he comes back, he's got a warm, damp towel from my bathroom. He wipes me gently, and out of nowhere, I feel tears welling up in my eyes.

What the heck?

I don't understand why I'm crying. Maybe it's because I've never felt so close to someone before, or maybe it's the way he's taking care of me, so tender and thoughtful. It's overwhelming, this rush of emotions, feeling so cherished and safe. Before I can stop them, the tears start to fall. Bradley notices right away, his face full of concern.

"Amelia? Hey, what's wrong?" His voice is so gentle, it makes me want to cry even more.

"I don't know," I whisper, feeling overwhelmed. "This was perfect. You're perfect. I'm just... feeling everything."

He sits beside me, pulling me into his arms. "Fuck. It's okay. You can let it out. I'm here."

I feel *so* embarrassed. Is this what it's supposed to feel like? Don't get me wrong, that was bloody amazing. It was everything I could've hoped for with Bradley.

Disappointed? Absolutely not.

Relieved? Maybe?

Complete? *Definitely.*

Gosh, am I supposed to be crying? Is this like those cheesy romance movies where the girl cries after the perfect night? Except, I'm not sad or upset—just overwhelmed in a good way. Crying after sex isn't exactly the sexiest thing, is it? But then again, Bradley's reaction is sweet.

This feeling, though, this *connection*—it's like he's seeing right through me, and I'm not sure I've ever felt so vulnerable yet safe at the same time. Is this what people mean when they talk about being truly intimate? It's overwhelming, yet I don't want it to end. Bradley's tenderness, his care—it's breaking down walls I didn't even realise I had. And here I am, baring my soul in a way I never expected.

"*Ughh,* I'm so embarrassed," I mutter, trying to hide my face.

He *tsks* at me, gently lifting my chin. "You never have to feel embarrassed for feeling emotions, sunshine. Don't bottle anything up." His thumbs wipe away my tears gently, and then he leans in to kiss my lips softly.

"You should take your own advice, you know," I say softly, not meant to tease, but glancing up to see him smiling.

"Touche, Mills."

"You really *should* try opening up more. I love talking to you, you know, about… everything."

"For you, sunshine, I'll try. I promise."

He guides me up, urging me to stand. I watch as he heads to my tallboy, rummaging through for underwear and pyjamas. When he finds them, he returns to me, gesturing for me to lift my arms so he can slip my top on. Then he bends down, gently coaxing me to lift my legs, sliding on my underwear and shorts in one smooth motion. As he pulls them up, his lips brush against my most sensitive part, so tenderly that tears well up in my eyes again. He finishes pulling up my shorts and then swiftly strips off the dirty bed sheet, tossing it to the floor.

"Where do you keep your spare sheets?" he asks.

I point to my tallboy. "Bottom drawer."

He follows my direction, retrieving a fresh fitted sheet and placing it on the bed with care. When I move to help, he gently stops me. "Let me."

After he finishes making the bed, he takes my wrist, guiding me back toward it. I start to apologise again, but he interrupts me. "No more apologising, not to me, not to anyone. Ever."

I just nod, feeling his warmth enveloping me as he tucks me snugly under the covers. Resting my head on his chest, I hear the steady thump of his heart. His body is firm yet comforting, like the best cuddle ever. With his strong arms wrapped around me, gently rocking me with each breath, I begin to relax.

The rhythm of his heartbeat becomes a familiar melody, lulling me closer to sleep. In this quiet moment, as I feel his presence so intimately, I realise something profound stirring within me: I guess I've felt this for a while but couldn't quite find the words. Maybe all those butterflies weren't just about nerves after all.

I am completely and hopelessly in love with Bradley Mitchell.

As I wake, sunlight spills through my blinds. I stretch out my arms, expecting to feel Bradley beside me, but the bed is empty. Panic sets in. Did he leave? I could have sworn he stayed the night. I look around and spot a note on my bedside table.

Just went home to grab a change of clothes and freshen up.
Will be back soon. I promise. Xx

Relief washes over me. I quickly freshen up myself and head to the kitchen to make some coffee, the note still in my hand. As I boil the kettle, the sound of the front door opening catches my attention. I turn to find Bradley walking in, his hands full—juggling a parcel, a gym bag, and a small paper bag. His eyes light up when he sees me.

"Morning, sleepyhead," he greets with a warm smile, planting a kiss on my forehead.

I yawn, rubbing my eyes. "Sleepyhead? It's barely eight a.m."

"Yeah, and? I'm awake at the crack of dawn, sweetheart. It's midday for me now."

I pout playfully. "Since you don't drink coffee, how do you even function in the mornings?" I ask, my voice light and curious.

He frowns slightly, smiling as if trying to figure out what I'm really asking. I clear my throat, feeling a bit silly. "Like, what *drives* you to get things done? If I don't have a cup of coffee in the morning, I'm basically a zombie all day."

He chuckles, a twinkle in his eye. Then, with a smirk, he leans back. "My brain, I guess. It just doesn't stop."

I giggle, nodding. "Hm. Yeah that brain of yours does seem pretty clever. Makes total sense."

He grins, teasing, "Guess that means I'll now have to watch out for zombie-you on coffee-free days."

I laugh, shaking my head. "You might have to!"

He winks at me. "Oh, by the way, this parcel was at your door."

Huh? Parcel? Oh no, not another one. Surely this isn't from the girls again. I tentatively pick up the parcel, inspecting it, yet nothing indicates where it came from—just my name and address.

Odd.

Opening it, I freeze before clearing my throat.

"What? What is it?" he asks, going into all protective mode. I take a step back, embarrassment kicking in.

"N-nothing! It's just something for work," I stutter. He raises an eyebrow at me, not buying it. Yeah, *I* don't even sound convinced by that. Bradley moves closer, his curiosity evident. I quickly tuck the package behind my back, but it's too late.

He's *seen* it.

The pink wand vibrator with packaging is as clear as the blue skies this morning. Just a quick glance at it would have anyone recognising what it is. Oh, I'm going to *kill* the girls when I see them on Monday.

Bradley raises an eyebrow, a playful smirk forming on his lips. "Something for work, huh?" he teases, stepping even closer.

I swallow hard, my heart racing. "Yeah, well, sort of..."

He laughs softly, his eyes twinkling with mischief. "You're a terrible liar, Amelia." I bite my lip, trying to think of something to say, but my mind is blank. "If I knew toys were your thing, I would have bought you some." His voice is low and husky. Oh, God. Is it possible to be even *more* mortified than I am already?

I blink rapidly. "I'm not. It was... um, it's just a gag gift from Jamie and Kristie," I manage to say, though my voice wavers.

Bradley's smirk widens. "Some friends you got."

"Mhm, yep!" I reply, swallowing hard.

He brushes my hair to one side and places a kiss on my shoulder. The touch sends a shiver down my spine, intensifying the heat between us. He turns me around to face him, and my eyes drop to his mouth. He leans in, his breath warm against my cheek. "You know," he says, his lips ghosting over mine, "I could help you test it out." My breath hitches, my body reacting to his proximity.

"Is that so?" I reply, my voice barely above a whisper.

God, I wouldn't even have the tiniest clue how to use something like this.

Bradley's hand slides to the small of my back, pulling me closer. "Only if you want, sunshine," he murmurs, his eyes flickering with amusement as he takes the parcel from my hands. He opens the box and pulls out the vibrator, his smirk growing wider. My face is on fire, and I can barely meet his gaze.

"I... um, I don't even know how..." I stammer, feeling utterly out of my depth.

"Do you want me to show you?" he asks, and his voice is so deep and smooth it sends shivers down my spine. God, yes.

I nod a little too quickly, and a nervous laugh escapes my lips. Before I know it, he's pinning me to the bench, his lips crashing into mine and kissing me senseless. My thoughts scatter, my body responding to him instinctively. His hands roam over me, igniting a fire wherever he touches. I lose myself in the kiss, forgetting everything but the way he makes me feel.

Then he lifts me, carrying me to my bedroom and gently setting me down on the bed, his eyes never leaving mine. "I've got the whole day to myself," he says, his voice low and filled with promise. "I plan on having my way with you many, *many* times."

A shiver of anticipation runs through me. "Oh, really?"

He nods. "Mhm. Is that going to be an issue for you? Do you have other plans?"

"Oh, well, not sure. I'd have to double-check," I tease back, feeling a surprising surge of confidence overwhelming me.

"Oh, yeah?" he asks, and I nod at him, enjoying this new boldness.

"Not before I make you come, though."

"So sure of yourself, aren't you?" I retort.

"Do you doubt me?" He raises his brow, and I definitely do not. I like this game we're playing, and I'd be lying if I said I'm not turned on right now. I love teasing him.

"Hm. I guess you'll have to show me."

He scoffs a laugh. "My pleasure, baby. In fact, I'm going to show you just how many times I can make you come."

"And how many is that?" I ask, my voice quivering slightly.

With a wicked gleam in his blue eyes, he hops off the bed and steps out momentarily. I hear a bag open; the tap runs quickly, and then he returns, holding something behind his back. He pulls the pink vibrator out from behind him, but that's not all. He's holding a pair of handcuffs in his other hand.

Yes. *Handcuffs*.

My eyes widen, and my jaw drops.

"Second guessing yourself now, sunshine?"

I'm speechless, unable to say anything. I swallow the lump in my throat. "Bradley," I breathe.

"You had a lot to say just before. Let's put the theory to the test." He smirks, twirling the handcuffs around his finger. "Trust me?"

I nod without any hesitation, still unable to find my voice. This is so dirty. *Kinky.* And I absolutely love every bit of it.

He steps closer, his eyes never leaving mine as he gently cuffs my wrists, attaching them to the metal frame headboard. My breathing hitches, but I am so turned on right now, squirming against the restraints.

"Good girl," he murmurs, his lips brushing against mine. "We'll start off slow." He slides my pants and underwear off in one movement, leaving me bare and exposed. "Open for me, sunshine," he says, tapping my thigh.

I'll never tire of him calling me that. I do as he says and open my legs, not caring about anything else because I trust this man wholly. Who would have thought that this man, always so controlled and poised, had a kinky side?

Someone pinch me.

"So fucking perfect," he murmurs, dipping his head and placing a kiss on my sensitive flesh before parting me and diving in. His tongue makes lazy strokes, and I moan out loud. For a moment, he works me with his tongue, loosening me up. Then he inserts a finger, followed by another, and I arch into his touch. Just when I think I can't take any more, he removes his fingers and reaches for the vibrator. It comes to life quickly, the subtle hum filling the room. I swallow my nerves, anticipation coursing through me.

He presses it to my thighs gently, trailing it down to my inner thigh, straight to my clit—holding it there softly at first, gauging my response. I bite my lip, nodding for him to continue.

"Always so responsive," he murmurs, his voice dripping with

temptation. "Such a good girl."

The way he talks, the way he moves—it's intoxicating. Every nerve in my body is on fire, and I'm teetering on the edge of ecstasy. My wrists are screaming to be free, but I don't care one bit. The thrill of being restrained only adds to the sensation. He moves the vibrator slowly from my thigh, over to my pelvic bone, before dipping it lower. When it finally touches me, my body jolts forward, the handcuffs clinking against the bed frame. The vibrations pulse through me, building and building until I can't hold back any longer.

"Bradley," I gasp. "I'm so close."

He smirks, his eyes dark with desire. "Then let go, sunshine, and count for me. Let me see you fall apart." The intensity is overwhelming as the vibrator pulses against me, sending waves of electric pleasure that shoot through my core. The sensation is all-consuming, making my body tremble with each wave of stimulation. I cry out his name, lost in the sensation. My orgasm washes over me suddenly, making me jolt as the vibrator continues to rub softly against my clit. My body trembles with pleasure, each spasm heightening the exquisite waves of ecstasy.

"I don't hear you counting," he teases.

"One," I manage, and Bradley beams, a low growl rumbling from his chest. I glance down, noticing the impressive bulge in his trackies. In a flash, he's undressing, his cock springing free. With practised ease, he pulls out a condom from his pocket and swiftly sheathes himself.

"You ready to count again?"

"Oh, God. I don't think I can," I manage to whisper.

"Oh, yes you can, sunshine," he assures me, and with a smooth, slow motion, he's thrusting into me. I revel in the way he fills me up, the slight discomfort now quickly fading into a pleasurable sensation.

My hands strain against the handcuffs. The clinking of metal fills the air, blending with my moans and the sound of our bodies moving together. As he powers into me, he presses his thumb to my clit, and a second orgasm wracks my body, Bradley following along not long after, groaning through his own release. After not two, but *three* orgasms, I'm utterly spent. We both struggle to catch our breaths. He pulls out slowly and unlocks the handcuffs. I roll my wrists around, savouring the feeling of freedom, before falling back onto the bed with him.

He grabs my wrists and massages them where the restraints had once been. Bradley then collapses beside me, his chest heaving. I turn my head to look at him, a lazy smile playing on my lips.

Yeah, I could get used to this.

39

Bradley

As I think about these past few weeks with Amelia, I feel completely content. Between her place and our spontaneous, secret dates—picnics out in the bush, leading to multiple sessions of fooling around, to even fucking in the back of my ute one afternoon—we've been at it like teenagers discovering sex for the first time. I can't get enough of her, and she feels the same. For once, I'm completely full of happiness.

Somehow, we've managed to keep our relationship under wraps, even with our friends around. The other night at the Loose Lasso, the sexual tension between us was palpable. I just hope it wasn't too obvious to our friends. My mum's been acting strange, but Olivia... Well, she hasn't said or noticed anything. Thank fuck for that, at least for now.

But life always has a way of throwing curveballs, disrupting our rhythm.

A series of house fires have broken out in a town about an hour away, and all units have been called to assess the damage. Of course, that includes our station. I'm gearing up at the station now, ready to head out with the boys—Faulkner leading the case. Nerves start to prickle at my skin. We haven't had anything this drastic in years.

And this? This is bad.

The fire has spread wide, with five homes now a total loss and fifteen people severely injured. Casualties? We'll know when we arrive at the scene. I pull out my phone and dial Xavier's number. He answers on the first ring.

"Xavier?" I say, my voice tense.

"Bradley," Xavier's voice comes through the phone, full of relief. "We're all here—Isla, Liv, Mum, and Dad. I've put you on speaker so they can hear you. What's going on? We just saw the news."

"I'm good, Xav," I reassure him quickly. "We're about to head out there now. I can't say much more until we assess the situation. I just wanted to let you all know I'm safe." Mum's voice in the background cracks my heart. They shouldn't worry; I'll be fine. If anyone's sweating it, it's me, not them. All in a day's work, for a Friday.

But something deep down tells me this isn't going to be one of *those* days.

Xavier's voice snaps me back. "Okay, be careful, Bradley. Keep us updated. We love you." His words hit hard, crack something open, but I can't say it back now.

"Alright. Gotta go."

Dad's voice breaks in. "Son. See you back home later, yeah?" They act like they're not sure I'll be coming home. But we'll get it under control, with ambulance and fire services, surely.

"Yes, Dad. Relax, I'll see you soon."

"Love you, son."

"Yeah. You too."

Faulkner gives a quick nod, signalling to wrap it up. "Okay, gotta go. Bye." I end the call, a whirlwind of emotions swirling inside me—concern for the situation, gratitude for their support, and a steely focus on the task ahead. I know I gotta let Amelia know I'm alright, but the thought of her fretting tears at me. Those three little words are on the edge of my tongue. Do I feel that? Fucked if I know. Right now, all I know is I've got a job to do, and I need my head on straight.

Still, I pull out my phone and shoot her a quick text.

> **Me:** Called out to a fire. Will update you when I can.

A text from her pings back almost immediately.

> **Amelia:** Brad! Thank God.

> **Amelia:** Thanks for letting me know. Please stay safe! 🖤

> **Me:** I will, sunshine. See you back at home xx

> **Amelia:** I'll be waiting for you 🖤

I'll be waiting for you.

That's all I need to keep my worries in check.

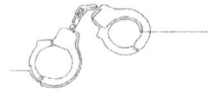

As we get closer, the glow of the flames paints everything in an eerie light, giving the whole area a spooky vibe. The houses, all lined up in a row, look like they've seen better days. They're off on their own, away from the busy town square. The rural Fire and Rescue Team is already there, with their bright red trucks and flashing lights standing out against the dark night sky, like a sign of hope in the middle of all this chaos. Faulkner walks off to meet a few of the other team members, and I join in on the conversation, Daniels and Reynolds following behind me.

"Faulkner, good to see you," Gerry Holmes, the Deputy Captain of the NSW Fire and Rescue Team, greets him, his voice tense. "We've got a real mess here. Looks like it started from one of these houses." He gestures to the row of homes engulfed in flames. Faulkner nods, his expression grave.

"We're trying to contain it, but the spread is rapid. We need to get everyone out of these homes," Gerry continues.

"We need to find the source fast. If it's a gas leak, we'll need to shut it off before it causes more damage," Faulkner adds.

Kurt Black, who I know to be the lead unit commander for

NSW SES team, joins in. "We've got ambulances on standby for any injuries. Let's get to work, boys." The three of them exchange determined looks, knowing the urgency of the situation.

"Let's do this," Faulkner says, rallying our team. "Safety first, everyone. Let's get these people out of harm's way."

Faulkner's voice cuts through the chaos as he directs Woody and Stokes to lead traffic control for all conjoining, adjacent roads and concealed driveways.

He then turns to us—Reynolds, Daniels, and I—ordering us on scene safety. "Ensure that the scene remains safe for firefighters, emergency service workers, and members of the public working in its vicinity," he commands. Faulkner's words put us right on the front line of the fires.

We're not firefighters, but our jobs are just as important.

Reynolds and Daniels both nod to me, understanding the gravity of the situation. We quickly gear up with our protective wear before heading closer to the fires, ready to do our part in ensuring the safety of everyone involved.

As we approach the fires, the intensity of the situation becomes palpable. The heat is unbearable, and the flames seem to dance wildly, defying any attempts to control them. The smoke billows thick and dark, making it hard to see and even harder to breathe.

In the middle of the chaos, the screams of people trapped in their homes cut through the air, making the situation even more urgent. Firefighters are everywhere, working non-stop to get the fire under control. Ladders are up, water hoses are spraying, and paramedics are on standby, ready to jump in and help.

Victims who have managed to escape the flames are being tended to by paramedics in their vans, their faces filled with shock and fear.

Reynolds shouts over the roar of the fire. "Fucking hell. They need to get these people out now!"

A firefighter beside us chimes in, his face grim with determination. "We'll go in, mate. Cover for us," one of them says, his voice steady despite the chaos.

Another firefighter adds, "We'll get them out. Just keep the area clear for us."

As they rush toward the house, a series of explosions erupt, sending shards of glass flying in all directions. The windows shatter one by one, adding to the already chaotic scene. The screams and wails for help echo through the air, sending a chill down my spine.

My heart drops out of my chest as I watch the firefighters disappear into the burning building, knowing the dangers they face. Reynolds and I stand ready, our eyes fixed on the house, waiting for any sign of the firefighters and the people they're trying to rescue.

Meanwhile, Woody and Stokes are doing their best to control the traffic, but the situation is quickly spiralling out of control. Faulkner's voice crackles over the radio. "We need backup! The fire's spreading faster than we can contain it!"

I grit my teeth, feeling the strain of the situation weighing heavily on me. "We need to work fast. Lives are at stake here."

As I say this, a firefighter returns, running out with a woman under his arm, covered in soot, and her clothes burnt and singed.

Behind him, another firefighter holds a young boy, who is screaming and crying. The boy looks to be around ten or eleven years old.

Fucking hell.

More screams break out as the team spreads out to the other home beside this one. Faulkner's voice comes through the radios strapped to our chests. "Stay focused, boys. We're sending more backup. Just hold on tight. I'll be there in five."

Suddenly, I spot movement in a window on the second floor. "Copy Radio. All units, I spot movement, second floor. There might be someone still trapped inside."

Faulkner appears beside me after a few minutes, asking, "Where? Point."

I point to the window, and as I do, the same woman we just pulled out screams, her cries louder than a banshee. "My HUSBAND! He's still INSIDE. He's with my d-daughter. Please HELP THEM!" Her voice cracks, and my eyes widen.

Without hesitation, I run up to the woman and ask, "Your daughter is still inside? And your husband?"

"Yes! Please help them!"

At the same time, a firefighter comes to her, saying, "We're doing everything we can, Miss. That part of the house has been compromised. The staircase leading up to that room has collapsed. We'll need to get them from the outside." She's inconsolable.

"NO! PLEASE! You have to go in. Please save them." The firefighter takes off his helmet. "I assure you, our team is doing everything we can right now." She starts wailing.

"How old is your daughter?" I ask, remaining calm.

"She's three. Please, *God*. She's only THREE."

My heart drops. Three-fucking-years-old.

At such a young age, this little girl can't comprehend what's happening, and she must be completely petrified. My heart cracks, and immediately my mind goes to Millie, Amelia's niece.

She's the same age. Fuck.

My body turns cold at the thought. Springing into action, I turn to the firefighter. "Get in there. Do what you need to do now!"

"Now, mate. Calm down. I have my boys assessing the situation."

"You don't fucking have time! She's three years old. Get to the window, get them to open it from the inside, pull them out."

Fuck, it's not my job to be thinking of this. It's *theirs*.

I understand they're in dire circumstances.

"Oi. I don't take orders from you," the firefighter retorts.

At that moment, my radio crackles. "Copy Radio. Mitchell, we need you here."

"Copy. On my way," I say as I sprint back to the scene, and as I do, Faulkner barks my name out. I keep running back toward Daniels and Reynolds.

As the firefighters start to move the ladders up to the window where the man and little girl are trapped, every step, every movement makes me hold my breath. The intensity of the situation is overwhelming, and I can feel the weight of responsibility pressing down on me.

I watch anxiously as the firefighters reach the window and try to open it from the outside. The mother's cries for help echo in my ears, and I can't shake the image of her husband and daughter trapped inside.

Suddenly, as they attempt to open the window, it shatters, sending shards of glass flying. The fire spreads rapidly over the area around us, the heat pressing against my face and body, suffocating and intense. I hear the crackling of the flames, a harsh, relentless roar that drowns out everything else. The smoke grows thicker, curling around us like a suffocating blanket, while the wind feeds the flames, spreading them further. The heat is unbearable, radiating off the flames and adding to the growing chaos.

"I'm moving closer. Fuck this. I need to help," I bark out.

"Are you fucking mental? Leave it to them," Reynolds yells back over the noise.

"Mitchell. Stop!" Daniels says, stepping in front of me.

"I can't just fucking sit here and watch." I push forward, throwing myself closer to the fire. I cover my face, coughing as the fumes enter my lungs, pushing forward despite the warnings from the firefighters behind me.

"All units, movement has been spotted. A young girl. She's alone. A body is near her, but no movement from the man. Copy." The radio crackles.

I'm not thinking rationally; I'm not thinking at all. All I see is that little girl trapped in there, her father not moving.

I see those sparkling brown eyes.

I see a little girl that I've come to know all too well just recently.

The little girl is clinging to the edge of the windowsill, probably trying to move away from the spreading flames. She looks down and spots me, her eyes wide with fear, before crying out louder. I manage to get just underneath the window and call out to her.

"Jump. I need you to jump, sweetheart. I'll catch you."

"I want my mummy. I want my mummy," she cries.

I weigh my options. By the time the firefighter repositions the ladder to get closer again, another burst might erupt. The second floor isn't too much higher up from the ground floor, probably about five metres, give or take.

"Your mummy is here. I need you to jump. I'll take you to her," I shout, trying to overpower the sounds of walls crashing and glass shattering.

"That's a police officer. Get him out of there!" a voice crackles over the radio.

A bunch of firefighters and men from the SES team run up beside me, barking orders. "What the bloody hell are ya doing, mate? You need to move before the house blows!" one of them shouts, grabbing my arm and trying to pull me away from the burning building.

"I can't leave her! She's just a kid," I protest, struggling against the firefighter's grip.

"We'll get her out, mate, but you need to move now! It's not safe. It could blow any minute," another firefighter insists, pulling me back as flames lick at the window above us.

"I'm not fucking moving. Help *me*. Get her to jump. I'll catch her," I bark at them, my voice desperate. They ponder it for a moment, exchanging quick glances, before nodding to me. One of them barks out orders for the rest to follow.

"Grab a tarp sheet, and move the ladder closer to the girl," he commands. Another firefighter breaks down what's going to happen.

"We'll position the tarp below the window. You stay ready to catch her when she jumps. We'll do our best to guide her out safely." I nod in approval, my heart pounding in my chest.

As they scream for her to jump, a firefighter creeps closer, climbing further onto the ladder as they move it slowly, inspecting where the father lies beside her.

"Copy Radio. Spotted the father. Moving closer. Over," the firefighter reports over the radio, his voice tense with urgency.

"Come on, sweetheart, you can do it! Jump!" I shout, my heart in my throat. Crashes echo from behind her, followed by a surge of smoke and fire bursting from the windows. The little girl screeches, hesitating for a moment, fear clear in her eyes.

But then, with a final, desperate cry, she leaps from the window. In that split second, I lunge forward, my body instinctively reaching out to catch her. I manage to get under her just in time, breaking her fall as we hit the ground with a thud.

Pain shoots up my arm and down my back as I crash onto my shoulder, but I push through it, my focus on the little girl in my arms. She's crying and shaking, but she's *safe*. That's all that matters. Tears prick at the corners of my eyes, a rush of relief and adrenaline surging through me.

I've never felt more alive, more aware of life's fragility.

In seconds, firefighters pry her from my grasp, wrapping her in a fireproof blanket and carrying her away. The intensity of the moment lingers, the sounds of chaos and rescue efforts filling the air as I lie here on the ground—feeling the weight of what just happened.

"Fuck," I grit out, as pain radiates through my arm when I attempt to stand. Someone grabs my shoulder, and I bark out in agony.

"Mitchell, you stupid cunt. That was fucking amazing." It's Daniels. Relief washes over me, but as the adrenaline fades, the pain in my shoulder sharpens, becoming nearly unbearable.

It could be dislocated. Or broken.

It takes *seconds*, just seconds, for everything to change, leaving us no time to comprehend what's happening until it's too late.

An explosion erupts nearby, the force of it causing my ears to ring and pain to shoot through my head. The blast knocks both Daniels and me back, sending us sprawling. Daniels hits the ground beside me with a grunt. Smoke engulfs us, thick and suffocating.

Muffled screams echo around us, chaos reasserting itself. I feel myself being dragged, a dull ache spreading through my body.

And then it stops.

Just like that, everything goes black.

40

Xavier

I pace back and forth in the living room, my anxiety gnawing at me as each minute passes without any word from Bradley or anyone else. "It's been five fucking hours. What the fuck is happening?" I bark, unable to contain my frustration.

I keep rereading the texts that have been coming in over the past hour in our group chat, *'Wattle Creek's Finest'*.

Harrison: What the fuck's going on?

Michael: Any news?

Imogen: Omg. I really hope he is okay. 🥺

Harrison: He will be. It's Bradley.

Michael: True. That cunt is one badass motherfucker.

> **Olivia:** I'm sure we'll hear from him soon. He's probably just so caught up. Give it some time.

Amelia had 'hearted' Olivia's text, before sending one of her own.

> **Amelia:** You're probably right, Liv. Positive thinking. 🤞

Her message stirs an uneasy feeling in the pit of my stomach. I can only imagine the fear she must be also experiencing right now.

"Calm down, son. He's fine," Dad says, trying to reassure me, but his words fall flat.

"Xav, baby—" Isla starts, her hand resting on my shoulder, but I can't handle any comfort right now.

"No! Fuck! Please, don't tell me to calm down. I need to know where he is," I snap, turning away from Isla to face my sister, who sits on the couch, her eyes wide with unshed tears.

"Xavier!" Mum's reprimand cuts through the air, reminding me to control my temper, especially in front of Isla.

I turn back to Isla, the one person who's supposed to ground me, and see her shock. "Isla, I'm sorry. I'm just... fuck!" I exclaim, my fist colliding with the wall beside me, the impact making a noise but causing no real damage.

Instantly, I regret my outburst, especially seeing Isla hold her bump with another hand on her hip, watching me with concern in her eyes.

"It's okay, Xav. I understand, baby. He's fine. Bradley is amazing at his job," Isla reassures me, her words barely registering as questions swirl in my mind.

Why does he do this? Why does he put his life on the line every day? Why did he choose this path? Why couldn't he just stick to the farm? Then none of us would be here, worried sick about him.

Fucking hell, Bradley.

As I think this, the news reporter appears on the TV, reporting live.

"I'm standing about one-hundred-fifty metres away from this scene that continues to unfold. We have three casualties who have perished in the fire, fifteen still confirmed to be injured," and behind her, I can see the fires continuing to spread, but it's mentioned that firefighters and all units have managed to contain two house fires out of the three.

Her voice continues, loud and clear. *"We currently have two police officers down."* My heart drops.

No. Fucking no way.

He's fine. He *has* to be.

I mean, it's Bradley we're talking about here.

She continues, "In a heroic attempt, an officer and multiple firefighters managed to rescue a three-year-old girl who was trapped inside a room. The mother and eleven-year-old brother are both being treated, and the forty-four-year-old male, who was seen with the young girl, is being rushed to emergency, in critical condition."

My breathing quickens, and then she announces that, "The two officers that were down are conscious and are being treated at the scene."

Relief washes over me, yet it's still not confirmed who these officers are. I pull out my phone and send my brother a text.

> **Me:** Bradley. You better be okay. Call me asap. Please.

The bond I share with Bradley knows no limits. Despite our differences, we're alike in many ways. I find myself wondering how well I truly know him. He's always been the quiet, moody type, lost in his own thoughts. As I shake my head, my mind wanders to Amelia. Glancing at Liv, I can't help but think about their situation. It was surprising, yet not entirely unexpected.

They suit each other.

Isla steps toward me, and as I lock eyes with her, I pull my phone out to text Amelia. Bradley texted her number to me after we got off the phone earlier today to have... just in case. Even though I'd had it saved since she was already in the group chat, it was a thoughtful gesture.

> **Me:** Hey, Amelia, it's Xav. Just wanted to check in with you. Hope that's okay.

> **Amelia:** Hey. That's okay. I'm alright.

> **Amelia:** I'm assuming you know... about the two of us?

> **Me:** I do. Brad told me a few weeks ago.

> **Amelia:** How are you all holding up? I'm thinking of you all.

> **Me:** We're okay, I guess. Thank you, I appreciate that.

> **Amelia:** Any news from him?

> **Me:** Not yet. I will let you know ASAP, though. You at home?

My heart breaks for her. She belongs here, with all of us. Bradley would have wanted that. Yet, she's on her own, facing these uncertainties solo.

But having her here would raise too many suspicions, I reckon. It's messed up, considering she's practically family, being Liv's best friend and all.

Isla steps up beside me, her eyes scanning the message, their softness evident. Yeah, she's aware. When she noticed Bradley acting all strange—like, unusually happy and shit—she didn't waste a second before asking what was up, so I'd told her.

She's my wife; naturally, I share *everything* with her.

> **Amelia:** Yeah. I'm home.

Isla understands the need for discretion, nodding in silent agreement before returning to the couch. Now, we simply wait, anxiously anticipating my brother's safe return home.

It's not a matter of if, but *when*.

He'll be back home soon.

41

Amelia

The silence in my apartment is deafening. I sit curled up on the couch, my phone clutched in my hand, staring at the TV screen as if willing it to offer any shred of good news. Hours have dragged by, each minute stretching into what feels like an eternity.

We have three casualties who have perished in the fire, with fifteen confirmed injured.

Two police officers are also down.

My heart sinks as I recite the grim news in my mind, each word hitting me like a blow. I replay the messages I exchanged with Xavier, my heart aching with every word. I can only imagine them all at home, consumed by fear and uncertainty, just like me. I wonder if he's okay, if he's... alive. I picture Xavier, most likely inconsolable over his brother. And Liv.

Oh, Liv. My heart shatters even more at the thought of her. I click on our text message thread and start typing.

Me: Are you okay? 😢

Liv: He'll be fine. It's Bradley.

Liv: Right?

Me: He will be. I know it.

This is her *brother*. She must be feeling so terrified.

I spent the night with my parents, who kept reassuring me he'd be fine. My mum kept chanting, "He's a strong, capable man," over and over, trying to instil hope and faith in all of us. Kat even FaceTimed us for a while, wanting updates, but we had *none* to give her.

I left not long ago, thinking I might be able to clear my head at home—but also hoping to get some sleep. Just as I was about to head out, my dad stopped me.

"*Amelia.*"

"*Yeah?*"

"*When he comes home, tell him I'll plan our hunting trip. Yeah?*"

My eyes had welled up with tears, and I nodded before kissing him on the cheek.

Not if, but *when*.

I try to keep myself busy in my lounge, but my mind is racing. The TV is on full volume, and my heart aches at the sight before me—those poor victims, elderly people, and young children. As I watch, the screen shows a drone flying over the area, capturing the full extent of the devastating fires. The image of a fireball erupting in the distance almost makes me choke on my tea. I quickly set the cup down, struggling to regain my composure. Tears well up in my eyes.

Oh, God, please let him be okay. He has to be okay.

Bradley, you're strong, you're capable.

You can't be one of those officers. You can't be.

I start nervously rambling to myself in my mind. What if he's hurt? What if he's... No, don't think like that. He's fine. He's got to be fine. But what if he isn't? What if he's lying there, needing help, and I'm just sitting here, useless?

I wrap my arms around myself, trying to hold it together.

Come on, Amelia, breathe. He promised he'd come home.

I'll see you back at home.

Home. He'd called this home.

The news reporter's voice cuts through my thoughts. "We've just received confirmation that the two officers who went down are now regaining consciousness. Both are receiving medical treatment on the scene. One officer has a dislocated shoulder, a couple of cracked ribs, and the other has a broken Tibia."

Relief floods my veins, and a tremor runs down my spine. Thank God, they're going to be okay. But as the relief washes over me, a wave of panic quickly follows. What if one of them is Bradley? What if he's more hurt than they're letting on? The uncertainty claws at me, threatening to pull me under.

I force myself to focus on the positive—the officers are alive, they're being treated. I cling to that, pushing the what-ifs aside. But the fear lingers, a reminder of just how fragile life is, especially in his line of work.

Time is too short.

And the minute I see him, whenever that is, I'm going to tell him. He has to know. I can only hope he feels the same way.

My phone buzzes from beside me, startling me awake.

I take a minute to gain my composure, scanning my surroundings in confusion. Where am I?

Oh. My couch.

I must've dozed off for a little while. I grab my iPhone and see there are text messages from Xavier.

9.39PM

> **Xavier:** Got an update! Paramedics treated his injuries on site, gave him some oxygen… but the stubborn fuck refused to go to hospital. Reckons he's fine and is on his way home.

Another text came from Liv not long after.

10.00 PM

> **Liv:** He's home! Thank God!

I check the time now which reads twelve oh one a.m..

But that was two hours ago! Yeah, that nap was definitely not a 'little while'. So that means he would still be at home now. I check our text message history to find nothing from him.

My heart drops. No, it's fine.

He's at his home with his family, where he needs to be. Despite this, I can't help but feel anxious. My eyes blur with unshed tears, threatening to spill over, but I blink them away, tilting my head back before they get the chance to.

I notice now that my TV is still playing in the background, but the sound is on low. *Very* low. My mug is no longer on my coffee table. Okay, now I'm really confused.

When did I...

My thoughts are cut off when I hear shuffling coming from my bathroom, and I turn slowly.

Panic settles in as I hear the shuffling from the bathroom. My heart races, and I feel a knot form in my stomach. Who could be in there? I didn't invite anyone over. I try to calm myself, telling myself it's probably just a neighbour or something.

But deep down, I know that's unlikely.

I slowly get up from the couch, trying to make as little noise as possible. I edge closer to the bathroom, my heart pounding in my chest. The door creaks open, and Bradley's frame comes into view—his arm is strapped to his chest, and another bandage is wrapped around his midsection.

All the air is knocked out of my lungs, and I gasp for air for just a moment. His beautiful striking features are creased in pain, but they soften once he spots me.

"Hey, sunshine," he says, his voice strained.

My breath hitches, and before I can think, I run up to him, wrapping my arms around him. Tears spill down my cheeks as I hold him tight. He grunts out in pain, and I pull back, realising what I've done. My mind goes blank, shock paralysing me for a moment. I can barely form a coherent thought, let alone a sentence.

"Crap. Sorry." I take a breath. "Bradley, I... You're... How did you..." I stutter, words tumbling out in a frantic mess so I clear my throat. "Are you okay? Why didn't you call? I was so worried."

He gently wipes my tears with both thumbs, his touch calming my racing heart.

"I'm okay, Amelia," he says softly, his voice soothing. "I'm here now."

"But you're hurt," I manage to say, my eyes fixated on the bandages. "I was so scared, Bradley. I thought... I thought—"

"Shh, shh," he interrupts, pulling me close again, despite his obvious discomfort. "I'm here. I'm fine."

In a moment of shock, I mutter, "I love you." My eyes go wide, and I can feel his body go rigid. He pulls back, his eyes searching mine, back and forth.

"What was that?" he asks, his voice barely above a whisper.

I shake my head before laughing nervously. "I said I love you?" I say it with uncertainty, like I'm not sure if I should have said it. What if

I've scared him away? I wonder if he'll think I'm too forward. Which is *very* ironic, because I, Amelia Brown, am never forward. But deep down, I believe he feels the same; maybe he's just unsure how to say it himself.

"Sorry. It's just that... don't scare me like that agai—" but he cuts me off, his hand finding the back of my neck as he pulls me in for a kiss.

When he breaks the kiss, he looks at me with such intensity that I know the feelings are there.

I search his eyes, finding the *unspoken* words in their depths. They shimmer with affection as he pulls me close again, resting his forehead against mine. I bask in the warmth of his love, feeling it emanate from his very presence.

"When did you get here?" I ask, curious about the time, but also seeking reassurance of his arrival.

"Not too long ago. You were sleeping so peacefully, I didn't want to wake you." His voice is soft, filled with tenderness.

The bond between us is undeniable, and it's enough.

We settle onto the couch, Bradley gingerly adjusting himself to avoid aggravating his injuries. I curl up next to him, my hand resting gently on his good shoulder. The relief of having him here, safe and sound, is almost overwhelming.

"What happened?" I ask softly, looking up at him.

He takes a deep breath, his eyes meeting mine. "Fucking hell, it was a rough night," he begins. "The place was already an inferno by the time we arrived. We knew there were people trapped inside, so we had to act fast."

I listen in awe, hanging on his every word. "*You* went in?"

He shakes his head. "Not inside, just close to the building. We found a little girl trapped in a room. She was scared, crying for her mum. I couldn't just leave her there."

My heart aches at the thought. "And your shoulder?"

Bradley grimaces slightly. "I dislocated it when I caught her, falling to the ground. I managed to block her fall, but the impact hit me pretty hard. Hence the cracked rib, too."

He pauses, taking a breath. "My partner, Daniels, broke his leg when some of the rubble fell on him from the explosion. We both got knocked, and the rest is all fuzzy."

Bradley's voice cracks, and my heart breaks at the sound. "I-I don't even know how I got out of there," he continues after a moment. "But they moved us away in time."

I can't help but ask in a hurry, "Why didn't you go to the hospital for further treatment?"

He scoffs. "I'm fine, Amelia. They popped my shoulder back, gave me some strong pain meds and some to take home. There's no need to go to the hospital, and for what? To take up a bed when someone else could be needing it more than me," he explains, shaking his head.

I smile. "You really are stubborn. Your brother was right."

He turns his head to look at me. "My brother, huh? So, he's been messaging you?"

"Yeah, he has. He also told me that he knows about us."

"You can trust him." Bradley says.

I nod. "I know. It's okay. It was nice of him to check in."

His face softens. "I'm glad he did, too."

I process everything he must have gone through and wince at the thought. "I still can't believe that all happened. It sounds so terrifying, but so incredibly brave of you," I say.

He shakes his head. "It's just part of the job. We got her out, though, and others. That's what matters."

I shake my head. "No, Bradley. That's really, *really* brave. You're like a *hero*."

"Nah, the real heroes are the fire service teams. They took most of the brunt of the fire." How can someone be so humble when he literally saved a young girl's life?

"Well, you're a hero in my eyes." I snuggle closer, feeling his heartbeat steady and strong beneath my hand. "I'm just glad you're here. Safe."

"Me, too, sunshine," he says, his voice soft and sincere. "Me, too."

We sit in silence, the weight of the evening settling around us. At some point, I'd changed the channel back to the news, and there, on the screen, in large bold letters, reads: *"Local Officer Rescues Young Girl from Burning Building."*

His name is mentioned afterward, along with a snapshot of his academy portrait. My heart swells with pride. His actions haven't gone unnoticed. This small town of Wattle Creek will forever remember the actions performed by Senior Constable Bradley Mitchell.

My *man* is a hero. I'll never forget.

After a few moments of silence, a thought occurs to me. "Wait. Where did you tell your family you were going before you came here?"

"Uh, that I needed to head back to the station to grab some things."

"And the overnight bag?" I nod toward his bag on the dining table.

"That was for visiting Daniels," he says, throwing up air quotes with his free arm. "You know, to be with him, for emotional support." He shrugs with a smirk.

I nod, a bit puzzled. "But haven't they been wondering where you've been off to these past few weeks? Like your mum, dad, or Liv?" *Well, it's been over a month now, or more, technically.*

"Nope, not really." He shrugs, and I can't help but feel a pang of curiosity.

As I sit there, basking in the relief of having Bradley safely by my side, my mind drifts to Olivia. She's been in the dark about our relationship, and it weighs heavily on me. I know she cares deeply for both Bradley and me, but the thought of telling her about us fills me with unease. It's a conversation that has been a long time coming.

I take a deep breath, gathering my courage. "Bradley, I... I think we need to tell Liv about us. Like *really* soon," I say hesitantly, my voice barely above a whisper. He nods, brows furrowed, lost in thought.

"I'm just... I'm concerned about how she will react," I admit.

"We will tackle it together," he offers.

I acknowledge his words with a nod, but a knot of unease tightens in my stomach.

"Okay."

As I lean into his comforting presence, I appreciate his support, but my mind is consumed by worry about the challenges ahead. This isn't a small matter; it's a secret we've been keeping for a while now. We've let it drag on for so long that I worry it might be too late to fix things with Liv. Her reaction could change everything, and I fear the consequences of our actions.

The knot in my stomach tightens with each passing moment, and I can't shake the sense that this conversation will lead to complications that we may not be able to overcome.

42

Bradley

Staying at Amelia's feels like a sanctuary, a rare place where my mind finds peace. At home, my thoughts swirl endlessly, and work brings its own barrage of distractions. But here, with Amelia, it's like I'm anchored, grounded in her presence.

She sleeps peacefully beside me, her hair cascading over the pillow, a picture of serenity. She's truly beautiful. Last night, sleep eluded me. Despite her offer to ease my mind, I'd declined—too drained, physically and mentally. I managed only a couple of hours of rest, but I'm thankful she slept well.

The covers have slipped down to her torso, revealing her flawless, pale skin. I lightly brush the back of my hand over her stomach, the touch sending shock waves straight down to my hardening cock.

Despite the pain I'm in, despite being uncomfortable, I shouldn't be turned on when she's with me, I can't explain it. But when I'm with her, it's like I have this primal desire for her—something I've never felt before.

My touch stirs her awake, and she blinks her eyes open, her gaze focusing on me. I can't help but smile at the way her eyes sparkle in the morning light. Moving closer, I nudge her with my cock, and her eyes widen.

"Straight to the point, I see," she teases, her voice laced with amusement.

"What do you expect when I wake up next to the most beautiful woman in the world?"

She blushes and murmurs, "Lies."

I lean in, pressing my lips to hers. "Not lies. It's the truth." Her soft chuckle is like music to my ears.

"A simple 'good morning' would have sufficed, you know," she teases, playfully scolding me.

"My apologies. Good morning, sunshine," I say, peppering kisses along her stomach. "My sweetheart." *Kiss.* "My girl." *Kiss.*

Each word is punctuated by a kiss, and I feel her body shudder beneath me.

Careful of my shoulder, I move up to capture her mouth in a kiss, my lips meeting hers with a hunger that never seems to fade. She responds eagerly, her hands moving to tangle in my hair as our kiss deepens. A surge of desire for this woman fills my insides and my heart pounds in my chest.

She is *everything* to me.

Her declaration of love still echoes in my mind. Since she said those words, it's been eating at me. I hate feeling vulnerable; it's one of my least favourite things. And yet, hearing her say she loves me, knowing that I feel the same, has made me feel raw and exposed. That fucking voice in my head keeps filling me with doubts. What if I'm not enough? What if I can't be what she needs? I don't like feeling like this, so open and uncertain. It's a struggle, this feeling of being so vulnerable, but the truth is, I wouldn't trade it. Not for anything.

"God, I missed you," I whisper against her lips, my voice husky with emotion. She smiles against my mouth.

"I missed you, too."

She pushes me back carefully, breaking the kiss, before straddling my hips, placing herself directly on top of me. I can feel the heat of her body against mine, igniting a fire within me that only she can quench.

I run a hand up her sides, feeling the curve of her waist, the softness of her skin. She leans down, capturing my lips again, and I respond eagerly, losing myself in the taste and feel of her.

She leans in from the side, her lips leaving a trail of soft kisses down my chest. Each touch sends a shiver through me. Her kisses wander lower, across my abdomen, careful not to press too hard, avoiding my ribs. A wave of anticipation washes over me as she moves down further, settling in front of my cock, which strains beneath the fabric.

She hesitates, and I ask, "What?"

"How's your pain?" she says, nodding to my shoulder and ribs. I'd taken off the bandage earlier this morning, iced it for twenty minutes, and then took a tablet for further pain relief, so right now, I'm not feeling much pain at all.

"I'm fine, Mills," I assure her. No amount of pain will deter me from anything.

"You sure?"

"Yes, babe. I'm sure," I reply. She smirks at me.

"I want to make you feel good," she says.

My already hardened cock throbs at her words, standing up tall for attention under my briefs. I can't help but encourage her with a grin. "I'm not going to stop you, sunshine. Go for it." She tugs at the waistband of my briefs, pulling them down my legs, and my cock springs free.

Her fingers wrap around me, her touch feather-light and teasing. I shiver at the sensation as she begins to stroke me slowly. Then she lowers her mouth, her warm breath sending shivers down my spine before her lips envelop me completely. The way she circles her tongue around the tip makes me fight the urge to groan.

Fuck, she's a natural. She's learned well, and it feels incredible—better than I ever expected.

Her hand pumps at the base, the pressure just right as she moves up and down. Each stroke drives me wild, and I can't help but grip her hair, pulling her closer. The way her mouth feels, warm and wet, sends me spiralling. Her soft moans and the sound of her sucking push me to the edge. To my surprise, she takes me even further, her throat opening to accommodate me. I groan in disbelief as she gags slightly before moving back up.

"Oh, fuck," I can't help but groan as she swirls her tongue around the tip, and I feel myself nearing the brink. Her free hand runs down to fondle my balls, and I nearly lurch forward from the sensation.

It's a new sensation, one I didn't teach her.

The feeling of her mouth on my cock, coupled with her hands massaging my balls, becomes too much. "Fuck, fuck. I'm gonna come," I groan out. Before I know it, I'm coming hard and fast. She doesn't pull away, though. Instead, she keeps going, sucking me dry as my orgasm crashes over me. I growl through gritted teeth, overwhelmed by the intensity.

She swallows every drop, then releases me with a soft *pop*, wiping her mouth as she pants, her chest heaving. Her face is flushed, and I'm hit with a powerful urge to kiss her.

"Come here," I manage to grunt, and she moves closer, rounding my side. I grab her by the back of the head, pulling her mouth to mine, but she hesitates.

"Wait. I just swallowed your—"

"I don't give a fuck," I growl, cutting her off as I take her lips in a fierce kiss. The mingling taste of my cum and her sweet lips ignite a primal hunger within me. I deepen the kiss, savouring the intoxicating blend of our flavours. Pulling away, I exhale heavily.

"That was... fuck. That was amazing."

"Well, I had an *excellent* teacher," she quips, a playful laugh dancing in her voice.

I growl playfully. "Damn straight, sunshine."

As I lie here, feeling her warmth against me, my mind drifts. I think about Amelia and my sister—wondering how she'll react to us being together—and everything else. Last night replays in my mind, each scene raw and vivid. I was sure I wouldn't make it out. When that explosion hit, all I could see were her brown eyes, her smile; just her.

Yet, here I am, breathing, feeling her breathing next to me.

I shake my head, trying to clear away the thoughts. I should be grateful, shouldn't I? Grateful for this moment, for her, for being alive. But the what-ifs, the could-have-beens, they linger.

I wrap my arm around her, pulling her closer, needing the reassurance that she's real, that this is real.

"Bradley?" Her voice breaks through my thoughts.

"Hm."

"I can hear you thinking."

I chuckle lightly, but the movement causes a twinge of discomfort in my ribcage. "It's nothing, babe."

She sits up. "Tell me. Please."

I huff a laugh again, but then stop myself short, wincing this time—not wanting to strain myself any more. She apologises for making me laugh, and I shoot her a look.

"What have I said about apologising?" She just rolls her eyes at me. I continue answering her question with a sigh. It's such a simple question, well maybe for her, yet the answer is so loaded. How could I ever truly explain what goes on in my mind?

"What isn't?" I say nervously, pausing to consider how to express the jumble of thoughts. "Just... everything. Last night, us..."

Her brow furrows slightly. "It's a lot, isn't it?"

I take a deep breath, trying to find the right words. "I was just thinking... about how fragile everything is. How quickly life can change." My words trail off, and I shake my head. Amelia studies me, her gaze intent.

"What are *you* thinking now?" I ask, wanting to know what's on her mind.

She shakes her head, unsure. "I don't know."

"Tell me," I urge, mimicking her works from earlier, wanting to understand.

"Has... has anyone ever mentioned that you might have GAD?" she asks tentatively.

"What's GAD?" I inquire, not familiar with the term.

"Generalised Anxiety Disorder?" she explains. "You know, because you're always thinking and worrying about things. I'd assume you overthink things in your head, play out scenarios. Am I right?"

I frown, considering her words. Fuck. Could she be on to something? Is that what I have? I've never been diagnosed with anything, and we're trained and put through tests at the academy, to ensure we're one-hundred percent.

Anxiety? No, that can't be it. I don't think so.

She smiles at me, watching my reaction.

"I'm doing it now, aren't I?"

She shrugs. "It's okay, though. I just assumed, but I could be wrong. I deal with lots of children with GAD. I know kindergarteners are different, but we see it in our older students."

Amelia continues to reassure me that it's normal, that this might be what gives me that *grumpy* vibe. She doesn't believe I'm a real grump, just that I'm so caught up in my head that I give off those *brooding* vibes—as she put it.

Fuck, how can someone know me so well? She sees right through me, and to my surprise, it doesn't bother me at all.

"Bradley," she says softly. "You can open up to me whenever you want. I won't judge you. I just want you to be yourself. Always." Her words wash over me, and I feel a weight lift off my shoulders.

She has this power over me. In her eyes, I can be myself.

"Come," she says, getting out of bed. "Let's make some breakfast." She gently pulls me up, and I follow her into the kitchen. But as we move, her steps falter, and she stops suddenly, a gasp escaping her mouth. I look up to see what caused it, and my heart drops.

Standing in the doorway, holding a set of keys, is my *sister*.

"What. The. *Fuck?*" Liv's voice cuts through the silence.

"Liv..." Amelia whispers, her voice barely audible. My sister just frowns, just standing there, not saying anything else.

Well, shit.

Her gaze flickers between us, eyes narrowing as she takes in the scene. We're not exactly dressed for company.

"What the FUCK is going on here?" Liv demands, her voice sharp. "Are you two… together?" she asks, her tone accusatory.

Amelia stumbles over her words, and I step in to confirm, "Yes."

Liv gasps, her disbelief evident. "What? I'm so fucking confused. No, this can't be real," she laughs incredulously. "You're fucking joking, right?"

"Liv, I didn't know you were coming by. I—" Amelia begins, but my sister cuts her off, her tone sharp.

"I texted you!"

"I'm so sorry, I haven't checked my phone," Amelia explains, trying to defuse the situation.

Liv's eyes flash with anger. "Of course you didn't. You were probably too busy fucking my brother," she spits, each word laced with venom.

Amelia recoils, her face paling. I feel a surge of protectiveness toward her, but I know Liv's anger is justified.

My sister directs her gaze toward Amelia. "How long?" she asks, her tone demanding. Amelia hesitates, not answering immediately.

"Liv—" I start, but she holds up a hand, cutting me off.

"You, shut the fuck up. I'm talking to her. How long, Amelia? How long have you been seeing my *brother* behind my fucking back?" Liv's voice is sharp.

Amelia takes a deep breath, her voice barely above a whisper. "A few months."

"Months?" She blows out a breath. "Are you for real?" Liv cries out, her frustration palpable. "It's been months. FUCKING MONTHS, and you never thought to tell me?"

Amelia's eyes fill with tears. "Liv, I promise you, we were planning on telling you. We just..." she trails off, unable to find the right words.

"Oh. You *were* planning on telling me?" Liv asks, her voice dripping with sarcasm. "When exactly?"

I step forward. "We should have told you sooner. We know. We both just got caught up."

Liv's fists clench at her sides. "I thought you were my friend, Amelia. MY BEST FRIEND!" She laughs nervously. "I'd suspected you'd had a little crush on him, but I never fucking thought it would get to this extent. Going behind my fucking back!"

As Liv's words cut through the air, I feel a sharp pang of guilt for the hurt I've caused my sister. What we've both caused. Her anger is palpable, yet amidst this, my heart breaks for Amelia, too. She stands there, pale and shaken, bearing the weight of my sister's accusations. I know she's feeling the same thing as me. She'd been concerned, and I'd selfishly brushed it off, saying we'd tell her when 'the time was right'.

Olivia's words hang heavy in the air, a stark reminder of the breach of trust between us. She backs toward the door, her expression hardened.

"Please, Liv... don't leave. Let's talk about this. Let *me* explain," Amelia's soft voice pleads, breaking the tense silence.

Olivia pauses, caught in a moment of contemplation, her eyes reflecting a mix of hurt and anger. "You know, Amelia, fair enough. I get it. You've never experienced being with a guy before, so you'd jump at any opportunity you get," she says, her voice laced with disdain.

"Liv, there's no need to be hurtful," I say through gritted teeth.

"But you," Liv continues, pointing at me, "you fucking disappoint me," she spits. "I can't even look at you. You both disgust me." Her parting words sting, the final blow to an already shattered moment, before she turns, slamming the door behind her, leaving us both standing there, hearts heavy with regret.

The weight of her words hangs heavy in the air, and I can feel the sting of her disappointment like a physical blow. As an older brother, the sense of duty to my sister weighs heavily on me, and I know I've let her down. I turn to Amelia, who now has tears streaming down her cheeks. I wrap my arms around her, pulling her close as she buries her face in my chest, her body shaking with sobs, and my heart breaks.

I feel responsible. *This is all my fault.*

"She hates me. Oh, God," Amelia says into my chest.

I hold her tighter, trying to offer what little comfort I can. "She'll come around. I know it," I say, hoping it's true.

Amelia sniffles, pulling away slightly to look at me. "I don't know, Bradley. This is a mess."

This is a mess. I couldn't agree more.

As I continue to hold her, rubbing circles on her back, deep down, a part of me fears that Liv's hurt runs too deep, that this betrayal might be too much for her to forgive. And if Liv can't forgive, I can't help but wonder how Amelia will cope with losing her best friend.

The thought gnaws at me, twisting my gut with worry. This mess has the potential to not only damage Amelia's relationship with Liv, but also to jeopardise whatever we have between us.

How do we move forward from this?

"Bradley," she whispers, her voice choked with emotion. "Maybe you should go home. Talk to her. You're her brother; maybe she'll listen. I just need some time to think." My heart sinks at her words, and I frown, realising my fears may have been correct.

I can't think of anywhere else I'd rather be but *here*, with *her*. But I respect her enough to do what she asks, as much as I hate it. I reluctantly release her from my embrace and head to her bedroom to change and grab my things.

Returning to the living room, I find Amelia still standing in the same spot, her eyes red and swollen with tears. I move to her side, gently tilting her chin up to meet my gaze.

"We're gonna be okay," I reassure her, my voice soft.

She looks at me, hurt evident in her eyes. "I-I hope so... I just need to fix things with her. I can't lose her."

I swallow hard, a pang of disappointment hitting me. *What about me?* I want to say, but I hold back, wanting her to ask me to stay, to reassure me as well.

But nothing.

With a heavy sigh, I acknowledge her request and press a soft kiss to her forehead before turning toward the door. Stepping out into the morning air, a sense of foreboding settles over me, and I'm left to ponder what lies ahead for us.

43

Amelia

It feels like forever since I last saw Bradley or Liv. Each day drags on, and the ache in my heart just gets heavier. I miss Liv—her presence, our conversations, our laughs, and jokes.

But God, do I miss Bradley even more.

I've been receiving messages from Isla and Xav, checking in on me. Even Imogen sent a text the other day, offering her own comforting words. She even mentioned that she's there if I need to vent. But I didn't have it in me to reply. *I feel horrible.*

I'm not one to be rude or dismissive. Not replying to everyone, when all they're trying to do is provide *some* comfort, is just downright bitchy.

But I just couldn't.

I chose to distance myself from everyone, not out of spite, but because if I engaged in those conversations, it would only make me feel even more terrible for my deceitful actions.

I'm embarrassed.

Before I knew it, the opening exhibition night at the gallery in Sydney came around, which brings me to the present—making my way to Wattle Creek Regional Airport. My parents opted to drive me here.

Yesterday morning, I had to carefully wrap my artworks individually and package them before shipping them off. Heading into town to our local post office, I'd bumped into Grace Mitchell, and our conversation plays out in my mind vividly.

"How you holding up, dear?" Grace had asked.

"I'm fine. What do you mean?"

"Honey, I know just about everything that goes on in my household and outside."

I smiled nervously. "I'm so sorry. I didn't mean to cause any trouble. I'm sure Olivia's told you by now—" But she'd cut me off.

"Olivia? Oh, no, dear. Olivia hasn't told me anything."

"Oh... but how do you know?" Grace had smiled warmly, placing a comforting hand on mine.

"Honey, I'm his mother. It's my job to know what goes on in his life. I've been watching him for the past month or so, dear. I knew from the start. Everywhere you'd go, he'd be there; you'd call, he'd be there. He lives and breathes you, honey."

I choked out a sob.

"I don't think you see it, but you are the 'something' that's been missing in his life. And that man hasn't been himself for a while. Then, all of a sudden, he's smiling more, talking more, and performing heroic acts. You did that, darling."

"But Olivia..." I had started, but Grace swatted the air.

"Don't you worry about my daughter. She'll see it, too, soon enough."

As we pull up to the airport, I take a deep breath, ridding myself of those thoughts, trying to steel myself for what's to come. I step out of the car, thanking my parents for the ride.

"Sweetheart, we're just a phone call away if you need us," Mum says, her voice filled with concern.

"I know, Mum. Thanks," I reply, forcing a smile.

After everything went down, after Dad kept asking when he was going to see Bradley again, I had to tell them what had happened. It broke my heart to see their faces droop as I told them. They really liked having him around, even if it was short-lived.

Dad remains silent, his expression unreadable. I can sense his disappointment, even though he'll never admit it. It breaks my heart to see him like this.

"I'll be okay," I assure them, trying to sound more confident than I feel.

"We love you, Amelia," Dad finally speaks, his voice heavy with emotion.

"I love you both," I say, blinking back tears.

"Kat will pick you up from the airport, okay?" Mum adds, her voice soft. I nod, grateful for my sister's presence in my life, especially now.

"Okay," I reply, grabbing my suitcase and backpack before heading inside the airport. As I reach the reception desk to check in and retrieve my tickets, I can't help but wonder if things will ever be the same again.

Pulling out my phone, I check for any messages from Olivia, but there's nothing. With a heavy heart, I open our text message thread and reread over the unread messages, my breathing hitching as I swallow the lump down my throat.

> **Me:** *Can we talk? Please!*

> **Me:** *I'm so sorry. I know I'm in the wrong, and I really want to explain things to you.*

Above our thread is my chat with Bradley, and the *last* messages that sit there are from him and me the day he'd gone off to help with the fires.

> **Bradley:** *I will. I'll see you back at home.*

> **Me:** *I'll be waiting for you.*

How can I be with him now if Olivia never wants to talk to me again? As the airport announces my flight is ready to board, I take a deep breath and gather my things. The airport bustles around me, but I feel disconnected, lost in my thoughts.

I find my seat and settle in, staring out the window. The engines hum to life, and the plane begins moving, slowly making its way toward the runway. As we take off, I feel a sense of weightlessness, both from the plane lifting off the ground and from the weight of the past week lifting off my shoulders.

The cityscape below me shrinks as we climb higher into the sky, disappearing beneath the clouds.

I try to distract myself with my Kindle, but my mind keeps drifting back to Bradley and Liv. I wonder if she'll ever forgive me, if things will ever go back to how they were. The flight attendant interrupts my thoughts, offering me a drink. I politely decline, lost in my own world. The hours pass slowly, each minute dragging on as I replay our last conversation over and over in my head.

Did I do the right thing by leaving so soon?

Maybe I should have cancelled going to the exhibition. I'm conflicted. The uncertainty gnaws at me, making it impossible to find peace.

Eventually, we begin our descent toward Sydney. My stomach churns with a mix of anxiety and anticipation. What will I find when I get there? A part of me hopes for clarity, for some kind of sign that will tell me what to do next. But another part of me is terrified of what that sign might be. I stare out the window, watching the cityscape come into view, and take a deep breath.

I can't shake the feeling of regret for not telling Liv sooner, for going behind her back. The thought brings tears to my eyes.

Whatever happens, I know I have to face it head-on.

This is my mess to clean up, my mistakes to own.

44

Bradley

One whole week it's been since I last saw Amelia, and every day feels like a lifetime. One *long* fucking week of trying to distract myself so I don't lose my shit.

It's like I've been thrown back to those months before I started hanging around her. I wake up, head to work, come home, struggle to sleep—well, the lack thereof—and repeat. I've been pushing myself, throwing everything into work.

My body screams for me to stop, to rest, but I can't. My shoulder's a dull ache now, where it was once dislocated, and my ribs are doing better. I can breathe easier now, well... in the *pain* scheme of things. The doctors are pleased with my recovery, especially this quickly. I no longer need pain meds, but I occasionally still ice my ribs now and then.

Right now, we're getting rid of old furniture from the station, making way for new desks and facilities. I'm out back, tossing some old stuff from my desk into the skip bin.

"Easy there, tiger. Need a hand?" Daniels asks.

"No," I grunt, lifting a chair with my good arm, tossing it in. I look back at Daniels, who's standing there with a moon boot and sporting crutches.

My eyes soften for a moment, and I feel a pang of guilt for my mate. His injury is on me. If I hadn't moved closer to that house, Daniels wouldn't have come to get me, and he wouldn't have been hurt. I stare at his boot.

"Hey. Don't do that."

"Do what?" I say, my tone clipped.

"Don't beat yourself up over it. It's cool, mate. Protect and defend our own. Always," he says with a nod.

Protect and defend our own.

If only I'd done that for Amelia. If only I'd done that for my sister. If only I'd listened to myself over the past few months and not pursued her. The one time I make a sacrifice, the one time I do something for myself—something I'd been hesitant to do—and look where it's gotten me.

A sister who won't talk to me, won't even look at me; a mother who looks at me like she knows something but won't say it; and now Amelia—I feel like I'm losing her, too.

I feel as though maybe I already have.

I failed her. I failed everyone.

I sigh, the weight of it all bearing down on me. I shouldn't be lifting anything too heavy, but I don't give a fuck. The pain only spurs me on more to keep going.

My ribs now scream in protest, but the *ache* in my chest is worse. I busy myself, trying to push through the pain, both physical and emotional, but it's no use. It's always there, gnawing at me, reminding me of what I've done and what I've lost.

Daniels breaks the silence. "The council wants you to join some of the firefighters in addressing them about the incident."

I just shrug.

"They're calling you the town's local hero."

"They're wrong. I did nothing."

Daniels scoffs. "Who are you tryna bullshit? Because it ain't working for me, mate." He goes silent for a moment. "Is this about Amelia?"

My body goes rigid. "What?"

"Reynolds told me about her. Sorry," he says, raising his hands in mock surrender. "Says that your foul mood might have something to do with her leaving." *Leaving?* What's he talking about?

"Leaving?"

"Yeah, she went to Sydney. For some exhibition or some shit. I dunno."

Fuck. I *forgot* about her exhibition. I could kill Reynolds right now.

"What else did he tell you?" How the fuck does he know?

"Dunno, man. Go and ask him," he says, nodding to the station.

"Fuck," I mutter to myself.

"Hey, for what it's worth, she made you *happy*, Bradley. You changed over these past few weeks. Whatever happened between the two of you, get it sorted." Daniels says with a crooked smile.

How could I forget about her exhibition? She had asked if I'd be there, and I had told her I would be. And yet, I fucking forgot. How pathetic. That's the only word that comes to mind.

My heart sinks as I think about how disappointed she must be feeling. How could I have been so careless? I storm inside, not wanting to hear any more.

"Reynolds!" I bark out, searching for him. Woody and Stokes look up from their desks, confusion on their faces. They both point to the lunchroom, and I barge in.

"Bradley, what's up?" he says with a smile, sitting at one of the tables with another constable.

"How do *you* know that *she* left?" My voice is sharp, demanding answers.

His brows furrow for a moment before recognition forms in his eyes. "Rose told me. She said Amelia ran into her in town the other day and they spoke about everything."

"Everything?" I ask, not putting two and two together.

"Yeah, Amelia said she's taken more time off than she needs to, just to get away, to think and just wait..."

His words trail off, and I growl, "Think about what? Wait for what?"

"To see if things sort themselves out," he finishes, shooting me a knowing look. Does she mean my sister, or does she mean me?

I fucking told her I'd wait for her.

And I *meant* it.

I'd wait a fucking *lifetime*, for her, if it meant she'd come back to me.

45

Amelia

Today has been a day. I'm exhausted.

I can't remember the last time I did this much walking. My Fitbit tells me that I've walked over sixteen-thousand steps, and I almost passed out when we got back to my sister's place.

I had ended up taking a whole week off work, instead of just a few days—with the kids going on holiday soon, my boss didn't make a fuss about it. I just needed some *extra* time away.

I need to give *Liv* some more time.

Kat has been amazing, keeping me busy for the past couple of days. Yesterday, she took me out to the harbour. We saw the bridge, the Opera House, and discovered some amazing little nooks and crannies I never knew existed.

Today, Kat and Millie took me to The Rocks. We grabbed a coffee, browsed through some bookstores, and stumbled upon a small art shop. I stocked up on pencils because I've decided to take a break from painting. I want to try graphite and charcoal.

Change of scenery, change of style, I guess.

As I sit here now, sketching on a fresh pad of paper, I can feel a bit of the weight lifting off my shoulders. The change of pace is nice, and the distraction helps, but the ache is still there. Every stroke of the pencil reminds me of what I left behind, what I'm trying to forget, even if just for a little while.

I focus on the details of the person's face, working meticulously on the eyes, making sure to get every detail right. Millie is keeping me company while Kat makes dinner inside. We're nestled in the spare room, which is my bed for the next week.

"What's that?" Millie asks, pointing to the paper.

"It's a drawing, munchkin," I explain to her.

"Can I draw?" she asks so innocently, and my heart swells. How I hope to have a daughter like her one day—always so eager to try things, so polite, and just so incredibly cute. I grab her cheek and blow a raspberry on it. She squeals and giggles.

"You sure can. You can draw with Aunty Meli," I say, ripping a page out of the book and handing her a lead pencil.

That's how we spend the next twenty-five minutes, nestled on the bed, showing Millie how to draw simple shapes while I work on my own pencil skills. When I finish the rough sketch, I look at it and my lip quivers.

"Bwadey, Bwadey. Where is Bwadey Bear?" Millie asks.

The drawing captures his likeness so vividly. It's from his chest up. He's not looking directly at me; his face is off to the side, with a hand behind his head, as he does when he's thinking.

Seeing his image there on the paper brings a fresh wave of emotion, and I struggle to hold back the tears. This is the man I love, the man I might not be with again because of everything that's happened. Because of my mistakes.

I hope Liv can eventually get past it. If not being with Bradley will help salvage our friendship, then I'll do what I need to. I need to sort this out with Liv before I can even think about going back to Bradley.

No. I need to *stop*, to *breathe*. But my mind won't listen. It keeps replaying every memory, every shared laugh and intimate moment. My heart feels heavy with the weight of it all, the uncertainty of what lies ahead.

But how do I find a way back to the simplicity we once had?

46

Bradley

I'm on my third Jack and Coke, not giving a single fuck—seated at the bar of The Loose Lasso. It was a long fucking day at work, dealing with the aftermath of the press release this morning. The weight of upholding the hero image the town expects from me is heavy on my shoulders. Dealing with the public, with the townspeople, it's all just exhausting.

But right now, none of that matters.

"Need a refill?" the bartender says, nodding to my now-empty glass. I nod to her, feeling a buzz warming my body. Just as she starts to make my drink, a young woman sets herself on the bar stool next to me, her thigh brushing against mine.

Her touch does nothing for me.

"Why is a handsome man like you all alone tonight?" Her voice is sweet and her perfume wraps around me—but it's a sickly sweet scent; I fight the urge not to scrunch up my nose.

It's not floral, nor is it cherry.

"Just enjoying a drink," I say, my tone clipped.

"I can see, and all alone, at that. Want some company?"

"No thanks. Not in the mood."

"Why not?"

"It's complicated," I reply, hoping she'll finally drop it. I'm not in the mood for company, especially not *hers*. But she seems undeterred.

"Wanna talk about it?" she says, her hand lingering on my arm.

"No, I don't," I state firmly, finishing my drink, leaving a fifty on the counter, and heading for the door. As I stride out of the bar, someone calls out my name.

"Hey, it's Bradley Mitchell," they say, followed by another voice, *"Fuck, that guy's a gun. A hero."*

I pay them no mind, my focus solely on getting home. As I leave the bar, the buzz from the drinks makes me realise I am in no state to drive. I reach for my phone to call for an Uber instead, making a mental note to retrieve my car in the morning. Before long, the Uber pulls up outside, and I hop in, heading home.

Once inside, I beeline straight for my father's liquor cabinet, grabbing the half-empty bottle of Jack Daniels. More alcohol isn't the best idea right now, but it might just help numb the ache I'm feeling.

Outside, I seat myself in one of the outdoor chairs, not caring if I'm being too loud. I take a sip from the bottle, the burn of the whiskey barely registering. Pulling out my phone, I open my text messages with Amelia, the *last* one from me *unanswered*.

Taking a deep breath, I press the call button next to her name. My heart lurches forward as anticipation kicks in, but it goes to voicemail.

Fuck. I type out a text instead.

> **Me:** Why didn't you tell me you left for the exhibition?

After what feels like an eternity, a reply finally comes back.

> **Amelia:** Why would I need to tell you?

> **Me:** Because you told me about it. You asked me to be there, and I said I would.

I fire back, my fingers tapping on the screen with agitation.

> **Amelia:** I know, but things have changed. It doesn't matter.

It doesn't matter? How can she say that? I fight the urge to crush the bottle in my grasp.

> **Amelia:** I've been reflecting on everything, and I believe we should take a step back for a while. It's not easy for me to say this, but I think it's necessary for now.

I think the fuck not. I blink hard, trying to clear the blurriness from the alcohol, and manage to type out a coherent text. It takes a moment for the words to come into focus, but I finally get it right.

> **Me:** For who? You OR my sister?

Amelia: I'm not sure. Maybe both?

> **Me:** Not really thinking about my sister right now. Thinking about us.

> **Me:** I care about us.

> **Me:** You are your own person. So is she. She'll get over it in time.

I wait for a response, but none comes.

With a growl of frustration, I pick up the bottle of Jack Daniels and throw it, wincing as it smashes to the ground. The light turns on from the kitchen, and surprisingly, Olivia steps out.

"What the fuck are you doing?" she demands, her voice cutting through the air. It's the first time she's spoken to me in a week.

I turn to face her, my frustration boiling over. "You done fucking sooking?" I snap, my tone sharp.

Her eyes narrow, and she stands up straight. "Excuse me?"

"You heard me," I reply, my voice challenging, the alcohol fueling my defiance. Fuck this. I'm not in the right state of mind to deal with her right now.

Turning away without a word, I storm toward the stairs, each step fueling the rage boiling inside me. I can feel Olivia's eyes drilling into my back, but I ignore it. I reach my room and slam the door shut behind me, the sound echoing in the quiet house.

I collapse onto my bed, my body trembling as the room spins around me. The weight of everything crashes down, each thought of betrayal, each confrontation with Liv, each frustration with Amelia, overwhelming me. The silence of the room is suffocating, the weight of my thoughts crushing. I long for a moment of peace, a respite from the storm raging inside me. But for now, all I can do is lie here, lost in a sea of emotions, hoping that, somehow, we'll find our way back to each other.

I bury my face in my hands, trying to block out the chaos inside me, but it's futile.

Amelia

We're all sitting at Kat's dining table, after having a late dinner, the TV running softly in the open lounge room. I've been quiet, with Kat and John doing most of the talking. My mind is still reeling from my recent conversation with Brad. I can feel tears threatening to spill, but I fight them back. Not here, not in front of everyone. Especially not in front of Millie. Kat had been there when Brad was messaging me, offering support and encouragement. I really struggled to find the right words, and it hurt more than I expected. Thank goodness for Kat—she practically told me what to say when I couldn't find the words myself. I don't know how I would've managed without her.

Trying to lighten the mood, Kat asks if she can see the *new* drawings I've been working on. I smile softly at her and say, "Not yet."

"Bwadey drawings. Can I see?" Millie's voice chimes in, and I force a smile at her.

"Soon, munchkin."

"Bradley drawings?" Kat questions softly.

"It's nothing," I reply, my voice barely above a whisper, my sadness seeping through.

Just then, the TV changes to a news report. At the mention of fires, police officers, and a hero, I turn my head. Millie squeals, "Bwadey. Bwadey."

My heart sinks.

It's a news recap of a conference from the morning, with the local hero of Wattle Creek front and centre. Bradley in all his glory. Without thinking, I stand and walk over to the back of the lounge, listening intently. His voice fills the room as he expresses his gratitude for the community's support, and for the support of local officers, firefighters, and all services.

"*It was sheer will and instinct that led me to make those reckless actions,*" Bradley says on the TV. "*The only thing driving me was someone special to me, driving me to make those decisions. If it weren't for her, I probably wouldn't have made it. She was the light that kept me alive.*"

He's talking about me, on live television, to *everyone*. Oh, God.

I gasp, my hand flying to my mouth as I stare at the screen, stunned. Hearing his words on live television feels like a punch to the gut, especially when I think about how I brushed off his text messages earlier. The contrast between his words and my careless responses hits me hard, and I'm suddenly drowning in regret.

Tears well up in my eyes, and I can't bear to hear any more. I rush to the spare room, closing the door behind me, before curling into a ball on my bed as sobs wrack my body, the flood of emotions overwhelming me completely. Through my cries, I hear Kat and Millie's voices at the door.

Millie asks, "Meli, what's wrong with Meli?"

"She's just upset, baby. She'll be okay. Come."

"Bwadey will help her," Millie says innocently, and this only intensifies my sobs.

47

Bradley

The next morning, I wake up groggy, the events of last night slowly filtering back into my memory. I called in sick for work, not wanting to face the day with a hangover. As I stir awake, voices fill the space around me.

"How long has he been like this?"

"I dunno. He got pretty drunk last night."

"Bradley, drunk?"

"Yeah. I know, right?"

Fuck's sake.

"Wake him up."

"No, *you* wake him up."

I bury my face farther into my pillow and groan aloud. "I'm already awake," I grumble, my voice muffled.

"Rise and shine, sweetheart," I hear a familiar deep voice say, and I blink my eyes to find my brother and sister standing above me.

"What the fuck?" I say, my voice groggy.

"Bradley, get up," Liv says.

"No, piss off."

"Don't make me jump on you, Brad. I will," Xavier warns. Oh, I'm *so* scared.

"Don't, he's still injured," my sister says. I feel my lips turn upward at her words. *So, she does still care.*

"So fucking what? More of an incentive to do it," Xavier retorts. *He's such a fuckwit..*

"I'm getting up. Fuck off," I grumble.

"What's this I hear about you getting drunk?" he asks, genuine concern in his voice. As I sit up, still feeling the effects of the hangover, Xavier's words sink in.

I shrug, not wanting to admit to the mess I've made. "Nothing."

"And smashing bottles? Mum had to clean up *your* mess this morning," Olivia adds, her disappointment evident.

Fuck's sake.

"I'm sorry," I reply, feeling the weight of their words. I need to sort myself out, but right now, I just need to get through this hangover. I look at Olivia, the question burning in my mind. "So, you're talking to me now?"

"I guess so," she shrugs.

"So, what does that mean?" I ask, furrowing my brows. Olivia ponders my question for a moment, and Xavier just stands there, watching the exchange.

"Do you love her?" Olivia's question catches me off guard, but instantly I know who she's referring to.

"Is that a trick question?" I emit a snort of amusement.

"No. Answer my fucking question," she insists.

"Oo, feisty," Xavier chimes in, earning a glare from Olivia.

As I sit there, contemplating Olivia's question, the truth hits me like a ton of bricks. *Do I love her?* It's such a stupid fucking question because the answer is so blindingly obvious. One that I hadn't been able to voice.

Until now.

"Yes. I love her," I finally admit, my voice barely above a whisper.

"But how do you know?" Olivia questions me, crossing her arms.

Without hesitation, I reply, "Because I've loved her from the very moment I saw her."

I pause, taking in a breath before continuing. "All these years, I've put up boundaries, told myself she was off limits, but it became too fucking hard to ignore. She's not just someone I love; she's a part of me, a part of my soul. And I'll continue to love her, no matter what."

Olivia gasps, a look of shock on her face. I'm stunned, too, by my own confession.

Xavier breaks the silence with a simple, "Well, I'll be damned."

"Then what the fuck are you still doing here?" Olivia questions so casually.

Confusion mars my face. "Huh?"

"Why haven't you left already? Fucking go and get her," Olivia says, her tone casual yet firm.

Xavier chimes in, "She thinks you don't *care* anymore. It's been a week, and she hasn't heard anything from you."

I'm getting frustrated. How does everyone seem to know more about this situation than I do? It's starting to really piss me off.

"I fucking texted her. Saying I'd wait for her," I explain, pulling out my phone to double-check that message.

> **Me:** This isn't over. I'll be here, waiting for you. When you're ready.

But next to it is a red exclamation mark indicating it *wasn't* delivered. *For fuck's sake.*

In my drunken state last night, I mustn't have noticed when I'd checked our texts.

"She didn't get it," Olivia confirms the obvious. I sigh, feeling defeated.

"I spoke to her last night, though," I add, but the words feel hollow as they leave my lips. There was no confirmation in our conversation. I feel a sinking feeling in my chest, the uncertainty of where we stand weighing heavily on me. She never responded to my messages. Olivia shoots me a sympathetic glance.

"This is what she sent me last night," she says, lifting her phone to show me a series of texts.

> **Amelia:** I'm unsure where things will lead for Brad and me, but I want you to know I truly love him. I really do. He never said it back, so you don't have to worry. Maybe it wasn't meant to be.

> **Amelia:** I can't begin to express how sorry I am for hurting you, for betraying your trust and our friendship. I never meant for any of this to happen. I hope we can talk soon and work through this.

> **Amelia:** I truly am sorry. I love you, Liv.

"Fucking hell, Liv," I mutter, staring at the messages on the phone. I don't bother reading the rest, and I groan in frustration, feeling a surge of anger and desperation. "How could you not see that?" I can't help but raise my voice, my emotions boiling over. "I love *her*." I choke on my words, shaking my head.

But it's too late. The words, while spoken, don't have the same impact because they're not being said to the person who *needs* to hear them. It's fucking devastating, and I'm left feeling crushed, knowing that I may have lost her forever.

"Oi! Listen here, don't fucking blame me for not *seeing* anything!" Olivia screams back, making air quotes. "If there's anyone to blame, it's yourself. Why didn't you fucking tell her you love her back, huh?" She shoves my chest. "You led her to believe you don't fucking love her. Why wouldn't you tell her?"

I stand here, stunned.

She's right. I never told her I loved her. I've been such a coward, stuck in my head, letting fear and vulnerability dictate my actions.

Since when do I fucking cower away from doing what's right?

I should have told her I loved her back when I had the chance.

It was the right thing to do, and I just... didn't. I drop my head to my chest, absorbing my sister's words while my brother stays quiet beside me. Deep, burning embarrassment runs through me.

I fucking hate the way I am.

I fucking hate being so caught up in my head all the time. I pinch the bridge of my nose, trying to fight off the chaos swirling in my mind. Hearing it all out loud is a brutal wake-up call.

It's like everything is now finally crystal clear.

"Bradley?" Olivia's voice is softer this time, laced with concern. I take a deep breath, exhaling loudly as I wipe at the tears that have begun to prick the corners of my eyes—tears I hadn't even realised were there.

I lift my head, meeting my sister's gaze. Her eyes are glistening with her own tears. "I'm so sorry," she says, her voice trembling. "I was so fucking hurt, blinded by my own pain, that I didn't even see you both were hurting, too." She reaches up to gently wipe the rogue tears that have started to fall down my cheeks.

Hearing Liv's words, a sense of relief washes over me, yet it does nothing to ease the ache in my chest. We've been stumbling around in the dark, each of us hurting without even knowing the full extent of our own pain.

"How do I even get there?" I ask, frustration seeping into my voice. "I don't even know where she's staying."

"One step ahead of you," Olivia says, typing on her phone. Xavier, who's been silent throughout this whole ordeal, does the same. In an instant, an address in Sydney appears on my screen, along with an email from Xavier containing a link.

I frown and click on the link—a return ticket to Sydney. Time of departure: ten fifteen a.m..

I glance at my phone. Eight thirty-five a.m.

"Fuck. I need to get dressed. I don't even have a suitcase."

Just then, Isla, who must have been standing at the door, walks in unannounced.

"I'm sorry, I wasn't eavesdropping, but I brought this by," she says, with a small suitcase at her side, wheeling it into my room. "Xavier sent a text saying you'd be needing it."

My heart swells with love for these people—my family. There's just *one* person missing.

"Go get your girl, brother," Xavier says, clapping me on the back. I pull him into a tight hug, tears welling up in my eyes.

"I love you, Xavier."

Xav freezes at my words, his breathing quickening as he tightens his embrace. "I love you more," he replies.

I hear Isla sniffle, and I pull away from Xavier to find her wiping at her eyes. "Sorry, pregnancy hormones," she says with a shaky laugh, and we all chuckle.

Xavier glances around and says, "Did we all catch that? Bradley just said he loves me—out loud." He points at me while nodding with a grin.

I chuckle and reply, "Fuck off, you idiot."

"I truly am sorry, Bradley," Olivia says, her voice cracking. "I acted so immature. I was just hurt."

"I know, and I'm sorry, too," I say. "We both meant our apology. Amelia loves you so much. She cares about you a lot."

"I know. I care too," she says softly. "So, we're good?"

"Yeah, we're good," I reply, giving her a gentle punch on the shoulder.

"If you ever lie to me again, I'll chop your nuts off," she warns, half-jokingly.

"Yeah, yeah. No need for drastic measures, princess," I chuckle, trying to lighten the mood.

"Guys, hate to interrupt this beautiful family moment, but... time's ticking," Isla chimes in.

"Oh, fuck," I say, springing into action, filling up my suitcase with the essentials. We all pile into Xavier's Tacoma, the tension thick in the air. The engine roars to life as he heads toward the airport. My pulse races, matching the rapid blur of the scenery outside the window. Unease fills my mind, overthinking everything—*what if she doesn't want to see me? What if I say the wrong thing? What if it's too late?*

Nausea creeps up as I think this, twisting my stomach into knots. I grip the edge of my seat, my knuckles turning white. One word comes to mind: anxiety. It's anxiety I'm feeling. Ever since Amelia mentioned it, I've been thinking about it more, and she was fucking right.

She always is.

I've come to accept it. Anxiety gnaws at me, tightening my chest and making it hard to breathe. I swallow hard, trying to push it down, to focus on the task at hand.

As I board the plane, my heart pounds in my chest. I grip the armrest, my fingers tapping nervously as I settle into the cramped seat, my legs pressing uncomfortably against the seat in front of me. I shift, trying to find a more comfortable position, but my tall frame takes up most of the space. I thank God this flight is only an hour or so long. The engine hums softly in the background as I close my eyes, picturing her sweet face—her *smile*.

I can't wait to hold her in my arms again, to make things right, to start anew. The thought of seeing her, of fighting for us, is the only thing keeping me grounded.

Amelia has always been more than just someone I care about; she's the one who understands me in ways no one else ever has. Her kindness, her quiet strength, and the way her eyes light up when she talks about something she loves—it's all etched into my memory.

I think about the little moments we shared, the quiet conversations late at night, the way she fits perfectly against me when we cuddle. I miss her laughter, her voice, the way she makes even the worst days feel bearable. Every day without her has felt like an eternity, and I'm determined to show her just how much she means to me, and that I'm willing to do whatever it takes to win her back.

I know I missed my opportunity to tell her I love her.

I didn't understand the full extent of my feelings until I'd lost that chance. But now, I'm ready to be the man she deserves, the one who will stand by her no matter what. I want to build a future with her, to share everything—the highs and the lows.

She's my heart, my home, and I'm ready to prove that to her.

48

Bradley

After a restless flight, I finally touch down in Sydney. The journey felt like an eternity, my mind racing with thoughts of seeing her again. Now, as I hop into a taxi, I announce the address that I assume is her sister's house.

Nerves kick in, full-blown and trembling with anticipation. God, I could vomit. Swallowing hard, I tell myself, *Fucking get a grip, Bradley. You're fine.*

I fight the urge to spew into this taxi as we continue on. The taxi pulls up outside a small, modern federation-style home, its exterior painted in soothing shades of grey and white. I take a deep breath, trying to calm the nerves that threaten to overwhelm me. Stepping out, I make my way up the pathway, each step feeling heavier than the last. Finally, standing in front of the door, I raise my hand and knock, the sound echoing through the quiet street. I hear a voice from inside call out, "Coming!"

The sound of footsteps approaches the door, and it swings open. Kat, Amelia's sister, stands there, her expression a mix of shock and relief.

"Bradley?" she gasps, her voice barely a whisper. I can see the emotions swirling in her eyes, and I know my presence here has caught her off guard.

"I'm sorry to barge in unannounced, I—" I begin, but she cuts me off with a knowing smile.

"I know," she says softly before pulling me into a tight hug. It's a surprise, but I welcome it, knowing how much Amelia means to her.

"*Thank you* for coming," she says, and I nod, feeling a glimmer of hope.

I ask about Amelia's whereabouts, and she tells me that she's at the exhibition, getting ready. She hands me a small paper with details and urges me to get going.

"She's been a mess. Go get her," she insists. Curiosity gets the best of me, and I ask why she's not with Amelia.

She chuckles, explaining, "She wanted to do this on her own. So stubborn, that woman."

I can't help but smile at the thought. We're so alike, in so many ways.

"Here, take my car," she adds, tossing me the keys. I catch them instinctively, appreciating her trust.

As I head to the car, she calls out, stopping me in my tracks. She runs up to me, breathless, handing me a few sheets of paper. "Here. She'll probably kill me for giving these to you, but fuck it. I know she'd want you to have them."

I look down and my heart lurches in my chest. In my hand are drawings, multiple drawings, all of me, some of Amelia and me together.

They're in pencil, and they're breathtaking.

Each stroke captures moments—me caught in a rare, unguarded laugh, me lost in thought, my eyes full of intensity, looking away. There are sketches of us together, our expressions raw with emotion. These drawings weren't done in the moment; she drew these from memory, and it takes the breath out of my lungs. With a lump in my throat, I nod to Kat, silently thanking her for this precious gift.

"I'll make things right," I promise, my voice barely steady.

"I know you will," she replies softly.

Driving to the gallery, memories flood my mind. It was years ago, watching from afar as she came over to see Liv, always full of sunshine and smiles. She had this way about her, something so captivating that it knocked me off my feet.

Our love, our connection, it's like two hearts intertwined, each beat echoing the other. She's the only one who can ground me, breathe life into me.

I can't remember what life was like before her.

Today, I hope to mend what's broken and show her that my heart hasn't always *just* been hers, but that it's been *branded* with her name in a way that can *never* be undone.

After punching the address into Kat's car, it takes me exactly fifteen minutes to get to the exhibition. The streets in Sydney are a nightmare. First time here and I'm driving around blind. All my common sense and good judgement went out the window the minute I hit these roads. This is definitely not the country. Fuck, you couldn't pay me to live here.

Is this what Mills wants? Can she see herself living like this? The thought stirs in my gut, wrenching it tight. I'd do anything for her, but can I really give her this life?

Stepping into the gallery, someone immediately hands me a small booklet with information about the exhibit. I flip through it quickly until I find what I'm looking for on page four. There, in bright colours, is a portrait of *my* Amelia with the title of her series, 'Stolen Moments.' My heart pounds as I scan the walls, looking for Amelia's name among the artworks. How the fuck am I going to find her pieces in this maze? There are heaps of them.

Portraits. She paints people. *Look for that.*

But fuck me, the place is chockers, and I have to squeeze past people. My six-foot-four frame towers over most of the crowd, all dressed in fucking suits and expensive outfits, while here I am in torn-up jeans, steel cap boots, and a flannel, looking every bit the outsider in this fancy joint. Butterflies erupt in my stomach at the thought of seeing Amelia. I'm so fucking nervous.

More than ever.

As I scan the crowd, I don't spot her until I move forward and find her deep in conversation with a younger woman, her back to me. I keep my distance, not wanting her to see me. Not yet. Just the sight of her from afar takes my breath away. She looks stunning—tight black dress, denim jacket, and those damned boots I adore. My mind races. I wonder what her paintings could be about, what moments she chose to capture.

The thought that she poured her heart into these works, capturing moments that mean the world to her—it hits me hard. This isn't just about art. It's about her sharing her world, her emotions, and her memories. I need to find her pieces, to see what she sees, and to understand the depth of her art. Continuing to walk around, keeping my distance, I spot a series of works to my left. I do a double take because I could've sworn I saw myself. Nah, surely not. *Wait.*

I walk closer, and my breath is knocked out of my lungs. There on the wall are huge fucking paintings of me. Next to them is a painting of her parents hugging, and another of Millie—little Millie blowing bubbles. All images caught in the moment, but it's the artworks of me that make me freeze.

The first painting is from the night we went to Clifftop Haven. I'm glancing away in my favourite sherpa jacket, the details so precise it feels like I'm right back there. The second one is just my face, serious as hell, brows furrowed, and eyes intense. She's captured the blue in my eyes so bloody well, they're piercing even in a painting. Seeing myself through her eyes like this, it's overwhelming. I've got no idea about art, but this? This is different. My heart races, emotions welling up inside me.

She's managed to capture something raw, something real. It's not just about the likeness, it's about what's beneath it. The way she sees me. The way she feels about me.

And then it hits me—these moments she's painted aren't just random. They're special to her. They mean something. And knowing I'm part of that, that I'm one of those significant people in her life? It's more than I can wrap my head around. My breath catches, tears pricking at the corners of my eyes. I never thought I'd be standing in a gallery, staring at paintings of myself, feeling this damn moved.

But here I am, and it's all because of her. My fucking Mills. *Mine.*

I turn to see where she is, and she's standing on her own now, a worried look on her face. Why is she worried? A tall, older woman walks up to her, and a small smile plays on Amelia's face. She says something to her, and Amelia nods. After the woman leaves, Amelia pulls out her phone and starts typing. Now's my chance. I decide to text her, nerves dancing as I type out:

> **Me:** How's the exhibition going?

> **Amelia:** It's going.

> **Me:** What does that mean?

Is she not happy here? Just go up to her, you wanker.

> **Amelia:** Idk. I feel so out of place here.

She's so wrong. She fits right in. Her talent is phenomenal, the best work that's here, to be honest. I couldn't care less about the other artworks.

> **Me:** I think you fit right in.

> **Me:** You look beautiful. Especially in that dress.

She looks around before turning to face the other way, looking toward the front doors. I start walking toward her, nerves kicking in as I get closer.

49

Amelia

As I stand in the bustling gallery, surrounded by the vibrant art scene of Sydney, I can't help but feel overwhelmed by the possibilities this city offers. The crowd is larger than I expected, and the energy here is electrifying. Despite the allure of this new environment, my heart remains tethered to Wattle Creek.

It's my comfort zone, where familiar faces and a close-knit community await me. The drive into town, the sense of closeness and distance all at once—it's home.

Yet, inevitably, my thoughts circle back to Bradley. I know I handled this all so poorly, but what's done is done. I keep telling myself that things happen for a reason. I'm a firm believer in this.

If Brad and I were truly meant to be together, then things would have worked out differently. I've tried to remain positive, but that doesn't stop the ache in my chest, the desperate prayer inside me that things might still change.

Yet, deep down, I'm not sure anymore.

What surprised me the most were the texts from Olivia. She'd questioned my feelings for him, and I'd confessed *everything*—telling her it was too late.

Her response, "We'll see," still lingers in my mind, cryptic and unsettling.

Shaking off those thoughts, I focus on the task at hand: greeting people and mingling. *Two* tasks I'm familiar with. This can't be too hard, right? But as I survey the room, insecurity creeps in. Everyone is dressed in trendy, expensive clothing, while I'm wearing a borrowed dress from my mum—a figure-hugging black midi dress paired with a distressed denim jacket and worn-out ankle boots. Kat did my hair in loose curls and applied light makeup, but still, I feel out of place.

Taking a deep breath to steady myself, I catch the eye of the gallery owner, Valerie, as she makes her way over to me.

"Nerves kicking in?" she asks, her words smooth yet thick with an accent I can't quite place.

"You bet," I reply nervously, with a forced laugh.

"Don't be," she reassures me. "Your works are phenomenal."

I glance around the room, taking in the packed gallery. It's surreal.

"Grab a drink and mingle. I'll catch up with you later."

I nod at her, and my phone vibrates.

Kat: How's it going?

I smile and quickly type back.

> **Me:** Good, I guess. You guys can come whenever you want.

I had told her not to come initially, wanting to handle this on my own, but as time ticks on, I realise I want them here.

> **Kat:** We are already on the way. Had to wait for John to pick us up.

Of course they are. Wait...

> **Me:** Why didn't you just drive?

> **Kat:** Oh, my car wouldn't start...

Huh? But she drove it this morning.

> **Me:** Oh, it was fine this morning, though?

> **Kat:** Yeah, life just loves to throw you surprises. See you soon.

I pay no mind to her words. Just knowing they'll be here is enough for me. I smile at someone passing by, and they smile back. My phone vibrates again, and this time my heart skyrockets when I see a text from Bradley.

Bradley: How's the exhibition going?

Despite everything that has happened, just seeing his name on the screen sends a rush through me. Butterflies erupt in my chest, and I can't help the way my pulse quickens. He still has this effect on me, no matter what.

Me: It's going.

Bradley: What does that mean?

Me: Idk. I feel so out of place here.

He's still so caring, so attentive to my feelings. I should have told him to come. I'm such an idiot.

Bradley: I think you fit right in.

My breathing quickens. Heart racing. *How could he know that?* He's not here to see how incredibly nervous I am. *Is he just saying that?* Trying to make me feel better? His words are just… They mean so much to me. But they also twist the knife of longing in my chest, reminding me of what could have been.

> **Bradley:** You look beautiful. Especially in that dress.

My heart drops. I look around quickly, eyes wide. How does he know what I'm wearing?

He can't be here. Is he here? No.

> **Bradley:** Behind you.

I spin around, and there he stands, right in front of me. My breath catches in my throat, and I struggle to breathe.

All the restraint I've maintained seems to shatter, and I battle the urge to cry and rush into his arms. Speechless, I watch as he strides over, towering above me. He's impeccably dressed in a black shirt, my favourite plaid jacket of his, black jeans, and his steel-capped boots. Despite the crowd in suits and fancy attire around him, he's all I see, rugged and handsome as ever.

"Hi, sunshine."

Don't cry. Please, don't cry.

"Brad..." is all I can manage to say. My voice wavers as I stutter, frowning. "Wh-what are you doing here?"

"I caught a flight this morning," he explains. "Kat gave me the keys to her car, and I came here as soon as I could." So that explains Kat's car situation.

I shake my head, trying to process everything. "You... you came all this way?"

He nods, a small smile playing on his lips. "Of course, I did. I *needed* to see you, Amelia."

I blink back tears, my heart pounding in my chest. "But…"

Bradley steps closer, silencing my words. "I couldn't stand being apart from you any longer. I've been a fool. I let you go when I should have held on tighter. For us," he says, his voice earnest.

I swallow hard, my throat tight with emotion. "I'm so sorry for how I handled things. I—"

But he shakes his head, his words cutting through my apology. "Don't be sorry. I should be the one apologising."

"But what about your work?" I manage to utter.

"Forget work. You wanted me here, so I'm *here*. That's all that matters." He gently lifts my chin, his touch sending shivers down my spine.

"I love you, Amelia."

His words hit me like a ton of bricks, stirring up a wild mix of emotions inside me. Relief, longing, it all comes rushing in at once, swirling through me.

"And I'm so fucking sorry it took me so long to say it back," he murmurs, his words piercing through the air. "You breathed life back into me when I thought I was doing fine. You made me realise how much I had been missing. My whole life, I had this nagging feeling that something was off. That there was an emptiness, something I couldn't place my finger on, until you came along." Cupping my face in his hands, his touch is a lifeline, grounding me in the moment as his words wash over me like a gentle tide. "I've been so stubborn, so blinded by fear, by my own rules and expectations, that I failed to see what was right in front of me," he murmurs, gently wiping away the tears streaming down my cheeks. I know my makeup is probably a mess by now, but I couldn't care less.

"Y-you love me?" I manage to ask, my voice wavering.

"With every fucking fibre of my being, Mills. I'm yours."

I let out a shaky breath, and my hands tremble as I reach up to touch his face. "I've waited so long to hear you say that," I whisper.

Before I can utter another word, he crashes his mouth to mine. I grip his back, pulling him closer, needing him as close as possible. The world around us fades away, and I don't care that we're in a crowded gallery. I hear a few whistles break out, but I ignore them, lost in the kiss.

Lost in him.

His hands slide down to cup me from behind, effortlessly lifting me up. I cling to him tightly, and he holds me there, his lips never leaving mine, the kiss deepening. I bury my hands in his hair, feeling the soft strands between my fingers, before moving them to the nape of his collar, pulling him even closer.

I'm breathless, overwhelmed by the intensity of the moment, but I never want it to end.

He breaks the kiss, holding me there, both of us breathing hard, our foreheads resting against each other. Slowly, he lowers me back to the ground, and the crowd erupts into a fit of whistles and applause. I bury my face in his chest, feeling it rumble with laughter.

"This is the second time you've kissed me in public," I mumble, feeling a blush creeping up my cheeks.

Bradley chuckles, his arms around me tightening slightly. "So? I just can't help myself around you."

"Since when are you into *PDA*?" I tease, looking up at him.

"Since you," he says, leaning down to place a soft kiss on my forehead.

The laughter, whistles, and applause begin to fade, and I feel a light tug on my dress. Turning around, I see Millie standing beside me, her face beaming.

"Meli! Bwadey!" she exclaims with a big smile.

"Hi, princess," Bradley says, a huge grin breaking out onto his beautiful face. "Did you miss me?"

Millie nods enthusiastically.

"And she's not lying. She hasn't stopped calling your name ever since Meli came to stay with us." This comes from Kat, who appears by our sides with John.

"She likes you more than me now," I say, tilting my head and crossing my arms.

"Ah, is that so? Who could blame her?" His wink makes me flush with heat.

"Well, I missed you, too. And your aunty Meli. I'm here now, and I'm not going anywhere," he says to Millie before standing back up.

"What about Liv? Any news? Did you speak to her?" I ask, my

voice tinged with worry.

"I did," he replies, his tone reassuring.

"And?"

"She's the one who booked my flight to come here. Well, her *and* Xavier."

"What?"

"Yep. She's okay. *We're* okay. Said she wants to speak to you when we get back," he replies, his gaze steady and reassuring.

I take a breath of relief, feeling tears start to prick at the corners of my eyes. "Oh, thank God. So, we're really okay?" I ask again, needing that extra reassurance.

"We're good, Mills," he says, his voice firm and comforting.

"And you're really not going anywhere? Don't make promises you can't keep," I tease, my smile mischievous.

He raises his brow, his expression challenging me back.

"I promise."

"So, does that mean you'll be around for morning kisses?" I ask, looking up at him with a playful grin.

"Every single morning," he promises, pressing a tender kiss to my lips.

"And goodnight kisses?"

"Yes, Amelia," he murmurs, pressing a kiss to my cheek. "And midday kisses, too," he adds, kissing my other cheek.

"Midday? But we both have work," I point out, amused.

"You think that'll stop me? I'll leave the station every day at noon if it means I get to kiss you," he vows, love shining in his eyes.

"Forever?" I ask, my eyes lighting up.

"Forever."

Ten years ago, I locked eyes with a boy whose blue eyes were like the summer sky—so far out of my league, yet I didn't care. His rare smile was infectious, and his laughter, though infrequent, was a melody I never wanted to stop hearing. All those years of wishing to be noticed, of longing for a man who felt like a breath away but seemed so unattainable, have led me to this moment. Now, here I am, loving that same man unconditionally. Every day with him feels like a gift, a beautiful blend of shared dreams and endless possibilities.

As I look into those familiar blue eyes now, I'm filled with a sense of peace and joy. I'm content knowing I'm going to spend the rest of my life with him, building our dreams together, and perhaps starting a family of our own one day. This is our forever, and I couldn't be happier. My heart is full, and my future looks brighter than ever.

It's not just a hope; it's a certainty—I *want* to spend the rest of my life with him because my heart has always been his, and I wouldn't have it any other way. I now know that some things, or some people, are destined to be together forever after all.

Epilogue

Amelia

November

Spring is in full swing here, with flowers blooming everywhere, and I feel like my life is just perfect right now. Bradley and I are back in Wattle Creek, and I'm absolutely glowing with joy. I can't wait to see what our first summer together as a couple will be like. It feels like the start of something truly special.

After the gallery night, we had an impromptu longer stay in Sydney. We ventured around the city, making memories and spending time with Kat, John, and Millie. We visited the Sydney Opera House, took long walks by the harbour, and even had a few picnics in the Royal Botanic Garden. Bradley and I explored hidden cafes, laughed over silly souvenirs, and shared countless moments that made my heart swell with happiness.

We made new memories that I'll cherish forever.

The townsfolk were thrilled to have us back, welcoming us with open arms. I'd been hesitant to come back home after everything that *happened, but the minute Brad and I landed back in Wattle Creek, our whole family was there waiting for us—Mum, Dad, Bradley's parents, Olivia, Xav, Isla and Imogen. I'd promised Bradley that I wouldn't cry, but the moment I saw my best friend, the waterworks just wouldn't stop. Liv rushed over and had given us both a tight hug. The three of us shared our sorry's and I love you's.*

It was such a heartfelt reunion, making me realise just how much I missed our tight-knit community. I fumble with my keys as I unlock the door to our apartment. Well, technically, it's still *my* apartment, but Bradley moved in as soon as we got back from Sydney. He fit right into my little space, and it feels more like home with him here.

Just as I'm dropping my bag by the door, my phone buzzes. It's a text from Bradley.

Bradley Bear: Hi Sunshine. Meet me out front in 5

A blush creeps up my cheeks. This man will never stop making me blush. I love how he knows my schedule, knows exactly when I get home and when I leave for work. Every day since the gallery, he's met me for lunch at school, still keeping his promise. My face heats at the thought. I glance in the mirror, smoothing my hair and touching up my lipstick.

My heart pounds in my chest. It seems that even five months later, my heart *still* skips a beat at the thought of seeing Bradley.

I step outside, and the warm spring breeze lifts my spirits even higher. He leans casually against his Navarra, ruggedly handsome in worn jeans and a flannel shirt that clings just right to his frame, showing off those strong arms. My heart flips at the sight of him. His eyes light up when he spots me, that familiar spark dancing in his gaze.

As I approach, the scent of his cologne mixes with the fresh spring air. He pushes off the car, meeting me halfway with that lopsided grin that always makes my knees a little weak. His hand finds mine, fingers intertwining, and it feels like coming home. Before I can speak, his other hand cups my face, thumb brushing my cheek. I barely have time to gasp before his lips capture mine in a kiss so fierce it sends tingles down to my toes. He bends me back slightly, his arm supporting me. My hands grip his shirt as I lose myself in the kiss.

The world fades away, leaving just us in this perfect moment. His lips move against mine with a mix of urgency and tenderness, and I melt into him, feeling the depth of his love in every touch. When we finally pull apart, his forehead rests against mine, both of us breathless, sharing a smile that says everything. His eyes hold an emotion so deep it makes my breath hitch.

"Hi, sunshine," he murmurs, and I can't help but smile, feeling like the luckiest girl in the world.

"Hi," I say, my voice a little breathless from that kiss. He grins at me, eyes crinkling at the corners in that way I love.

Bradley steps back and opens the passenger door. "After you," he says, teasing, but with that warm look in his eyes. I slide into the seat, the familiar scent of his car wrapping around me like a hug. He shuts the door and walks around to the driver's side, and I can't help but wonder what he's up to. Bradley hops in and starts the engine.

"So," I begin, turning to look at him, "what's with all the secrecy? You've been acting all mysterious and sneaky today." I raise an eyebrow, trying to figure him out.

He smirks, glancing at me with that twinkle in his eye. "Can't I surprise my girlfriend once in a while?" His voice is playful, but there's this excitement in it that gets me curious.

I laugh, the sound bubbling up from my chest. "I guess you can. But now you've got me all intrigued."

Bradley chuckles, his hand reaching over to give mine a reassuring squeeze. "Good. That's exactly what I was going for." He pulls out onto the road, and we head off—the world outside a blur of colours and light.

As we drive, I keep sneaking glances at him. The way his jaw tightens with concentration, the easy confidence in the way he handles his ute, the gentle curve of his lips when he catches me looking—all of it makes my heart swell with love and anticipation. Whatever he's planned, I know it's going to be special, just like every moment we've shared since that day at the gallery.

He turns down an unfamiliar road, and I furrow my brows, trying to figure out where we are. We're a good fifteen minutes from town. Bradley suddenly pulls over on the side of the road, and I glance at him, confused.

"What's going on?" I ask, my voice laced with curiosity.

He turns to me with a mischievous grin. "Trust me, I have a

surprise for you." As he says this, he pulls out a blindfold. My breath hitches, my pulse quickening.

"A blindfold?" I stammer.

"Do you trust me?" he asks softly, holding the fabric out to me.

I nod, swallowing hard. "Always."

This has become our thing. *Trust*. And oh, how I trust him with my life.

He's taught me so much—not just in the bedroom, though there's been plenty of that—but about *life*, about being street smart, about protecting myself. He's shaped me into the woman I am today: strong, confident, and ready to tackle whatever life throws our way. With him by my side, I've learned to embrace my strengths and know my worth. Sure, I still have my moments—like when I nervously yap to myself and anyone within earshot. But hey, Bradley loves me just the way I am, quirks and all.

And let's be honest, who doesn't need a bit of comic relief now and then?

He gently ties the blindfold over my eyes, and the world goes dark. My heart pounds as the car starts moving again, every sound and sensation amplified in the absence of sight. What is he doing? What kind of surprise? My mind races with possibilities, and my senses heighten, making every detail feel more intense.

As we drive, Bradley's fingers begin to toy with the hem of my dress, sending shivers up my spine. His touch is light, teasing, as he trails his fingers along my thighs. "You look incredible in this dress," he murmurs.

"Bradley..." I whisper, my breath catching as his hand inches higher.

He chuckles softly, continuing to tease me, making the drive feel like it's stretching on forever. Without sight, I have no idea where we are, and the suspense is almost unbearable. Finally, the car slows to a stop, and he announces, "We're here."

I hear him get out, then my door opens. He helps me out, guiding me with a steady hand. "Careful," he says, leading me up a pathway and then a set of stairs. My heart races, my mind spinning with anticipation as I follow his lead, wondering what he has in store for me.

Bradley takes a deep breath. "Ready?"

I nod, my heart racing. "I think so."

He gently removes the blindfold, and I blink, adjusting to the light. My breath catches as I see it—a stunning two-story white house that looks like a dream.

"What...?" I whisper, stepping out of the car, eyes wide. The house is a perfect blend of rustic charm and modern elegance, with a wrap-around porch draped in lavender and vines.

"B-Brad, what are we doing here? Whose place is this?" I ask, still trying to process.

He grins, holding up two keys. "Ours. This is our home."

I'm speechless. "But... when? How?"

"I met with Rose a couple of weeks before you left for Sydney," he says, stepping closer. "I signed the papers last week. Got the keys this morning. Mills, I bought this for us—because you're the one I want to spend my life with."

Tears well in my eyes. "Bradley, you... bought a *house* for *us*. This is... I can't believe it."

"I knew straight away when I saw it for sale," he says, stepping closer. "It was a decision I made right then and there. I didn't even think about it; it just felt right. I'm sorry I didn't talk to you about it. I didn't mean to overstep. I just know it's you I want. We could get married, start a family, grow old together here—"

Before he can continue, I break into a huge smile and cut him off with a kiss, tears streaming down my cheeks. I pull back, "Brad. I'm not mad, and you didn't overstep. This is... perfect. You're perfect. I love you so much."

He wraps his arms around me. "I love you too, Mills."

I smirk playfully and tease, "Who's the nervous yapper now?"

He chuckles and replies, "No one can know."

I mime locking my lips and tossing away the key. "Come on, I'll show you inside," he says, already pulling me toward the door and unlocking it. I let him guide me inside, my curiosity sparking and heart racing. To my right, I spot a charming wooden love seat and a Monstera plant. As I step further in, Bradley closes the front door, revealing a cosy living room with wooden furniture, white couches, and a large antique rug. Natural light pours in from the sash windows, bathing the space in a warm glow. He follows me into the kitchen, where I trace my fingers along the smooth marble countertop. The cream wooden cabinets and grey-tiled backsplash complement the white walls and gleaming sink.

Bradley stands close behind me, brushing my hair away to kiss my neck, sending shivers down my spine. "Brad, this house is amazing," I say, turning to face him.

He smiles, his hands sliding to my waist. Before I know it, he lifts me effortlessly onto the counter. The cool marble against my thighs makes me shiver. His lips find mine again, deepening the kiss. His fingers trail up my dress, brushing the inside of my thigh until they reach my underwear. I freeze. "Wait. What are you doing?" I whisper-yell, though there's no one else around.

"What's it look like? I'm going to fuck my girl in *our* kitchen," he murmurs against my neck. "Want me to stop?"

I release a shaky breath. "No."

His fingers slip beneath my underwear, and I instantly know I'm drenched. Just one kiss or touch from him has me completely aroused.

"Always so wet for me," he growls. He eases a finger inside, and I moan as I arch my back. Another finger joins, moving in deliberate, measured strokes. Pleasure radiates through me, narrowing my world to just this moment with him.

His pace quickens, fingers working with increasing speed. I bite my lip to stifle my moans, but too he's pulling his fingers away, leaving me panting. My eyes snap open as I hear the distinct sound of a zipper.

Bradley hoists my dress higher and tugs my underwear down, which I kick off onto the floor. I pull at his t-shirt as he swiftly pulls out his cock, lines himself up, and thrusts deep inside me. His movements are forceful and rhythmic, driving into me with quick, deliberate thrusts. He tugs at my straps to free my breasts, each motion intense and urgent.

My head falls back, and I cling to him. He whispers in my ear, his breath hot against my skin. "Tell me you love me again, Mills."

"I love you," I gasp, barely able to speak. "I love you, Bradley. I love you so much." My words spill out in a fervent stream, like a prayer.

He growls, his thrusts gaining intensity. One hand braces on the bench, the other grips my hip. I lean back, letting him press me into the bench, his length pushing deeper, rubbing deliciously against my tight walls. The pressure builds to an unbearable peak.

"More, I need more," I beg, my voice desperate.

Bradley takes a breast in his mouth, biting and sucking, making me moan loudly. He moves to the other, his mouth hot and insistent.

"Bradley, oh God," I cry out, overwhelmed by the sensation. His pace quickens, each thrust sending waves of ecstasy through me. His thrusts become erratic, and with a final, powerful thrust, I shatter around him, my release crashing over me and soon he's following me over the edge, groaning my name as he comes deep inside me.

The hot rush of his release fills me, and I feel it drip onto my inner thigh. I'm on the pill now, have been for a few months, but his words about starting a family keep echoing in my mind. The idea of stopping it, of one day feeling a baby growing inside me—his baby, our child—sends a thrilling shiver down my spine.

One day.

Bradley stays inside me, our breaths mingling. His forehead rests against mine, eyes locked. "I love you," he whispers, filled with emotion.

"I love you too," I reply, my hands sliding up his back. "More than anything."

He grins that lopsided grin. "You're amazing, Mills. You know that?"

"You're not so bad yourself, Bradley Bear." I rub my nose against his. "Thank you. Thank you for everything, for buying this house."

He shakes his head, a tender smile on his lips. "No, thank *you*, Amelia. For coming into my life. I can't thank you enough, so I'll spend every day of the rest of my life proving how grateful I am that you exist and that you're mine."

My heart swells with his words. "I can't wait to see what's next," I whisper.

Bradley's eyes sparkle. "Neither can I. So... should we christen the rest of the house, or do you want to take a break first?" Bradley's lips curve into a devilish grin as he bites my lower lip and gives my behind a sharp, playful smack.

I smirk, teasing, "I don't need a break. Do *you*?"

He arches an eyebrow. "You think I can't handle a few rounds?"

"Not sure. You're going to have to prove it, Officer Mitchell," I say sweetly.

With a growl, Bradley sweeps me up effortlessly, my dress hitched up and his pants still undone. "To the bedroom it is then," he declares, our laughter and excitement mingling with the promise of new beginnings as he carries me through the house.

Bradley

I jolt awake to the shrill ring of my phone, cutting through the quietness of the room. I squint at the clock—five twenty-five a.m.—and see Xavier's name flashing on the screen. Panic knots in my chest as I blink away sleep. Shifting carefully to avoid waking Amelia, who's still tangled in the sheets beside me, I press the phone to my ear.

"Xav? What's up?"

His voice comes through, strained and hurried. "Brad, it's Isla. She's in labour. We're at the hospital. Mum and dad are on their way, but... how fast can you get here."

I glance at Amelia, who stirs beside me, her eyes blinking open.

"I'll be there in ten," I say, then hear him sigh through the phone.

"Okay, see you soon."

"Who was that?" Amelia says with a yawn.

"Xavier. Isla's gone into labour." Amelia's eyes widen, and she's already up, getting dressed.

"We have to go now," she says, urgency in her voice. I smile at her determination as I get dressed quickly and then we're out the door and speeding—responsibly, *of course*—to the hospital. We make it in record time.

Inside, the harsh fluorescent lights are a jarring contrast to the early morning gloom. I stride up to the reception desk, heart pounding. "I'm here for Isla and Xavier Mitchell."

The nurse types away, nodding. "They're in the Acacia birthing ward. Take the lift to the third floor, and follow the corridor to room 305."

"Thank you." As we head to the lift, Amelia grabs my hand, sensing my nerves. I lean down and kiss the top of her head. We reach the third floor, and just as I take a step out, I spot Dad further down, waiting just outside a door.

"Jeez, you got here fast," I call out, and he whips his head around, squinting even with his glasses on.

"Yeah well, your mother was going ballistic," he says, pulling us into a quick hug as soon as we reach him. "They're in there, but only a few people can go in at a time."

"How's Isla doing?" Amelia asks, squeezing my hand.

Dad smiles. "She's a champ. Your brother, on the other hand," he nods at me, "needs someone to hold his hand."

We all laugh, easing the tension. The suddenly door opens, and Xavier emerges, his face lighting up at the sight of us. "Oh, thank fuck!" he exclaims, pulling us into a hug. "I'm so glad you're here." He keeps a hand on my shoulder and turns to Amelia. "Isla would be *so* glad to see *you*. She's threatening to strangle my balls for putting her through this. I'd prefer to keep them intact."

We chuckle, and Dad shakes his head with a smile. Amelia nods and steps inside. As the door closes, I hear Isla's groans and the soothing voices of Mum and the nurse encouraging her. I ruffle Xavier's hair playfully.

"Look at you, panicking like a kid. You've got this."

"Fuck off," he says with a smile, shoving me back. "I just didn't expect any of this. I feel so unprepared." I've never seen my brother so nervous.

Dad steps closer, placing a reassuring hand on Xavier's back. "Son, no one's ever truly prepared for this. You just gotta rub 'er back, do those bloody breathing exercises... just be there for 'er—even when she's cursing at ya."

Xavier nods, looking between us. Just then, Imogen barrels down the hallway, breathless. "How's Isla doing? Is she okay?" She skids to a stop in front of us, looking worried. "How's she holding up?"

"She's alright," Dad says with a chuckle. "It's Xavier who needs the support."

Imogen rolls her eyes but smiles. "Typical."

Xavier defends himself, "Hey, I'm the one being threatened in there for getting her pregnant. It was a *consensual* act."

"Yeah, well, you try pushing a baby out of... your... *dick*," she says with a shrug and arms crossed, "and *then* see if she eases up a bit." *Ouch.*

Xavier's face contorts in pain. "Yikes. Not sure how that's the same."

Imogen shakes her head. "Don't worry about it. I wouldn't expect *you* to understand."

I can't help but chuckle, the sound escaping before I can hold it back.

At the sound, she turns to me, a hint of surprise in her eyes. "I don't think I'll ever get used to hearing you laugh."

I roll my eyes, but before I can respond, she playfully smacks my bicep. "Don't worry, big fella, it suits you."

I can't help but smile at her, and she grins back, satisfied.

"Anywho, I'm going in to check on Isla," she says before knocking on the door and walking inside. The murmur of comforting voices fills the hallway. After a while, now seated on the waiting lounge, a nurse steps out, her expression serious but calm. "Dad, Mum is ready to push."

Xavier's eyes widen, and he claps his hands together, taking a deep breath. "Alright, this is it."

"Go get 'em, tiger," I say with a smirk.

Amelia and Imogen join us outside as Xavier heads inside. Amelia immediately moves to my side, and I wrap an arm around her shoulders, pulling her close. We stand together, waiting in anxious anticipation.

The room buzzes with a mix of nerves and excitement, everyone glancing at the clock every few minutes. Just as I'm starting to lose my patience, the midwife from earlier comes out, a broad smile on her face.

"Congratulations everyone, we've got ourselves a girl! A healthy baby girl!" she announces, and the group erupts into a chorus of awws. Mills and Imogen squeal in excitement, hugging each other. Th nurse's eyes then scan the room. "Which one of you is Bradley and Amelia?"

We stand, hands entwined. "That's us," I say.

"Mum and Dad want you inside."

Amelia and I exchange a glance, then follow the midwife. Inside, Mum and Xavier are by the bed. "Hey, there they are," Xavier says, his pride shining through.

Isla, though exhausted, smiles as she cradles their baby girl. Amelia steps closer, her voice warm. "Isla, she's so beautiful. How is she?"

Isla's tired eyes brighten at Amelia's words. "Thanks, girl. She's doing great. It's been a long night, but we're over the moon."

"How are *you* holding up?" Amelia asks.

Isla smiles softly, her gaze fixed on her daughter. "I'm exhausted and sore, but it's all worth it. Seeing her makes everything feel right."

I step forward, peering at the tiny, perfect face. Her eyes are closed, tiny fingers curling and uncurling. "She is beautiful," I say, my voice cracking slightly.

"Thanks, man," he replies, his usual bravado softened. "Isla's a bloody warrior."

"Damn right she is," I say, winking at Isla.

Isla looks down at her daughter and then back up to us. "This is little Callie, Cal for short," my heart swells at the name. *Callie*. Cal, like Isla's *dad*. "And there's something we'd like to ask you both," she finishes.

Xavier steps forward, placing a hand on my shoulder. "Brad,

Amelia, we'd like you to be Callie's godparents."

Amelia's eyes widen. "Wait, what?"

"Godparents?" I ask, taken aback.

Xavier nods. "Yeah. There's no one else we'd trust more with this role. You've always had my back, and I know you'll have my daughter's too. And Amelia, and you're part of our family. Isla and I know you'll show the same love to little Cal that you've always shown to us. We couldn't think of better godparents for Callie."

Tears prick at my eyes. I pull Xavier into a rough hug. "Thanks, Xav. That means the world to me. We won't let you down."

Amelia's eyes also shine with tears and I wrap my arm around her as she says, "Thank you both. We're honoured to be Callie's godparents."

"You know, Xav, if she inherits half your charm, we're all in trouble," I joke.

Isla laughs softly, looking at her daughter. "Oh, trust me, she's already got a bit of her father's charm. And his eye colour, too."

"That's the Mitchell genes for you—strong sperm," Xavier says proudly. *Idiot*. Mum, standing nearby, smacks Xavier gently on the arm and we all laugh. She then hugs both Amelia and I warmly, congratulating us.

"I'm so proud of you both! Now, let's get cracking on more grandkids, chop-chop!"

I smile nervously, glancing at Amelia. Her eyes light up, a true ray of sunshine. Holding her close, surrounded by family and our new goddaughter, I realise how much this moment means to me. I think about the possibility of one day having a daughter or son of my own. With Amelia by my side, I feel a deep sense of fulfilment and certainty.

  Together, we have everything I could ever want.

Acknowledgements

As I sit here reflecting on the fact that Branded Hearts is now my second book, I'm filled with a mix of disbelief and gratitude. If writing one book seemed like an insurmountable challenge, the idea of having completed a second still feels utterly surreal. This journey has been an unexpected one, but storytelling has always been a quiet passion of mine, simmering beneath the surface, waiting for its moment to be shared with the world.

To my loving friends and family—your unwavering support has been the bedrock of this entire experience. A special thank you to Michelle, whose dedication to reading and reviewing every word I write is unmatched. You truly are the best alpha reader, and I'm so grateful for you. And to my booksta girls, my thirst trap girlies—you know who you are—I will forever cherish your words of encouragement and the camaraderie we've built together.

A heartfelt thank you to my partner, Thomas. Your restless brain, always buzzing with ideas, has been my endless source of inspiration. Thank you for answering my never-ending questions with such merit, and for inspiring every character, every quirk, and every thought that has found its way into these pages. I have so much love for you.

Just like *Lassoed Love*, these characters are incredibly special to me. They represent pieces of myself—my thoughts, quirks, and flaws—as well as those of the people I hold dear. Bradley, in particular, holds a special place in my heart. His internal struggles and thoughts are a reflection of someone very dear to me, and I wanted to capture that in the most heartfelt way possible.

Thank you to *everyone* who has been a part of this journey. Your love and support have made this dream a reality.

About the Author

Elle Mariah is a teacher turned Romance Author from Australia.

Growing up, her ambition was also to be able to inspire others and educate young individuals on the beauty of art and literature. For the past four years, she has successfully been able to do just that, educating young minds on the world of Creative Arts through Painting, Photography, Graphic Design and more! Recently she has embarked on this journey to put pen to paper and pursue her dream of becoming an author, where she could still continue to inspire others, although this time, through fictional worlds and characters.

Elle Mariah enjoys writing heartfelt, swoon-worthy, raw romance about extremely relatable characters with snarky humour on their journey to their happily ever afters.

Instagram: @ellemariahauthor
Website: www.authorellemariah.com

Printed in Great Britain
by Amazon